This book is dedicated to all the souls who know who they are inside, and who bravely choose to live that truth even when faced with the true demons of the world.

Your light sends the shadows running. Keep shining.

THE RIP FILES

CASE OF THE DEMON DRUMS

BETH ANNE CAMPBELL

Beth Anne Campbell LLC
Virginia, USA

Love and heartfelt gratitude to my husband, Sean, for his undying support, and for being the guy who decided it would be fun to sign up with a ghost hunting group all those years ago. Thank you for being my rock and for kicking off *The RIP Files* by drafting the early pages of chapter one.

Thank you to the family who inspired the Mackenzies. Although this tale is fiction, it arose from the emotion of a real family. Wherever life has brought them, I hope it comes with much happiness and love.

And to everyone out there who doesn't fit into the mold that someone else has created for you, thank you for being an inspiration and voice for progress. Keep fighting and keep being true to yourself. You are worthy. You are deserving. You are loved

The RIP Files: Case of the Demon Drums

Demons, Drums, & Dysfunction

Monday, September 23, 9:30 pm
Series of Unexplainable Events, 2nd Major Occurrence
Mackenzie Residence, Starry Knob Lane, Roanoke, Virginia

ratta-tat-tat

Sue Mackenzie hears the soft tapping of the snare first, like a faraway Johnny-come-marching home drummer at the end of a bloody Civil War battle. It reminds her of a movie she saw back in the eighties; or maybe it was a miniseries. She doesn't remember. Her mind is fuzzy and distant. *What time is it? How did I get here?*

She is standing in front of the kitchen window, her hands immersed in a sink full of warm, soapy water. There is a broken coffee mug shattered at her feet. Sue vaguely remembers dreaming that the cup flew out of the bubbles by itself and smashed onto the floor. As it hit the old linoleum, it sounded like a cymbal crashing. Or did she hear an actual cymbal? A lot of crazy things have happened over the past few weeks, ever since the party. The sound of snares, cymbals, and bass drums coming from nowhere. Random objects flying through the air. Something foul stroking her hair. *Voices whisper on the stair. Hands on my neck, an icy pair.* Edgar Allan Poe would be proud.

ratta-tat-tat

Sue cocks an ear toward the basement door. *Did I imagine it this time? Am I still dreaming?* The tapping is faint and so very far away. She strains to hear it, holding her breath. Clumps of stringy hair cling to her collarbone with a sticky sweat that drips down the front of her t-shirt, leaving salty streaks across the giant screen-printed letters: **Isaiah 35:4 BE STRONG, DO NOT FEAR; YOUR GOD WILL COME!** She pulls her hands from the water and dries them on a dish towel hanging on the junk drawer knob to her right. The towel is filthy. She should have changed it out for a clean one last week, but Sue Mackenzie's got bigger fish to fry right now.

She walks around the island that separates her small kitchen from the living area. The speckled laminate was once the pride of a seventies housewife but now sits dingy and worn with a fringe of crackle along its edge. Sue stops at the corner of the bar and sends out a shallow prayer that emerges only as a sigh: *Be with me, Lord. I can't do this again.* Another faint *ratta-tat-tat,* another skipped heartbeat, and then the drums fade away. *For now.* But they will be back. Just like last time. The drums come first, and then… *the demons.* Sue tries to inhale deeper but can't. She is going into a panic. Again.

They're coming.

Sue's vision begins to collapse like she's in a tunnel. *Fuck, here it comes.* As the room spins, her knees abruptly give out and she falls forward, catching herself on the island. She leans forward, resting her head on her forearm and looking down through the oak bar stools. The dirty moss carpet swirls from below like a black hole, threatening to suck her into its void if she doesn't get it together. *Good God, what is wrong with me?* Her throat is thick and dry, but she manages to squeak out a cry for her daughter.

"Josephine!"

And then they start again. *The drums.*

ratta-tat-TAT

This time there is no mistaking them. They crash suddenly in a tidal wave—first the snares, ear-shattering and unforgiving. Their strike is sharp and taunting, growing louder and louder, *ratta-tat-TAT, you bitch, RATTA-TAT-TAT!!!* Then the bass shakes the duplex—*BOOM, BOOM, BOOM*—crashing glass against glass in the kitchen cabinets until the doors fly open and dishes launch into the kitchen like missiles. CRASH, CRASH, CRASH! The cymbals explode; a light bulb in the hallway shatters. The drums pound deep and penetrating, like a heart attack inside Sue's head. She lets out a gasp and covers her ears to drown out the noise as she stumbles blindly into the living room, falling back into the worn-leather recliner just as the toms kick in all at once in a macabre "Wipe Out!" crescendo.

Then… nothing.

Sue sits panting until her vision clears. A few minutes, maybe more, maybe less. Her veins are sleet. Every cell in her body is being squeezed by frosted hands as she sits stunned in the silent aftermath. The house has turned into a meat locker, and she can see her breath in the dim light of the stale living room. Sue watches in horror and awe as her big, flatscreen TV—almost fully blocking the picture window directly in front of her—suddenly cracks like ice on an almost-frozen pond. She flashes back to a scene on that winter planet from that *Star Wars* movie, except she doesn't have a warm, stinking yak carcass to crawl into. Just cold all over her body, like a frigid vice compressing her bones. She tries to say the 23rd Psalm, but it comes out in stuttered, short-breathed staccato. She stops abruptly, almost forgetting where she is. Sue calls for Josie again, but nothing comes out. Her chest rises and falls like a piston on a steam engine. The dizziness returns. She calls out once more, this time finding her voice.

"JOSIE!"

There is no reply. Her daughter's bedroom door is shut, not ten feet from where Sue now sits in the middle of the living room. Either Josie is too scared to answer, or she slipped out to meet her friends at The Hollow. Sue would bet money it's the latter; certain she heard the front door click quietly shut when she got out of the shower after supper. But she's not mad, not this time. She prays that her youngest hasn't heard the demon beat after so many days of silence, so many days thinking the nightmare was over. For once, Sue would rather Josie was hanging out with her lowlife friends—drinking stolen beer and smoking cigarettes over a bonfire—than be here in this stifling cave of madness.

Sue pulls her cell phone from the front pocket of her jeans and taps on Josie's number in the recent calls list. It rings and rings, but no one answers. *Is something wrong?* Josie always answers. Not texts (God forbid; she always ignores Sue on those), but she knows to pick up when her mother calls. It's a nonnegotiable that Sue has drilled into her daughter since she got her first phone when she was eleven. It's probably nothing (and Josie will get hell for it later), but Sue *is* worried. Did the demons follow her? Or is she ignoring her mother's call, maybe because they argued about her friends over dinner?

Sue shoves her phone back into her pocket. She honestly doesn't know if she is more pissed or panicked.

"Jesus help me," she whispers through a salty tear. She breathes in silence for a few minutes, wishing she had grabbed her pack of smokes before she bolted out of the kitchen.

RATTA-TAT-TAT

Sue jumps out of the recliner like it's a trampoline, grabbing her Bible from the end table next to her and clutching it to her chest as she sprints toward her bedroom. *Our Father, who art in heaven, hallowed be thy name.* The drums pound as she stumbles through the doorway, leaps onto her old mattress, and curls up with eyes squeezed shut under a painting of the Holy Christ watching from the wall above. The image is massive, spanning almost the width of the double bed—an oversized head-and-shoulders Jesus gazing out with hands folded in solemn prayer. His cornflower eyes match the Wedgewood blue in a faded quilt passed down to Sue from her great-grandmother, so the bedroom seemed like the perfect place for him. Sue bought the painting last summer at the starving artist show in Floyd. At first, she thought it was just a lucky find, but now she wonders if God himself led her to it. Her bedroom is her sanctuary, and blue-eyed Jesus is there to protect her. Demons cannot hurt anyone in the presence of the heavenly Lord and Savior.

Everyone knows that.

And tonight, Jesus does not disappoint. As Sue lies huddled in her bed, holding a chain of rosary beads in one hand and her Bible in the other, the drumbeat stops sharply as if recoiling from the judging stare of the Holy Son. *Amen, Jesus! Hallelujah!* The room is now silent, broken only by Sue's desperate sobs and sputtering breathing. She is a woman nearing defeat. For just a few seconds, she opens her eyes and looks frantically around the room (just to be sure), then closes them again. She curses herself for not having done more to protect the house. Pastor Bill gave her a shoebox full of old plastic crosses that had been gathering dust in the basement of Cave Spring Lutheran Church, waiting to be thrown out with the Monday trash. Why hadn't she put them out? If anything happens to Josephine...

She sighs and gives up. There is no point in entertaining regret. *Shoulda, woulda, coulda.* She and Josie have gotten soft since the demons showed up just over two weeks ago. They let down their guard; got distracted by life. Sue will not let that happen again. She drops the rosary beads softly onto the quilt beneath her. Her best friend, Gina Baymont, gave them to her after the first encounter, after they had the house blessed by Gina's priest, Father Rick. Sue isn't Catholic, but she was ready to try anything. It seemed to have helped a little. It hasn't been as bad as it was on the day of the party. But tonight? It feels like the demons are coming back with a vengeance. Sue hopes she is wrong.

She reaches wearily over to a small table next to her bed and grabs the last remnant of a joint sitting in an amber-glass bowl. A bit of ash falls onto the faded lavender scarf used as a makeshift tablecloth, but Sue does not wipe it away. The butt has been cold for days, and it's not the first time a little burned-up Mary Jane has marred the chiffon. She pulls a Zippo lighter from her back pocket. Her jeans are too tight, and it takes a few seconds to get it out. *Mom jeans*, she thinks, disgusted at her expanding waistline. She rubs her finger over the laser-engraved cross on the front of the lighter before flicking the flame. The joint is lit, and in two long tokes Sue Mackenzie goes from manic to mellow in the soft glow of Jesus's love.

She stays collapsed on the bed with her head resting at an awkward angle against the fake wood headboard for several minutes. Or maybe it is an hour. She is losing track. What time was it when she started rinsing the dishes—when the sudden tapping of the demon drums startled her, and she dreamed about dropping the mug on the floor? Or the mug crashed itself. She isn't so sure anymore. She reaches for her phone again to check the time. It's almost ten. Sue looks through the crack in her bedroom curtains. The days are getting shorter now, even though it still feels like summer. Has it already been two hours? She squeezes her eyes shut and concentrates. She and Josie ate dinner around seven—late because Josie got detention again and Sue couldn't get her a ride home until Gina finished her shift at Staples. Sue blames her ex-husband. It's all Randy's fault. *Bastard.* If he weren't such a dick about needing his van back, she wouldn't be in this position. She silently curses him and prays that the good Lord will find it in Himself to place a nail in one of those tires; it will serve the asshole right. Then she retracts it, because that's not what a good Christian woman does. *Sorry, Jesus.*

Back to the time lapse. Sue clenches her eyes tighter and tries to remember. After dinner she took a quick shower, and then… and then she indulged in a little of that sweet dope she got last week from Pastor Bill's son, Cliff. He's not supposed to sell it (personal use only), but that's their little secret. Cliff gets a little something under the table; Sue gets a little something to take the edge off her stressful life as a mom and front desk manager at Courtyard by Marriott. She needs a little homegrown relief now and then to deal with the assholes of the world—who might be her own teenager, or they might be difficult hotel guests. Depends on the day. Cliff has some robust pot growing out on Buck Mountain Road. Downright wicked. Best she's had in years.

Holy shit.

Sue sits up with her swollen brown eyes wide open. She took a few hits from Cliff's joint, which she then carefully snuffed out and stashed on top of the cabinets in the kitchen to finish later (more than a toke or two of his special blend will put her in a coma). Then she sat down in her recliner for a few minutes. She was looking forward to watching *Friends* reruns until she nodded off. And after that? Totally blank. The next thing she remembers is standing in front of the sink with a wet sponge in her hand and a broken cup on the floor, hearing the drums for the first time in almost a week. She must have lost… what? An hour? Almost two? It's beginning to make sense. What the hell is Cliff growing over there? LSD weed? Sue suddenly realizes what happened. She laughs from way down in her gut, so hard she can't breathe. She sounds like a horse with a pack-a-day habit, and that makes her laugh even harder.

She wheezes for a full minute before blowing a kiss at blue-eyed Jesus and hoisting her perimenopausal body off the side of the bed. She's got a great story for Gina, that's for sure. *Two hours.* She lost damn near two hours. The last time she had a reaction like that to marijuana was back in her early twenties in Ohio, when her roommate brought back a questionable dime bag from a trip to Cleveland. Sue didn't think Cleveland was the hub for fierce weed, but apparently, she thought wrong. It took a full weekend to recover from that one. And now here she is, a quarter century later, blacking out just the same but this time waking up in front of a sink full of dirty dishes instead of on the sidewalk two blocks from her apartment in Akron.

She is full of confidence now (*FU drums!*) as she walks—no, *struts*—back into her living room, flipping on several lamps to break the darkness (just in case). She looks over at the hall light between her bedroom and the bathroom. Still intact. No shattered bulbs or broken light shades on the floor. The TV looks perfectly normal—more evidence that the drums were a pot-fed paranoia. That and stress, most likely. It's been a banner year here at the old Mackenzie household.

But I'm back, baby.

Josephine will be home in an hour, and Sue wants her to know that her mother is waiting. An eleven o'clock curfew is plenty late for a fifteen-year-old. Sue is confident that it was THC causing the drums this time, and not the demons (although she is certain they have not left). Still, she dials Josie's cell again. Just to be sure she's safe and alive. As the other end of the connection rings, Sue looks around and realizes that Pepper is nowhere to be seen. Her old Yorkie is usually napping on the living room couch or huddled beneath the counter under a bar stool. He is in neither spot. For a moment, Sue has a horrifying thought that maybe something happened to him while she was "out." *Did I leave the front door open?*

As she heads toward the kitchen, Sue notices the basement door is slightly ajar. She vaguely recalls going downstairs to do laundry just after Gina dropped Josie off. Pepper may have gotten himself lost down there, and it would not be the first time. He likes to shadow his humans when they head down the steps and sometimes gets disoriented amid all the junk piled up behind Josie's hangout couch. Sue figures she'll find Pepper in the massive cardboard fort in the far corner. She hangs up her unanswered call to her daughter (compartmentalizing her anger for the moment) and makes her way toward the stairs in a quest for her canine and a basket of clean clothes.

As she reaches for the doorknob, it shakes violently in her hand. She gasps and recoils, then curses herself. *I'm not falling for that again.* It makes sense how she conjured up the scary drums; they have been here before, legitimately. But a shaking doorknob? Where did she come up with that? Sue rolls her eyes and smiles at her paranoia. It's probably just mad old Alice Winchester from next door. In this duplex, the basement is shared, with each tenant having their own stairwell. This isn't the first time her retired neighbor has trespassed onto Sue's territory. The first time was shortly after Sue and Josie moved in, when Alice came over (through the basement, unbelievably) to borrow some sugar. *Do people still do that?* Apparently so. Another time it was to deliver some misdirected mail. Rather than just put it in Sue's mailbox like a normal person, Alice felt the need to come up the *inside* staircase again and bang on Sue's basement door. *Damn near gave me a coronary, stupid old bitty.* It's about time to put a stop to this. She throws open the basement door like she's mad at it, ready to give Alice the gears.

But there is no one there.

She pulls a chain hanging above the second step to turn on the stairwell light and see if Alice retreated to her own territory (it's not likely she could move that fast at her age, but stranger things have happened). The bulb flickers and then goes out, leaving Sue with an empty stairwell. All she can see are the first few slabs of bare pine. *Goddammit,* she thinks, then quickly apologizes to God for taking his name in vain. She meant to replace that bulb earlier, when it was still daytime. A faint glow from the front house lights comes through the basement windows, slipping through the sides of the faded plaid curtains that provide moderate privacy from passing critters. It's not enough light to prevent her from killing herself on the steep stairs, so she goes back to the kitchen, pulls a flashlight out of the junk drawer, and continues her mission.

"Alice?" she calls out softly. No answer.

"Pepper?" Sue hears rustling from the back of the boxes. Then a high-pitched bark. Yep, there he is.

She descends slowly, sidestepping the rusty nail sticking out of the fourth step from the bottom. Yet another item on her to-do list that she hasn't gotten around to. When Sue reaches the end of the stairs, she pans the flashlight around, looking for her lost pooch. The gleam of the beam reflects off a cymbal hanging on an old drum set left there by one of the previous tenants. Sue's heart jumps out of her chest for a second as she flashes back a few weeks to her grandson Finn's birthday gathering when they first heard the drums. Cliff's pot might have caused tonight's mental episode, but there was nothing on this God's green earth that could explain what happened that day. No one was in the basement, yet the drums had come from inside the house. And there were other things. Sue doesn't want to think about them.

Something moves in the corner. Sue shines the flashlight over toward the boxes. It sounds larger than a Yorkie, but Pepper *is* getting chunky. Sometimes he tries to jump up onto one of the empty cardboard cubes and gets trapped inside.

"Come on, Pepper! C'mere, boy!"

She gets no response, but suddenly the rancid stench of urine and fecal matter overpowers her. The air is thick and pungent, and she lets out a cough, placing her hand over her nose and mouth to numb the effect. *What in the ever-loving hell???* Something slithers across her ankle, and she is about to scream when she realizes it is Pepper. He circles twice, then stands with hair on end, growling into the darkness at the far corner of the basement… behind the drums, behind the old couch where Josie sits and doomscrolls for hours. It is pitch black over there, and Sue does not want to reveal anything with her flashlight, let alone walk over there by herself to pull the chain on another light bulb.

ratta-tat-tat

Pepper barks sharply and continues growling as Sue swings the flashlight around, reluctantly pointing it toward the drum set that sits in front of the couch not six feet from where she is standing. *It's just the pot; it's just the pot.* One of the cymbals is swinging back and forth like a maniacal pendulum. Sue's breath quickens, and she pivots the flashlight away, clutching the bottom of her t-shirt with her other hand. If only she had brought her Bible. *It's just the pot; it's just the pot.* She is having trouble convincing herself. Pepper is barking violently now, and the smell of piss and shit is unmistakable. Sue is ready to get out of there, so she turns to head back toward the stairs. But there is something blocking her way, something that wasn't there before. She stumbles to the stair rail, and in the wave of the flashlight beam she sees a snare drum on its stand, separated from the rest of the set and somehow moved to where she was just standing. *How can that be?* It wasn't there before; she would have walked right into it. Yet here it is, alone and unmoving as the *ratta-tat-tat* continues, getting louder and louder even though the drum set and its rogue snare remain untouched.

Untouched by anything visible, that is.

RATTA-TAT-TAT RATTA-TAT-TAT RATTA-TAT-TAT

The rapping is so loud that Sue can hardly hear her own rattled breath whispering a slur of prayers. She feels the hammering at her core, even louder than her heart, which is about to burst out of her chest. Something lets out a long hiss.

Sssssuuuuuuuuue. A manma ungho artee masho manma suuuuuuu

Sue's knee buckles under the weight of fear as she tries to go up. She can't stand, so she turns and sits, facing the black nothing. Pepper flies upward, leaving her alone in the dungeon with the goblins.

Sssssuuuuuuuuue. Masho nima suuuuuuu

"WHAT DO YOU WANT FROM ME?" she yells into the darkness.

She lifts her backside up a single step, struggling to hoist herself into a wobbly stand. Heading toward the basement door above would be the quickest way back to safety, but she's not about to turn her back on the unknown.

Sssssuuuuuuuuue.

It whispers on her neck. Not in the dark caverns of the basement; not over by the snare drum that beats without moving; not in the blackness or under the stairs or in the pipes or over by the water heater where Sue doesn't go at night even on a good day.

It is near her. No… it is *on her.* Like a demon lover holding her frozen in an invisible grasp so it can whisper sweet, rotten nothings in her ear. It is heavy, solid, and creaking on the stair, yet there is nothing there but shadow. The booming drum song suddenly softens to a delicate tap, as if to make sure Sue hears its death whisper.

Sssssuuuuue… A manma ungho artee… come closer…

ratta-tat-tat

I have something to

ratta-tat-tat

tell you

ratta-tat-tat

GET OUT!!!

She narrowly misses the protruding nail as she turns and flees upward toward the light.

Two doors slam simultaneously. Sue Mackenzie reaches the top of the stairs, shoves the basement door shut, and pushes in the lock on the doorknob just as her daughter Josephine comes into the house through the front entrance. As Jo throws her old military backpack into the corner, she spots her mother across the room. Jo is home well before curfew, so she thinks she is safe. She takes a step, brushing her hands down the front of her hot-pink hoodie to get rid of any crumbs or wrinkles that might trigger her mother. Some days, that's all it takes. Jo shifts her shoulders and wiggles them back and forth like she's uncomfortable in the fleece. And she *is* uncomfortable for many reasons. The pockets are too small to be of any use (because that's how they make pockets for girls, apparently), and her arms are stuffed like sausages into the fuchsia sleeves. Pink is most definitely not her color, and even though it's a plain zip-up, it's still too feminine for her tomboy tastes. She only wears it coming and going. A more comfortable long-sleeved Salem Red Sox T-shirt is hidden in her pack, the baseball logo and drab gray much more Jo's style. She slipped into the sports top once she was out of her mother's watchful eye, then changed back into the more mom-friendly hoodie when she was heading back home. Anything to avoid a fight. If Jo let her mother have her way, she'd still be wearing lacy ruffles and white patent leather Mary Janes.

Jo stops cold when Sue collapses onto the kitchen counter. From across the room, she can see her mother's crucifix dangling over what is likely the remains of Jo's dinner. The leftover pork stew might become tomorrow's breakfast as punishment for Jo not finishing her meal. Or it might get tossed. Like everything, it depends on the many moods of Sue Mackenzie. Sue coughs deeply from her Marlboro lungs and looks over at her daughter. Jo won't move until she is sure of the situation. It is always a crapshoot what state Sue might be in. Is she upset over another phone call from Jo's half-brother Jared? Is he drinking again, or worse? Or is it Jo again, not being the perfect daughter? Jo glances sideways at the oversized clock above the sofa on the inside wall of the living room. The cross-shaped hands read twelve minutes after ten, well before her eleven o'clock curfew. So it can't be that.

Sue shivers as if startled, like she only just notices another person standing in the living room. Her face is blotchy and red, and Jo can tell she has been crying (or smoking dope) even behind the straggled hair matted across her forehead and half-covering her bloodshot eyes. *Shit.* Jo takes a step back, feeling the heel of her sneakers skim the bottom of the front door. Her intuition kicks in and she goes into defensive mode. What is intuition but the culmination of being in a certain situation so many times that you can sense it coming? Jo has been in this situation far too many times. First it was Jared's addiction. Now it is her own disease, an acute case of "not good enough for Mom." She has learned to trust her gut. Sure enough, Sue suddenly pushes away from the counter and rages toward her daughter like a rabid dragon. Jo is caught in the corner between the door and the wall, unable to escape the real-life demon coming at her with full force. She sucks in her breath in instant panic, raising her arms to protect her face, but not before her mother slaps her hard across her left cheek—and then again, almost too quick to be humanly possible. The second one hits Jo's forearm, but it still makes its mark.

Jo is beyond stunned. She can't remember the last time Sue laid hands on her. *What is happening?*

"Where have you been???" Sue cries as Jo shrinks into the dark corner. "I've been trying to call you all night!"

Jo bites her lip and breathes quietly into the sting now pulsating throughout her cheek. She does not look up. She tries to make herself sound like the sweet little girl her mom wants her to be. As much as she is able at fifteen.

"I'm sorry! I texted you I was going out. I was at Julie's house with her and Shaun."

She regrets it as soon as it comes out of her mouth. Jo is well aware that her mother hates texting and hates her friends, especially Shaun. Sue predictably fumes, and Jo almost expects smoke to come out of her nostrils.

"If I call, you will pick up the phone! I have told you that a thousand times!"

"I couldn't answer; we were watching a movie! It was too loud!"

Jo scrambles for an excuse because she knows she messed up. She makes herself as small as possible, cupping the cheek where her mother's wrath still burns. Her eyes are watering, but she chokes back the tears.

Sue explodes. "Are you an idiot? Did your brain cells get cooked up with your popcorn? THEN WALK INTO THE OTHER ROOM WHERE IT'S QUIET!"

She takes a step toward her daughter. Her adrenaline is in overdrive now, but she can't let it go too far. The last thing she wants is to have Child Protective Services on her ass. They'd already been through that a few times with Jared and his drugs. Sue takes in as much of a breath as she can muster and tries to control the rage that shakes her entire body.

"What were you doing?" she asks me through gritted teeth. "Were you doing drugs? Or other… things?"

Jo almost rolls her eyes. *Here we go. She thinks I'm off getting pregnant with criminals and smoking crack like she smokes cigarettes.* This is what goes through her mom's head. All. The. Time. And Jo finds it hypocritical coming from someone who gets her dope from the pastor's son. It doesn't matter what Jo tells her. Sue is going to believe what she believes.

"What were you doing with that… *girl?* And hanging out with that pillow biter and his slut mother? Do you know what God is going to do to you for this?"

Sue is right up in Jo's face with her finger pointed, almost touching the same cheek she just slapped. Sometimes she can't stand the sight of her daughter, who looks like a boy with her short hair and ugly high-tops poking out from under her baggy pants. Gina was right; Jo's behavior is pathetic and embarrassing. What Sue doesn't know is that Jo is well aware of what her mother and her mother's best friend think of her. She overheard them talking a few weeks before. Jo was in the basement and opened a window to let in some fresh air. Gina and Sue were out on the front steps and didn't know she could hear them.

"Your daughter is headed down a path, Sue. It is not God's way. The Bible is clear on that."

Jo isn't entirely sure what Gina meant, but she knows it's not good. And what's worse, her mother didn't even defend her. All she could say was, *"Uh-huh. I know it, girl."*

That hurt more than anything. That her own mom wouldn't stand up for her. And it has only gotten worse since then.

"You're not leaving this house again except for school. Do you hear me? TWO WEEKS!"

The sound of Sue's voice pushes Jo from fear into fury. She forgets her swollen cheek and prepares to go apeshit (and didn't she learn that from the best?). She's had enough of her mother's craziness and wild mood swings. It was bad enough when they first moved to this shithole neighborhood two years ago, but ever since Sue met up with that Jesus freak Gina and her bitchy little dog, things have gone over the top. If Sue is a religious nut, then Gina is the entire nut tree. But Jo doesn't dare say anything about her mom's new BFF. She tried that once, and it didn't turn out well. When the two women first started hanging out, Jo accused her mother of being gullible with Gina. As a result, her phone was taken away for a week. Right now, she needs that phone more than ever. You never know when you may have to jam.

"Why don't you leave me alone? I HATE YOU!"

Jo pounds her right fist into the wall behind her (luckily not penetrating the drywall), but doesn't take a step toward the beast, even though she has twenty pounds and two inches on her. Sue is stunned at the level of disrespect coming from her daughter. Her teeth are clenched so tightly that Jo wonders if they might crack.

"I am your mother! You will not talk to me like that in my house! MY HOUSE!"

She spits as she yells, a spray of droplets hitting Jo in the face and neck. *Fuck this!* Jo catches her breath and lets loose a primal scream thick with rage. She thrusts her contorted face toward her mother, fists clenched. Sue takes a step back in surprise. Taking advantage of the half-second it will take her mother to truly comprehend her outburst (which will be interpreted as gross insubordination), Jo skirts around her and escapes into the doorway of her bedroom a few feet to her right. She slams the door behind her and wishes she could lock it— lock her batshit crazy mother out of her room and out of her life forever. But Sue won't allow locks. *Oh God, no.* Locks are for drinking and drugs and fornication, and a litany of sins Jo has heard about every day almost since she could understand language. *Locks are for secrets, and there will be no secrets in this house.*

Jo sits at her tiny desk, taking deep breaths and trying to calm down. She wants to hide under the bedcovers, but that will leave her too vulnerable. She needs to stand; it is the best defensive mode to face her mother's rage. But standing upright is impossible right now. Her legs are weak, like unfired clay. So, she sits in the desk chair that has been too small for her since she was twelve. Her hand is shaking as she lifts it to her cheek, hiding the red mark and swelling. It hurts like hell. But she will not cry. *Fuck that.* Jo doesn't have much, but she has her pride. She would rather die than give that up.

Sue's anger deflates at the sound of Jo's bedroom door slamming. She is conflicted, torn between anger at her daughter for disrespecting her and her instinct to be a protective mother. There is still something here in the house, something bad. It is burrowing its way inside both of them like a malignant tumor. Changing Josie into something she is not. Turning Sue into a demon herself. *I shouldn't have slapped her.* Sue knows that… so why did she do it?

This is not me. I am not that woman.

She is still a mother. Whatever that thing is in the basement—whatever demon hound of hell is in this house—it didn't follow her up to the main floor. This time. For that, she is grateful and silently prays. *Thank you, Jesus.*

As much as she wants to confront Josie right away, she needs a moment. The demons have won this battle. She retrieves her cigarettes from the kitchen and plops down on her recliner. It is a little tattered, like her Bible, and nearly as much comfort as The Good Book in these past few years. As she lights up, she looks over to the couch where Pepper is curled up. He seems to have only two moods lately: hyperactive and coma. His state fluctuates almost hourly, and right now he is firmly entrenched on the sleep side of his bipolar personality. This makes no sense. Pepper is a deep sleeper for sure, but he always wakes up at loud noises. Given a warm, soft cushion, he'll sleep like an old man. But if someone walks by on the sidewalk or the neighbor's dog comes out, Pepper is at the window barking deep and fierce like he's a wolf. Yet somehow, he fell into a nap in the middle of Sue's fight with Josie. He didn't even move when Josie screamed. That's crazy, because Josie is his world.

Something isn't right.

Sue pinches the top of her nose to relieve the pressure building under her skull while she tries to think. He hasn't been acting like his normal self for a while; it isn't just tonight. He won't go into Josie's room, not since that damn party. My poor little old guy hasn't been himself since the drums started.

"Pepper!" she calls quietly. He doesn't move. "Pepperoni? Pup-pup?"

When he doesn't respond to his favorite nicknames and louder calls, Sue leans over to her curled-up bundle of wiry fur and nudges him from the recliner. Pepper doesn't move; doesn't snort or stir or lick his chops like he is eating a squirrel. She pushes again, harder. Nothing. His chest is rising slightly, so at least he is breathing. He was awake not ten minutes ago! She presses even harder. Still, he remains motionless.

Her eyes fill with tears. "Fuck."

It's not just the dog. Sue rarely spanked Josephine as a child, but her behavior these past six months has been troublesome. At first, Sue thought it was just a phase—the bad influence of a crowd she'd started hanging out with over summer break. They are very much part of the problem. Maybe even the cause. Especially Shaun Rivers. Sue went to school with his mom, Cheryl (Bodard, before she got married—or as

Sue used to call her, "Cheryl Rode-Hard… and put away wet"). She was rough, that's for sure. Still is. Nasty girl with an even nastier personality as an adult. And that little fucker Shaun is just like his mom. "*Severely lacking any breadth of culture or manners,*" as Sue's late father would have said under his breath from behind a newspaper. And often did about her own friends, but that's another story. Shaun has been banned from the Mackenzie house since Josie's movie night last spring when Sue's favorite gold-plated bell vanished. That little snake stole it, no doubt about it. He was the only one in the room, and Sue noticed it missing right away. She hoped he'd come to his senses, but he is a dark one. She'll never see that bell again. It isn't worth squat, and that's the worst part. He just did it because he could. Because he's a heathen like his mom.

The rest of Josie's friends are a motley bunch of misfits, outcasts, and losers, and why she spends time with them is beyond Sue's comprehension. Josie has a tested IQ of 125, and she's hanging out with dimwits. She once had friends who were on the honor roll. Now she has friends with criminal records. And she acts just like them, wearing boys' clothes and trimming—no, *buzzing*—her beautiful blond hair like she's going into the Army. She even told Sue she doesn't want to be called Josie anymore. Imagine that! She has been Josie all her life! Baby Josie, then Little Josie, then Sweet Josie, Josie Boo, Jo-Josie, Jo-Jo. What now? Rebellious Josie? BOY Josie? She is running with a dangerous crowd, and Shaun is a homosexual. Sue would bet her life on it. Honor roll Josie is now just "Jo," hanging with thieves and gays and worthless delinquents who smell like old laundry, body odor, and misery.

But Sue knows the real reason Josie associates with these lazy sons of bitches. She knows why her daughter started skipping school and got her first detention (ever) just three weeks into the school year. She looks over her shoulder at the locked basement door, shuddering at whatever lies beyond. *The demons caused this.* Those fucking demons. They are the reason Josie wears boys' basketball jerseys to school, why she secretly smokes Camels and parties every weekend, and why she has a personal relationship with the truancy officer. The demons have done it. They caused Sue's son to go back on heroin. Jared had been doing so well—taking classes at the community college, working at the bakery, going to his group therapy like a good recovering addict. Trying to be a decent dad. And then he relapsed, and it was right around the time of that damn party earlier this month when they celebrated the first birthday of Jared's son.

The day the demons arrived.

Sue pauses for a moment, as if frozen in thought. The drums are gone for the moment, but the demons are never far away. Something happened on the day of the party. Something unearthly awakened or tore open, releasing a piece of hell into her house. Before that day, they were doing just fine, thank you very much. Jared was clean and sober, taking responsibility for his new baby and working to better himself. He even got one of his articles published in a biker magazine: "To Hell and Back" by Jared Mackenzie, published author. A mother was never so proud. Josie started her sophomore year in high school, coming into it with a solid 3.9 GPA from last year. That psychopath bully Luke Sizemore—who tortured Josie during most of her freshman year—moved to Amarillo, Texas, with his dad after his parents split, so he was out of the picture. And it was lucky for Luke too, because Josie gained three inches and nearly thirty pounds last year, not to mention some fighting skills she learned from Jared, who once studied taekwondo. Everyone else was behaving, mostly. Even Sue's ex, Randy, seemed cooperative. He let Sue borrow his van when her geriatric Impala took a tank in the middle of Main Street in Buchanan on a sleepy Sunday last July. Didn't bug her about returning it either.

But something happened. Something dark. It started at the party… before they heard the footsteps in the basement, before the drums came. It was when Sue and Josie fought after Josie came out of her room dressed like a boy with her hair all buzzed off. Looking like a damn carpet muncher. Sue can't keep the bile from rising into her throat just thinking about it. Josie *is* different. She is going down a path that will end in damnation if she isn't careful. Last week she failed her first test ever, and it wasn't even a hard one. Algebra II. She aced that stuff in her first year of junior high! And she has been dressing like a boy since the middle of summer. Even acting like she wants to *be* one sometimes. Hanging out with those little fuckers. Staying out late, skipping school.

"Lord Jesus, be my strength," Sue prays through tight breath and tears. "Guide me, protect this family. Watch over my baby boy so he doesn't have to go back to rehab. Protect my grandson Finn and his little chubby cheeks."

She inhales her Marlboro Gold, holds it for a moment while the cigarette quivers in her unsteady hand, then blows out the smoke slowly.

"And help me bring my daughter to reason. Help guide her to the right way, bring her back to her senses. Show her the way so that she may someday enter your kingdom and see your glory. In Jesus's name, Amen."

With her free hand, she softly fiddles with the cross around her neck. She'll have to go in and soothe Josie in a minute. Even though her daughter brought this on herself (she's nearly sixteen; she knows better), Sue is still the gatekeeper. She is the mother, the wise force in the household. She must take the first step in reconciliation. Sue asks Jesus to help her remain calm. God knows, getting angry only pushes Josephine away even more. She needs to keep it under control.

But it is so hard.

When Josie walked out of her bedroom that morning before Finn's birthday party, with her military haircut and University of Virginia jersey, she looked just like Jared did ten years ago. *Like a boy.* Sue doesn't want to admit what she fears is going on, but she can no longer deny it. And she can't let that happen. Maybe she will have to send Josie to one of those rehab camps like Gina recommended. Get her back into God's good graces. Is that even possible? Sue doesn't know, and it frustrates her to no end. She is confused, and she doesn't know why. She knows what God says. The Good Book spells it out. But it feels… off. If Gina were here, she'd know what to say. Gina knows the Lord's word better than anyone Sue has ever met outside of the clergy. And Gina has complete conviction in her beliefs. Sue is confident that her friend will help her work through the doubt.

Sue sighs and looks to her right. She notices her Bible sitting on top of the end table on the opposite corner from the ashtray. *Didn't I leave that in the bedroom?* She shakes her head. *Nope. Not falling for that again.* Cliff's shit is taking its sweet time clearing out of her system, making her forget things. The Bible is showing its age. Sue's father gave it to her on the day she graduated from high school. He got it from his father, passed down through generations since the early 1900s. She touches the top for good luck and for protection. She doesn't know what might still be here in the house with them. But the infernal demons will have to wait. Now she must get up and deal with the hormonal ones inside her daughter.

Josie's door isn't locked; Sue doesn't allow that. Still, out of courtesy, she knocks before entering.

"Jo-bean?" Sue uses the nickname Jared called his sister when she was still a little girl, back when she wore ruffles and bows and didn't fight her mother about every damn thing.

Josephine's double-bed sits pushed against the front wall of the house, with too many pillows piled against the antique wood headboard. *The more pillows you have, the richer you are.* That's what Sue's mother used to say, anyway. Another lie. Josie has given up her defense posture and is now curled up on the bed hiding under her old yellow comforter. The quilt has seen better days, and the delicate daisies seem ironic given the changes over the past few months. She is sniffling. Sue can hear it from the doorway. Good. This is a positive sign. Remorse is the first step in repentance.

"Get out of my room," Josie says flatly from behind her posy blanket. She pulls it tighter around her, as if to reiterate her demand.

Sue takes a step forward, preparing herself for the worst. Which she probably deserves. *Keep it calm, keep it cool. You already crossed a line. Now is not the time to double down.*

"Josephine, I'm just doing what's best for—"

She stops. The air around her is cold as a January midnight. Her heart quickens, but she checks herself. It felt the same when she was hallucinating in the aftermath of Cliff's joint, and that turned out to be a whole lot of nothing. Still, it gets her neck hairs on end. When they first heard the drums at Finn's party, the air turned to ice just like this. It was so cold that they could see each other's breath even though it was early September. Still summer, officially. Yet, it had felt like dead winter. Sue breathes into the memory rather than trying to suppress it, praying that what she feels now is just her imagination or more weed effects. She doesn't want to give herself a reason to believe otherwise.

But her body is shivering. It betrays her confidence. *Please no, Jesus, Mary, and Joseph, please protect us, not again, not again, not again…*

Nothing happens, and when she finally looks over behind the edge of the headboard, Sue notices the window has been cracked open a good eight inches. Her shoulders drop in relief, but only for a few seconds before her patience is cracked a few inches, and the tension sneaks back in. *For fuck's sake! What now?* She sniffs around. The room doesn't smell of smoke. The window isn't open enough for Josie to sneak out, and she's just as likely to walk out the front door. It's getting chilly outside, so why on earth would she let all that cold in?

"What in the hell, Josephine?"

She stomps over to the window and slams it down.

"Do you think we're made of money? Who do you think is paying for the damn heating bill?"

Sue hasn't even turned the heat on at night yet, but still. She spits out "damn" with emphasis. Sue doesn't like to swear out loud, but lately it's hard not to. Well, that isn't quite the truth. She loves to swear, but she knows God doesn't approve, so she tempers her mouth in certain company.

Josie's voice is muffled under the covers. "I was just trying to get some fresh air! It smells like roadkill in here."

Sue walks back to the foot of the bed and sniffs again near the closet and bedroom door. She can't smell anything, though her nose is like a bloodhound's. Josie is lying. But her tall tales take a back seat when Sue looks over at her desk and gets triggered by the heathen rock T-shirts and sports jerseys strewn over the back of the chair. Who is she kidding with all her heavy metal Slayer/Anthrax crap? Devil's music is what it is. And what a farce! Josie listens to Gaga and Tay Tay Swift all day, every day. Sue has been hearing it from behind the bedroom door for years. Who knows all the words to "Poker Face" and "Cruel Summer?" Josephine Mackenzie, that's who.

The sports stuff is even worse. Sue bought Josie all kinds of blouses and skirts this past year. Where are those? She has half a mind to tear through Josie's closet, and it's all she can do to keep her displeasure contained. Heating bills and messy rooms are bad enough, but this whole teenage angst thing is about to send Sue on a detour down Losing-My-Shit Lane. She reminds herself that she must be the better person. Lead by example. *I am her mother. I am THE mother.* Repeating this mantra temporarily compartmentalizes her growing rage. *We WILL deal with this later.*

Sue stands at the edge of the bed, ready to do better. Immediately, Josie goes stiff, pulling her legs closer to her body and using the buttery quilt as a shield. Sue can feel her daughter's tension skyrocket. Or maybe it's her own stress. How can a mother love her child so deeply that it hurts… and some days wish she had never been born? Sue accepts the understanding and patience that are necessary to address the unacceptable behavior. At the same time, she literally wants to strangle Josie with the vacuum cord right now.

God, please help me guide this child back to herself; give me the patience.

"Josie." She exhales. "I apologize for losing my temp—"

Josie flips back her faded flower blanket and screams at her mother with bloodshot eyes and the imprint of Sue's hand fading on her cheek.

"GODDAMMIT, GET THE HELL OUT OF MY ROOM!"

God is not helping Sue with her patience one bit. *Why hast thou forsaken me?* She is mad. Mad at Josie, mad at herself, ashamed of it all. *I have failed her, and I have failed myself.* The compartmentalizing falters, allowing the anger and frustration to boil over as she tries in vain to quiet both the raging teenage volcano and the one erupting inside her own body.

Josie pulls the covers back over her head and screams into her flat, dingy pillow—the same one she's had since she was a toddler, when she'd suck her thumb and chew the corner until it was the color of mud. She'd cry bloody murder if anyone dared mention washing it. The memory softens Sue for a split second, and then she knocks it aside because she's all fury again. She stands up and yanks the covers back.

"Don't you ever talk to me that way, do you understand? EVER! You will not curse the Lord's name in this house!"

She leans over to grab Josie's arm, intending to drag her out of bed. BANG!

The bedroom door slams shut, jolting Sue out of her red zone as Josie pushes herself back into the corner of the bed and cowers against the wall like a four-year-old.

ratta-tat tat

The back of Sue's neck prickles, and she realizes she can see her breath. The room has dropped to arctic levels, just like it did at the party. It isn't nearly this cold outside. This isn't from an open window on the second day of fall in the southern US of A. She looks at her frightened daughter balled up in a pile of pillows. Her gut seizes, and she honestly isn't sure if it's because of Josie or because of the thing terrorizing their house.

ratta-tat tat RATTA-TAT TAT

It sounds like it is coming from inside the room, but how is that possible? Pepper barks from behind the door, having emerged from his coma and now returned to protective mode. For a split-second Sue entertains the thought of opening the door and letting him in, but her daughter is the more pressing matter. Something tells Sue to focus on her human offspring.

Josie peeks out from behind the quilt and stares wide-eyed toward the door with tears streaming down her face, her lips pressed together tightly. *She heard it too.*

"Josie, give me your hand."

Sue reaches across the bed.

BOOM BOOM BOOM BOOM

The sound of a bass drum shatters the icy room, shaking the walls and windows like an aftershock. Josie's bedside lamp falls off the nightstand. As the lampshade hits the dark green carpet, the room darkens. The bass drum pauses, as if taking a moment to appreciate its accomplishment. There is just enough silence for Sue's shoulders to relax; just long enough for her to think maybe it's over.

BOOM *RATTA-TAT TAT* BOOM BOOM BOOM *RATTA-TAT TAT*

The drums abruptly start again. Sue nearly falls backward at the pounding bass, now accompanied by the snare, which mocks her as it fills the upbeat with a frenzied rage.

"JOSIE!" she yells with a cloud of frosted breath that fades underneath the crescendo of the drums. "GIVE ME YOUR HAND!"

Josie hesitates, not wanting to make herself more visible to the growing darkness invading the room. Finally, she reaches out, and their fingers entwine. The front window suddenly slides up and wind whips through the opening like a dust devil, tossing the curtains about and toppling an old teddy bear off Josie's oak dresser on the other side of the room. Sue can see the trees outside in the streetlamp's glow. They aren't moving.

BOOM *RATTA-TAT TAT* BOOM BOOM BOOM *RATTA-TAT TAT*

Something sharp grabs the back of Sue's neck. It feels like fingernails, sharp and bitterly cold, squeezing her flesh and shoving her forward onto the bed. She releases Josie's hand and uses both arms to brace herself against the mattress. Something is holding her down. *Pushing* her. Sue strains to look over her right shoulder. She doesn't want to see what's there, but she needs to see what's there. There is nothing, just like in the basement. But she can feel it. The wind whips harder as the invisible hand grips Sue's neck more firmly, and she can't turn her head anymore. It forces her down with the strength of a professional wrestler, crushing her violently into the bedsheets. Her face sinks into the mattress until she can't open her left eye. The unseen hand seems to want to shove her right through to the floor.

BOOM *RATTA-TAT TAT* BOOM BOOM BOOM *RATTA-TAT TAT*

Josie lets out a half-scream, half-gasp. Sue turns her eyes upward and can just make out her daughter cowering in the corner of the bed. Her heart sinks at the thought of her baby girl being so terrified, but she is unable to break free from the ghostly force that restrains her.

"Jesus, please help me," she mumbles from her mashed mouth. She is sobbing and desperate and cries out in anguish.

Suddenly, it stops. The room is dead silent. The monster on Sue's back is gone, and she is free. She takes a desperate, tear-filled inhale and looks up at Josie, who is cupping one knee and rocking back and forth. The daisy quilt has fallen—or been pushed—off the bed. Even in the dim light, Sue can see a large handprint forming on her daughter's exposed thigh. *Did I do that?* No, that's impossible. Josie was crouched against the headboard. There was no way Sue could have reached across the bed; her hands were pinned under her shoulders.

BOOM *RATTA-TAT TAT* BOOM BOOM BOOM *RATTA-TAT TAT* BOOM BOOM BOOM *RATTA-TAT TAT*

Sue jumps up, not waiting for the demons to turn their attention back to her. She leans across the bed and again reaches out to Josie.

"JOSIE, NOW!"

It isn't rage in her voice this time, or disappointment, or guilt. It is a desperate order, the instinct of a mother. For just a second, Sue recognizes the woman she lost long ago. Josie clenches her mother's hand as Sue pulls her off the bed, putting her arms around her daughter protectively as they head toward the door. Josephine Suzanne Mackenzie is a little girl again, and Sue wants nothing more than to make all the bad go away and keep her safe. If that is even possible.

BOOM RATTA-TAT TAT BOOM BOOM BOOM RATTA-TAT TAT

They reach the bedroom door, and Sue has a brief pang of horror wondering if it will open. Mother and daughter will be locked in this room of terror with a typhoon of demons swirling around in madness. But the latch gives, and the two stumble into the living room as the drums continue their demonic rant. The beat has grown faster now, as if the drummer is on a rampage. A tom kicks in, far off from its snare and bass siblings, but almost more sinister in its quiet patience.

BOOM RATTA-TAT TAT BOOM (tom) BOOM BOOM RATTA-TAT TAT (tom)

Suuuuue… little giiiiiiirrrrllll

Sue blocks out the voice at her ear and pulls Josie toward the front door. She grabs her purse from the floor, tucked just behind the TV stand. Her mother taught her to keep her valuables at the ready, *just in case.* This is *just in case,* and Sue is vaguely grateful for having learned the value of a quick getaway. The drums get even louder as they make their way through the doorway, staggering down the driveway to Starry Knob Lane and running toward the main road at the entrance to the subdivision. It is dark, but the moon is bright, and they are close to a strip mall with lights beaming in the parking lot. The mall will be closed for the day, but there is a Marathon station next door. Sue pulls Josie through the thick grass along the shoulder, oblivious to the cars passing them at sixty miles per hour on Rte. 220. Sue has only one thought, and that is to get them to safety. The gas station is the nearest populated place, and right now she is desperate not to be alone. A semi whizzes by as they near the pumps. They slow down now that their refuge is in sight. Josie is still crying.

Sue can still hear the drums pulsating behind her as she dials Gina's number.

We Need SSSome Help

Wednesday, September 25, 6:30 pm
Initial call to Roanoke Investigations of the Paranormal (RIP)
Bean Residence, Saddleridge Rd, Roanoke, Virginia

Walter Bean

I have just put a tray of frozen taquitos into the microwave when my cell phone rings with an unknown local number. *Shit.* It might be spam, or it might be someone seeking help from the paranormal investigation team I run with my wife, Libbi. The 540 area code sways me in favor of it being a potential client versus "I've been trying to reach you about your car's extended warranty!" While I would love to send the caller to voicemail either way, my inbox is full. I don't want to lose out on a good haunting case, yet it's been a long day at work, and my stomach is rumbling. I ask myself: *What would Libbi do?* She would answer without hesitation, which means I will reluctantly do the same. *Damn.* I hope this is quick.

"Hello, this is Walter." I nearly drop the phone trying to punch in the cooking time on the microwave pad.

"Is this Roanoke Paranormal Investigations?"

The caller sounds roughly female, though the voice is on the husky side. You never know in today's world. A smoker would be my guess. There is a strange tone in her greeting. It's a little shaky, and "Investigations" comes out like there is a snake in the middle of the word—*Invessstigations.*

If I'm being honest (and I usually am), she sounds a little drunk. Which means it's some joker who found my number on our website *RIPafterdark.org* and just wants to talk about their ghost stories without an actual investigation. Like that guy last week—what was his name? Danny, that's it. Danny and his self-investigation, full-body apparitions, and untreated bipolar disorder. That's an hour I'll never get back. As much as I want a good, down-and-dirty haunting, I am already kicking myself for taking the call.

But the deed is done. I can smell the taquitos, but they will have to wait. I take a mental and physical deep breath.

"Yes, this is *Roanoke Investigations of the Paranormal.*" She gets our team's name wrong (like many people do), so I correct her mistake with emphasis. "This is Walter Bean speaking. How can I help you?"

The caller coughs deeply. Smoker's cough, I was right. Or maybe hair of the dog. She could be wasted.

"I have something… sssomething really weird going on in my house. I don't even know how to exssplain it. I'm not sure what to do and I was hoping you could help."

Though her speech is slow and drawn out, I don't think she's drunk. She sounds tired or maybe medicated. Great. This is a strong start.

The front door opens, and Libbi walks in with our three-year-old silver Labrador retriever, Fenny. Short for Fenrir. Fenrir is a wolf in Norse mythology and therein lies the irony. Our dog is about as far from a wolf as a modern canine can get. Bull in a china shop? Most definitely. Out-of-control baby rhino? Absolutely. Hungry, hungry hippo? Every second of every day. But a wolf? Not even close, in body or personality. I give her some pets with one hand as I put the caller on speaker with the other so Libbi can hear. The microwave dings. Story of my life.

"I'm sure we can help, ma'am." I'm being extra polite now that my wife is in the kitchen to witness my behavior. "Could I get your name and city you're calling from?"

"Sue Mackenzie. I'm in Roanoke."

A local client, and for that we are grateful. Having a dog that wakes us up at the butt-crack of dawn for a walk and first breakfast takes a super-late night to a new level of exhaustion. And by "us" I mean "Libbi," because Fenny knows she isn't getting her daddy up before ten o'clock on a weekend.

Sue, the caller, asks, "How much do you charge?"

"We don't charge anything for our services, Sue."

I repeat the standard response displayed in big, bold font on the home page of the RIP website. I also repeat her name, which is a tip a former boss and sales associate once gave me to make a stronger connection with strangers—and more importantly, to help remember people's names. Which is important in this case, because my instinct will be to forget this woman as soon as I hang up the phone.

"One hundred percent free. Why don't you tell me what you've been experiencing? I've got my wife Libbi here too, and she's going to take some notes."

I know what you're thinking. No, I'm not volunteering my wife for the administrative duties of our team because she's a woman. I'm volunteering her because she's a type A director of getting shit done. She's already given Fenny a treat and retrieved her MacBook Pro from its resting spot in her office down the hall. She is tapping the keyboard almost before I get the words out of my mouth. How is this sorcery possible? I don't know, but I'm married to it. She types the name *Sue Mackenzie* into one of our blank digital interview forms (honestly, I don't even know where she stores those forms) and pivots her laptop so I can view the screen if needed. From some parallel universe, she has also obtained a blank *printed* copy of our standard interview questions, which she slides across the cold quartz countertop to me— for reference, should I need it. And I will need it. That's Libbi. She doesn't miss a beat.

"Hi Sue," calls Libbi, leaning against our speckled counter with hands on *ASDF JKL;* ready to type.

"Hello." Sue sounds awkward. At least I hope it's awkward and not high.

I roll my eyes at Libbi. *Whack job,* I mouth silently. She shakes her head back at me. *Stop.*

I can be the problem child of our small ghost-hunting team. Libbi and I are the founders, and we both describe ourselves as healthy skeptics. I simply show my disbelief more openly (and with very little— okay, zero—tact). In our seven years of leading the group, we've run into more than a few "whack jobs." Meaning, a little *out there.* Borderline crazy or sometimes just seeking attention. Like the aforementioned Danny. When we first started our supernatural journey nearly a decade ago (with another group), our clients sincerely wanted to get to the truth. Now with all the TV shows, movies, and readily available phone cameras, everyone fancies themselves a paranormal investigator. Few people seem to want the truth. Instead, they want the professionals to prove they have a ghost or to do an exorcism.

So yeah, I'm a little jaded, and it comes out sometimes.

"Whereabouts are you in Roanoke?" I ask Sue, trying to channel some politeness so Libbi won't yell at me or give me the evil eye.

Sue clears her throat. "I'm over on the southeast side, just off 220 near Walmarts. Starry Knob Lane, in the Blue Ridge Estates subdivision."

Blue Ridge Estates is a small community on the southern edge of the Roanoke County line. Libbi and I frequent the Walmart in that area (or as the locals call it, "Walmarts" plural). I am somewhat familiar with the subdivision; one of my coworkers lives there, and last spring I gave him a ride to work for a few days when his car was in the shop. Blue Ridge Estates is an older neighborhood, built in the seventies, and the word "Estates" is misleading. It's more cookie-cutter ranch houses, lots of modest duplexes or divided houses, and average-sized lots surrounded by trees and farmland. Not ideal for investigating, but subdivisions never are. They usually have a lot of activity going on, and the houses (at least the ones built in my lifetime) are often constructed with cheap materials. Thin walls make noise pollution almost guaranteed.

"I know the area," I say, putting my phone on the counter between me and my wife. "So, tell us what you have going on?"

Sue takes a breath, and I can hear her telling someone in the background to be quiet.

"Well, where do I start? I live here with my daughter Josssephine and we've been having some weird ssstuff going on for the past few weeks. The mossst recent—and the worst—was the day before yesterday."

She tells us the events of two nights ago, spewing drunkenly (that's my best guess for now) for several minutes in one huge run-on sentence: drums crashing to the song "Wipe Out"; the smell of human urine (how can you tell that it's human, I wonder?); something evil whispering in her ear; a voice screaming "GET OUT!"; the fight with her daughter; her dog being put into a coma by demons; doors slamming by themselves; a handprint on her daughter's leg; even a snare drum that apparently worm-holed through space and time to a different location in her basement. By itself.

Libbi is frantically typing while I talk. Even her fingers can't move that fast. She points to the basic information on the printed form. I'm picking up what she's putting down. *Get the critical stuff.* We'll get the details at the in-person interview should we decide to take on this case.

"How long have you lived there, in your house?" I ask.

"We've been here just over two years, I think. Yeah, that's right. Two years ago, June."

"And how old is your daughter?"

"She's fifteen," says Sue.

Libbi glances my way, and I'm sure she is making a note to consider poltergeist activity. According to the lore, poltergeist entities gravitate toward teenagers. Also, we had a case once where a pair of rebellious fourteen-year-old twins were pranking the parents, making them *think* they had a ghost. Kids are assholes. I'm glad we never had any.

"Anyone else living in the house?"

"No, just Josie and me."

"Is this a private home you own or rent?" We ask because sometimes people call us on behalf of others. We need permission from the homeowner or renter.

Sue hesitates for just a second. "Yes, it's a private home; we are renters. And it's a duplex. Side by side, and we share a basement, laundry, and some ssstorage with an older woman and her dog."

I sigh imperceptibly and give Libbi another eye roll. Her eyes are on her laptop, so I am spared *the look*. This investigation will be tricky if we accept. Sharing walls and a basement might factor into reported events. We must always consider the most logical explanation for things. Out-of-control neighbor activity turns up more often than you might think.

"Okay then. And then—"

"Oh, I forgot. We alssso have the dog I mentioned before. A Yorkie mix named Pepper."

"Got it!" Libbi calls out. That was our next question (*Are there any pets in the home, and if so, what type?*), which Sue already answered in her ramble. The name is not relevant, but now we know.

We go through a few more high-level details about the house. When was it built? Is there any known history of the house—like, did someone die there? Has there been any major remodeling done recently (which can trigger paranormal activity)? Sue doesn't know much about the house since it's a rental, and they have not done any renovations.

"Has the house ever been blessed or cleansed by a priest or other clergy?"

Sue responds, "Yes."

Sigh. I am not a fan of cleansing. Worthless as tits on a boar hog.

"Okay, can you tell us about that?"

"Um, I had a friend bless the house with sage about… oh, geez, almost two weeks ago, when we first ssstarted experiencing stuff. She just went around each room with a sage bundle and sssmoked it good."

I'm sure she did, I think. *Et tu, Sue?* Is it possible you smoked a little of something as well?

Sue continues. "And then I had the house blessed by a priest from St. John's. I'm not a Catholic, but my friend is, and she got sssomeone to come out. Father Rick Mallory. Thisss was about a week and a half ago. He blessed the house and told the ssspirits they were unwanted. He… he told me not to provoke them, and to say the 23rd Psalm. Which I have been doing every day since then."

I glance over at Libbi, who is giving me the double thumbs up with an exaggerated smile. Sarcasm. She knows me too well. I can almost hear her brain whirling. She has done a sage smudge in every house we have ever lived in. Two decades back and forth from Michigan to Virginia, Roanoke to Charlottesville, then Staunton, and a few more in between before we landed back in Roanoke and finally bought a house. That's a lot of rentals and a lot of sage. But in her defense, we have never had paranormal activity in any of those houses, sooo…

I return my focus to the task at hand. "Just a few more questions, Sue. How long has the activity been going on? When did it start?"

"Hmmm." She pauses for a few seconds. "About two weeks, I think. Two and a half weeks. It was the Sssunday after Labor Day when we first heard the drums—multiple times—and footsssteps running up and down the stairs in the basement. Except no one was down there."

I look at the RIP interview form. Libbi likes us to complete the first page on the phone before we accept the caller as a client. One more question.

"And how often are you having events now?"

"Daily," says Sue. "Well, almost daily. Ssseveral times per week. Mostly it's been just drums and footsteps and smelling urine, poop. Something touching us, and we hear voices. We had a bad event on Monday. That's why I called you. Feels like it's essscalating."

Admittedly, I am intrigued by the events where she and her daughter claim to have been touched by an unseen entity. I ask if she has any photos of the handprint. She does not. Now I am less intrigued, because everyone has a camera on their phone, so why wouldn't you take a photo? I'm back to my original prediction: *whack job*.

I hear someone in the background, the daughter Josephine if I were to guess. "Mom, don't forget about the party and the Bible!"

Sue shushes her, and I start talking before we go down a rabbit hole. "I think that's all we need for now, am I right, Libbi?"

My wife knows when it is time for her to step in. She senses the taquitos getting cold in the microwave and probably heard my stomach growling, so she knows my patience is dwindling. The details can wait for our in-person interview, which will be much more comprehensive.

"Yep, that's all we need for now," says Libbi. "Sue, what I'd like to do is set up a time when we can come out and do an interview, check out the home, and maybe even talk to your daughter if she is available."

Sue agrees, and Libbi pulls up our RIP team calendar. Moments later, we have a date set to go out to Blue Ridge Estates and meet Sue and Josephine Mackenzie in person. I'm grateful to my better half for making the arrangements. Fenny is sniffing at my feet; she knows her daddy is about to down some good Mexican food.

As for the investigation, I have a funny feeling that this one is going to be nicknamed Whack Job Central.

Excerpt 1 from the *RIP After Dark* Podcast
Episode 72: Case of the Demon Drums

This podcast was broadcast one year after the actual investigation.
Client names and identifying details have been changed to maintain privacy.

Libbi: *In case you're just joining, this is RIP After Dark coming to you LIVE, and tonight we're covering a case we did just about a year ago. We started off discussing the initial call we got from our client, who claimed she had demons in her house. What were you saying, Walter?*

Walter: *Just that they never get our name right. Why do we even bother?*

Libbi: *I know, right? We should have made our tagline "It's RIP, not RPI!" for as many times as we have to say it.*

Walter: *Even when they aren't whack jobs, they slaughter the name.*

Libbi: *Everybody's a whack job to you. Especially when they interrupt your dinner. You gotta just let those calls go to voicemail.*

Walter: *That is a fact. If you recall, my voicemail inbox was full. Otherwise, I would have ignored it.*

Libbi: *Your inbox has been full for the past five years.*

Walter: *Hurtful.*

Libbi: *Truthful.*

Walter: *Sometimes letting them go to voicemail is counterproductive too. Remember that crazy manic-depressive—*

Libbi: —*bipolar.*

Walter: *Right, the bipolar guy? Can't remember his name, but he left a ten-minute verbal dissertation about his ghost infestation.*

Libbi: *Let's call him Charlie. And then we ended up on the phone with him for over an hour.*

Walter: *I rest my case.*

Libbi: *For our audience, Charlie (not his real name) called us about a haunting in his apartment. I was curious at first, and he almost had me until I asked if he had ever been diagnosed with a mental illness or experienced hallucinations.*

Walter: *Yes, to both, if memory serves.*

Libbi: *Correct. And no, he was not on any medication or undergoing any type of therapy. It can be awkward asking these kinds of questions, but we have to factor in every logical reason that might explain the things people experience. Like it or not, a diagnosis of a bipolar disorder that isn't being treated is a consideration.*

Walter: *Turns out we were right in his case.*

Libbi: *At least he didn't mention smudging his apartment with sage. I know how you love that.*

Walter: [scoffs] *Don't get me started. You are the sage queen. We must have had at least six rentals in ten years, and you smudged every one of them.*

Libbi: *Damn right! And we have never had a haunting. You're welcome.*

Walter: *I cannot deny.*

Libbi: *Well, whether or not you agree with smudging, it did not work with—what did we call her again?*

Walter: *Nancy Hobart. Because she looked like your middle school bus driver, same name.*

Libbi: *Yes, that's right. It clearly didn't work at Nancy Hobart's house. The demons just kept a-coming!*

Walter: *"Demons" in air quotes. I admit I was skeptical when we got the first call. I thought we might even turn her down after the interview.*

Libbi: *When are you not skeptical?*

Walter: *Again, I cannot deny. But you have to admit, it sounded like she'd had a few too many beers. Or something more pharmaceutical in nature.*

Libbi: *You're right, and I had my doubts too. But in the end, the case was most definitely NOT a dud. In fact, I think it was an amazing experience.*

Walter: *It was an experience, no doubt about that. So, let's dive into what happened after the call.*

Happy Birthday, Baby! How It All Started

17 days earlier, Sunday, September 8, 1:00 pm
A Series of Unexplainable Events, 1st major occurrence
Mackenzie Residence, Starry Knob Lane, Roanoke, Virginia

Sue Mackenzie

Picnics and holidays are supposed to be fun. Josie just started her sophomore year at Cave Spring High School, we're on the cusp of fall (pumpkin latte here I come!), and I am excited to kick off the season with my son Jared and my one and only grandbaby coming down from Blacksburg. It's Finn's first birthday next week, so we're going full tilt. Everyone gets invited, even the ones I don't particularly care for. Like my son's girlfriend—sorry, *fiancée*—Danielle. I am not a racist. I just don't care for her. If she weren't the mother of my grandchild, she wouldn't be on the priority list. I don't like my recovering addict son hobnobbing with another ex-junkie. It's not a recipe for lemon teacakes; I'll just say that. But I have no choice at this point. They procreated, so I'll tolerate her. For now.

It might be a little different for my friend Gina. I get the impression she doesn't care for anyone more than half a shade of brown—which is odd because Gina also claims to be one quarter Cherokee. But haven't I heard that about a million times? Every brown-eyed brunette in my high school said they were half Indian. Or I guess it's Native American now. I'm sure Gina gets her looks from her Italian side. Her maiden name was Giorgiantonio according to her Facebook page. She does kind of look like Cher with her long black hair and skinny hips and all, but so did my great-grandmother, and she was one hundred percent German.

Gina has not met Jared or my grandson in person, although I've talked about them so much that she might as well have. So, I invited her. Plus, she's been a tremendous help in the never-ending struggle with my daughter, Josephine. That girl is the walking poster child for rebellious teenagers. Gina doesn't have any kids, but she knows a lot about teenage behavior, and for that I am grateful—even if her ideas are a bit extreme. It will be fine. Gina usually sits around and chain-smokes in quiet solitude. A people watcher of the highest caliber. If it weren't for her yippy, rat-fanged varmint of a dog, she might almost blend into the background. Unfortunately, little Tinker with his baby shark teeth goes everywhere Gina does.

I invited my immediate family to the party, and they all responded in the affirmative. Good food, family, and cute babies—all the ingredients needed for a successful gathering. Unfortunately, things go sour right from the get-go when it starts pouring rain at noon. So much for the new boho blouse I bought for the occasion. The floral print will turn see-through after a few seconds in this deluge. And the temperature is dropping fast; might as well just throw on a hoodie. I utter a few mild curse words, then grab a gummy from a bag I have hidden in my kitchen. The cabinets stop short about a foot from the ceiling, and a tiny rail runs along the edge at the top. It's thick enough to hide my secrets and keep them from falling onto the counter. The cherry-flavored cannabis nugget should kick in just before the guests roll in at one o'clock. Jared already called to say they were coming, rain or shine. No doubt it's going to be the former for most of the day. This isn't the sort of storm that just blows over. We are in Roanoke, which sits in a bowl-shaped valley surrounded by mountains. Once a weather system hits the city center, it will sit for eons.

Well, isn't that a pisser?

I feel a hot flash coming on, and I'm fairly certain it's not related to hormones or edibles. I don't deal well with plans that go sour. There was not a lick of rain in the forecast as of last night. Otherwise, I would have moved us indoors. I did *not* move us indoors, and now Mother Nature is emptying her bladder on the folding table and chairs in my backyard. I'm watching the deluge from my back door and getting more frustrated by the minute. Even if it stops, the yard will be a muddy pond. There aren't enough towels in the neighborhood to dry off the chairs and tables adequately.

I try not to let it bother me, but it does. This isn't happening on purpose just to tick me off. And Lord knows I've had my share of rained-out holidays in the past. It's simply a matter of revising the plan for an indoor event. Beer does just as well in the fridge as it does in a bin of ice. I can cook the brats and dogs *en masse* in the oven. Everything else is done, just waiting to be unwrapped and devoured. I didn't invite an army, and I've got plenty of seating in the living room if I bring a few of the lawn chairs inside. The speakers are on the windowsill; I just need to turn them around and blast the party music inside instead of out. Problem solved, right?

So why is my blood still boiling? I just want it to go right for once. It's been a crazy summer. Josie is turning the corner into the "I hate my parents" phase, but she's not all the way there yet. My baby boy now has his own baby boy, and who knows what happens now? Danielle graduates from Virginia Tech this year, and with a computer degree, the three of them might end up in Seattle, for all I know. This might be the last gathering where we sit together as a family. I don't want to think about it. But it's coming. I want this to be perfect.

Josie has been in her room for over an hour, getting ready and cleaning up (after much nagging on my part; why is it so hard for her to just put her damn dirty clothes in the bin three feet away from where she throws them on the floor?). I need to get a few of those lawn chairs inside to dry off, so I call to her while I am trying to shove my stash of gummies back up in their hiding spot. I don't get a quick answer, so I turn my head over my shoulder to project a little more loudly.

"JOSEPHINE SUZANNE, GET YOUR ASS OUT HERE."

The bedroom door flies open, and my petulant daughter (obviously not in the mood to be helpful) yells something about how she can't clean her room and help set up at the same time. I shake my head and bite my tongue, silently asking Jesus to give me the strength to keep from strangling my only girl-child right before we are about to start a family party. *Breathe*, I tell myself as I bring my arm down from the cupboard top.

"It wasn't a request," I say loudly but calmly.

I look out the back window. If I give her an umbrella, might she survive if I banish her out into the monsoon while the rest of us enjoy ourselves without her shitty attitude? Most of her smartass mouth comes from me (I cannot deny it), but it's getting a little annoying. One of these days, the shit is going to hit the proverbial fan. I turn around and head into the living area, preparing for a mild pre-party showdown. Josie finally emerges from her bedroom, grumbling about some crisis or other. I repeat my demand.

"We've got to go get some of those chairs and bring them—"

I stop short as I catch sight of my daughter, seeing her for the first time since breakfast. I'm horrified and disgusted by what is before me. *Oh, HELL no!* My jaw tightens, and I blink rapidly. The gummy hasn't kicked in yet. Better hurry.

Josie looks like a professional basketball player. Not the Women's NBA, which would be bad enough. What stands before me is Larry Bird minus a foot in height. She's wearing a burgundy Virginia Tech jersey with an orange long-sleeved t-shirt underneath and matching shorts that reach almost to her knees. She's even got high-tops on. Where did she get those? Freaking Randy, that sonofabitch. It's just like him to throw money at her as if it can take the place of being an actual father. I am beyond livid. This is not my little girl.

But that isn't the worst part. I've grown accustomed to her increasingly neutral clothes. The real shocker is further up. I look at her head, searching for that beautiful bundle of blonde curls that normally bounces off the back of her head in a ponytail. She never wears it down, God forbid. And now she can't… because it's gone. Her long, springy curls are all gone. Josie cut her sweet golden locks—no, *shaved* them, on the sides. The top and back still have a bit of hair, but it's only a few inches long. My stomach curdles. She looks like a redneck teenage boy from 1987.

"Are you kidding me right now?" I cry out in anger.

Guests will arrive any minute. What am I going to say to them? How do I explain this? What is Gina going to think? She's going to blow a gasket. This is exactly what she warned me about. She kept asking me if I thought Josie was a dyke. That's the word she used. *Dyke*. She spat it out sideways like it tasted bad. I told her Josie is a tomboy. She's always been a little on the rough side. *"Tomboys keep their hair long."* That's what Gina said. I thought nothing of it. Gina's a little over-judgmental in several categories. I could never tell her I almost got an abortion at sixteen when Curt Babcock put his "bad-cock" inside me and knocked me up after prom junior year. The Lord called my fetus to glory before I got the chance, but I would have done it. Gina holds signs in front of Planned Parenthood and laughs when she scares a young girl enough to turn around and get back into her car. I, however, understand what those girls are going through.

We don't agree on everything. But here I am with a daughter who just chopped off over a foot of virgin curls, so maybe Gina's got the number on this one.

"I asked you if I could cut it," Josie says from her doorway. "You said it was okay!"

Is she for real?

"You said, 'Can I *trim* my hair?' and I said yes, you can give it a TRIM because it was getting long! I thought you meant like one of those wolf cuts from Instagram! I did not say you could go all achy-breaky *Stranger Things* mullet on me!"

This is not happening. I don't even know what I am looking at here. I might excuse the haircut as an adolescent mistake. You cut too much on one side, so you trim up the other… but now that side is too short. Before you know it, there's nothing left. But the hair *and* the basketball head-to-toe uniform? Where is my little girl? Where are the cap sleeves and butterflies? I want to see baby blue Vans with white ankle socks. Not black high-tops. I almost dry heave thinking about it. She's supposed to be turning into a woman, not a *dude.*

This is too much for me on top of the weather disappointment. My heart is beating fast, and I can feel the sweat pooling under my bra. I'm going to burn up. I pull the floral blouse over my head so I'm in just a white tank top. My pits are stained wet. Fuck menopause. Fuck insubordinate teenagers. *No daughter of mine is…*

I can't even complete the thought.

"There is no way in hell you are wearing that." I say with my teeth gritted. "No way. Go change your clothes. Right. Now."

Josie just stands there, her lip trembling but with defiance in her eyes. She seems at the same time fearful beyond words and uncharacteristically courageous. I don't know how to react at this moment. I feel like I'm in some screwed-up after-school special.

"This is not you—"

Josie cuts me off.

"It *is* me, Mom. This is who I am."

My face is hot as a Florida sunburn in July, and I think might have a heart attack right here in the living room.

"Josephine Suzanne," I hiss. "Get in your bedroom and put on a skirt. It's Sunday. Judas Priest, you are not a boy, and I won't have you dressing like one, not for a party on the holy day."

She looks at me like there's nothing more horrifying than wearing a skirt right now. Too bad. She'll just have to make it work with the new haircut. Tears are running down her face. I can tell she's more angry than sad. They warned me about the terrible teens, but I thought nothing of it until these past few weeks. Where is my little girl? It's so surreal. I feel like I'm caught in one of those Salvador Dali paintings, melting off the side of a table.

But then my daughter decides she's going to make her stand, right now with guests about to pull into the driveway.

"I don't even have a clean skirt," she says, wiping her eyes. "I'm wearing this."

"No. You are not." She doesn't even want to listen.

"Why?" she asks, getting louder. "What is wrong with—"

"I don't owe you an explanation, Josephine. You will do as I say!"

I cut her off. Again. I am so tired of this. I feel myself getting red-faced. I am supposed to love her unconditionally, but sometimes it's hard. I can't help it. Right now, I want to punch her. I want her to punch me. And I want her to be as far away from this house as possible and let me have some peace for just one goddamn minute.

"I'm *not* changing my clothes," she says defiantly. Then something bursts inside her, like she just broke out of prison lockdown. "I AM NOT CHANGING MY CLOTHES! GO FUCK YOURSELF!"

She is out of her damn mind!

I'm on fire now. I'm genuinely afraid I'm going to hurt her. She just told *me*—the woman who gave birth to her, raised her, fed her, kept her alive some days—to go fuck herself. Someone is going to have to call the cops because this girl is dead.

"HOW DARE YOU! I am your mother! You will not talk to me like this, Josephine Mackenzie!"

To my utter disbelief, she doubles down. "I have told you a million times, I want to be called JO!"

Something whizzes past Josie, coming from the bedroom behind her. It hits me squarely in the chest. I stagger backward and grab the back of the recliner to keep from falling as the object bounces to the floor in front of me. It lands with a dull thump. Josie turns to look behind her, and I do too, expecting to see someone standing there with their arm splayed like they just let loose a fastball. There is no one, and I know this because Josie and I are the only ones in the house. I see nothing in her room but dirty clothes and furniture.

She turns back to me. I am clutching my chest, more in awe than pain. I see it lying there on the floor. My father's Bible, old and frayed from years of being squeezed and grasped and tucked under my arm when I'd rock back and forth on the edge of my recliner in our Michigan house when Jared was using—when he'd somehow make it home alive from his parties and stumble into his bedroom yelling profanities at us both. I would recognize my solace anywhere.

"My Bible? My precious Bible?"

I am beyond rage but also suddenly afraid. Something is happening. The room is noticeably darker. Clouds are moving in, the rain is picking up, and I can feel bad weather coming. But it's not just outside. The storm is in here… with us.

"THIS… IS NOT… YOU!!!" I scream.

A crack of thunder shakes the house, lighting the outside like a spotlight for a split second. I duck instinctively, putting my hand on top of my head as if the ceiling is about to fall in. Josie hasn't moved. She glares at me in the growing darkness. Lightning strikes again, and I see another flash through the front window. It reflects briefly in my daughter's left eye, and for a second, I think she is possessed.

As suddenly as the thunder comes, the storm stops. One minute it is swirling around us, then abruptly, it isn't. The rain ceases, the wind dies down, and there is not a sound to be heard except my raspy breath and my heart beating out of my chest. Josie still looks like she has murder on her mind. It feels unnatural in here. Like there is something unseen but all around.

ratta-tat-tat ratta-tat-tat

The sound of a drum cuts into the silence. Its sharp tapping comes from behind me. Josie hears it too. She finally breaks out of her murderous trance and turns toward the basement door.

ratta-tat-tat ratta-tat-tat ratta-tat-tat ratta-tat-tat

It's louder now. I try to think. Is someone downstairs? Is someone playing the drums down there? That old set has been in the basement since we moved in, sitting right next to the old couch Josie sometimes uses as an escape when Gina comes over.

ratta-tat-tat ratta-tat-tat RATTA-TAT-TAT RATTA-TAT-TAT

BOOM *RATTA-TAT TAT* BOOM CRASH BOOM BOOM *RATTA-TAT TAT* BOOM CRASH

The drums explode, and it sounds like cymbals are joining the party. It only takes a few seconds before they go from distant to deafening, like we are in front of the speakers at a rock concert. Josie and I both put our hands to our ears instinctively. I look around, trying to make sense of it. It feels like we are inside it. I have a moment of utter confusion, almost vertigo.

"What is happening?" Josie yells, but I cannot answer. I am suddenly frozen with my eyes open wide, staring straight at my youngest. Fear has taken over. I cannot move my body; I have turned to stone. Terror runs through my chest like a burning wave. I am scared shitless. Our house shakes like it's at the epicenter of an earthquake.

BOOM *RATTA-TAT TAT* BOOM CRASH BOOM BOOM *RATTA-TAT TAT* BOOM

Suddenly I am thrown forward toward my daughter—violently, savagely, and with unimaginable force. It feels like I just got pushed by the Hulk. There is a hand on the back of my neck, cold as ice and with a bony grip like an old man. It shoves me hard with a strength I could not have resisted even if I had sensed it coming. I don't know how I can know this, but the force feels malicious. *Like it did when Jared's father did it.* It shoves me forward like a rocket, taking me airborne for a second until it slams me down onto the thick carpet below. Josie jumps back in horror. I hit the floor with a thud, crying out as the air leaves my lungs and my body flattens. It feels like I just got thrown from a car onto the asphalt after a crash. For a few seconds, the adrenaline floods to my face like a wave of fire as I try to comprehend what just happened. I look up at my daughter, perplexed. I know it makes no sense, but I think she is responsible for this. She was in front of me when I was shoved from behind, yet she is to blame. My breath is stuck in my ribs, and I fear I will die right there in front of her. Josie stands with her hands over her mouth and tears streaming down her face. A different fifteen-year-old girl would have black mascara streaks tattooing her cheeks, but Josie is bare-faced. Sadness and terror are the only other colors in her blue eyes.

The doorbell rings.

My breath finally comes. I inhale deeply, pushing the air hard a few times until I think I am returning to sanity and no longer at death's door. I hoist my thousand-pound body up, taking a moment to rub my shin before going completely vertical. It hurts, but I don't think it's badly damaged. It is quiet now. Whatever was here before is now gone. I don't understand what just happened. I am still partially in shock, but I better snap out of it quickly. I wipe my tears and take a step past my weeping child, heading toward the front door just as it rings again. My impatient family, no doubt. As I pass Josie, I am seething through gritted teeth.

"Go clean yourself up. We'll talk about this later." Josie turns and runs into her bedroom, slamming the door behind her.

"I'm coming!" I call out, then quickly reverse direction back into the kitchen to pull a handful of paper towels off the roll. A deep breath, a swipe of sweat and tears, and then I'm slowly walking back into the living room to retrieve my Bible, my blouse, and my smokes. The guests aren't going anywhere, and I thank baby Jesus the door is locked. My security OCD comes in handy sometimes. I need a minute to focus; a minute to flush out the visual of my daughter—or something— throwing the Holy Book at me. A minute to forget the frigid grip I felt on my neck from something that could not possibly be there.

The house activity is almost normal for the next hour, with guests bustling in and about. Gina arrives with Tinker in tow and immediately senses that something is wrong. She asks if I'm okay, but it feels more like she wants to feed off the drama than to console a friend, so I wave her off and start fluffing pillows even though I've fluffed them plenty already. Danielle and Jared arrive soon after, with the birthday boy Finn. Jared is fighting some sort of bug, so he heads straight into the kitchen to look for some Pepto-Bismol. Danielle settles in like she lives here and starts chatting it up with Gina like they are besties. I'm annoyed that my future daughter-in-law is effortlessly pretty, all Bohemian in her turquoise maxi skirt with pink butterflies scattered around the bottom; her curls tied up perfectly with a hot-pink bandana. Not a hint of makeup but for a sheen of gloss on her lips. She takes Finn out of one of those big baby scarves wrapped around her chest and hands him to me. She knows the grandmother gets first dibs; that's one good thing I'll say about her. I've been sitting in my recliner trying to forget the events that took place just before everyone arrived. I'm grateful for all the activity. It is a welcome distraction. Finn stands on my knees and bounces up and down. That won't last long. Most one-year-olds don't want to be held much, but he's going to have to deal with a little cuddling before I let him loose.

My younger sister Tina is here with her husband Earl, who looks like that actor John Leguizamo (except a little taller and a little darker). Tina is a plain Jane like me but thinner and with short hair that's already gone mostly gray. Tina and Earl are wearing matching white hoodies with "Hakuna Matata" printed across the fronts in rainbow bubble letters. Yes, they are "those people." They have been happily married for seventeen years (disgustingly so sometimes), and they go to Walt Disney World at least twice a year. They arrived a short while ago with their daughters, my nieces Sierra and Jayde.

My oldest niece, Sierra, is twelve and perfect. Straight-A student, athlete, good manners, and looking cute as a button in her baby-blue sweater with sparkles on it. Her dark hair is perfectly styled in a wavy little bob; she looks like a young Rita Moreno. I hope she stays this way. Sierra is almost at the age where the teenage rebellion kicks in. It's a roll of the dice whether she stays cute and nerdy or goes Goth and trades in her white flats for combat boots. Either way, I will enjoy her perfection while I can. Sierra sits quietly and awaits her turn with her baby cousin, occasionally catching his eye and making faces at him. She's going to be a great mom someday, with a career as a veterinarian or nurse.

Her younger sister, Jayde, will work at a gas station. Or maybe a strip club; it's too early to tell. She is a wild child who likes to climb trees and boulders and refrigerators. She'll be a natural on the pole. Jayde is nine and showed up in dirty overalls with an unintentional rip in the right knee. Her hair looks like it hasn't been brushed (or washed) in a month. She is enamored with Josie and has been running around like a rabid raccoon, asking me about every two minutes when her cousin is going to get here. I didn't tell her that Josie is already here, shut inside her room getting her shit together. Jayde has a fantasy; I'm not going to burst her bubble.

Everyone is fussing over the baby. He's the most beautiful little cherub I've ever seen, looks just like Jared did at that age. All pinchy-fat and giggles. I'm still bouncing Finn on my knee when Josie finally emerges from her room. She's changed from the basketball uniform into some cargo shorts and a plain, white V-neck T-shirt—one she no doubt pilfered from her dad's underwear drawer last weekend. The high-tops are gone, and instead she is wearing slip-on Birkenstocks. It's too cold and rainy for sandals, but I'm going to pick my battles, and this isn't one of them. She's wrapped a red and blue paisley bandana around her head, which almost hides the shaved sides. It's at least in the ballpark of feminine and gives the illusion that she still has hair. I'm relieved that she put on a bra, but annoyed that she's hunching forward as if to hide her womanhood. *You are your mother's daughter,* I think, as I glance down at my own balloon bosom. She refuses to look at me and instead beelines for the kitchen where her brother is standing against the sink, bent over slightly.

"Hey kiddo," I hear him mutter as she reaches his side.

Jared did not look well when he arrived, holding his stomach as if he were about to hurl when he staggered through the doorway. I immediately went into smothering-mother mode. *sMother.* That's what he calls me. Typical of my eldest child, he got defensive. He's always been a little too independent, and at twenty-two, he hasn't yet reached the age when he adores his mom again. I offered him a homemade peanut butter cookie, his favorite. He refused. My food is my love, so that stung, but okay. I get it. I offered him ginger ale. He just waved me away as if I were a fly and seemed irritated by my presence. That pinged me a little too. But I'm still his mom, so I pushed through the hurt and showed him the Pepto on the inside door of the fridge. When he snapped at me again, I decided I was done, retiring to my chair and my grandson's better attitude. Jared has been standing at the kitchen sink ever since. When Josie gets there, he's hunched over with his head rested on his arm.

"Leave him be," I call out. "He's not feeling well, no sense in spreading his germs all around."

I'm ashamed to admit how it hurts me when Jared allows his sister in as easily as he dismisses me, the woman who gave him life. Maybe that's why I want her to step away. But it's more than that. There's something eating at me. I'm glad I'm facing away from the kitchen because if I were to look at my two children, there would be a rock in my stomach. I would be the one needing an antacid. Even with bouncy Finn in front of me, I feel something inside that wants to come out. A little niggle in my brain that is me… but also not me. A faraway voice in my ear that asks me questions to the answers I already know but don't want to know. Like why Josie wears boys' clothes and how she could throw a Bible at me when it was nowhere near her—and I would swear on that very book that she never picked it up to begin with. Or how there were drums playing plain as day when there were no drums and no drummers nearby. How Jared isn't sick, not with the stomach flu or food poisoning, anyway. He is sweaty, his skin gray and clammy like a dead octopus. The way it looked before he stopped using.

Something wants me to believe all this like I believe the sun will rise in the morning. Something wants me to be angry about it. Something wants me to lose control because it means it can then take that control away from me. I can almost hear it in my ear.

I'm coming for all of you.

I put Finn down on the floor next to Sierra, who is eager to play with her bubbly cousin. I grab my Bible from the end table and stand up from my chair (with some effort; the knees have been going downhill the past few years). As I shuffle past Sierra and Finn, I catch Gina's eye and nod toward the front door. Time for a smoke break. She understands the assignment and pulls her lithe body from the couch to follow me, keeping Tinker under her arm. I walk to the front door and open it, allowing a wisp of fresh air into the house. Gina and I step out under the awning. The overhang is just big enough to keep the two of us dry. The rain has cooled everything down, and the breeze feels good on my face. I'm back in the moment again. For now.

I reach back in through the doorway and pull a half pack of Marlboro Golds from my purse. When I step back out, I leave the front door open a bit. Enough for the cool air to freshen the house, but not enough to let all the smoke in. Gina lights up her Virginia Slim. She's dressed in her usual supermodel outfit—long boot-cut jeans on her legs for days and a black knit shirt that hugs her slim frame. Today she's topped off her Kendall Jenner look with a crocheted wrap in shades of warm colors draped over her neck and shoulders like a big sunrise bib. I used to hate girls like her—girls with small tits and even smaller waists who have never had to use a safety pin between the buttons on blouse for fear someone might see their bra through the gaps. Even just a few years ago, I would have avoided Gina like the smallpox, but she has been a godsend of support these past few months. A little over the top sometimes, but she's got strong opinions, and as scattered as my brain has been lately, I need that conviction to counter my confusion.

I take a drag on my cigarette and let it out slowly, staring through the doorway crack into the black hole of space that tears right through my living room and into infinity. Josie and Jared are still talking in low voices in the kitchen. The sound of the drums is still echoing in my head. I clutch my Bible and close my eyes. *God will not let this happen. God will provide. He will watch over us and protect us. Please help us, Jesus. Amen.*

"Is your son okay?" asks Gina in a low voice. She has her arms crossed, with one up in the air, waving her smoke in the general direction of Jared. "He looks a little whacked out."

I bite my tongue and blink slowly. She's overstepping a bit, and I would rather she just shut her piehole. I say nothing for a few seconds as I give her the side-eye.

"Jared is fine. He has a stomach bug."

That might be a lie, but Gina doesn't need to be up in *all* my business.

"Okay, so you say," she says, putting her cigarette to her pursed lips and inhaling. "Just seems a little off."

I hear Finn giggling inside, that kind of hard belly laugh that makes everyone else giggle too. It comforts me. But not for long.

"I didn't want to say anything in front of everyone, but did Josephine cut her *hair?*"

I bristle. She says it like it revolts her; like she just found a dead rat under the sink. I can almost feel her dry gagging inside. I'm not happy about it either, but Jesus H. Christmas. It's not like her own head of hay is anything to write home about. I could sweep the floor with her split ends.

I stay silent but give her a stern look as I take one last toke from my shrinking cigarette.

"Girl, it ain't your fault," she says, touching my arm gently.

There it is. *That's* the Gina I need.

"Hell, I dyed my hair blue when I was fourteen, and my mom never saw it comin'. I always knew when she was mad at me 'cause she'd use my full birth name. 'Georgina Frances Giorgiantonio,' she'd say, except this time I think she threw in a few extra names 'cause she was speaking in tongues. She was quite a spitfire, and I didn't help."

I laugh, feeling a little of the weight of the day falling off my shoulders. Gina always has a way of bringing me back to the here and now. I'm still a little spooked from my fight with Josie earlier, but I shouldn't take it out on my best friend. She's just trying to help.

Gina leans in and half-whispers under her breath. "All I'm saying is, be careful. Don't let it go too far before you get her some..." She blows out a lungful of smoke. "... help. Today it's short hair, tomorrow she's bringing home a girlfriend or asking about testosterone. She's a good kid, but she is not on the Lord's path."

She startles me with her last sentence. Is my baby girl on a fast train to hell? I throw down my cigarette and smash it out with the toe of my sneaker, leaving it to smolder in the mulch. I'm breaking my cardinal rule about leaving butts on the lawn, but it's my house, so I suppose I get to decide which rules I abide by and which ones I don't.

I pat Gina's arm to let her know I am picking up what she is putting down, then gently pull away and head back inside to join the party. Sierra has claimed my chair and is leaning forward, holding Finn's waist as he stands on the floor, balancing himself against the pine coffee table and slapping his chubby fingers on the top. He squeals as he looks at me, like he's proud of what he accomplished. I smile at him and ask him what he's doing in my best high-pitched voice.

"Meee!" he squeals, and I pretend he is saying *Mimi*, my chosen grandmother's name. I nearly get choked up thinking about the circle of life, so I give him a quick wave, blink back the tears, and head toward my children. Josie and Jared are still in the kitchen, standing on opposite sides of the double sink, talking in low voices. Jayde is sitting on one of the counter stools (waiting, no doubt, for Josie to break away and pay her some attention). Jared looks a little better from afar, but the closer I get, the more I see the telltale signs of an addict in need of a fix. His jeans are baggy and wrinkled, and he looks like he slept in his navy zip-up hoodie. One of the hood strings is pulled all the way down while the other is cinching up one side like a Slinky. He is balancing himself on the sink edge with one hand and holding a cigarette in the other, which is shaking slightly like he's in the early stages of Parkinson's. He looks like he's going to pass out or puke. Josie stands listening with her arms crossed, hiding her chest like she does. When I get to the edge of the island, she sees me and immediately stops talking. *Can't let Mom hear,* that's what I figure. I'm no longer part of the club, and that stings a little.

But I guess that's what motherhood is about. You can't be your kids' friend; you have to be their parent. Sometimes you're both Mom *and* Dad, especially if you can't rely on the other one to wipe his own ass at the appropriate place and time.

I skirt around the island, telling Jayde to go play somewhere else for a minute. My children stare at me like I'm some dumb shit. The sink window is open a few inches; at least Jared hasn't lost all his good sense and is venting his smoke away from the kids. Josie wants me to disappear into thin air. She won't look at me directly and seems pissed that I have interfered with her sibling bond. No matter. My house, my space, my rules. I position myself between them—my addict son and my confused daughter—and put one arm around each of them. My Bible rests on Jared's shoulder.

"Lord Jesus," I whisper, bowing my head. "Make this all go away. Heal this family. Amen and thank you."

I feel them both prickle and tense up. Josie maneuvers her shoulders out of my embrace violently and pulls away. Jared responds to my loving hug by barfing into the kitchen sink. I have never felt so unwanted and unvalued in my life.

"FUCK!" I yell and step back from the stink, throwing my arms up in the air. I feel the room go silent and everyone's eyes upon me even though my back is to the living room. I smell my son's rancid vomit and see the hatred coming from my daughter. I am bona fide losing it with this family.

"Goddammit, Jared, what is wrong with you?"

Jared coughs like he's got pneumonia. "Jesus Christ, Mom! I'm fucking sick!"

BANG! BANG!

The door to the basement opens with such fury that it hits the wall on the other side and ricochets shut. Jared jumps back toward me; Josie nearly leaps over the counter.

THUMP THUMP THUMP thump thump thump

Someone is running up the stairs. Now down the stairs. It sounds like an entire football team.

THUMP THUMP THUMP thump thump thump

The sound gets louder as they come up the stairs, then muffled as they stomp back to the basement.

I stand for a moment, confused. Did I lose track of anyone? I take a quick tally of my guests. Gina is in the living room on the couch, sitting cross-legged at one end with Tinker wrapped up in her arms (shocking). Almost as if on cue, he barks, pointing his little rat-dog yip toward the basement door. Gina shushes him, but he only snaps at her and keeps it up, trying to jump out of her arms. Danielle is on the floor on the far side of the coffee table near the TV, balancing Finn as he wobbles on his unsteady legs. Finn is staring at the yapping Tinker with a quivering lip. A second later he is full-on crying and turns to his mother, who pulls him into her arms. I can only see the top of Sierra's head behind the back of my recliner, but Jayde—who is leaning against the chair arm trying to see something on Sierra's iPad—does not hide her annoyance at all the noise. She puts her hands over her ears, pinches her eyes shut, and opens her mouth wide with nothing coming out—somehow instinctively knowing that if she also yells, it will just make things worse.

THUMP THUMP THUMP thump thump thump

Tina and Earl are on the couch looking at me. My sister mouths, *what the fuck?* I shrug my shoulders and shake my head. All accounted for. Who is in the basement?

BARK BARK BARK BARK

WAAAAAAAAAA

THUMP THUMP THUMP thump thump thump

Rinse and repeat. I catch Gina's eye.

"Could you take him outside, please?" I yell over the noise, unable to mask my exasperation.

I point to the front door. I can't think with that damn rodent screaming like a jungle animal, and Finn won't stop crying until the dog is gone. Order of operations. I glance over to the floor next to the couch where my own four-legged boy is snoozing on his doggie bed, like he's stone cold deaf (which he most definitely is not). Something isn't right. Gina reluctantly gets up from the couch with a huff I can hear over the ruckus. For just one second, I want to throw something hard at her. *For fuck's sake, help a girl out without the eye roll, would you?* Tinker looks fit to be tied, and Gina almost drops her cigarettes as she attempts to keep him from jumping away from her and attacking the basement door or whatever might be in the way before he gets to it. Finally, she gets him out of the house and slams the door. It's raining a little harder, and I'm not sure if the awning will keep the two of them completely dry, but right now I don't give a fuck. She can go sit in her car with her five-pound noisemaker, for all I care. In fact, I'd love it if she left that miniature honey badger locked up for the rest of the afternoon.

THUMP THUMP THUMP thump thump thump
thump thump thump THUMP THUMP THUMP

Finn's crying tapers off into sniffles as soon as the front door shuts. Everyone else has gone silent, as much from fear of their host as from any concern about what is making all the racket in the basement

THUMP THUMP THUMP thump thump thump

There is only one other way to get into the basement, and that is through Alice's door on the other side of the duplex. There is no way she is making that noise. Alice knits and crochets and goes to church every Sunday. She also uses a cane, so it can't be her running up and down those steps like she's trying to win the fifty-yard dash. But she does have a tween grandson named Caleb who visits his Nana once a month. I have definitely heard him thump downstairs more than a few times. The kid has a wild streak, that's for sure.

thump thump thump THUMP THUMP THUMP

I have had the "pleasure" of Caleb's acquaintance ever since he broke my back window the summer before last. He and one of the neighbor kids were hitting pop-ups out in the backyard. I went out to buy some smokes (locked my doors; you never know what kids are up to these days). When I got back, the boys were gone, but one quarter of my back window was shattered all over the kitchen counter and onto the floor. I found the evidence—a dirty baseball—nestled under one of the bar stools at the kitchen island. Caleb said it was the neighbor kid; the neighbor kid said it was Caleb. Alice paid for it, but I never trusted that little gangster after that.

THUMP THUMP THUMP thump thump thump
thump thump thump THUMP THUMP THUMP

That little fucker isn't going to get away with it this time. Spare the rod, spoil the child, right? I stand at the basement door waiting for the thumping to get closer and louder. Sounds like he is running up and down Alice's stairs, then up and down mine. When the sound is at its peak, I fling open the basement door and cry out, "GOTCHA!"

There is nothing but blackness. I stand there for a moment looking into the dark. The thumping has stopped, and the rest of the house is dead silent.

ratta-tat-tat

I jump back at the sound of the tapping and damn near knock over Jayde, who has crept up behind me. It's the same snare drum Josie and

I heard earlier—faint, but still loud enough for my heart to race when I hear it. I turn back to my children with a puzzled look on my face.

"Did y'all hear that? That drum?"

Jared looks at me with disgust and shakes his head. I don't know if that means "no, I don't hear it" or if he's just fed up with his crazy mother. His cheeks are damn near gray. Maybe he has food poisoning after all. Josie is half hidden behind her brother, like she's using him as a barrier. She heard it. I can tell by her clenched eyebrows. She's scared. I turn back around to the black stairwell. Should it be that dark? I can't see anything beyond the first two steps. It's overcast outside for sure, but it's afternoon. Still full daylight. I should see the bottom of the stairs, certainly halfway down, lit up by the kitchen light. But it goes pure black after the second step.

ratta-tat-tat

My adrenaline is pumping, but I'm not sure if it's anger or fear. That little fucker Caleb is down there somewhere, messing around with that old drum set. He shouldn't be over on our side. He's probably with his little juvenile delinquent friend. Goddamn kids. I'll bet that's what we heard earlier too. I'm sweating again because the rage is building. It's bad enough that our parade is being rained on, literally. Now we have one, maybe two crazies playing games. My patience is fleeing fast.

Enough.

ratta-tat-tat

I take two steps down the stairs and suddenly I'm in total darkness. I take another step and feel for the chain on the light bulb that should be hanging right in front of me. I've run into it dozens of times coming down the stairs too fast. Freaks me out sometimes; I think it's a spider hitting me in the face. I finally find it and tug, praying that it works. It doesn't feel normal in the middle of all this black. The air is wrong. It's usually moist and musty down here. Now it's dry and putrid, like old rot. I imagine it would be like this if someone opened a coffin that had been buried for a hundred years. It's getting into my lungs. The bulb flickers once, then turns on. It's dim, but the stairwell brightens enough for me to avoid killing myself on the way down. The air seems to freshen a bit as the light hits it.

Just before I take another step down, I grab the kitchen broom hanging on the stairwell wall and lift it off the hook, turning it around so the sweeping end is behind me and I'm holding the handle end like a bat. Just in case I need to deliver an old-fashioned ass-whooping to Alice's misbehaving grandson. As I descend to the next stair, I dip my head a bit and look around the dimly lit basement, certain I will see the culprit giggling over on Alice's side of the cement floor.

grrrrrrr

I freeze as a low growl echoes from below. It sounds like it's coming from under the stairs. Pepper is still upstairs, comatose on his couch-bed, and Tinker is outside. I can still hear his faraway yaps from outside. Alice's beagle can hardly make it out the front door, let alone down that many steps, and I've never seen it in the basement in over two years. It must be Caleb.

"What is it?"

Josie's voice comes from the top of the stairs. *What*, not *who*. Was that intentional? I shush her.

As I turn back around, I am hit with the overwhelming stench of urine. Instinctively, I put my free arm up to my face to cover my nose, but I stand my ground. This is human urine; I would stake my life on it. Did those boys relieve themselves in the basement? The audacity of people with dicks. They whip it out and pee wherever they want just because they can. I'm beyond livid now. It's one thing to be obnoxious and loud and disruptive. It's quite another to be pissing in the common area. Alice is going to hear about this.

ratta-tat-tat

The tapping is still faint but clearer now, as if it is coming from somewhere close by. I can't tell for sure. It must be Caleb tapping on the dusty snare drum, sitting on that nasty old couch. I creep further down the stairs, listening for the telltale sounds of mischievous young boys—snickering, shuffling, whispers. The only noise comes from the top of the stairs as my clan murmurs from above. *"What the hell is she doing down there? When are we going to eat?"* Helpless morons. I reach the bottom step and round the corner to the right, where the old drum set sits about six feet away. Even with the stair light on, it's nearly pitch black over here. All the better. I intend to catch Caleb red-handed. I hold my breath and listen.

ratta-tat-tat ratta-tat-tat

Louder now. Okay, now we are getting somewhere. I make a mental note to put a padlock on my basement door as soon as I can get out to Walmarts to buy one. The knob already has a push-in lock, but everyone knows they are worthless; any self-respecting kindergartener knows how to jimmy one of those with a wire hanger. How that unruly child has the nerve to come up MY stairs and come into MY side of the basement is a question yet unanswered, but I am now convinced that he was the origin of the loud drums that Josie and I heard earlier.

It's a long shot, but I wonder… could he have been inside our half of the duplex? Did Caleb throw the Bible? My thoughts are getting crazy now—enhanced by adrenaline and the gummy, no doubt—but I imagine Caleb hiding in Josie's room and throwing the book through the bedroom door. Maybe his friend was hiding in the living room, and *he* pushed me down. It seems impossible, but it makes more sense than the alternative. That the Bible came from nowhere. Or from something unseen.

I round the corner, find the bulb chain over the lounge area, and flip it on as I yell, "HA!"

There is nothing there. Nothing amiss, no snickering boys, no sign of any human presence whatsoever. I suck in the sides of my cheeks and breathe in deeply through my nose, trying to calm myself. *WTF?*

ratta-tat-tat

There it is again, this time coming from across the basement where Alice has a pile of old moving boxes sitting in the dark. The boys must be over there. I glance back at the drum set, now lit. It looks intact, with nothing obvious missing. Nothing that I can see, anyway. I don't know how they are doing it, but I don't care. They must be hiding in the boxes. I would normally honor the sanctity of keeping to my side of the cellar, but I'm done with respect. I creep over to the pile of boxes and quietly reach for another light switch chain.

"GOTCHA!" I scream as the area illuminates.

There are only empty boxes and a few dusty tote bags resting on the concrete floor. There is nowhere to hide. No misbehaving boys, no drum, no cause.

I am beyond red at this point. I walk around flicking on all the lights, still holding up the end of the broom. Nothing. My face gets even hotter, and I can feel it turning red as a fire poker. What is happening? I close my eyes and drop my arm, letting the broom handle hit the cement floor. I rub the bridge of my nose, trying to ease the growing tension in my head. If no one else had heard the stomping, I might think I'm losing my ever-loving mind. After a moment I hear someone upstairs mumble, *"Should one of us go down there?"* and I decide to end this once and for all.

I walk through the dim cellar to Alice's stairs and stomp up as hard as I can until I reach the top. If I am making half the noise that those thugs made a few minutes ago, I'll die smiling. I am seething, and I pray I am interrupting Alice's day as badly as her damn grandson has interrupted mine.

BOOM BOOM BOOM BOOM BOOM

I pound on Alice's door with full force. And again.
BOOM BOOM BOOM BOOM BOOM
"ALICE! Open the door, it's Sue."
I pound a third time, not caring that Alice is older and doesn't get around as well as me, a generation younger. Finally, I hear her telltale creak and sense her gnarled, arthritic hand on the doorknob. The lock turns, and the door opens to reveal octogenarian Alice Winchester—borrower of sugar (which she never did pay back) and grandmother to heathens. It is mid-afternoon, but Alice is still wearing her bathrobe—a pale pink chenille gem perfectly appropriate for someone her age. I'm pretty sure my grandma wore this same style thirty years ago. Alice looks groggy, as though she just woke up, which would not be surprising, since she is prone to napping. Napping after nipping, as they say.

Alice," I say with clenched teeth. I am standing on the top step, my chin level with the top of Alice's hair, which is a lovely shade of church-lady powder blue. "I have had just about enough of your grandson's pissing around down here, and now he's gone too far."

I pause and purse my lips together, trying to control my anger.

"I would like to have a word with him, please. I know he's inside; please ask him to come to the door."

I am not sure yet if I am going to get old-school physical with the little shit or just rip him a new one with my mouth, but either way, he is going to get a piece of Sue Mackenzie.

Alice looks confused. But then, Alice always looks confused. "Do you mean Caleb?"

"Yes. Caleb." For fuck's sake, he's the only grandson she has.

"Caleb isn't here, Sue. He's gone to visit his dad in Richmond this weekend." She slurs a bit.

I shake my head in doubt. "Now Alice, I damn well heard him not one minute ago running up and down my stairs! Don't lie to me; I know he's in there."

Alice stares at me with an almost curious look. She pauses for a few seconds, and I want to slap her hard.

Finally, she replies. "Sue, you are fucking losing it."

Well. That was unexpected.

"Come on in if you don't believe me, take a look for yourself."

She moves aside to let me pass. I don't enter. I'm trying to process.

"Now listen here, Alice... you tell that little—"

"'*That little*' is not here. I'm not telling him anything."

She is surprisingly coherent and oddly direct. I didn't realize Alice was such a badass, and for a split-second I am humbled with respect. But I don't know if I believe her. Maybe she had one too many afternoon cocktails and—

ratta-tat-tat

I turn and look down the stairs. The sound is coming from behind me. My face tingles, and I swallow hard. The stairs fade under me as the adrenaline kicks in with even more intensity. I turn and run down Alice's stairs before I fall, which is a good possibility right now. My head is spinning; the darkness of the basement is swirling like a vortex that is closing in on itself. I might be having a panic attack. Before it hits full on, I stumble to the laundry area by the front wall and look between the washer and dryer. I scope every corner, every nook and cranny, even the ones not half the size needed to hide a tween boy. But there is no one here. Someone is playing a game with me. Someone is trying to get under my skin, and I am not having it. Not in my house.

"Sue?" Tina calls from above. "What are you doing down there? You need some help?"

I briefly wonder why no one has come down to assist of their own volition, but then I realize they are afraid of me in my current state.

"I got it."

I got to get my shit under control, that's what I got. I balance myself on the washer while I stare at the floor for a few seconds until the world around me stops spinning and gets a little brighter. I flip off the laundry room light, then continue with the other bulbs around the basement until just the stairwell is lit. I look out into the darkness. It stares back in bleak indifference, as if it doesn't even notice me.

"Fuck you." I flip the bird into emptiness.

I turn and climb the stairs, pushing through the small crowd of onlookers at the top as I walk into the kitchen, slamming the basement door behind me. I still have the broom in my hand, so I toss it into the corner by the back door. I will take care of it later. I am silent as I make my way to the kitchen sink and pour myself a glass of water from the faucet.

Gina approaches with Tinker snuggled in her arms. I give her the side-eye as I lift my glass to my mouth. I don't know why she didn't put him in her car. It's cool enough, and better that he annoys the occasional passerby than this house full of screw-ups.

"Who was it?" she asks.

I drink the full glass until it is empty, exhaling hard after the last gulp. "I didn't see—"

ratta-tat-tat

Goddammit! I push Gina out of the way and hurl my empty glass at the basement door. It misses my sister by six inches and shatters against the wood.

"FUUUUCK YOU!"

Whoever—whatever—is torturing me, I am literally going to kill them. Murder, right here in my home. Maybe I am going crazy. I look at Gina.

"Did you *hear* that? The drum?"

Gina has a deer-in-the-headlights look as she shakes her head back and forth, pulling Tinker closer and taking a step backward. The dog is panting hard. I hope it's from me. I hope I scared the red zone right out of his little rodent ass.

"Drum? I heard the door slam and someone running up the stairs, but—"

"But did you hear the *drum*?" I am pleading with her now.

Tinker lets out a sharp bark as he tries to squirm out of Gina's arms. I am going to lose my shit on someone before this day is over. I wave my hand at Gina dismissively.

"Take him outside."

"Well, it's raining, so—"

"Gina, please! I can't take his barking! Get him out of here! A little rain isn't gonna hurt him! Put him in the fucking car!"

I look at my friend as if she is the stupidest being on the planet. Maybe she is. Right now, I just don't know. My family members are all frozen in awkward silence, staring at me from various points in the living area. Gina doesn't go outside; she just moves into the living room and sits on the couch next to Tina and Earl, which calms Tinker down a bit. Good thing too, because I might have choked her. That right there—her not taking him to the car when I am literally pleading for her to do so—feels like a big *fuck you*. I look around. Jared is no longer in the kitchen. I don't know where he is. Danielle is walking around the living room with the baby, bouncing him and trying to calm him down. My nieces look perplexed and a little scared; they avoid looking at me directly. I turn to my only salvation left.

"Josie, did you hear it? Did you hear the drum?"

She is still standing near the sink, arms folded as she shakes her head once and looks down. My heartbeat picks up. She is lying. Her face is pale with fear; I am familiar with that look. I saw it a hundred times during or after the fights with Randy before the divorce. I've seen it recently when Josie and I have gone at each other maybe a little harder than moms and teenagers normally do. She is afraid. Her lying about it makes me even angrier. If the girl is going to dress like a man, then she should act like a man. I want to strangle my daughter right now for her hypocrisy. You want adulting? Then be a damn adult.

RATTA-TAT-TAT RATTA-TAT-TAT RATTA-TAT-TAT

I jump because it's loud, so loud, like it's coming from all around us. No one says a word. No one seems to hear… except Josie. I see her glance toward the basement door. It's quick, just a split second—no more than a blink—but I see it. All the fear and rage and disappointment in me bubble up as I stand inches away from the teenager who just bold-faced lied to her own mother.

"DID YOU HEAR IT?"

I am up in her face now. I scream with an intensity that I don't even recognize in myself. My face is burning, and my eyes feel like they are going to burst out of my head. My fists are clenched at my side, and I am struggling to keep them down. I will not be made a fool!

Josie shrinks back toward the kitchen sink. Tears stream down her cheeks as she slowly nods.

"Yes," she whispers through quivering lips. She looks at the floor.

"I can't hear you," I say, seething.

Josie's expression sinks, and she slowly raises her head until her eyes meet mine. Her eyes have gone from fear to "fuck you." I think she is done with me.

"YES," she cries. And then, everything pent up inside her explodes. "YES! I FUCKING HEARD THE FUCKING DRUUUUMS!"

She is yelling, and it feels unnaturally loud in the surrounding silence. I am suddenly aware of the eyes on us and let out the breath I have been holding. The tightness in my jaw eases a bit.

At least I'm not insane.

I look around the room again. No one speaks except the rain, which beats down on the roof relentlessly in defiance of whatever evil energy is invading the house. Jared is in the bathroom; I can see that the door is shut. His absence is his tell. I have an idea of what he is doing in there. Not taking a shit, that's for sure. Snorting something illegal, most likely. Gina looks confused because Gina is easily confused. Josie is someone else. Tina and Earl are up gathering their jackets while Sierra and Jayde stand stiffly by the door. Danielle avoids my eyes and continues hugging Finn, not knowing what else to do. The cause of the stairway ruckus is now secondary to the rage they all know is brewing inside their hostess. A rage that they understand all too well and don't want to be a part of. Danielle starts to pick up the baby's toys and pack them into her diaper bag. Tina tells the girls to get their things.

The party is over.

Cross-Examination With Crosses

Saturday, September 28, 4:00 pm
Paranormal investigation interview, in person, with Sue and Josephine Mackenzie
Mackenzie Residence, Starry Knob Lane, Roanoke, Virginia

Libbi Bean

Walter and I pull up to 1031 Starry Knob Lane for our client interview and find a young man playing basketball in the driveway. He is wearing a high-end Detroit Pistons basketball jersey with matching shorts, and he is making most of his shots as we near the house. I assume this is Sue's son, the one who recently (allegedly) relapsed into addiction because of the "demons." He looks healthy to me, so maybe he got his act together. Good for him. He tucks the ball under his arm and moves aside as we enter the short, steep driveway. I wave; he waves back, and instantly I get a good vibe from him. I'm not a psychic or sensitive, but I like to think I can read people well. I've been told I have high emotional intelligence; maybe I do. This guy is looking confidently at us, not trying to avoid direct contact as so many of the young'uns do these days. There is no phone in his hand for doom scrolling, and he's engaged in sport. And he follows a Michigan sports team. Walter and I grew up in the Great Lakes State. It's a great start to the investigation. I turn off the Zen Wagon—my ten-year-old Subaru Impreza Sport hatchback in light metallic blue and silver—and step out. Walter exits the passenger side as I grab my laptop from the back seat.

I am immediately struck by how much this young man does *not* look like a mid-twenties current (or former) drug addict. At all. And then I realize he's not a young man. *She* is a young woman. Her hair is short, nearly military length, with an undercut and a fluffy, messy mullet. A little disheveled, as if she hasn't quite figured out how to work it yet. I get ya, girl. Short hair is a blessing and a curse. Been there, done that. The presumed Josephine Mackenzie is rocking her high-tops, and her smile is infectious.

"Hey," she calls and dribbles the ball twice, then half-waves again. "I'm Jo."

She extends her arm for a handshake. What? She's fifteen! What fifteen-year-old shakes your hand? This one does. I like this girl. I like her a lot.

"Nice to meet you, Jo. I'm Libbi" I take her hand. It is firm but not manhandling. There is an art to a good handshake. Too strong, and it becomes a power move, usually rooted in insecurity. Too loose and it's like shaking a wet rag, which means the other person is snooty, weak, or doesn't give a shit. Jo is the Goldilocks of handshakers.

Walter comes around the front of the car holding a notepad in one hand and tugging down his long-sleeved navy T-shirt with the other.

"Walter Bean, at your service," he says, putting out his free hand to Jo. "You've got some skills there; you play varsity?"

Jo blushes and dips her head sheepishly. "Nah, mostly just for fun."

"You a Pistons fan?" Walter points to Jo's jersey.

She nods. "Yeah, we lived in Michigan for a couple of years."

"You don't say? Libbi and I both grew up in Michigan. I'm not into basketball, but I keep an eye on the Pistons. They did all right this year."

"Yep," says Jo, nodding again.

"Where did you live in Michigan?" I ask. It's always fun to meet someone from our home state.

"You probably never heard of it. It's a little town called Grass Lake, near Jackson."

She tucks the basketball under her arm and raises her right hand, pointing to the bottom center of her palm with her left index finger. The lower peninsula of Michigan is shaped like a mitten, and we locals often use that to our advantage. It's like having a built-in map.

"Jackson? Hey, home of the prison!" Walter says. "Did you hear that, Lib?" He turns to me with his eyebrow raised in feigned excitement. "That's your hometown!"

I grew up in Jackson County, Michigan, just south of the city. There is a big correctional facility on the outskirts, which has gone by many names over the years. Many of us still affectionately refer to it as "the Jackson prison."

"Yep, good old Jackson," I say sarcastically and scoop my arm like I'm in a vaudeville skit. "It has some lovely parks."

Jo nods. "I liked it there. I'll go get my mom."

And there's the teenager. Still. I think this kid has a story.

Sue Mackenzie comes out of the duplex, which is a side-by-side model—her half being on the right as you look at the house from the road. It's modest, maybe a thousand square feet max on either side, and very similar to the next few houses down the street. I see a lot of ranch-style homes with small decks, a few carports, and lots of awnings. Very working class. The houses aren't as close to each other as I've seen in other planned subdivisions, so they have that going for them. There are many mature trees and overgrown hedges cutting off the view on three sides of the Mackenzie casa. Across the street, behind the houses on that side, is farmland as far as I can see. Looks like corn. I make a mental note, because even though we are in the off season, it's easy to misinterpret farm chemicals and livestock activity in paranormal events.

Sue holds out her hand. She looks like a typical middle-aged working-class mom, wearing cutoff jean shorts and a T-shirt screen-printed with the cover of Journey's *Escape* album. A cigarette is hanging from the side of her mouth. Her face is bare of makeup, and her long, mousy hair is pulled back into a ponytail. My mother used to say that our selection of jewelry reveals our true soul. If that is true, Sue's soul is devoted to Jesus. She's got gold crosses in her ears and not one, but two around her neck. I also can't help but notice a crown of thorns tattoo on her right forearm. I shake the hand at the end of that forearm, as does Walter.

"Thanks for coming. Come on inside; we can talk in here. Looks like it's gonna rain."

The four of us walk through the front door directly into the living room. At once, several things hit me. First, the smell of marijuana is distinct. I don't imbibe much, even with pot being legal in the state of Virginia, but I will occasionally pop a gummy for stress relief. My cousin grows "the green" in Michigan, so it is usually abundant during our family gatherings. As such, I am well acquainted with the odor of pot. Someone in this house indulges. My guess is that "someone" is not the tomboy daughter.

The second blaring observation upon entering the Mackenzie abode (and not surprising, given her cross adornments) is that Sue is extremely religious. The living room is open concept and modestly sized, so it would be hard to miss all the Christian decor: multiple pictures of Jesus staring from the walls; an old Bible sitting on an end table next to a recliner; and a clear, glass ashtray shaped like a cross nudged up against The Holy Book. Who has a cross-shaped ashtray? Sue Mackenzie, that's who. There is a Bible quote print hanging just inside the entryway and a poster of da Vinci's *The Last Supper* a few feet to the left. I observe and will record this later. Religious devotion is a powerful factor in reports of paranormal activity. The more religious the client, the more outlandish the reports will be, and the more likely the words "demon" and/or "exorcism" will be mentioned.

Sue motions to a worn floral couch pushed against the side wall (a wall she presumably shares with her duplex neighbor). Walter sits at the end nearest the front window. I perch next to him, and I'm only a little ashamed to admit that my first thought is hoping my clothes don't smell like that crucifix ashtray when this is done. I subconsciously brush my hands over my jeans and hoodie just in case I already got some on me. Some of what, I don't know… but I know there is something.

As we settle in, I notice the furry pillow to my left, which is not actually a pillow. It is a small, scruffy dog whose nap we are in danger of interrupting. This must be Pepper. I wonder if it is deaf, because having a dog at home myself, I find it inconceivable that Pepper did not even flinch when strangers entered the house. Whenever Walter and I have visitors, Fenny will give out some warning barks, but then quickly graduate to jumping and bouncing around like a kid on Christmas morning with her new best friends. Pepper, conversely, seems dead.

Sue sits in the worn recliner (which I imagine smells like her ashtray) and lights up a cigarette right there in the living room. It astounds me that people still do these things. My stepdad smoked in the house when I was a kid, but it has been a long time since I was in an enclosed space where people puffed so casually. No judgement, it's just how the world is now. Josie has followed us into the living area and sits on a wooden bar stool she pulled from under a cluttered counter in the adjacent kitchen.

I open my laptop and pull up our interview form. It is only partially filled out after our call with Sue the other day; we still have four pages of questions to go through. There are a lot of factors in paranormal experiences—what the client hears, smells, feels, touches, even tastes sometimes. There is a lot to capture. Fortunately, technology has blessed us with the ability to take a lot of notes with a keyboard versus a pen. I am a fluid typist (compared to my husband's two-finger hunt and peck style), so we will get through this quickly.

Walter starts us off. "Sue, first of all, thank you for inviting us to hear your story. We've got a little questionnaire we want to go through to get more information, if you don't mind."

Sue exhales her Marlboro Gold smoke. At least she has the courtesy to point her head toward the center of the house, away from us.

"Fire away."

She is calmer and much less agitated than she was on the phone. Her brown eyes look slightly bloodshot, and I suspect she had a little something-something to take the edge off before we arrived. At least she isn't slurring again.

I begin the interview by asking her to give us a quick overview of the events from September 8—the party she alluded to on the phone, when the events first started. I ask her to keep it at a high level because we'll get into the weeds when we pick back up with the detailed interview questions. Sue is a little more coherent than she was the other day and gives a cohesive summary of the gathering. She and Josephine had an argument; a Bible flew across the room; something unseen allegedly pushed Sue from behind; later, they (and some guests) heard loud footsteps coming from the basement; and of course, the drums. Josie interrupts a few times, and each time she does, her mom shushes her. At first, I wonder if Sue is worried that Josie will reveal something that Sue doesn't want her to. But after the fourth or fifth time, I realize this is just their mother-daughter dynamic. Eager, talkative teenager versus annoyed, controlling mom. Sue is trying to keep it brief; Josie wants to do a minute-by-minute playback. She reminds me of Walter's ten-year-old nephew Eric talking nonstop for hours about his video game adventures. We get the minute-by-minute rundown, every detail down to the gnat's ass. *"And then the giant cockroach from Andaria jumped out of the bushes, and I had to pull out my jeweled sword and take a bottle of health potion to prepare for the battle."* It was kind of like that.

When Sue finishes the party recap, I pick back up with the interview questions.

"First, I'm going to ask you about any sounds you've heard during your experiences. At the party, when you went into the basement, or at other times. Be as specific as you can be. The drums, of course—"

"The drums were the first thing," says Sue. "They started on the 8th when Josie and I were getting ready for the party, and we got into a… a fight."

She gulps and looks down. Jo also averts her eyes. *What was that fight about*, I wonder.

As if on cue, Sue tells us. "Josie cut her hair short—like a *boy*—without my permission. And I wasn't happy about it." She glares at her daughter.

"Jesus, Mom!" Josie huffs, rolls her eyes, and looks uncomfortable.

"Don't take the name of the Lord in vain! How many times do I have to tell you?" She turns back to me. "We were in the middle of having words when all of a sudden, there was a loud drum sound."

"Can you describe the drums?" asks Walter. "Was it like a tribal drum? Or more like a drum set from a rock band?"

"More rock band," says Jo, leaning forward. "Like with drumsticks and cymbals. There's an old set in the basement I used to mess around with when we first moved here. It sounds like that."

They have a drum set in the basement. I type that on my form. *Very interesting.* I don't type that, but I think it.

"Yes, like she says, it was a modern drum sound. Snare! That's it. A loud snare. Like a Revolutionary War drum. After we first heard it the morning of the party—while we were fighting—it stopped for a while. But then later that day it came back, snare and cymbals and the big drum all together, over and over. The weird thing is, I don't think anyone at the picnic heard it but for Josie and me. And then two days before I called y'all, it started again. That was Monday. It was just me at home at first. It got bad that night. I swear it was playing the "Wipe Out" drum solo. Not just the snare, but the entire set was going off…cymbals, bass, everything."

"Wipe Out" is a famous song by the Surfaris, popular in the 1960s, and it contains one of the most recognized drum solos today. I imagine it would be intense hearing that full blast in your house from unknown origins.

"Have you heard the drums at any other times?"

"A few times off and on, just the snare mostly. We've been hearing it faintly every couple of days."

"Okay. What other sounds. Anything like voices?"

Jo starts to say something, but Sue cuts her off again. "Yes, lots of voices, whispers. Conversations that I can't quite make out, or they are in a foreign language. Last Monday I definitely heard a voice—sounded female to me—hissing at me, and then it screamed '*GET OUT!*' We heard it later in Josie's room."

Sue wrings her hands almost like an autistic toddler, flinging ash out into the open space next to her chair. I can tell she is distressed about this. I hope the carpet doesn't catch fire.

"Mom, don't forget about the growling and the footsteps."

Sue waves her daughter away. "I'm getting to it, keep your pantyhose on. Yes, we have heard growling, like a demonic growl. A couple of times, just out of the blue."

As I am thinking it, Walter asks it. "What makes you think it's a demonic growl versus, say, a dog?" He nods his head toward Pepper, who is still out cold. "How do you know it's from a demon?"

"I just know," says Sue, a little exasperated. "It wasn't a dog. I know what my dog sounds like. Anyway, we heard some footsteps and banging at the party, like I said earlier. It sounded like someone running up and down the basement stairs. I thought it was my neighbor Alice's grandson Caleb, but when I went downstairs, there was nobody there. Alice said Caleb wasn't even over that day, but I don't know, maybe she lied. I still think it might have been him."

"He wasn't here," says Jo under her breath. Sue follows up with an irritated "HUSH!"

"Any other noises that you can think of?"

Sue can't think of anything we haven't already covered, so we move on. I ask her about anything she or Jo has seen with their own eyes. Sue reports seeing shadows out of the corner of her eye, the extreme darkness of the basement when she went down to find Pepper, and a basement light that goes on and off by itself. She cannot recall any similar issues with the light prior to a month ago, when the alleged activity started.

I record the events but mentally pay little attention to things like shadows and lights blinking. We will check into them, of course, but if I had a dollar for every client who claimed ghosts were causing their random light flickering and then we found blatant electrical issues, I could buy us a nice dinner at Red Lobster. As if on cue, my stomach rumbles.

Next on the questionnaire is smell. Oddly enough, we get reports of smell as much as or more than sight or hearing experiences.

"Yes," says Sue when I ask about odors. "I told you about the urine. We smell that regularly. Human urine. It is very strong, lasts about a minute, and then it disappears. Excrement too. I've smelled it in the basement and here in the living room."

"I smelled something rotten in my bedroom," says Jo.

I smell no urine or other bodily waste as we sit in the living room, but admittedly, the reek of stale pot is still strong and could be overwhelming other odors. I also wonder about Pepper, the senior dog sitting next to me on the couch.

"I have to ask this, so please don't take offense… but is it possible that your dog is peeing somewhere that would cause the urine smell? Or pooping, for that matter?"

Sue takes the last drag on her cigarette and presses the butt into the ashtray.

"It's not Pepper. I know dog pee. This isn't dog pee. And Pepper has been housebroken since he was a puppy."

I leave it at that. But I also note that the house is very close to farmland, which could be a possibility. Farm chemicals are notoriously poop and pee scented because, well, they basically use poop and pee as fertilizers. It isn't growing season, but some farmers use fertilizer in the fall.

"Fair enough. Any other smells that you can think of?"

Sue shakes her head no and starts fidgeting with one of the crosses around her neck. I would bet money she's on the spectrum.

"Okay, what about touch? Can you elaborate on the experiences where it felt like you were being physically touched? Or was something else moved or touched?"

"I got touched," said Jo suddenly. "It left a mark on my leg."

"I already told them that!" says Sue.

"I wouldn't mind getting Josie's perspective," I say matter-of-factly. I feel for the girl. Sue shrugs and waves her hand toward her daughter. I look at Jo. "Tell me what happened."

Jo relates the incident from two days ago. She was on the bed—this was while Sue was being pushed into the mattress by something unseen—and felt her leg become icy cold about halfway up the upper thigh. After they left the house, Jo pulled up her shorts and could see a handprint on her middle thigh. She said it felt like something was gripping her leg. She pulls up her shorts to show me, but there is no bruise or imprint. I ask her to show me the position of the hand, and she puts her left hand on the inside of her right thigh, twisting her wrist so her thumb points toward her knee.

"It was like this, and I had a bruise the next day."

Unfortunately, they took no photos. But it is interesting how she put her left hand on her right thigh with the fingers pointing down. That suggests the hand came from someone or something that was facing her or perhaps next to her, on her right.

Sue tells us that on the day of the party, while she and Josie were arguing, she was pushed from behind so hard that she fell to the floor. Another night, something played with her hair while she sat on the recliner. She also recapped when something forced her down onto Josie's bed and held her down during the event on Monday. And of course, the Bible flew by itself on the morning of the party, hitting Sue in the chest.

Walter is writing his thoughts and observations with a pen on a small notepad. He will need to interpret his notes for me later because his handwriting is atrocious. Which is a blessing, because I'm sure he has written *whack job* at least once on the paper. I can't say I fully disagree on this one. We both like to come into these things with a healthy skepticism and an open mind. But there are so many factors here that raise red flags. The pot, religion, outlandish reports of touch (which are uncommon). The most troubling is the contentious relationship between Sue and Jo. Paranormally, we could be looking at poltergeist activity given Jo's age and the stress she might be experiencing. Psychologically, I can't help but wonder about the conflict between a very religious mother and a gender-alternate daughter. I certainly don't know Jo's business (and it's not my place to ask), but since Sue revealed the cause of the argument the day of the picnic (Jo's hair and appearance), it is possible that Jo is finding herself. And "herself" might not be the sweet little posy wearing a pink gingham pinafore who is smiling in a family photo on Sue's end table.

We finish with incidents involving touch, so it's time to move on. I put a check mark next to "No" for "Plumbing issues reported." There have been none other than "the normal kind that one deals with." I don't ask. Both Sue and Jo say they experience a lot of temperature changes. Jo's room is often twenty degrees colder than the rest of the house, but Sue admits this is just an estimate and she has not actually taken a temperature. I ask if they are using any air conditioning. Although the temperature is more fall-like today, the past few weeks have been unseasonably warm. It is that time of year when one might have their heat on at night and the AC on in the afternoon. Sue says they have window units but aren't using them this time of year. Too bad. You can't put a price on comfort.

"What about Pepper?" Walter asks. "Has she ever displayed any reaction to anything? You mentioned a coma on the phone the other day."

"It's he," says Jo.

"I apologize. You mentioned that *he* had been put into a coma by whatever it is you believe to be haunting your house."

Sue lights up another cigarette and gets visibly choked up. It takes a few seconds to find her voice.

"YES!" she finally blurts out, then starts a deep, wet coughing fit. I don't know if it's from the smoke or the emotion or both, but I wonder if she will ever catch her breath as she wheezes and spews mucus from her worn recliner. I glance over at Walter, who is in full-on cringe. Jo doesn't flinch and seems lost in thought as her mother is on the verge of vomiting. She probably witnesses this regularly. Finally, after what seems like an eternity (but was probably only thirty seconds), Sue recovers. There are tears in her eyes.

"Pepper has been terrorized! Most of the time, he just wants to hide in the pillows. His entire body quivers, and his eyes get so wide I can see the whites. Sometimes he shakes like he's having bad dreams."

Sue becomes animated while she speaks, ashes flying everywhere as she waves her hands around. I wonder if she will report smelling burnt shag carpet as part of her paranormal events. She suddenly stops and flicks her ash into the tray, almost as if she heard me thinking. I try not to look in the general direction of Pepper, who is finally awake (sort of) and groggily stretching beside me. Decidedly *not* terrorized and very much alive as his dog-mom cries out "Amen, Jesus!" now and then.

"Mom, tell them about the thing in his eye!" Jo suddenly comes back to the here and now. I am intrigued by this very polite teenager, who does not seem nearly as defiant as Sue described her on the phone.

"It was one of the nights when we smelled the urine and heard a wolf growl," says Sue. "There was a black mark in his left eye. And he knows when it's coming. He barks before stuff starts, before we hear voices. Barks at nothing or just starts growling at the dark."

As Pepper pulls himself out of his nap, I lean over and look closer at him. He opens his eyes wide and wags his tail. His left eye pupil is a little larger than the right one. I mention this to Sue. She says this only started when the paranormal events began. I type the details and shudder briefly.

"That is unnerving," I say casually. I get freaked out when Fenny barks at the window at night, even though I know it's probably just a raccoon or deer. It is still unsettling. If she were to growl at something invisible, I'd shit my pants. Don't let anyone tell you that ghost hunters are fearless. We are just as frightened of this stuff as anyone else.

Sue nods, takes another drag, and continues. "The worst part is, sometimes I can't wake him up. It's like he is in a trance or a coma! He'll bark and bark and growl, then hide in the couch... but then I can't wake him up. I shake him and nudge him and even roll him over. He won't move. It's like something put him under a spell!"

"How old is he again?" Walter asks.

"Fifteen, almost sixteen."

Walter pauses, then cocks his head. "Is it possible he's getting old and deaf and just sleeping more deeply?"

Walter likes to rule out the obvious right away. But Sue isn't biting. She is leaning forward, shaking her head no.

"It's not that. If he's deaf, why doesn't he wake up when I push him? And this only just started a month ago. Plus, he isn't that old. Little dogs live longer. I had a toy poodle mix that lived to be nineteen, still went on a walk every morning until the day she died."

She flops back into the recliner. Walter scribbles (and I mean literally scribbles) some notes. I type.

"Sue, you mentioned on our call the other day that your daughter was having nightmares. Can you tell us some details about those, or maybe Jo can tell us herself?" I nod toward the teen, whose face has gone a little gray.

Sue waves her left hand toward her daughter as if to pass the microphone. Jo takes a breath.

"I had some dreams where, like, there was a face of a demon. I was looking into its eyes, and then I woke up sweating."

She does not remember what the demon looked like, just that it was a demon.

"Then, a few nights ago, I dreamed about the demon again. It kept coming after me and grabbing me, like it wanted to pull me through the wall or something. Then it was... inside me or possessing me. It was controlling my body. It wanted me to—"

She pauses and looks down, as if she doesn't know how to say it.

"Just spit it out, child," says her mom. "Let's get it all out on the table."

"Okay. It wanted me to kill my mom."

Whoa. That is heavy.

Sue throws both arms up and exclaims, "There you go!" I can tell she is upset by the prospect of her daughter dreaming of murdering her. I don't read much into it. Walter and I don't believe in prophetic dreams. But the psychological implications might be worth exploring. A child dreaming of being possessed and wanting to kill the parent... if we twist it a little, we have a child who is not feeling like she's herself, not comfortable in her own body, in conflict with her mother's beliefs, and wanting to lash out. I wonder if there isn't some connection between Sue's very conservative religious beliefs and her daughter perhaps not being cisgender and/or not heterosexual. I don't like making assumptions, and I'd love to explore further, but this is not a subject we can easily approach without opening a big can of worms. Best we keep it on the back burner for now.

"Josie has always…" Sue searches for the right words. "… sensed things. When she was little, she would have dreams, and they would come true. I, I can't—"

She is visibly shaking. When she brings her cigarette to her mouth, she almost misses. I ask her if she remembers any examples of Josie's childhood dreams that came true. She looks to Jo for help. Jo shrugs and appears embarrassed.

"I don't know. A few years ago, I dreamed about cats a lot. And then two different cats showed up at our doorstep, so we adopted them. This was when we lived in Michigan, and we had to give them away when we moved. That's the only one I remember."

"Remember the one about your dad." It was a directive from Sue, not a question.

"Oh yeah, that was before the cats. I dreamed my dad was yelling at my mom, and he threw her Bible at her. It hit her in the head, and she disappeared in this, like, black cloud of smoke or fog."

Sue steps in. "Two days later, my husband told me he didn't believe in God. We had a horrible fight, and he threw my Bible across the room. It hit the wall and shattered a family picture of us. The Bible hit me—the 'me' in the photo. On the head. You could tell by how the cracks were. It scared the shit out of me so much that I choked on my cigarette."

"The black smoke," says Walter in a monotone that reeks of skepticism. He doesn't believe it for one second.

Sue nods. "You got it."

"Personally, I don't think I sense stuff," says Jo. "And we learned in school that dreams are supposed to help clean out our brains from all the junk we see during the day. I mean… I definitely don't want to kill my mom."

Ah, I do like this kid. A ton.

I nod and rest my hands on my Mac. "You know, dreams can be a little wonky. Sometimes when there is death in a dream, it means the death of a concept or something we're doing, like a job. I think dreams are helpful in helping us recognize what we are dealing with in daylight, but I wouldn't take them literally. Once when I was fourteen, I dreamed I was a vampire sitting in my living room. I knew I was going to kill people and suck their blood, so I decided—in my dream—that I needed to kill myself. I wasn't suicidal in real life and certainly not a vampire. It was just how my unconscious brain interpreted something that I experienced."

Jo nods her head as if that makes perfect sense. Her mother is not so accepting.

"She senses things, and that's just one dream example. There's been others, that's all I will say. Ask her dad."

She crushes her second (third?) cigarette into the glass cross. I feel sorry for Jo; that's all *I* will say. We go through more questions. Neither Sue nor Jo has been diagnosed with a mental illness like bipolar disorder or schizophrenia—although Sue tells us they are both taking prescription medication. Jo is on something for her ovarian cysts, while Sue is getting some help with menopause symptoms via a bioidentical hormone treatment. Neither of their medications has known side effects like hallucinations or sensory impairment, so I note it on the form, but it doesn't raise any red flags.

I ask if they have had previous paranormal investigations, and the answer is no. We are the first ones. This is always a relief. Many people who experience unexplainable phenomena often bring in multiple ghost hunting teams. They are looking for some validation that they didn't get with the last, so they call another.

As I type up the details, Walter asks, "Is there anything else you can think of that we haven't already talked about? Paranormal, or maybe major life events?"

I buckle up for this one. There is a lot more. Sue goes on for a good five minutes, with Jo interjecting and the two bickering periodically about the other's recollection of events. I can hardly keep up with typing. This has not been a smooth year for the Mackenzie family. Sue lost her job at The Garden Inn in Hollins when it was sold to a couple who are turning it into a nursing home. That was in April. It took her over four months to find another position, and it came with a pay cut. Jo has gotten in trouble for a few things, most frequently for skipping school (Sue is on a first-name basis with the truancy officer, Tom). The school absences are apparently due to Jo's medical issues (and also because of the demons, according to Sue). We get more detail about Sue's son Jared, Jo's older brother. The short of it is, he is a recovering addict who allegedly had a relapse around the time of the unexplained activity on September 8. Sue isn't one hundred percent sure about that because she hasn't spoken to Jared since that day. However, she believes that the demons in her house caused the relapse even though it sounds like it had already occurred when Jared showed up for the festivities. There is no accounting for logic when your house is infested with evil.

At least one other person—that being Sue's friend Gina Baymont, whom I gather is a frequent guest at the Mackenzie casa—heard the bass drum once when she was visiting. She wasn't sure if it was a car bass or an actual drum. Sue insists that when she heard the "Wipe Out" solo, it was coming from *inside* the house. Not from the outside. I press a little, wondering if it could have been one of their neighbors. Both mother and daughter insist that the neighborhood is just a bunch of old people who are usually quiet. But sometimes old people play their TVs and radios loudly, and sound can travel far and fast.

I record all the events in as much detail as I can, cursing myself for forgetting my mini recorder, which would have spared me all the trouble. Walter wraps up his notes too. There is almost too much going on here. I never thought I would hear myself think that. Usually, we have precious little activity to go on. But not in this case. There are so many details to sort through. I am both excited (because we *do* have a lot of specific events to investigate) and a little nervous (because it's a little overwhelming). We will need to bring some of our RIP team members along for this one.

Walter and I gather our things as we wrap up. Sue pulls out yet another cigarette as we stand up and get ready to leave.

"Sue, thank you so much for your time," says Walter with his hand outstretched.

"Yes, thank you! Both of you," I say, nodding toward Jo. "We're going to talk to our team, go over the events with them, and then we can schedule a time to come out. We might even be able to do next weekend, depending on availability."

"That would be great," says Sue through a cloud of smoke. "The sooner, the better. I don't know how much longer we can live here with this going on."

I sense the weariness in her voice.

"I'll give you a call tomorrow," I say. "Take care now."

Walter and I head down the driveway to the Zen Wagon, holding our respective note-taking devices close as Sue and Jo stand soberly under the awning.

Walter mutters under his breath. "This one is going to be interesting."

I agree and turn to wave goodbye to the Mackenzies. They have already gone inside.

Excerpt 2 from the *RIP After Dark* Podcast Episode 72: Case of the Demon Drums

This podcast was broadcast one year after the actual investigation. Client names and identifying details have been changed to maintain privacy.

Libbi: *It's so weird that they spent time in my hometown. Well, more accurately, near my hometown. But still. Jackson isn't exactly a well-known Michigan city.*

Walter: *Unless you're a felon.*

Libbi: [laughs] *Well, there's that. "Please do not pick up hitchhikers."*

Walter: *As the signs say.*

Libbi: *And we listen.*

Walter: *I'd almost rather spend time in a Jackson Prison cell than in the Hobart house. I'm pretty sure a prison cell smells better than ole Nancy's living room.*

Libbi: *Come on. It didn't smell* that *bad. Just smelled like pot.*

Walter: *Two years of Marlboro Golds and reefer madness under the eye of Our Lord and Savior. Do you think Jesus would approve of having joints snuffed out in a cross-shaped ashtray?*

Libbi: *More importantly, who manufactures cross-shaped ashtrays, anyway? I tried to look it up. I couldn't find a single one.*

Walter: *Somebody probably made that in Glass Blowing 101 circa 1974. Or in the prison.*

Libbi: *And Nancy probably found it at a garage sale in Jackson, Michigan.*

Walter: [laughs] *Speaking of 1974, isn't that about when the Hobart house was built? That carpet had to be at least fifty years old.*

Libbi: *Ew. Icky. The landlord should be ashamed.*

Walter: *Can you imagine when Nancy got pushed down by the demon hand before her party? Not only is she dealing with a terrifying paranormal force, but she's got her nose shoved into that nasty rug.*

Libbi: *No wonder she called us.*

Walter: *Hey, did she ever mention having another ghost hunting team investigate? I can't remember.*

Libbi: *Nope. As far as I know, we were the only ones.*

Walter: *Good thing too, considering how many of our cohorts are ready to do an exorcism at the drop of a hat. I can just see them now: "You guys, she has DEMONS! Get the holy water ready!"*

Libbi: [laughs] *Oh my God. It's funny, but it's not funny. I mean, how many exorcisms can regular, non-clergy people perform in a month?*

Walter: *Our listeners might be surprised.*

Libbi: *You mean Lucifer isn't living in the bedroom closet?*

Walter: *You mean it's just mice scratching on the drywall? Not a demon claw?*

Libbi: [laughs] *That shape in the paneling? It's the face of Beelzebub!*

Walter: *And this, folks, is why we work hard to keep it real.*

Team Briefing Over Homemade Biscuits

Tuesday, October 1, 6:30 pm
Cracker Barrel Restaurant, Troutville, Virginia
Walter Bean, Libbi Bean, Stan Katagucci, Maya Hill-Goldberg

Walter Bean

It is Tuesday evening, and Libbi and I are driving to the Cracker Barrel restaurant just outside of Roanoke for a case briefing with two of our RIP team members: Maya Hill-Goldberg and Stan Katagucci. It's a half-hour drive from our home in SW Roanoke when there is no traffic (and there is always traffic), but Maya and Stan both live an hour from downtown Roanoke proper, so we threw them a bone and picked a place that is more in-between. Libbi is at the wheel of my calypso red Hyundai Santa Fe as we head down the death trap known as I-81. About halfway to our destination, she pulls out of the late rush-hour traffic (that we have both come to know and hate) and turns onto the parallel U.S. Route 11. The interstate is faster, but also much more prone to nasty accidents, particularly those involving semi-trucks. We often take the older Route 11 to extend our lives a few more years.

We talk about the Mackenzie events as we slow down for the two-lane road. I am very much on the fence about this case. I love the fact that there is a lot of evidence to debunk. Almost too much. It's going to be complicated. We have multiple people witnessing (or not witnessing) the reported events. Then there's the religious stuff. The whole mother-daughter dynamic, which I cannot relate to. I'll leave that to Libbi. She believes there's something going on with the mom connected to the daughter being *different*. Jo dresses like a boy, cuts her hair like a boy, and shoots hoops in the driveway. Not that girls (sorry, *young women*) can't have short hair or wear basketball shorts or be good at sports. But Libbi doesn't think this is a tomboy situation, and she might be right. Or it could just be a normal parent/child thing.

We pull into the parking lot a few minutes early, and I pray one of the others got here first to put our name in. The restaurant is always packed. This isn't the worst I've ever seen it, and I am relieved that there are no tour buses around (which would almost guarantee a wait time). A noisy chain restaurant isn't the ideal place for a meeting, but it's Stan's favorite, and he practically begged us to come here. Plus, it's a good in-between location. Libbi and I walk past a few people waiting outside and head into the store with our laptops in tow. We almost reach the host stand when both of our phones go off. It is a text from Maya, who is already seated in the dining room. She is sitting near one of the front windows, and as we head toward her, I can see she has ordered water for the four of us and what looks like a couple of Diet Cokes for me and Libbi.

Maya is a psychology major at Hollins University who, like Libbi and me, leans toward the skeptical side. Her background has helped us weed out normal psychological reactions from the truly crazy. Her expertise is a good level-setter because I just assume most clients are borderline lunatics. We met Maya at a paranormal investigation conference in West Virginia two years ago. She was investigating with a group out of Blacksburg who, according to Maya, seemed "a tad extreme." After talking over lunch at the conference, Maya said she liked our *X-Files* "The Truth Is Out There" philosophy. We asked her to join RIP, and she has been on dozens of investigations with us since then. Great asset to the team.

Libbi and I sit down and look at the menu. So many good options. I'm pretty sure I'll end up with the meatloaf. When the server arrives to check on us, my wife orders a sweet tea for Stan, who hasn't arrived yet. She then pulls out her computer and opens a file labeled *0076 Mackenzie Interview*. I take a moment to reflect. This is our 76th case since we started RIP seven years ago. Most of those investigations (about seventy-five percent) are residential client cases like the Mackenzies. The rest are public places like cemeteries, businesses, and well-known haunting spots such as Mansfield Prison in Ohio. Before RIP, we worked with another Virginia group: the Charlottesville Ghost Chasers. We spent three years with them before we moved to Roanoke. It doesn't seem like we've been investigating the paranormal for that long, yet my joints remind me daily how much time has passed.

Just as Libbi opens the Mackenzie interview form, I look out the window and see Stan with his Cracker Barrel trucker hat crossing the parking lot and heading toward the front door like he's trying to outrun a tiger. He's wearing a plaid shirt and jeans because that's what Stan wears. Winter, spring, summer, fall, it doesn't matter. Stan will wear a plaid shirt and either shorts or jeans. He is nothing if not predictable. I nearly shit myself once when he showed up to an investigation with a Hawaiian shirt. The "flowers" printed on it were photos of his late pug Dalek (named after the robot villains from *Dr. Who*). When I pointed out his uncharacteristic outfit (okay, mocked him for it), he said it would have been Dalek's seventeenth birthday, so he wore the shirt in his honor. That is the only time I've ever seen him out of the plaid combo.

I roll my eyes as he enters the dining room, not intending for anyone to see, but Maya snickers and Libbi kicks my leg under the table. I deserve that. I don't know what it is about him, but he rubs me the wrong way. Stan has never been married (he's in his late forties), and he is obnoxiously loud (which is my theory as to why he's never been married). His voice is like fingernails on a blackboard projected through a megaphone. Stan is also our legit problem child. He likes to use provoking language during investigations (which we explicitly discourage) and he's stubborn as a mule. He thinks everything is supernatural and never listens. Unfortunately, he is also a tech wizard and can set up our equipment in a quarter of the time the rest of us can. And his mom was married to Libbi's late dad for over twenty years, so he's family. Sort of. Still, I have been on the verge of firing him from the team at least half a dozen times.

Stan waves and yells, "HELLO, RIP TEAM!" as he enters the seating area and barrels through the tables, nearly hitting the elbow of a large, bearded man about to take a bite of pancake. Stan is like Fenny: a bull in a china shop and about the same level of intelligence. I take a sip of my Diet Coke and fake smile at Plaid Jeans. I'm going to need something stronger from this point on. Unfortunately, Cracker Barrel does not sell whiskey, and smoking cigars inside is illegal. It's going to be a long dinner.

Libbi Bean

Stan comes flying over to our table like a typhoon. I give him a blue ribbon for "Most Enthusiastic About Ghosts" on our team. He's the oldest on the team at forty-eight. He also has the most exposure, having been chasing the paranormal with various groups for almost twenty years. Unlike the rest of the team, he gravitates toward some of the more extreme ghost-hunting philosophies. Everything is evidence of a haunting. Every other case is demon possession. He assumes a place is haunted and will cater any evidence to that conclusion, even if it makes little sense. Stan is more like some of the investigation teams you see on TV. They are artificially ramped up, both physically and emotionally. *"OMG WHAT WAS THAT? SOMETHING JUST TOUCHED MY FACE! DID YOU GET THAT ON CAMERA???"* One of the main reasons we keep him around despite his overzealous nature is that his mad skills with equipment and tech are untouchable. He built us a spirit box, which is a modified FM radio that scans stations to detect otherworldly noises. A couple of years ago he bootlegged a multi-spectrum lens onto a standard video camera, and we still use it today. So, we let him be on the team even though we are forced to shut him down occasionally.

My husband isn't as understanding as I am. He barely tolerates Stan, and I am not exaggerating. I periodically bribe Walter with a bottle of Irish whiskey and a pack of expensive cigars to keep Stan on the team. If I can keep my stepbrother to a dull roar, it works. When it no longer works, Stan is probably out.

Stan sits next to Maya, and she gives me an amused look. Maya tolerates everything. She is as chill as can be. I mean, the woman partly pays her way through college by dressing up as famous cartoon princesses and holding parties for little girls (and occasionally boys). Anyone who can put up with a dozen seven-year-old kids hopped up on sugar can put up with just about anything.

"Hey guys!" says Stan, removing his denim-blue hat. "How's everybody doing?"

When he's not focused on finding demons, he can be quite charming.

"How's Fenny?" he asks, looking at me. Stan has a weird affinity with dogs, and despite his questionable paranormal investigation skills, he is a canine magnet. Fenny cannot get enough of her uncle.

"Still a baby rhino," I respond cheerfully. "Always my heart and soul."

"Aw!" he says. "I gotta come up and give her some snuggles. So, what do we got? Is it a good one? You said demons, right?"

Stan is already over the dog. I think he might have attention deficit hyperactivity disorder (ADHD). He moves from topic to topic like I move from entrée to entrée at a Chinese buffet.

"Yes, this is a good one, Stan," says Walter, starting us off. "There are a lot of events reported, so even though the actual house is relatively small, we are inviting the entire core team."

The core team members are Walter and me, Maya, Stan, and Dana Tennant. Dana is our sensitive—which means she can sense things that the rest of us can't. She's a medium, a psychic, and a clairvoyant all rolled into one. I was skeptical of her claims at first, being that I am the co-founder of a logic-based, truth-finding group. But Dana has proven herself time and time again over the past five years. I have seen her come up with some truly freaky shit, stuff that defies all logic. Dana rarely attends our debrief sessions because she wants to know as little as possible about the case before the investigation begins. That way she can go in clean with no preconceived ideas or knowledge, which makes validating her talent that much easier.

The server arrives to take our order. Country-fried chicken with mashed potatoes and gravy for me, all day, every day. When we are done, Walter continues with the recap.

"The investigation will take place this Saturday evening, with the four of us and Dana. We'll meet at the client location at 7:30 for setup. I'll send you all a text with the address."

Stan is getting antsy. He wants details, more than what's in the interview form. Reluctantly (because I know him too well), I give them to him.

"The client is a woman in her late forties, and she has a fifteen-year-old daughter. They have both experienced some pretty intense stuff and had two major incidents (so far) where things escalated. Multiple minor encounters."

I scroll through the interview form on my MacBook Pro using the trackpad. "One of the main things reported is loud drum noises, including one incident where they heard the "Wipe Out" drum solo. Are you familiar?"

I look at Maya, who shakes her head and shrugs her shoulders. "I looked it up on YouTube." She's twenty-two; she gets a pass. Stan is nodding yes.

"Epic," he says.

"It's one of the most recognizable drum solos I am aware of, anyway," I say. "They hear other drum sounds periodically as well. Snare drum tapping, cymbals, bass drum."

"We should point out that they have a set of drums in their basement," says Walter. "And they live in a duplex with an older lady on the other side. The basement is shared."

Maya nods, understanding the context of "we hear drums and there are drums in the basement." She sits up and pushes her long chestnut hair behind her ears. It is comfortably cool but not yet cold in this part of Virginia, yet Maya is wearing a thick blue cardigan with a turtleneck underneath. There is a wool peacoat draped over the back of her chair for when she goes back outside, because Maya has zero body fat on her petite frame. She's probably freezing here in the temperature-controlled environment inside Cracker Barrel. Fortunately, her body temperature regulation does not interfere with her ace investigation skills.

And I have a feeling her psychology expertise is going to come in handy in this case.

Maya Hill-Goldberg

It is freezing in this place! Stan smells like he's been outdoors all day, which he probably has because he's a meter reader or repair person or something like that. I can't believe there are meter readers left in the world with all the technology these days. The dials at my apartment complex look like you could play video games on them.

"We have a lot of things for potential debunking," says Libbi. "There's a list at the bottom of the interview form I sent out. Urine and feces smells (sorry, hope that doesn't spoil your dinner), growling, hearing voices, cold spots, banging, footsteps. We've got the whole shebang here."

Walter says, "Yeah, so let's just remember to focus on getting to the root cause. That's our mission."

Walter is a quality manager, so getting to the root cause is probably in his blood. I like this group a lot because they seek the truth and don't freak out over every shadow or cold draft. Being a psychology major has helped me recognize how many of our cases are rooted in fear. Many people who have challenging stuff going on in their lives—like divorce, stress, abuse—use hauntings as a deflection. It distracts them from thinking about their own struggles. If the haunting is bad enough, it gives them something else to focus on. From what I read in the interview report, this case is a perfect example of a psychological haunting. Hey, I like that phrase! I might have to write a book.

Stan responds to Walter's list of items that likely have a logical explanation. "Yeah, but those could also be caused by spirits or demons."

"Fair enough," says Walter. "But we need to start with the most logical explanations—"

Stan cuts him off. "When I was with Lexington Ghost Chasers, we had a case with growling and whispering, and that place was definitely haunted. I mean, we got multiple clear EVPs and tons of orbs!"

I wince softly and hold my breath, waiting for Walter or Libbi to respond to the orb comment. Like me, they feel strongly that orbs— circles of light reflection that sometimes appear in photographs or video—are *not* paranormal. They even did a YouTube video where they recreated hundreds of orbs by shaking out a dirty rug into their dining room and taking photos. I can sense Walter cringing, but thankfully the server appears with our food, and the controversy is momentarily sidelined.

"Let me know if you want a bite of my meatloaf," Walter says to me, gesturing with his fork toward the pile of dead flesh on his plate. He's joking. He knows I'm vegan (mostly). I opted for the country vegetable plate as it is one of the few things available here without meat or dairy (I am skeptical of this claim; I would bet good money that there is butter somewhere in this mix). I'm not anal about the vegan thing (as a non-religious Jew, I'll even eat a little brisket at the family holidays), but I do like to limit the negative impact on the environment and my lifespan. The country vegetable plate is as good as it's going to get for this outing.

We all start eating as Libbi continues between bites. Her battered, deep-fried chicken looks way better than my green beans and corn.

"This client is a little… different. Maya, I think you'll have a lot to say about her once we get over there. The main thing is, she is super religious—like, Jesus and crosses everywhere. She was wearing at least four crosses when we went out there. Bible on the nightstand, even had a cross-shaped ashtray, I kid you not. She had the place blessed by a priest even though she's not Catholic. Sounds like she has a friend who is even more religious; I think that's the connection."

"Oh, geez." I make a mental note. I am Jewish but more cultural than religious. I don't really understand the need for people to broadcast their religion through any means available. You'd think there wasn't a church almost literally on every corner. Yet the second you put up a rainbow flag, you're "shoving it in their face."

"And here's one for the psych books. The daughter Jo—Josephine—looks like a boy. Like, seriously. Short hair, wears sports clothes, the whole shebang. No joke, when we drove up for the interview, she (as far as I know, that's the correct pronoun) was out playing basketball, and I thought it was the son, the former drug user. She looks like a boy. Not a tomboy. *A boy*. Take a super-religious, pot-smoking mom and add a possibly gender-nonconforming daughter. What do you get? You do the math."

I nod while I finish chewing. "Okay, I'm intrigued. I just did a class presentation a few weeks ago about the dynamic between parents and children when one or the other displays behavior or traits that are misaligned with the parent's core beliefs. That could be religion, dating someone of a different race, LGBTQ+, and others."

Libbi says, "So if you combine a few of these factors, it could be a ticking time bomb."

"Exactly," I say.

"Or it could be a demon!" Stan will not give up on his push for a paranormal root cause, but I guess that's why we are here.

I ignore him and address Walter and Libbi. "Did you get any indication when you were there whether the daughter's behavior and appearance were a problem for the client? Was there tension?"

Walter shakes his head no. "Not that we witnessed. They bickered a lot, but it seemed like typical mother-daughter stuff. In fact, even though Sue reported on the initial call that she had argued with her daughter about her boy clothes and haircut, Jo was wearing a basketball jersey and shorts when we did the on-site interview. There wasn't any unreasonable tension, but I also think Sue was high during the entire thing, sooo…"

"Hmmm," I mumble, taking a bite of mashed potatoes. "I am very much looking forward to this case!"

Stan Katagucci

It's annoying when the others lose their focus. This is a paranormal investigation, not a therapy session! I understand we need to look at all angles, but geez-o-Pete! Every time, it's debunk, debunk, debunk, and sometimes they come up with the craziest stuff. Are they trying to imply that this is all just a mother-daughter relationship thing? A religious parent with a defiant teenager who doesn't dress appropriately is every family on the block. That has nothing to do with a demonic haunting. Although now that I think about it—

"Isn't it possible that the tension between the client and her daughter might *cause* paranormal activity? Or attract it, like a poltergeist? Seems like the perfect storm."

A poltergeist is a mischievous spirit. In my opinion (and of many other experts), they are not ghosts. They are something entirely different, though it's not entirely clear what. Some even believe that teens or tweens (especially girls) can actually *be* the poltergeist or cause events through telekinesis or other psychic energy.

"Sure, it could be a poltergeist," says Walter through his oversized bite of meatloaf. I'm a little disgusted with his eating habits. Pretty sure no one is going to invite him to the royal palace for dinner anytime soon. "It could be a demonic presence, or it could be Lucifer himself. But we have a lot that we might easily debunk, so I'd like to start there. If we can't find a logical explanation, then sure. Maybe it's a poltergeist."

Libbi continues, "So in case you missed it, I put the summary of reported incidents at the end of the interview, in that last section. It's mainly the events that are the strongest candidates for us to actively debunk, like the urine smells. They have a dog, and they live across the street from a shitload of farmland, that sort of thing."

"Fair enough," I say. "Although it's not farming season. But okay. Debunking urine smells or random knocking is one thing. Someone being choked or touched where there's a bruise? That's not so easy."

"I agree," says Maya. I silently thank her. At least someone at this table has an open mind.

She continues. "I wish they had gotten a photo of the mark. While I think there might be something psychological here, I'm intrigued by the poltergeist theory. What if Jo is manifesting these events and doesn't even know it? The tension with her mom—if that is a real thing (to be determined)—could attract paranormal energy or even trigger it. And if—IF—she is struggling with her sexual or gender identity, that could mean stress hormones, teenager hormones surging, etc. I think it's worth exploring."

Maya and I rarely agree out loud, so I'm thrilled that she's backing me up on this.

Libbi nods. "We won't rule anything out for sure. I think Walter and I are just saying that it's not a no-brainer. Some of what they report sounds intense and otherworldly, but also a lot of it might be things they would brush off as normal if they were not under so much stress about it all."

I sigh. This is almost ruining my pot roast.

"Okay, okay. Balance, right? Isn't that what you always say?"

Libbi laughs. She reaches over and puts her hand on my forearm. I suppose she's trying to reassure me.

"Yep, that's right, big brother. Balance is the key." She winks.

I feel in my gut that this is going to be an epic investigation. I'll go along with the team mission to find the truth, but we can't just deny that the truth might be something other than farm fertilizer or dog poo. Debunking is fine, but I'm not going to ignore evidence that clearly points to a paranormal source.

"Okay, sis," I say, humoring her. "Balance it is. But I got a feeling about this one!"

Walter Bean

Stan has a feeling about every investigation. That's why we only bring him along when we need the bodies or the technical expertise. Everything is an evil spirit to him. Look, I believe there *is* something after death. I believe in ghosts. I try to go into every case with an open mind. But it's hard when we have Professor Paranormal ready to jump to a conclusion at every shadow and bump in the night.

There is a great quote from the literary character Sherlock Holmes: "*When you have eliminated the impossible, whatever remains, however improbable, must be the truth.*" I have my own saying about ghost hunting, from the Walter Bean library: "*When you eliminate the obviously possible, whatever remains might still be perfectly explainable… but okay, maybe it IS paranormal. Maybe.*" Libbi and I founded this group on the idea that not every event is a haunting. It's our job to find out what causes (or might reasonably cause) the things our clients experience. We gather information that helps us determine one way or the other if a situation is paranormal. But we almost never come to a rock-solid conclusion. Rather, we find evidence that tells a convincing story. And that story is always open to interpretation, even when the evidence seems overwhelming.

That's just how it works with the supernatural. Until we die, we won't know for sure.

Libbi goes over a few more items from the interview until we've exhausted every detail and our plates are clean. The bill comes; I let her take it. I didn't find our server to be that great, and my wife (a former waitress herself back in the day) will give me the stink eye if I don't tip enough. It all comes from the same account, but I feel better if she completes the transaction.

"Does anyone have any more questions?" asks Libbi. "If not, but you think of something later, just shoot me an email and let me know."

She always has it under control. I imagine she used that very same phrase at the end of every one of her meetings during her sixteen years in corporate and consulting—until the last company she worked for was bought out and her position eliminated. Even though she now pursues more creative endeavors like podcasting and writing books, Libbi will forever be the quintessential planner/organizer. She will document the shit out of just about anything, and I'm certain she's had an affair with at least one spreadsheet.

Maya and Stan are shaking their heads; they have no questions.

"And thank you both for helping with this on short notice. I don't think it will be too late of a night, but if anyone needs to crash at our place after the investigation, please do. We have plenty of room."

I hate even offering because Stan just might accept. Nothing rounds out a bad investigation like waking up to the Katagucci volume on a Sunday morning. My stomach gurgles at the thought, and I silently pray that Stan will prefer the hour drive back home. I will do everything in my power to get this case completed expeditiously if we can avoid a stepbrother sleepover.

"As long as you don't mind lots of licks and cuddles with Fenny," adds Libbi.

I visibly cringe when she mentions our dog. I'm trying to deter Stan from taking advantage of AirBNBean! Reminding him of Fenny won't help. We always issue a disclaimer about our attention-whore dog, who loves people more than life itself. She is a needy girl when it comes to human affection. Stan doesn't give a shit, but on the chance that Maya takes us up on our offer (which she has never done so far), it needs to be stated. The dog comes with the accommodations.

"We'll bring our standard equipment—recorders, cameras, the Blu-Lus, full-spectrum camera, flashlights, etc.," I say.

Blu-Lu is short for *Blue Illumination*, which is our preferred night vision video camera. They are cheap, highly rated on Amazon, and easy to use, so we have several of them. They were originally marketed as a kid's toy until the ghost hunters got wind of them. Stan is probably sporting a woody right now at the mention of "equipment."

Almost as if on cue, he pounds the table with excitement.

We get up to leave, stopping in the Cracker Barrel store for a box of Hot Tamales (me) and a bag of Getz Caramel Cremes (Libbi) before heading to the cashier to pay the bill. Maya and Stan wait by the door as Libbi signs the receipt, probably adding double or triple the tip I would have paid. We head out into the parking lot, where it is dusk and not too cold yet. I try to forget that winter is on its way, choosing instead to remember warm summer days with Fenny in our pool. That puts me in a mood that even Stan can't break.

My Santa Fe is closest, so we say our goodbyes there. Maya heads off to her trusted candy-apple red Nissan Sentra, while Stan tags his twenty-year-old Ford F-150 in the next aisle over. I'm not sure what color it was when he bought it. Now it's more or less "shabby chic skid mark." Libbi waves as we get into the car.

As we roll out onto Rte. 11 toward Roanoke, she asks, "So what do you think? Haunting or hell?"

That's our standard pre-investigation bet. Is this going to be an exciting ghost hunt with lots of intriguing evidence? Or will it be a dismal failure, with difficult working conditions and zero evidence found? This one is a toughie. On the one hand, we have a lot of reported events and (on the surface) I'm tempted to let myself get excited. But my Spidey sense is also telling me the client is a nutjob of the highest degree. I rarely play into the psychological aspect of paranormal events (that's for Maya and Libbi) but in this case, they may be onto something. I'm just hoping we find *something*. As much of a curmudgeon as I can be, I truly do *want* to believe. I *want* to get evidence that strongly suggests a haunting.

"What do I think?" I reply. "I think this case is going to be anything but typical."

And with that, we head home to plan the party.

Excerpt 3 from the *RIP After Dark* Podcast
Episode 72: Case of the Demon Drums

This podcast was broadcast one year after the actual investigation.
Client names and identifying details have been changed to maintain privacy.

Libbi: *Welcome back to the RIP After Dark podcast, coming to you from Roanoke Investigations of the Paranormal central (AKA our living room), where we are in the middle of discussing Case 0076, The Demon Drums. Before the break, we were diving into our pre-investigation mindset about the case. Which I think is always an interesting perspective.*

Walter: *Yeah, it's always good to set a baseline before we get the results.*

Libbi: *Spoken like a true quality manager.*

Walter: [chuckles] *If the shoe fits... but yes, to your point, we always go in with an opinion based on the facts at hand. And almost always we come away with a different perspective. I think this case was a great example of that.*

Libbi: *Exactly. I know you went in thinking this was going to be a trip down Lunatic Lane.*

Walter: *Whack Job Central*

Libbi: *I was convinced it was purely psychological. The mother-daughter thing.*

Walter: *Which you could write a book about.*

Libbi: *No doubt. RIP, Mom. I love you, but sometimes...*

Walter: *A topic for another day—*

Libbi: *Anyway, I thought it was a lot of that dynamic. Or maybe one of our favorite types of cases: "Come hell or high water, you WILL prove that my house is haunted!"*

Walter: *We have had a lot of those. For our audience (and we've talked about this ad nauseam), while we have many legitimate cases in our bag, we also get more and more people demanding that we prove that they have a haunting even when we find zero credible evidence.*

Libbi: *Like that guy at Smith Mountain Lake who was trying to rent out his cabin as a "haunted house."*

Walter: *Okay, that guy was the king of crazy. Didn't he claim that another paranormal group ran out of his house in the middle of their investigation screaming, and never came back?*

Libbi: *Uh, yes. He claimed that. I can't imagine any reputable group ever doing that. What did they do, just leave all their expensive equipment sitting there? Ridiculous.*

Walter: *They probably ran out screaming from the sound of his colossal burps.*

Libbi: [laughs] *Oh my god, that's right! Nasty body sounds all night long.*

Walter: *I got a little throw-up in my mouth just thinking about it.*

Libbi: *Anyway, back to the tale. We met with our team and went over the case. It was just Stan and Maya there.*

Walter: *That's right. Dana doesn't like to hear any of the details beforehand.*

Libbi: *For new audience members, Dana is our team sensitive. A medium of sorts.*

Walter: *I think we met her when we created our Facebook group, right? We had that meeting at Parkway Brewing Company.*

Libbi: *"Beers & Orbs" back before we realized what a scam orbs are.*

Walter: *Yeah, friends and listeners, side note: Orbs are just dust or mist reflecting in your camera. They are not ghosts.*

Libbi: *We did a video about this. I'll put the link in the show notes.*

Walter: *I think orbs might be in the top five of reported events in our cases. Oddly, not in this one, but just about every other.*

Libbi: *Yep, orbs, sleep paralysis events, and people claiming that their house was built on a Native American burial ground. Almost every time.*

Walter: *If anyone out there ever wakes up and sees a dark figure, or feels like they are being choked—*

Libbi: *—sat on, strangled, suffocated—*

Walter: *—it's just sleep paralysis. Perfectly normal. Google it.*

Libbi: *I'll put another link in the show notes.*

Walter: *So back to the case... Dana wasn't there. Maya thought it could be a psychological fear thing but was open to it being paranormal.*

Libbi: *And Stan was sure it was a demon, at least at first. Then he suggested that maybe it was a poltergeist.*

Walter: [sarcastically] *I can't remember, did he recommend we do an exorcism?*

Libbi: *Okay, be nice. He has gotten a lot better now that he's with us and not that team out of Lexington.*

Walter: *Fair enough. Sorry, Stanley. Okay, so Stan thought it might be a poltergeist.*

Libbi: *Yes, which wasn't a bad hypothesis given the mother-daughter conflict. Poltergeists are notorious for targeting young women for some reason. Of course, the term gets thrown around for any event where there's noise, banging, things moving around.*

Walter: *Which was the case in this case.*

Libbi: *Exactly! So as much as we want to make fun of Stan for his assumptions... was he right this time?*

Walter: *We will have to wait until after the break to find out! Back in a minute.*

Shit's Getting Real

Tuesday, October 1, 7:15 pm
Series of Unexplainable Events, 3rd major occurrence
Mackenzie Residence, Starry Knob Lane, Roanoke, Virginia

Sue Mackenzie

ratta-tat-tat

Josie and I both freeze as we enter our home and hear drums the moment the front door closes. The entire day has been one disaster after another, and this is the last thing I need. My shift at the Courtyard front desk was especially shitty (thank you, rich bitch, who didn't like her water pressure and thought the hot tub needed cleaning), and I've been battling a whole slew of problems with my cell phone. It was mysteriously locked this morning, and even my tech-savvy daughter could not get it to awaken. That resulted in a call to customer service and about an hour of agony as the patient rep worked through the issue. But then the phone crashed again when I was trying to use my child-support credit card at lunch. And it didn't stop there. While I was waiting for Gina to pick me up, I saw I had received several emails saying bills hadn't been paid (which they most certainly had). Dealing with all of this on top of my daughter's insolent mouth (which disputes everything) made for a no good, very bad day.

And now here they are again. Those fucking drums. They've been silent for a few days, and we thought maybe it was over. I almost don't care anymore. I am so tired of it, tired beyond words. Sometimes I just want to sit in my chair and let the demons take me. Just get it over with and let me move on to the promised land. God knows, it isn't a birthday party down here on Earth.

Except there's Josie. My instinct as a mother always kicks in, no matter how battered my relationship is with my daughter. It's what keeps me going, frustrating as she can be. She and Jared are the only things preventing me from giving up altogether.

"FUCK YOU!" I yell into the living room. "We aren't going anywhere!"

"Goddammit, I am so sick of this!"

Josie shoves past me and heads into her bedroom, hurling her backpack onto the floor as she slams the door. This sets me off. What doesn't these days? It's like the demons are in my head. I go from saint to sinner in half a second over the most minuscule stuff. It's like I can't help myself. I don't know how or when I became this person. I wasn't always this way.

"Do not take the name of the Lord in vain!" I yell for the millionth time, banging my fist on Josie's wall.

Does she have any clue what I put up with these days? I throw my purse on the floor and pull my lighter out of my pocket. I'm going to need something stronger than a cigarette to end this day, so I head to my kitchen and reach up to my special shelf above the cabinet. My fingers search until they find an old tin box with blue flowers on the outside and a half-dozen hand-rolled joints on the inside. I open it and select a tube that I am confident is not of the variety acquired from Mr. Cliff Gerber, then put the box back in its secret spot.

ratta-tat-tat

I light up and take a deep inhale of the magic leaf before walking over to the recliner, where I collapse with one arm dangling over the end table. *Nope. I'm done.* I don't want to cry, but my eyes well up. *Am I scared or just exhausted?* I honestly don't know which. Both, maybe.

ratta-tat-tat ratta-tat-tat ratta-tat-tat BOOM BOOM BOOM

The drums get louder and longer as I wait with my eyes closed, hoping they will eventually stop on their own. If I sit here with my back to the chair, nothing can get behind me and shove me like before. That's what I tell myself, anyway. I pray with all my devotion for Jesus to protect us, but I am cursing him at the same time. My faith is declining. *I'm sorry, God. I can't do this.*

I am startled back into reality when Josie rushes out of her bedroom with something in her hand. I blink to clear my tears because I can't believe my eyes. It looks like the bat she used in junior high softball a few years ago. I would recognize it anywhere because it's cotton candy pink with a neon green stripe running down the side. I threw it out after she quit the team in eighth grade, but here it is—like a full-sized accessory for a giant Major League Baseball Barbie. She must have taken it out of the trash. I want to ask her where she had it hidden. Probably the closet; that's the one area of her room even I won't enter.

But that will have to wait. Josie is on a rampage. Her face looks more satanic than I imagine the actual demons to be. And she is crying. She is on a mission, heading toward the basement like a bat out of hell with a bat in her hand.

"SHUT UP!" Josie yells as she stomps across the carpet.

"Josie, calm down! What is the matter with you?"

I shove myself out of the recliner, dropping my still-smoking joint into the ashtray. Josie is already at the basement door as I reach out to grab her arm. She jerks away, her youth and size meshing nicely with a rush of adrenaline to create a teenage Godzilla. With one thrust, she opens the basement door and rushes down the steep stairs into the darkness. She almost stumbles but recovers near the bottom by jumping over the last few steps onto the concrete below. The drums continue—*RATTA-TAT-TAT BOOM BOOM BOOM RATTA-TAT-TAT*—and they get louder as I follow her into the dark, musty underground.

Suddenly—CRASH! And another. And more, BANG, BANG, CRASH!

I find the chain to the ceiling bulb in the lounge area and pull. The demon drumbeats have stopped, replaced by the maniacal, untamed collision of Josie's pink club bashing the old drum set into an almost unidentifiable pile of wood, mylar, and metal. I don't dare get any closer lest I become an accidental victim of the flying debris. I can only stand and watch while this creature—who is and is not my daughter— exhausts every ounce of energy pounding the demonic instruments to a dusty, metallic pulp. If I weren't so afraid of her right now, I might be proud of her courage.

Josie's movements become slower and less powerful with each swing as her breath becomes more labored. Finally, she stops, hanging frozen in mid-swing like Babe Ruth waiting for the pitch. Her face is full of sweat; she looks like a statue made of wax that got too hot and started melting.

"Josie?"

I take a tentative step toward my rigid daughter. She doesn't move. Her eyes are open and staring at drums that are no longer drums. There is no *ratta-tat-tat*. There is only painful silence. Josie seems unable to move, possessed by some force that holds her in her fury—as if to remind her who holds the power here. I am petrified. But I repeat her name again and again, praying for a response.

Finally, she blinks and drops her arms to her sides. The bat falls to the cement floor with a loud CLUNK. She slowly straightens up, looks at me with an impossible combination of admiration and disgust, and turns slowly toward the stairs. Her sneakers shuffle across the cold, damp floor in a muffled echo that sounds eerily like the *ratta-tat-tat* of the demon drums if they were played inside a padded room. I wonder if that isn't where my daughter belongs. Maybe both of us. Josie disappears up the stairs, and I decide it is time for me to go too. What she did to that old drum set will need to be addressed, but that can wait. Right now, I need to get my thoughts together.

Just before I pull the chain to shut off the light, I look down and realize my watch is gone. I don't even look around. It is in the same place as my daughter's sanity. Somewhere in the dark.

Libbi Bean

When we arrive back home after the team briefing at Cracker Barrel, I notice a voicemail that must have come in while I was in "do not disturb" mode during our drive. It's from Sue Mackenzie. I put her message on speaker so Walter can listen while he greets Fenrir. Our pup is ecstatic to see her daddy (rather "meh" about Mom) and runs zoomies around our living room to release her big Labrador energy. I mumble "traitor" under my breath as I push the play button on my phone. The voicemail starts; Sue's voice sounds weary. That seems to be her thing, but it might also be a sign of how these events are affecting her.

"Uh… Hi, this is Sue Mackenzie from Starry Knob Lane calling about the investigation. You told me to let you know if we had any more incidents, and, well, we just had one. We're okay, just a little shook up, so if you can call me as soon as possible, I'll get you the details. Thank you."

Walter and I walk out onto the back deck so Fenny can go potty on our one-acre wooded lot. It's dark out, and it smells like autumn. A gentle breeze kicks up as I redial Sue's number while my husband stands next to his favorite cigar chair—a white Adirondack-style handmade by an Amish woodworker in nearby Fincastle. I put my phone on speaker again and wait for Sue to answer. My introvert husband is undoubtedly counting the minutes until he can sit out with Fenny and a stogie, decompressing from the drive and the social interaction. For now, he just listens.

"Hey," says Sue from the other line. "Thanks for calling back."

"No problem," I say, holding the phone horizontal and out from my body in case Walter cares to speak. Probably not. "Sorry I didn't answer the first time; we were on the road. Everything okay?"

I'm not sure if it's a burp or grunt or acknowledgment, but a bizarre sound comes through the phone. It sounds like Charlie Brown's teacher coughing. Very electronic.

"Pardon me?"

"I didn't say anything," says Sue. "But my cell has been acting up all day. I don't know what's going on or if it's related to the demons… but we just had another event. That's why I wanted to call you."

Uh-oh. "What's going on?"

Sue tells us the drums came back, and then her daughter went apeshit on the old set in their basement. As per usual (because we have now established a trend with Sue), she is a little slurred, a little breathy (smoking?), and a little all over the place. I gather that she and Jo heard drums, Jo flipped out, and beat the old drum set in the basement to a pulp. And when she did, the drum sounds stopped.

Coincidence? Maybe… maybe not. At the very least, it is something to add to our investigation plan. If the sound was coming from those specific drums (even paranormally), then would this be the end to any reoccurrences of "Wipe Out?" Who was playing them? Sue said there was no one in the basement when her daughter went off. Could this be some sort of poltergeist energy originating from Jo? Would things now escalate (or maybe slow down)? Did she get it all out of her system, or is this just the beginning? And psychologically—drums and demons aside—what does it mean for a fifteen-year-old girl to flip out like that? Honestly, if that were my kid, I would be scared shitless. I would lock my bedroom door at night. I guess that's another reason I'm glad Walter and I never reproduced.

But this isn't about me. This is about Sue and her daughter, and they need us desperately. I try to console Sue, but I'm getting the impression she is already consoling herself with something more… medicinal-*ish*.

"Sue, you mentioned your phone. What's going on there?"

Walter audibly mutters, "Jesus Christ!" I flip him the bird, which he can surely see because I turned the deck lights on before we came out. He points to the phone and then spins the same index finger next to his temple in the universal sign for crazy.

"Well, I'm probably just being paranoid, but last night I plugged in my phone just like I do every night. Nothing different. This morning it was all locked up. I had to call tech support on Josie's phone to get it running again. Took over an hour."

I give Sue a few "uh-huh" responses to let her know I hear her. My husband just shakes his head as Fenny returns from her potty break, jumps up onto the deck, and spins around in her post-poop happy place.

"Then this afternoon I was trying to use my child support credit card from my phone at Krogers, and it wouldn't work. Just flat out wouldn't work. I thought that was a weird coincidence given the phone problems earlier, but okay. Whatever. I called the number on the back, and they said my card had been reported lost or stolen. Well, I didn't do that! How the hell did that happen?"

"Huh. That *is* weird," I say, trying to be sympathetic but also knowing from my previous roles in corporate technology that sometimes people just don't know how to use the internet, and that's not something I can teach on a phone call.

"Right? Isn't that odd? But that's not all. Then I see I got not one, but two emails telling me I didn't pay bills. One from AEP and one from Xfinity. I paid both of those bills right from my phone last weekend, I swear I did. Didn't I, Josie?"

I do not hear any response in the background, but I'm not surprised. Jo is a fifteen-year-old who likely cut her teeth on a smartphone, so she's probably thinking what I am right now: *Phones can suck and they mess up. It's not paranormal.* Where is Sue going with this?

"I feel like there's a lot of weird stuff going on with my phone, like someone was messing with it. We've had trouble with the basement lights going on and off. Do you think they could be related? I mean, ghosts can make lights flicker; everybody knows that. Is it possible they could screw up my phone?"

Almost as if on cue, Sue's voice cuts again, same as before. It sounds electronic and alien, like when you get too far from your phone with your Bluetooth buds in your ear.

"Sue, are you there? Hello?"

There is a pause of about ten seconds as I am calling her name repeatedly. Finally, I hear her say in an exasperated tone, "Yeah, I'm right here!"

"Okay, that was weird," I say. "You cut out for a few seconds. I could hear some wonky sounds, but you weren't responding."

"I was right here; I heard you," she says, as if I'm the dumbest person on the planet.

I hear Sue exhale. She's smoking something. The question is… what? Or maybe I don't want to know.

"Well," I say. "To your earlier comments about the phone… sure, it's possible. Electrical and electromagnetic disturbances are often reported in suspected paranormal situations."

I deliberately use the qualifier "suspected" because we haven't come to any conclusions yet. Sue seems like the type of person who might latch onto that minor distinction. And my statement is absolutely true. While Sue's phone issues might be unrelated, it is also possible that paranormal energy *is* affecting her cell.

"But it's more likely that you have some problems with your phone, and we should rule that out first. Have you had any internet issues lately, or have you done an update recently? Or do you need an update? Sometimes those things can cause the type of glitches you're describing."

"I haven't had any problems with this phone, and I always keep it up to date. It's not that. I could understand if it were just one thing, but it's a bunch of things all around the phone. It's something else. Maybe them. I don't know…"

She trails off. I want to be sympathetic, but damn. It's a cell phone. My iPhone is almost brand spanking new, and it still acts up sometimes. That's what phones and apps do.

"I suppose it's possible," I say reluctantly. Walter, thankfully, is engaged in a game of fetch with Fenny out in the yard. He might have grabbed the phone out of my hand and hung up at that point.

"Did anything else happen?" I ask, not wanting to open that door but feeling like I must for the sake of getting all the details.

"Yes. My watch. My watch is missing, and I haven't been able to find it. I looked everywhere. I was wearing it when I picked Josie up from school, but now it's gone. It went missing when I was in the basement, after Josie let loose on the drums. She was already upstairs. I didn't even feel anything. I looked around, but I couldn't find it anywhere."

I hope Sue isn't making a correlation between her phone and the watch. She does not. At least, not out loud.

"Anyway, that was it," she says.

"Okay, thanks, Sue. If anything else happens, let us know— especially if you feel you are in immediate danger. Otherwise, we'll be out there around seven o'clock on Saturday. We'll get to the bottom of it."

Sue thanks me wearily, and we hang up just as Fenny comes bounding back onto the deck with a nasty old tennis ball in her mouth.

"Where'd you get that?" I cry in my high-pitched, dog-friendly voice. She responds by dropping the ball at my feet and backing down the stairs to wait for the next fetch. I happily comply. Walter and I need a break from all the paranormal talk. We've got a heavy couple of days coming up, so I'll take any relief I can get.

Excerpt 4 from the *RIP After Dark* Podcast
Episode 72: Case of the Demon Drums

*This podcast was broadcast one year after the actual investigation.
Client names and identifying details have been changed to maintain privacy.*

Libbi: *I must admit, it was creepy when the phone started warping like I was talking to an alien. Right as she was telling me she thought the demons had messed with her cell.*

Walter: *Correlation is not causation.*

Libbi: [sighs] *I didn't say it was. I just said it was creepy.*

Walter: *I think Nancy simply didn't know how to use her phone. It's like my grandma with her email machine. She couldn't manage the entire internet. It was too much for her. So, we got her something just for email. Even then...*

Libbi: *Well, in any case, we didn't dismiss it altogether because there are paranormal events that manifest as electrical issues.*

Walter: *Like EMF.*

Libbi: *Like EMF, which for those out there who don't know, stands for electromagnetic frequency. Lots of devices and machines—appliances, heaters, televisions, for example—can give off high EMF. High EMF levels have been linked to issues with the brain and nervous system—*

Walter: *Hallucinations.*

Libbi: *Right, exactly. And the belief is that when spirits manifest, or when there is paranormal energy present, EMF levels can rise temporarily.*

Walter: *Which is why one of the first things we do before we start an investigation is walk around the area and measure anything that is normally emitting EMF to rule it out... and also to note if anything has an abnormally high reading where it might cause problems for anyone exposed for long periods of time.*

Libbi: *We use several types of EMF detectors to measure levels. Digital and analog. We'll get readings from multiple devices to verify.*

Walter: *Paranormal investigation isn't all full-body apparitions and disembodied voices, folks. A lot of it involves collecting enormous amounts of data that need to be analyzed.*

Libbi: *It is a lot of work. Hey, a question for you, Walter. What EMF detector is your favorite?*

Walter: *That's easy! For me, it's the KII. I like the visual aspect of the lights.*

Libbi: *Yeah, I can see that. The KII is a digital EMF meter that doesn't give an exact EMF level. Instead, it lights up green, yellow, orange, or red depending on the intensity. I would call it a detector for kindergartners.*

Walter: *[dryly] Ha ha. Maybe that's what the K stands for.*

Libbi: *Ooh, good call! The Kindergartener II! Learn your ABCs at the same time as you detect a ghost.*

Walter: *It's not precise, but it's a good visual. And we always follow up the KII with a more specific reading on another unit.*

Libbi: *My favorite EMF detector is the analog Gauss Master; in case you were wondering.*

Walter: *Tried and true. I don't even think you can buy those anymore, except maybe on eBay.*

Libbi: *A true loss for the world. Okay, time to take a quick break! We'll be back with more RIP After Dark in just a minute.*

Libbi: *A true loss for the world. Okay, time to take a quick break! We'll be back with more RIP After Dark in just a minute.*

Setup Surprises

October 5, 7:00-9:00 pm
Equipment Setup, Baseline Checks, Investigation Prep
Mackenzie Residence, Starry Knob Lane, Roanoke, Virginia

Walter Bean

Libbi and I arrive at the Mackenzie's just before seven—a little early so we can talk briefly with Sue about the plan before the others get here. Our advanced arrival is strategic. We told the others to be here at seven-thirty. Maya will be on time or a little early; Dana will roll in just before eight; and Stan will show up in the next five minutes. I've lost count of the number of times we have pulled up to a location only to find that Stan is already there and planting his wild-ass ideas in the client's head. That's why we take some liberties with the times. It's a necessary evil.

I don't see the van that was in the driveway during the interview, and there is no garage attached to the duplex. I wonder if Sue's ex-husband reclaimed his ride, but I quickly decide I'm not going to ask. That is a door I do not want to open. Libbi grabs two black equipment cases from the back of the Santa Fe while I pull out the monitor, some cords, and a large fishing tackle box from the back seat. The tackle box makes the perfect organizer for smaller items like memory cards, batteries, matches, flashlights, and spare walkie-talkies. Sometimes a bottle of Tums and some No-Doz.

Sue comes to her door with Jo right behind her. They both give us a half-hearted wave of acknowledgement. The sun is almost set, just peaking over the Blue Ridge Mountains. Which is good. We'll have four strange cars parked on the street after everyone gets here. No sense in alerting the neighbors to the bizarre activities taking place at the Mackenzie house. The near darkness should camouflage most of our investigation.

Jo stays outside as we enter the duplex. Inside it smells like teen spirit—a mix of cigarettes, dope, onions, and lack of airflow. Now that I say it, it's more like mom spirit. Pepper doesn't seem to mind the thick air or the ruckus from us hauling in our equipment. He is sleeping soundly on the sofa. I wouldn't even have noticed him if it weren't for his snoring. Sounds like a mini wood chipper.

"I cleaned off the counter if you want to put your stuff there," says Sue. She appears surprisingly normal tonight. No red eyes, only slight shaking, and she's relatively calm. I wonder if she's laid off the drugs or maybe upgraded to better ones.

"Any new activity over the past couple of days?" asks Libbi. She opens the first black case and starts putting recorders, cameras, EMF detectors, and other equipment on the old laminate counter. I snatch the KII and place it in my pocket. The early bird gets the worm.

"Nothing major," says Sue. "Just lights flickering a bit but no drums, no bangs, no footsteps."

There is a large West Virginia mug filled with something the color of a grizzly bear on one end of the otherwise cleared counter. The mug looks like something you'd pick up at a rest area gift shop on the interstate. We aren't far from the WV border, so it's possible that's where she got it. The coffee (I assume that's what it is) looks old and potent, but it is steaming as Sue grabs the handle and takes a sip. I remind myself to bring in our bag of snacks from the Santa Fe, which includes a Monster drink for myself. It's going to be a late night; caffeine will be on everyone's menu.

As Libbi and I pull out more devices, we go over the plan with our client.

"Sue, you're planning on heading out until after midnight," I say, more directing than asking. "And you're taking your dog too?"

Sue nods. "Yep. My friend Gina is going to stop by in a bit and pick us up. We'll drop Josie off at a… a friend's house… and then I'll hang out at Gina's until you're ready for us."

When Sue says, "a friend's house," she pauses and chokes out the words. Jo's boyfriend? Doubtful. I would bet my paycheck that the daughter is not into dudes that way. Or maybe the friend is one of the borderline criminals Sue thinks are turning Jo into a teenage outlaw. Unknown, but her distaste is apparent.

"And Josie? Is she going to be coming back with you afterward?" Libbi asks. My wife calls her Josie around Sue but Jo when we talk about the case. I suspect it's intentional.

"Yep, we'll pick her up on the way back."

The plan is solid, and Sue seems to understand. Sue and Jo will go to Sue's best friend Gina's house, which is just on the other side of town. Pepper will go with them, and they will stay away from the duplex until after midnight. We have invited them to come back then, to do some EVP sessions with questions we provide. EVP stands for *Electronic Voice Phenomenon,* and the sessions are when the investigation team asks questions of the so-called spirits. EVP is any captured sound or voice that might be interpreted as paranormal. We have a rigid process around these sessions for good reason: We don't like letting the rookies have free rein with the spirits. Some people—clients, guest investigators, and, well, our own "favorite" team member, Stan—like to provoke spirits by getting angry and yelling at them. The jury is still out for me on whether the harsh tone actually hurts an investigation and makes the ghosts mad. But it doesn't reflect well on us as a team, so we choose to err on the side of caution. Libbi came up with a list of neutral questions, which helps us (or more accurately, her) keep control of the process.

I hear a knock on the door. It's Stan. So much for having some time before the rest of the team shows up. I take a deep breath and wonder which of his personalities we'll have to deal with tonight.

Stan Katagucci

Walter's SUV is parked in front of the third house down from the entrance to the subdivision, so I pull up behind it. I can't wait to tell them my idea. I was so excited about it that I forgot to pack my Ovilus and Frank's box receiver. Unfortunately, by the time I remembered, I was too far down the road to go back and get them. I left home early hoping I could get here before the Beans did so I could talk to the client. I wanted to get her support before everyone else got here, but I guess Walter and Libbi are looking to get a head start. No matter. A good idea sells itself.

I grab three rolls of cable and my equipment case from the back of my pickup truck and head up the driveway. There is a boy sitting on the front steps scrolling on a cell phone. Doom scrolling is what I think they call it. I'm not into the TikToks or Facebooks, but I do get lost in paranormal chat rooms and websites regularly. The boy looks up from his device. I would wave if I had an arm to spare, so I just say hello and ask if this is the Mackenzie residence.

The boy says, "Yes, it is. I'm Jo Mackenzie."

Okay then. Slight mental flux. This is the daughter. Didn't get that one right, but good to know. Libbi mentioned that Jo is quite the tomboy, but I guess I expected pigtails and overalls. That was a tomboy back in the day. But hey, to each their own. Makes no difference to me.

Jo gets up and opens the door for me, no doubt sensing my disadvantage lugging all this equipment. Libbi and Walter are inside talking to a woman wearing a dark blue hoodie and smoking a cigarette. I take a breath as I step in. I don't care for cigarette smoke, especially inside. I enjoy a campfire or pile of burning leaves; cigars and pipes are tolerable because people smoke them outside. But cigarettes gross me out. And indoors? Who does that anymore? Sue Mackenzie, I guess that's who.

Walter motions for me to drop the cables and equipment case near the counter, where we will set up the monitoring station. I read the entire setup form several times (and fed back my thoughts to Libbi), so I'm comfortable with the arrangements. Walter goes back to talking with Sue about whatever they were talking about when I walked in. I hate to interrupt, but I might not have a better opportunity to reveal my idea.

"Hey guys, I got something I want to run by you," I say while Walter is in mid-sentence. He stops and gives me the look. *The Walter look.* Like a frustrated parent trying not to lose their temper. The look that wants me to go away. At least, I think that's what it means. I'm not the best at recognizing facial expressions unless they come with words to back them up. I should have waited until he was done.

"I'm Stan, by the way." I hold out my hand. "Stan Katagucci, I'm the technical guy. You must be Sue."

"Nice to meet you," she says through the cigarette she has transferred from her right hand to a holding spot between her lips. She briefly takes my hand, then fills it again with her cancer stick.

"Sorry," Walter says to Sue. "Stan, why don't you start the bedroom setup with cameras and mic? We'll be with you in a minute."

He gestures toward the doorway behind me, where the daughter-boy is now standing. I ponder his request for a millisecond but then decide I need to get this on the table sooner rather than later.

"Okay but let me just tell you. I was thinking maybe we should do a seance after the Mackenzies return tonight. I think the spirits are attached to someone in this house, and—"

Walter grabs my arm and leads me away from the counter toward the bedroom. He is being a little aggressive about it, if I am being honest. Libbi is trying not to cringe; she knows her husband is about to give me a lecture. I've been in this position enough times to recognize *her* facial expression.

"Sorry, Walter," I say. Then I call back toward Libbi and Sue. "But this is a great idea! We could do it right here in the living room. We could make a connection like we did at the Churchville house last year."

One of our recent cases was at a restaurant set up in a 1920s building just outside of Staunton, Virginia. The place was empty when we investigated, and we weren't getting much on recorders or cameras, so Libbi and Walter agreed to try a seance. I believe I have some psychic abilities. Sometimes I feel things—maybe not as much as Dana does, but *something*. I thought I could channel whatever (or whoever) was in the restaurant. We didn't end up catching much on the equipment, but I felt a presence that night.

And this place? Holy hell! The Mackenzies have experienced many consistent events. As I walk around the house, it feels dark. Not dark as in without light (although it isn't the brightest living room ever). But dark feelings, like there's a thickness in the air. There is something present in this house, and a seance might help us identify who or what it is.

Walter isn't happy. I don't think he cares to hold a seance. Aside from his not believing in them, it's because the idea comes from me that he doesn't like. He puts up with me on account of Libbi, but we wouldn't be friends if we didn't both have a connection with her.

"Stan, let's get a level-set here, okay?"

We are in what I think is the daughter's bedroom now. Walter's voice is low and calm. He doesn't want Sue to hear. I must be messing up big time.

"We have a plan already, and that plan does not include your black-magic necromancy crap. Okay? We're going to stick to the plan."

Plans are necessary. But sometimes they are an impediment to progress.

"Walter, I understand, but can we talk about this? There is so much going on, and it sounds like the spirit is attached to one of them. If we could communicate, we could learn something about whatever 'this' is!"

Walter takes a breath. "Stanley, we don't even know if there is a 'this' yet. And I want to remind you that one of these people who might have an 'attachment' to any alleged 'spirits' is a fifteen-year-old child."

He uses air quotes to mansplain this to me. I have already considered this.

"A *child*," Walter repeats, with emphasis. "We are not pulling a legal minor into any voodoo Ouija board shenanigans, not without a well-thought-out plan. And we don't have time for that. Here we are; look about you."

"If you would just listen for a second—"

"No. The answer is no."

I sigh, defeated. "Fine, I'll just go and set—"

Sue interrupts from the counter. "I like the idea of doing a seance," she says.

Walter rolls his eyes and sighs in a huff. He doesn't even try to hide it from me. He is defeated, and he knows it.

"My friend Gina is going to be with us, and she's got a little experience with seances. I'm all in."

"Are we having a seance?" says Maya, who has just arrived and is walking through the door Jo is holding open. She has her tiny Maya-sized equipment bag in tow.

"Apparently, against better judgment and the actual plan, we are now exploring the idea," says Walter as he turns back to the kitchen counter. "I'll let you all figure it out."

Walter is annoyed, and I hope our clients don't pick up on it. It's poor customer service. But I don't care. I will take his defeat in exchange for my victory. I say hello to Maya and head back out to my truck to get the rest of my gear: tripods, more cable, and a spare monitor in case Libbi's craps out like it did on our last case. I told her to get a new one, but she said it has been working fine. Some days it's like a major movie production putting all the equipment up. I like this part of the job; it's where I feel most respected. I know how to connect all the cables, and I can troubleshoot and fix most of our problems. When a camera won't focus or the microphone sound is wonky, I'm the guy they call. When I want to pursue something different or innovative outside of tech, I usually get the eye rolls, especially from Walter. It's all bogus to him.

But you know what? I don't care. I am going to get my seance!

Maya Hill-Goldberg

I pull up to the Mackenzie house at a quarter past seven and park my Nissan Sentra (aka The Japanese Bitch) in front of Libbi and Walter's SUV. I am grateful for plenty of curb before the next-door neighbor's property begins. I always feel like I'm encroaching on someone's personal space when I park in front of their house if I'm not actually visiting them. Streets are public, but it still feels funny. I take a moment to look around from inside the car. I'm seeing lots of small, ranch-style homes and a few duplexes (I presume, based on the double front doors), each sitting on about a half-acre (which is my estimate based on ten seconds at dusk with an admitted lack of spatial context).

Before I head in, I finish a snack pack of peanut butter sandwich crackers that I started when I left my apartment. I live in Bedford, which is roughly halfway between Roanoke (where I go to school at Hollins University) and Lynchburg, where my boyfriend Dimitri works as a middle-school teacher. I wipe some crumbs from my jeans and swallow the last of my crackers, quenching the dryness with a sip of bottled water. Someone usually brings food for later, but I had some pangs. Plus, it's hit or miss on whether I can (or will) eat the team offerings. Stan sometimes brings venison sausage or meatballs. No thanks. I'm okay with some fake cheese squirts and over-preserved snack pastries, but I draw the line at deer meat.

I reach into my back seat and push aside a plastic bin with blue and yellow tulle spilling over the top. I support my college and life finances partly with student loans and a small scholarship, and partly by dressing up as famous cartoon princesses and hosting parties for children. It doesn't put me on the Forbes list or anything, but it pays my rent and essentials with a little left over for fun. Still, I'm not as well off as the others on the RIP team, so I don't own a lot of equipment. I have one handheld digital recorder already in my jeans pocket, and my iPhone. I rarely use my cell for investigations, but it's good to have a backup, and these days the phone cameras are as good as or better than some digital cameras (and a lot more portable).

From behind the princess bin, I pull out a green hoodie with HOLLINS UNIVERSITY written in gold on the front. It's already cooler than I expected, so I slip it over my head before I step out of the car and head up the sloped driveway. The only movement is from a large beagle lying in a mulch bed dead center between the two duplex doors. It is frantically licking its crotch. Must be the neighbor's dog. I recall from the interview notes that the client's dog is a Yorkie mix; this is not a Yorkie anything. Once I reach the house, I get a second perspective on the neighborhood from my elevated position. It looks like a typical older subdivision. The cars on the street and in driveways are all the standard variations of pickup trucks, mid-sized SUVs, and compact sedans. Someone is running a saw or maybe a leaf blower on a connecting street, and I'm picking up a little traffic noise from Rte. 220, the main road off the subdivision just about a quarter mile away.

The door on the right half of the duplex is ajar, and I when I get to the front stoop, I can see Libbi and a woman I presume is the client, Sue Mackenzie, standing next to a counter at the back of the house. I knock, and Sue motions for me to come in. The first thing that strikes me is the decor. As Libbi had mentioned, the walls are covered with Christian paintings, posters, and prints, and none of them are high quality. This is the kind of cheap art one finds in tourist shops or at church sales. At best, maybe one or two came from a mediocre art show. The living room is dark even though several recessed ceiling lights are on and it is barely past sundown. I would bet it's always dark, even when the curtains are open. It feels... *dirty*. Not visually dirty, at least not on the surface. In fact, it is visually neat as a pin. If I had seen a photo version of the Mackenzie living room, I would describe it as a clean house (albeit outdated). But it smells and feels stale.

Stan and Walter are just inside a doorway to my right. I overhear some of the conversation as I walk in.

"Are we having a seance?" I ask. I'm game. It doesn't exactly fall into my skeptic mentality, but seances can be fun. When I was a kid, I had a babysitter who fancied herself a psychic. She gave us Tarot readings and sometimes did little mini seances. My older sister and I never told our parents. They would have flipped out. My dad was very anti-occult and wouldn't even let us have a Ouija board in the house. He would have fired the babysitter on the spot had he known she was bringing the Death card into his family domain.

Walter mumbles something about the plan, and I gather this new activity is not something he agrees with. Not that Walter agrees with (or is enthusiastic about) much.

"Well, anyway, hello," I say. I am mouth-breathing. Eventually, I'll get used to the rank undertones in this house. If I were a spirit, I wouldn't want to live here.

"Hi Maya," calls Stan.

"How's it going?" I ask.

"Great! Couldn't be better!"

He is beaming with enthusiasm, and I wonder what has got his dopamine all fired up. But I don't wonder enough to ask. Once you have Stan's attention, you are in for the long haul. He walks past me and heads out the front door as Libbi gives me a cursory half-hug greeting. She's a hugger; I'm not. We compromise.

"Sue, this is Maya Hill-Goldberg. She is one of our RIP team members helping us out tonight."

Sue gives me half a wave and almost smiles (but not quite). I'm grateful that she appears to share my general aversion to bodily contact with strangers. Libbi resumes her discussion with the client while I put my purse on top of one of the bar stools. It sounds like they are finalizing the plan, which I am already familiar with. Walter looks down at the notes Libbi has put on the table.

"Stan is going to set up the cameras," he says, gesturing toward the daughter's bedroom behind me. "Starting in Josie's room. Then he'll do the living room with just the camcorder. Then the basement. Three cameras down there."

Perfectly timed, Stan comes through the front door with more cable and veers right into the second bedroom. He appears downright giddy.

Walter continues, "Maya, if you wouldn't mind taking initial readings in the bedroom and out here, that would be great. I'm going to cover the basement. Dana should be here by then."

"Yep, I can do that."

"Very good, thank you."

I grab a digital thermometer and analog EMF detector from the counter and shove them into my hoodie pocket. As I walk toward the bedroom, I pull out my recorder and open a folder I created yesterday labeled with the case ID: *0076-RIP-MACKENZIE*. I start my baseline by doing a general eye sweep of the room from just inside the doorway, to get the lay of the land (more or less). Also to let Stan finish his camera setup. Once he's done, it will be like a professional did it, but right now loops of black cable are spread out like waves over the evergreen carpet. The bedroom is rather small, and unlike the living area, the daughter's domain is cluttered and disorganized (although I'm guessing it smells better; not sure on that yet, as I haven't opened my nostrils). There are clothes strewn on a small desk, and the bed has not been made. A stray shoe is sticking out of the half-open closet, and it looks like it fell from a gigantic pile of dirty clothes. Someone needs a laundry basket (or two). From my vantage point, it looks like maybe Jo made a half-assed attempt to declutter, but being neat as a pin is obviously not her priority. I don't blame her. I was a slob at fifteen too.

The initial readings we take are temperature, EMF, any visuals to note, safety concerns, and anything that might cause a reported event. For example, do the windows have cracks? Is there an old heater on the other side of the wall that knocks when it turns on? Is there evidence of mold? When I started investigating, it surprised me how often we'd hear reports of things like cold spots, only to find hundred-year-old broken windows covered in plastic in the dead of winter. And the clients don't make the connection. Fear is more powerful than reality. Someone wakes up in the middle of the night and thinks they see a dark figure in their room (or hears drums). Fear kicks in, and suddenly they forget that the basement lights have never worked right, and the radio that keeps turning off by itself is fifty years old with a shredded cord.

While I am waiting for Stan, I have a moment to listen to Sue talking to the Beans. She has had a cigarette in her hand since I got here. Other than the nicotine addiction, she seems otherwise normal. A little nervous as she speaks, but who wouldn't be if they believed demons were possessing their house and possibly their child (and dog, apparently)? And she's about to hand the keys to the castle over to a group of strangers. That never ceases to amaze me. People will just vacate their homes and let someone they literally just met stay inside—unsupervised—for hours at a time. While many people nowadays have security systems, I would bet that the only cameras these walls have seen are the ones Stan is setting up now.

A short while later, Stan completes the camera setup and heads out into the living room. I step inside Jo's bedroom, placing my thermometer and EMF detector on top of a small lavender dresser on the wall opposite the door. The bureau might have been pretty at one time, but now just looks tired. It's not shabby chic; it's just shabby. I look around. As predicted, it smells a little better in here than in the main living area, although not exactly clean. Jo's room is a typical teenage girl's sanctuary, except that there are basketball posters and reproductions of rock album covers on the wall instead of teen heartthrobs. My childhood room was (okay, still is, even though I've pleaded with my parents to turn it into a craft room or man cave) plastered with Harry Styles, Zac Efron, and posters from the TV show *Supernatural.* Jo has Isiah Thomas, Rip Hamilton, and a vintage poster of someone named George Yardley, who looks like Nosferatu the vampire. I do not know who any of these people are other than they are basketball players judging from the uniforms. I don't care for sports; I don't follow sports. Even my boyfriend (who loves sports) doesn't care for basketball. But I give props to Jo for being herself. She may not be into pink party tulle, but at least she's authentic about who she is.

Looking around the room, I don't see any obvious red flags or safety issues. Stan has his cables secured to the carpet with yellow duct tape; the rest of the floor is clear of obstacles. There are two windows on adjacent walls, as this is a corner bedroom. The window facing the side of the house has a small air conditioner in it. It is too cool out to be using it now, methinks, but some people just leave their units sitting in the window all winter long.

"Initial readings, October 5, 7:28 pm," I say into the recorder. *"Front bedroom, normally occupied by the client's fifteen-year-old daughter. The Blu-Lu2 camera is set up just inside the doorway facing into the room."*

The room is small enough for the Blu-Lu2 to capture most of it, so no other camera is hooked up. We'll rely on our phone cameras if we need backup.

"Cables are secure, no obstructions on the floor. The AC unit in the side window has gaps where normally there would—should—be insulation. Noted, as this could account for temperature fluctuations."

I walk the perimeter several times to make sure I capture anything that could interfere with our investigation. I look up, down, contemplate looking deeper into the closet but decide not to. That feels like snooping. Nothing else is noteworthy from a visual perspective. I pause for a moment to listen. Nothing on the audio front. I pick up the thermometer and start taking readings randomly around the room.

"Wall temperatures are between 66 and 68 degrees, pretty consistent. The outside temperature is—" I lift my sleeve and check my smartwatch. *"—around 64°F and dropping. No significant fluctuations high or low anywhere."*

I circle once more just to be sure, touching the laser beam to the bed, windows, AC unit, closet door, dresser, chair, and random spots near the floor. Nothing concerning, all noted on the recorder. Now it's time to switch to the EMF detector. I have the Gauss Master, which is analog. I can get an approximate reading based on the meter guide on the front of the device. Someone will come around after me with a more precise digital meter (likely Stan, when he's done with the cameras). Still holding the recorder in one hand, I move the EMF meter around the room looking for anything concerningly high. A high reading doesn't necessarily mean there is a ghost nearby. In fact, probably not. But high EMF *can* cause physical reactions that might play into one's perception of events.

I notice no spikes in the electromagnetic field other than from the AC unit. It's not concerningly high, just something to capture, which I do on the recorded file. As I walk around for the umpteenth time, I notice a small sketchbook on the small desk that sits against the inside wall near the door. Closet snooping is a no, but a teenager's artwork? That's too juicy to take the high road. Plus, how private can it be? It's right here out in the open (albeit half-buried under a dirty T-shirt). I glance out into the living room before opening the book. Jo is outside; I can hear her bouncing her basketball on the driveway. Everyone else is engaged in prep activities. I quietly lift the cover. The sketchbook has a lot of random drawings, most of them of basketball players and buildings. I flip casually through the pages while shielding my thievery with my body so anyone looking through the doorway might just think I was taking notes. There are a few drawings in the book that might disturb me if I didn't know the context. Demons or gargoyles with blood dripping from fangs and long horns on their heads. Yikes! The detail is astounding. I spend a full minute lurking (and being borderline horrified) before I close the sketchbook for good. I make two observations. One, Jo has mad drawing skills. I can barely sketch a smiley face. Second, these beast figures are likely representations of her dreams. I am not a believer in prophetic dreams, but from a psychological perspective, I feel bad for the kid. I try to put the images out of my mind as I complete my rounds.

It takes about fifteen minutes to finish the initial review in the bedroom. I go back out to the living room to repeat the process. Stan is still setting up in there, but I decide to work around him as there is a bit more breathing room in this space. It's a little cooler in here, just a couple of degrees, and not surprising given the openness of the room and frequency of the front door being opened. The only EMF spike is from the large flatscreen television partially blocking the front picture window. A little high, but again, not unexpected. Not likely something to worry about given the distance from the seating area. Sue is the only other person in the room now, still standing by the kitchen island and still—unbelievably—smoking like a chimney. She's blowing her clouds in the general direction of the RIP monitor, which is only about two feet away from her. It's kind of cringe, but I say nothing. That's for Libbi and Walter to address; it's their equipment.

"Everybody just disappeared!" I say partly to Stan and partly to Sue, trying to break the awful silence. I place my thermometer and EMF meter on the counter among the other mobile equipment so they can soak in the smoke. Stan tells me that Libbi went outside to take some readings, and Walter went downstairs for the initial scan of the basement. I take that as my cue to go help Ms. Bean outside so I can help complete our prep and get some fresh air at the same time.

Dana Tennant

I pull into the Mackenzie residence just before eight o'clock. I'm late but not bothered by it. Other than work, I've never been a punctual person, and the highway is a bitch. I am last to arrive (shocking) as I see the others' cars along the street. Guess I can't blame anyone but myself for another crappy parking spot. I pull past the house and do a turnaround in the neighbor's driveway so I can face the subdivision exit. You never know when you might need to make a quick getaway. I pull my pickup truck nose-to-nose with Maya's Nissan and turn off the engine. Before I exit onto the curb, I take a deep breath and center myself. This is the first time I've been here, and I know nothing about the case. I want my mind and body to be relaxed and clear before I take a look-see. Pretty soon the action will start, so this is my best opportunity to pull all my senses together to get the lay of the land.

From my truck, the area appears to be a typical suburban neighborhood. Older, with lots of mature trees. The Mackenzie home has an enormous oak tree on the hill in the front. Just looking at it gives me a warm feeling. This girl has been around for many decades and hopefully will be for many more. I wonder what she's seen, but unfortunately my abilities don't seem to include channeling plants—just the spiritual energy of people, living or dead. Yet somehow, I know the tree is a "her." Weird.

After a few deep breaths, I say a quick meditation prayer, open the driver's side door, and step onto a thin layer of leaves lining the edge of the street. My truck is massive, but I don't use the running board step attached to the bottom of the frame. Those are for short people; I'm pushing six feet tall on a good day. My husband, Sawyer, hates driving my truck because he always needs to shift the seat forward a notch or two. He's a big boy, but his legs are like little tree stumps. Mine are like telephone poles. Sawyer is my number one heart and soul, followed by our boy Ralph (rhymes with chafe, which is what he does to my nerves sometimes). Otherwise known as Junior, even though he's not an actual junior. I would love to have the company of both my fellas for this case, but Junior is still in the paranormal investigation intern stage, and Sawyer wouldn't be caught dead on a ghost hunt. Sissy.

I see Libbi and Walter at the top of the driveway, so I wave. Good people, those two. Libbi is always on top of the planning—which, as a registered nurse in a busy hospital, I can appreciate. Walter is a hoot and very much aligned with my own snarky personality. Libbi too, but where Lib keeps it professional, Walter holds back nada. When he recognizes a situation is for shit, he will tell you. I guess that's why Libbi is the frontman. She knows how to temper her feelings in front of the client. Me and Walter? We can't hold back sometimes and that gets us into trouble.

Since it's just around eight o'clock on a Saturday and it hasn't turned ridiculously cold yet, I expect a certain amount of weekend activity in this type of neighborhood. Sure enough, somewhere in the distance I can hear kids playing, a leaf blower, and a basketball bouncing on the hard pavement. Hopefully, things will quiet down later tonight. It's hard to get clean recordings with a lot of uncontrolled noise, and I doubt the Mackenzie's stick-built duplex has super-thick, soundproof walls. For now, the buzz of the neighborhood doesn't interfere with my pre-investigation grounding. I pull a cigarette from the purse slung over my shoulder and light up. I won't smoke up near the house unless invited, but down here by the road it's harmless and helps me relax. I know. I'm a poor example of a nurse. But I probably wouldn't be a nurse if I couldn't smoke away the stress now and then.

I close my eyes and exhale the essence of Virginia Slims, counting backwards from ten and imagining myself walking down a flight of stairs toward a door at the end of the steps. When I arrive, I turn the handle slowly—focusing on my breath—and wait to see what comes to me. The visions I get might be spiritual, or they might be energy from living individuals. Sometimes it's obvious which one it is—like if I see a woman wearing a *Little House on the Prairie* bonnet. Sometimes it's a little more ambiguous. But I always figure it out in the end.

What I initially get from the Mackenzie house is a vague remnant of something old and dark and not of this world—and a strong, newer energy that is full of tension and conflict. The otherworldly shadow is faint, like a bat flying around a little too close on a summer evening. It's not inherently dangerous, but not something I want touching me either. The new, younger energy is like being hit in the head with a rock and buried alive at the same time. It feels a little like my head is inside a giant bass drum and someone is pounding on the outside. I don't know what this new thing is; I'm away from the house, and it's too early to tell. What I *do* know is that it isn't in control of itself and it senses me lurking. I take a drag from my Slim and relax my shoulders so that this energy perceives only curiosity.

After a few moments, I open my eyes. The sky is still clear, but it's almost full nighttime. Libbi and Walter are no longer in front of the house. No doubt they are wrapping up the equipment setup and working through the baselines. I stub out my cigarette on the asphalt with my waffle stompers and open the driver's side door to dispose of my bad habit in a half-filled can of Coke and ash.

Let's get this thing rolling.

Walter Bean

Stan is setting up the basement cameras, Maya is in the living room doing her walkthrough, and Pepper is asleep on the couch, so I take a quick inventory of the mobile equipment we have set up on the counter while Libbi and Sue talk. The kitchen island is huge; we've got nearly six feet of bare laminate to hold our crap. The duplex is relatively small—I'd guess a thousand square feet for this half, not including the basement. More like an apartment. Twenty years of watching HGTV with my wife has made me somewhat of an expert. Other than the open concept, it reminds me of my late grandmother's house. Smells like it too, under the cigarette smoke and not-so-faint memory of pot. I wonder if I could get a contact high just from smelling the furniture. It makes me giggle inside, imagining myself walking over to that old recliner and burying my nose in the cushion to get a deep sniff. Not something I care to test outside of my thoughts. The kitchen sink is against the back wall under a window that looks out onto a moderately-sized backyard. Parallel to the sink and cabinets near the center of the main living area is the counter, which I gather is where Sue and Jo eat, judging from the dishes and papers that were there when we did the interview last weekend.

I grab a couple of flashlights from the row of UV, IR, and LED units on the counter. Each one serves a purpose. The LED ones are for normal use. Infrared (or IR) we use when we are in full-on investigation mode, to allow us to see enough to avoid obstacles, but also prevent interference with the video cameras. There's nothing more frustrating than reviewing a night vision video and having someone flash their blinding hundred-watt LED bulb directly into the lens. The UV (ultraviolet) flashlight will come in handy in revealing any urine spots, especially in this case where urine smells have been reported. There are three Olympus digital recorders on the counter, but I leave them intact. My personal recorder and EMF meter are on my tool belt already. Yes, I wear a tool belt. Sometimes we have five, six, even seven pieces of equipment on hand. Some people use pockets or a bag. I use a tool belt. It holds my equipment like a champ, leaving me hands-free and ultra-masculine.

Stan emerges from the basement carrying spare cable. That's my cue to go down.

"I'm going to go do the basement walkthrough," I say to Lib with a nod to Sue.

I grab a digital thermometer and walkie-talkie, then head downstairs for my sweep. When we have a larger team working—especially if we have guest investigators, which we often do—we keep a check-out sheet for equipment. With just the core team, we're on the honor system.

Almost immediately, I find a big nail sticking out of one of the basement steps as I head down to the basement.

"Watch out for the nail!" calls Sue from above, almost as if on cue.

"Got it, thank you!" I holler back. Then I mumble to myself, "You could fillet a fish on that thing!"

I am kidding and don't think anyone heard, but thirty seconds later Sue flies down the wooden steps with a hammer and pounds the shit out of that little spear.

"All righty!" I say, walking away from the awkwardness of her sudden fury and into the musty cellar. "Crisis averted."

"Shoulda done that a long time ago," she says, out of breath. "As many times as I've darn near lost a toe."

She gives the nail one last bang with the hammer just to make sure it's flush with the wood and returns up the stairs with a grunt, shutting the door behind her. I continue into the basement with my recorder started. It's easier to capture conditions on audio and transfer them into the investigation log later.

"Walter Bean, basement walkthrough, October 5, 7:57 pm. The basement has a musty smell right off the stairs. Moderate urine odor—not unbearable, but something has peed down here in the past, and recently if I were to guess. It feels damp down here. There is a slight hum from the water heater, but otherwise it is quiet except for some creaking from above as people walk around. I can also hear voices, although I can't make out what they are saying. Sounds like Sue and Libbi."

I glance around and take in the greater room, which is lit by six or seven bare bulbs in the ceiling. Heading to the right off the stairs is a section they call the lounge area, although that is a stretch. There is an old couch perched perpendicular to the exterior wall, and I wouldn't sit on it with my good jeans. Or any jeans, unless there was a thick blanket between my ass and those disgusting cushions. A small table is at one end near the wall. If I were to guess, I'd say it was on trend in 1971—octagonal with a leather (I think) top that is badly peeling. The outline of an area rug is defining the space, but I can't verify if it's an actual rug because it is beyond filthy. The couch faces inward (toward the neighbor's side of the duplex), and in front of it to one side (closest to the stairs) is a pile of metal that I assume was the old drum set. I'm almost impressed with the number Jo did on those instruments.

Nothing is playable; it's all bent or broken brass, crushed wood, and mangled plastic. Someone took the time to put all the pieces in a pile, but they must have been scattered around the room right after the deed was done. I can almost taste the violence.

All three cameras—the full-spectrum, camcorder, and our Blu-Lu1 night vision unit—are set up at various angles pointing into the teen-cave. The full-spectrum camera is at the side of the stairwell, directed toward the back of the house; The Blu-lu1 is between the two stairwells pointed diagonally toward the couch and drum heap; and the camcorder is against the back wall pointed inward catching the lounge area and the stairs. Stan knows his angles. Although most of our cameras have built-in microphones, we will rely on our handheld digital mics for most of the audio. They record with higher quality and can be pointed in any direction.

As I continue my scan, I catch the faint but unmistakable scent of a plug-in air freshener wafting underneath (or maybe on top of) the faded piss smell. Folly, I think to myself. Much as I love my Glade PlugIns, it is a fact that they won't get rid of strong pet odors. This one must be on its last drop. Normally, those things are cloying. I log into my microphone to capture my finding in case anyone smells something during the investigation.

"In the lounge area of the basement near the couch and drum set, there is a slight floral smell, like Febreze mixed with turpentine."

I look around to see if there is indeed a plug-in air freshener nearby. There are a couple of outlets on the half-finished walls around the stairwell but no source for the odor. No matter. I am familiar. When Libbi and I were house shopping a few years ago, a lot of sellers used the same scent to mask their nasty cat piss. It got to where we would walk into a home, catch a whiff of the plug-in, and turn right back around. Nope.

I point the end of the EMF meter at the outlets on the stairwell and call out the readings.

"Outlets under the stairs, clockwise starting with the one behind the freezer. Green, green, yellow, green."

For now, I'm just looking for red flags. The yellow reading is the plug behind the freezer, not surprising. Getting an EMF outside of green on electrical equipment is to be expected. What I am looking for are readings that are in the orange or red (10+mG) or readings that have no obvious source.

I circle back around the lounge area, walking behind the couch counterclockwise toward the outside wall. When I get to the masonry of the foundation, the EMF meter spikes to orange. I raise the unit as high as I can and then bring it near the floor. Consistent orange spike. I'm about two feet from the outer back wall, and there is nothing electrical within six feet of me. No ceiling light, no lamp, not even a plug.

"The back wall in the lounge area—behind the couch near the basement window—is spiking orange. No apparent source of the EMF, it's just concrete and couch. It is consistent, so it could be something outside like a buried electrical line."

I complete my perimeter of the lounge area, passing around the other side of the rug, in front of the cameras, and past the heap of drum parts. The drum pile causes a brief blip—touching yellow but quickly going back down to green. I log it into my recorder and move on. I walk the circumference of the basement, covering both sides of the duplex and keeping the outer walls on my right. That's how I do it in video games too. If I keep the wall or border to my right, I rarely get lost. The rest of the back wall is EMF-clear, and there is nothing of note other than about twenty neatly stacked plastic bins and boxes, some of which appear to be filled with clothing.

I make my way to the other side of the house, where I am now directly underneath where Sue's neighbor Alice lives. No EMF spikes on the outlets. I pull out my digital thermometer so I can get readings in parallel and won't have to come back over again. I would hate to be lurking around Alice's dark stairwell and have her come down at that moment to do some laundry. It's in the low sixties Fahrenheit on this side of the building, completely normal and expected for a basement given the outside temperature.

I continue my path, observing a pile of toys and shoes behind Alice's stairs. I assume these belong to Alice's grandson. One pair of white(ish) women's canvas sneakers sits neatly to the side of the steps, with the distinct mark of a bicycle tire over the tip of each shoe. Did the kid run over his grandma's feet? Was he trying, or was it an accident? The alleged smoking gun (a Schwinn, by the looks of it) is leaning against the other side of Alice's stairwell. It is orange with a banana seat and looks like something you'd pick up at a garage sale today or at Sears & Roebuck in 1987. No hand brakes, just the old-fashioned kind where you backpedal to stop the wheels. Classic. Alice's grandson is lucky to have such a treasure; they don't make them like this anymore. I made much mischief with a similar bike back in the day.

Beyond the pile of misfit toys and hand-stamped shoes is the front wall. The community washer and dryer are side-by-side about dead center between the two side walls, and they look brand new. I find it ironic that the entirety of Sue's upstairs (the part I've seen) is dingy, worn out, and badly in need of an update (not to mention the borderline condemned lounge area down here), yet here in this dingy basement is a state-of-the-art front-loading Electrolux washer and matching dryer. High-end, if I were to guess, although I am hardly the expert. It looks fancy. Lots of buttons, and it shines even in the dull light.

To the left of the washer and dryer is a single sump pump; next to that, a utility sink with a slow drip. I try to tighten both the hot and cold handles, but someone has incorrectly installed the faucet so that the end of the handle hits the sink neck before it fully shuts off. It isn't enough of a drip to break the bank on the water bill, but I'll bet the sump pump goes off more than normal. I take out the pen and pad from my rear pocket and write *Have someone flush the toilet while we record in the basement near the sump pump.*

Before proceeding, I take readings of all the equipment.

"I am at the front wall near the washer and dryer in the basement. Temperature on the floor is 60°F; the wall is 62°F; ceiling is 63°. EMF is slightly into yellow both on the dryer plug and water heater on Sue's side of the house. All other EMF readings in this area are green."

Heading back to Sue's side of the duplex behind her stairwell, I realize how clean and organized Alice's side is in comparison. There is a lot of junk behind Sue's stairs—old lamps, tons of cobwebbed boxes, stacks of books that I wouldn't touch without hand sanitizer, and two oversized club chairs that should have been put out to pasture long ago. The obstacle course of worthless shit continues around and under the stairs. I'm relieved to discover no EMF or temperature anomalies, but I will need to warn the team to watch their step, especially when we turn out the lights. I note this all on the recorder with a caution in my notebook for quick reference.

Back around to the lounge area, I do a few more temperature and EMF readings but find little. I lean against the freezer by the stairs and look around. This is a typical unfinished basement—musty, dusty, probably full of mouse droppings, and not a place where I would care to have my man cave. But at least (so far) nothing has made me jump.

"HEY, WALTER!"

I stand corrected and nearly shit my pants when Dana calls out from the steps. It wouldn't be the first time I've nearly been frightened into a shart on an investigation, thank you very much.

"Sorry to interrupt. I'm just going to walk around and take some readings if you don't mind the help."

Dana, though she is our resident sensitive, is also a kick-ass investigator. She'll do her woo-woo, touchy-feely stuff but still pay close attention to all the things an excellent investigator should. Right now, it's not about a conclusion; it's about gathering data. Whether it's a dead person talking to her or a cold reading on her thermometer, she gets it all.

"Sounds good."

I continue my readings as we chit-chat. I'm careful to keep the conversation appropriate for all audiences. I've slipped a time or two in the past and made some comments about Stan that got caught on the camera audio (I called him The Exorcism Emperor and joked about his plaid shirts, if memory serves). It's nothing I haven't said to his face, but I sound like a colossal dick when I hear it back on a recording.

Dana starts on the other side of the basement. After a few minutes, we pass and overlap paths. Getting more than one set of base readings is always a good idea.

"How's Junior doing these days?" I ask.

"Oh, you know. He's a teenager now, and he's got a mouth on him for sure."

"Gee, wonder where he got that from."

"Ha ha. I'll try to keep it clean since we're being recorded. Ah, what the fuck am I saying; I'll drop a few f-bombs. See, already did."

"Just be careful when you're upstairs," I say in a low tone, wary of my own advice. "Jesus is watching."

"Yeah, from every nook and cranny, so far as I could tell." She laughs. "So anyway… Junior. He's too smart for his own good. They wanted to move him forward a grade, but I wasn't ready to let my baby be a high schooler yet. He still keeps a light on in the closet when he sleeps, and don't you dare tell him I told you that!"

"Junior? I don't believe it. He's fearless!"

We often take Junior on our practice investigations at cemeteries or well-known public places. He practically runs the show, and it won't be long before he's good enough to take over as our equipment guy. I'm counting on it, in fact. There is nothing I'd like more than to have zero reasons to keep Plaid Jeans around.

"He puts on a good show," says Dana. "He likes you guys, and he wants to impress you, so maybe someday you'll invite him on a proper investigation."

"I think we can make that happen soon," I say. "I mean, if he can manage it without a night light. We can't have any scaredy-cats running around on our highly professional cases."

"Hilarious. You just keep your damn mouth shut."

"I'm going to turn this light off for a second," I call from just outside the lounge area. Dana is checking EMF across the room by the neighbor's furnace and water heater, which is behind Alice's stairway toward the front wall. I pull the chain on the bulb over the couch and flip on my UV light to look around. The concrete area right around my feet looks clean-*ish*, but the rug could be a true-crime scene. With the light on, it looks like your run-of-the-mill filthy, matted floor covering. Something you'd see a professional rug cleaner tackling on a TikTok video. *"We found this one in a dungeon with decades of dust and mouse droppings embedded in the fibers."* In the UV light, however, it is quite easy to discern the pet pee design. There are dozens of spots on the rug—so many that they are overlapping into one giant spotted blob. It's like a piss Jackson Pollock painting. Most of the urine spots show faint in the UV light, meaning they aren't fresh (which is why they are masked somewhat by the air freshener that I still haven't found). But a few are bright enough to glow in the flashlight beam. I realize that one of my Skechers is dangerously close to the corner of the rug, so I quickly step back and dry heave a little (okay, three or four times). That is about as disgusting as it gets.

Dana calls out, "What the hell, you pregnant?"

"Careful on the rug over here," I say. "I think something has been using it as an outhouse. For some time."

"Hello urine smell." She mumbles something into her recorder.

I scan the UV flashlight around the general area outside of the couch and rug. There are more smears, as if someone tried to clean up the pee. I shake my head. They need to use enzyme spray; that's what Libbi tells me. That's the only way to break it down and get rid of the odor completely. I'm assuming at least some of these spots are from Pepper, and I also assume that either Sue, Jo, or both are aware of their dog's habits. How could they not be?

"Lots of other piss spots in the general vicinity," I whisper. "You have been duly warned."

Dana calls back, "Yeah, I found some black mold over here too. Just a little, but it's there."

She appears from behind the back of the stairs wearing a blue disposable mask over her nose and mouth.

"Better safe than sorry," she says in a muffled voice. "I'm not taking any chances over there."

The volatile days of the Covid pandemic are over, but many people still carry masks with them just in case. Dana is a nurse, so I'm not surprised she has a few on hand. Libbi always has a few in her bag, though we haven't needed them for a long time now. Me? I'm done with masks unless there's another deadly outbreak and a mandate. I'll take my chances with the mold.

We spend a few more minutes down in the pit. I check Stan's cameras again and run my LED flashlight along the cables, which are taped to the floor and running up the steps. I didn't even notice them when I came down. Stan gets a few brownie points for that; he knows how to get the tech going, and he makes sure it's all safe. I've tripped over my own setup more than once, so I'm glad to hand that all over to the stepbrother-in-law.

"I'm heading up," I call to Dana, who is talking to herself or something I can't see over by the kid's toys.

"Right behind you," she says but doesn't move, so I interpret that as "be up in a sec."

Just as I put my left foot on the stairs, I am startled by a small furry object whizzing past my ankles from above. For the second time in one night, I nearly poop my pants. Turns out it is Pepper, who is surprisingly nimble for such an old dog. I honestly thought he might have croaked on the couch upstairs when we first arrived. He did not move the entire time we were talking to Sue. But Pepper is awake now and on a mission. He hops off the bottom stair and heads toward the lounge area. He only gets a few feet from the steps when he stops and takes a piss. Not directly on the rug, but close to it. The urine stream is followed by a squat and pop. Yes, the little Yorkie mix just dropped a dookie on the cold concrete floor. So much for "my dog is one hundred percent housebroken," as Sue had insisted. The evidence is clear on that charge.

"That is GROSS!" whispers Dana, coming across the basement but stopping at the other side of the stairwell. Pepper gives himself a good shake head to tail and zooms up the stairs. He acts like he's on top of the world, which I totally understand. There's something about a good bowel movement.

"Should we clean it up?" asks Dana in a low voice.

"Fuck no," I mumble. "I'm not touching that. I'll let Sue know when we get up there."

Which would be now. Dana and I start up the stairs together. When we reach the third step from the bottom, I quietly point out the flattened nail that we are all safe from now, thanks to Sue's quick and vicious attack.

"She took out some rage on that one," Dana whispers. "I thought she saw a bat or something when she came back up the stairs with the hammer. Look, you can see the marks."

She points to the circular indents in the old pine.

"I gotta believe ole Sue has a few anger issues," I say under my breath. "She went at that thing like she was in a lumberjack contest."

The basement door above opens fully, and Stan steps onto the stairs heading down. Dana says hello while I let him pass without a word. I'm still pissed at him.

"Heads up on the pile of shit and piss between the stairs and the couch, to your right. Pepper just made an appearance. That rug is pretty nasty too."

"Oh jeez. Thanks for the warning."

I'm a little annoyed that Dana let him know about Pepper's gift to the investigation. I'd like nothing better than for karma to show up as a little doo-doo on Stan's shoe.

As Dana and I enter the Mackenzie kitchen, I see Sue standing near Jo's bedroom door smoking a cigarette. I'm slightly annoyed but not at all surprised. We did explicitly ask her not to smoke in the house before the investigation. Smells can be prominent in paranormal events, so it is important to have as clean an environment as possible. But honestly, I'm not sure how much that's going to matter. This entire night is going to be a shitshow, especially when Sue and Jo return after midnight. I need to let that feeling go.

"You have a little mold down in the basement," I call out as I turn to walk out the back door. It's just a courtesy. I look at light mold the way I look at radon: I don't think it's a problem. But I guess it could become one.

"Thanks," says Sue. She exhales and walks over to her recliner to put out the stick in her Jesus ashtray. She seems entirely unconcerned about anything, and frankly, I'm okay with that. The less chit-chat, the better.

Libbi Bean

I am standing alone near the top of the Mackenzie's driveway looking back at the house toward the center of the duplex.

"Well, that is very interesting," I mutter to myself. I feel like I just learned someone's deepest, darkest secret. An aha moment, as they say.

As I stand there, mouth agape, the neighbor's dog—not ten feet away from me—lifts his leg and lets forth a stream of unneutered piss under Sue's front window. The brightly lit sconce next to Sue's front door reflects against the beagle's enormous nutsack as he directs his piss toward the house. I can't quite believe it, so I shine my flashlight in that direction. There is no mistake. The recorder in my hand continues to clock, but it catches little in those thirty seconds but for the soft *whizzz* of a canine Austin Powers pee and the wind gently whispering in the trees.

Maya comes out the front door and heads toward me.

"Did you just see that?" I ask.

Maya shakes her head no. "What?"

I nod casually toward the neighbor's dog tethered between the two duplex doors.

"That dog totally just marked right in front of Sue's window. He still has his cojones too."

It is early fall in Virginia, which means temperatures during the day can still be in the low or even upper-seventies Fahrenheit. The picture window in front is flanked by two small windows that slide up and down. It is certainly plausible that one or the other (or both) has been open periodically over the past few weeks, possibly allowing the smell of the urine to enter Sue's living room—especially if a mild breeze kicked up. Maya and I look at each other, both of us having the same thought.

"That would explain the urine smell." Maya says quietly.

I can only shake my head in disbelief.

We pause a minute, letting it sink in. There is music playing from somewhere in the subdivision—a radio, I think. I heard it earlier, and it sounded like a DJ's voice. Now it's a song, although I cannot make out the tune; something from the nineties if I were to guess. I can just make out the patented grunge style of The Stone Temple Pilots or Soundgarden. It sounds like it's coming from far down the street. Sue's house is up on a small hill, so from the top of her driveway I have a great sight line. Sue and Jo reported hearing the "Wipe Out" song and voices speaking, so anything that might help explain those will be useful. Starting about a quarter mile away where Starry Knob Lane curves off into the rest of the subdivision, I scan the houses. I see nothing obvious that might be the source of the music. As I slowly drag my gaze along the street to the houses closer to us, I finally see something.

Wait, that can't be right.

Just then, Walter comes around the side of the house, and I lose my train of thought. He does not look pleased, but when does Walter ever look pleased? Maybe in the backyard on a summer night with a cigar in one hand and a glass of whiskey in the other. Listening to the NY Mets win a baseball game. That's about as pleased as my husband ever looks.

His expression is justified. "Be careful when you go downstairs. The dog just dropped a steamy at the bottom of the basement steps. There's a puddle down there too. And I don't think this is his first go-around."

Walter looks a little green around the gills. He doesn't exactly have a comfort level with pet bodily functions. Let's just say I'm the one who cleans up Fenny's dog puke and occasional hairballs.

"There's a big rug down in the basement," he continues. "It's right next to the bashed-up drums. Looks like ole Pepper has been using it as a litter box for a while. Could have brought down an airplane when I shined my UV light on it."

"Are you shitting me?" I ask. No pun intended.

He is not. Well, maybe the airplane thing was an exaggeration. But not the extent of the dog piss. This is perfect. It could not have turned out better. I live for debunking. Everyone else on the team has some level of belief in a spiritual afterlife. We are all (except maybe for Stan, still working on him) healthy skeptics. However, I am the only one of us who does not believe in any sort of spiritual or supernatural being. Dana is very Christian. Maya is a cultural Jew. Walter communes with his Nordic ancestors out in our backyard every month. Asatru, I think he calls it. Stan attends a Methodist church most Sundays.

I am a card-carrying atheist. Several cards, in fact: American Atheists, The American Humanist Association, and The Satanic Temple (which, despite its name, is simply a non-theistic organization). I even have a Flying Spaghetti Monster sticker on my Subaru. Many people have asked how I can be a paranormal investigator if I don't believe in a god or heaven. That's easy. One, I do this to find the truth and to help people. It is rare that we do not find at least a *possible* logical explanation for most of our clients' events. And two, as an atheist, I don't claim that it is impossible for there to be a supreme being or an afterlife. I simply assert that there is currently zero evidence of either.

Until if or when there *is* proof, I refuse to succumb to religious dogma. Religion has fucked up humanity in many ways. I *do* believe in energy. I believe there are things we don't understand. I believe in science and quantum physics and the multiverse. All these things are just as likely to explain paranormal activity as the disembodied soul of someone who didn't quite make it to heaven.

"Maya, would you mind asking Sue to come out here? I want to see if she is aware of this."

She heads back into the house while Walter and I linger outside. My recorder is still running, so I bite my tongue. I'm more than a little annoyed. Sue told us several times (and we did press) that her dog did NOT (and she was very adamant about this) go to the bathroom in her house. And she was not aware of any other source of the urine smell.

As we wait for Sue, I remember I haven't told my husband about the beagle's activity.

"Oh, by the way, since we're on the topic of dog piss, the neighbor's beagle just marked right in front of Sue's window."

I say it with a raised eyebrow, although I'm not sure Walter notices in the dim light. My better half looks over at the mutt, and rests his right elbow on his left hand, like *The Thinker.*

"That could also be why she smelled urine."

Fucking genius. Walter, you have crystallized my thoughts perfectly.

He continues, "Either that or the fact that her own dog uses the basement as his personal toilet."

Almost as if on cue, the neighbor's dog gets up and again marks the bushes under Sue's window for the second time in a matter of minutes. We both laugh in disbelief.

Both Sue and Jo report smelling a very strong urine odor with no apparent source. We have now identified two possibilities. This is outstanding. The skeptic in me rejoices. Of course, Sue was insistent that it was *human* urine, but how could she even tell? Is she a urine odor expert? I think not. I mean, she works at a hotel, not a urology lab.

A few minutes after Walter makes his announcement, we hear Sue yelling at Josie to get her shit together. Seconds later, Sue emerges from the front door with Maya. Though she is in her late forties, she looks older. She might resemble Janice Joplin if the famous singer had lived into her glory years. Walter and I walk over to tell her what we think is good news.

"So," I began. "I'm not sure if you are aware, but your neighbor's dog there has been marking in front of your window. Pissing, I mean."

It's obvious to me. Sue smells urine randomly for a few moments at a time. An unneutered male dog is marking regularly in front of the window. It is, as they say, a "no-brainer."

Sue scrunches up her face and shrugs her shoulders. Her head shakes back as if she is trying to say no but is hesitant to do so. There is nothing hesitant about Sue, as we have already ascertained. So, I press.

"I'm thinking this could be why you're smelling urine. As one option that might explain it. I mean, you know, the breeze picks up the marking, and you smell urine, even if the window is closed…"

I raise my eyebrows and open my eyes wide in a way that suggests I think this is painfully clear

Sue shakes her head no. "Nah, that's not what I smelled."

"Are you sure?" I push back politely. "I mean, dog marking can be potent. Or maybe it was your dog peeing in the basement. Which I think it just did. Another possibility."

Sue continues to shake her head, looking down and shuffling her feet. "Nope," she says firmly. "What I smelled was human urine. That's not it."

And there it is. There will be no budging. Not even a compromise. I can sense Walter looking at me even though I avoid his direction. I am sure he is rolling his eyes, and I can almost hear him thinking. *See, I told you… whack job.*

I can see where this investigation is likely to go, and although I am disappointed, I am not surprised. Sue is absolutely convinced that she has demons in her house. We can show her evidence that might explain some of the events she reported, but that's all we can do. We know from years of doing this that many of our clients would rather believe that something dark and evil and supernatural is causing all their problems, rather than accept that what they experience might just be perfectly explainable. I would love to prove (with irrefutable evidence) the existence of the paranormal. I would also love to prove beyond all doubt that there are logical explanations for every activity. But we rarely get that luxury. Most of our investigations fall somewhere in between.

Sue lights up a cigarette (when doesn't she?) and walks back inside. Walter disappears around the side of the house to check out the backyard. I ask Maya to follow me in the same direction. We stop at the front corner of the duplex.

"I want you to look at this," I say. I haven't forgotten my WTF moment from earlier.

I point to the beginning of a thick row of trees and overgrown shrubs along the fence that borders the sides and back of the Mackenzie property. Evergreens peek out from behind thick strands of bindweed and ivy. Decades ago, someone probably planted the pines for privacy, maybe even to dampen the sound of Rte. 220, which is in that direction. Even here with virtually no light seeping through the brush, I can hear a few vehicles careening down the 55 MPH road. Without the barrier, it would be annoyingly loud.

"Okay, don't turn around yet," I say.

We are facing the trees at the side of the house, away from Starry Knob Lane and the rest of the subdivision.

"Do you hear music?" I ask.

Maya nods. "Yes, sounds like a radio."

"Okay, good. Without turning around, point in the direction you hear it coming from."

Maya raises her left arm and points directly behind her, toward the end of the subdivision where the rest of the houses disappear at the curve. She is pointing right where I was looking when I heard the grunge guitar music a few minutes ago. Nearly a quarter mile down the road.

"Now turn around and look at that house with the lit garage almost straight across the street." Maya turns around. "The one with the little orange buggy in the driveway."

I point to the classic Little Tikes Cozy Coupe with the yellow frame and orange body. You can't drive down a residential street in the U.S. without seeing one of those in someone's front yard.

"Oh!" says Maya. "How is that possible?"

Attached to the gray house with the plastic toddler car is a garage on the side closest to us. There is an older SUV—maybe a Ford Explorer—halfway in the garage and halfway sticking out into the driveway. The hood is up and a man is leaning over it. It is dark out, but he has an industrial lamp in the garage doorway lighting up the vehicle engine. Just outside of the garage is some sort of dog—a German shepherd, maybe—snoozing on the driveway near the SUV. Either the dog wasn't out when we arrived, or it just isn't a barker because I would have noticed the sound. There is nothing unusual about this vignette of a dude messing with his car on a cool evening in early fall while his dog takes a nap at his side.

Except for one thing: The car is the source of the music. Once I make the connection, it clicks. The guy is even dancing to the beat of the current song as he backs away from the engine and gets a different tool from a red box just inside the garage. The music is coming from across the street. Yet it sounds like it is coming from the edge of the subdivision, a good thirty degrees clockwise and a quarter mile down the road.

The bramble of trees and shrubs and vines behind Sue's house is acting like the perfect amphitheater. The sound hits the tree wall, then bounces out. Or maybe it hits the tall arborvitae that line either side of the entrance to the subdivision. Sue's house is only the third one in from the main road. So basically, her trees and the community evergreens make a tiny Grand Canyon.

Sound is an amazing thing and not something to be downplayed in an investigation. There are birds that sound like cats or babies crying. Insects that make knocking noises. Engine braking can sound like growling. Music can come from an entirely different direction than you think. This is important for our investigation because anything that was reported as a sound might have come from a totally different direction or location than observed.

"That is the most bizarre thing," says Maya. "Is it possible that guy is just hearing something down the road too?"

We can both see him swaying to the beat of the music.

"No, I just watched him go inside the car and change the station a few minutes ago. The music is coming from that car right there. The SUV. It's just bouncing off something—maybe the thick line of trees behind the house."

"I wondered about that when I came in. Not so much the sound bouncing, but I thought maybe blocking it. Someone needs to call a landscaper."

"No shit. But… not my circus, not my monkeys."

Just to validate my theory about the sound, I walk down Sue's driveway to the road and up the street a few yards until I am almost in front of the neighbor's house with the car radio. There is no way I don't look like a creeper, so I stash my gun-shaped thermometer in my hoodie pocket and put my phone up to my ear as if I'm on a call. Awkward. I stop, and the guy waves, so I wave back.

"Is it too loud?" the neighbor calls out. "I'll be finished up in a few minutes."

"No, you're fine," I call out. "Thank you, though."

Lame. I pretend to finish my fake call and then I turn back to the Mackenzie house. A burgundy grocery getter minivan is just pulling into the driveway. A woman is driving with her window open, and a small dog is sitting on her lap with its head hanging out. The woman's long arm is half out the window with a cigarette dangling between her fingers. Safety first. This must be Gina. The van stops abruptly at the top of the driveway, whereupon the dog—a Chihuahua mix by all appearances and reports—starts yapping like his life depends on it. They say pit bulls, German shepherds, and Dobermans are bully breeds. I beg to differ. Chihuahuas are the worst. They will tear you a new one and laugh while they're doing it. Everyone thinks they are so cute and funny. *OMG, how sweet!* Meanwhile, you just lost a finger.

I take a breath and center my energy. Okay, rat dog. Bring it on. I head toward the duplex.

Walter Bean

When I come around Alice's side of the duplex, I see my lovely wife walking down the street in the middle of the road. Alice has been told that we will be in the house and why, according to Sue. Which makes sense, because if I were a single grandmother living alone and there were strange people walking around with flashlights at one o'clock in the morning, I would call the po-po. Alice assured Sue that she would be quiet; she and her dog, Roly Poly Oly (piss marker extraordinaire), go to bed early. Bonus: Roly is deaf as a doorknob. The grandson is not visiting this weekend. We should not expect any atypical noise from her side of the house. At least, not any human noise.

Maya has completed her rounds and is waiting for Libbi to return, so I walk over to compare notes. I found nothing noteworthy in the back other than a fence that is partially collapsed and held up only by thick vines and overgrown weeds. Maya tells me the theory about the shrubbery amphitheater.

While we are talking, a dark Chrysler Pacifica pulls into the driveway. The driver's side window is wide open, and I get a glimpse of the woman at the wheel—Gina, I presume. She is precisely what I would expect Sue's best friend to look like: bony, with long stringy hair, a cigarette hanging out the open window, and what looks like a large bat in her lap. If memory serves, its name is Tinker. Tinker's eyes are reflecting in the front light, and if there is a demon on this property, here it is. He is barking viciously, spraying droplets of devil spit from his creepy little mouth out into the night. Gina looks over at us, and I nod. Tinker barks louder. Gina nods back, but it doesn't seem friendly. I'm not the most emotionally intelligent person on the planet, but I would bet money she is sneering. Like she's disgusted. And then she spits out the window onto Sue's driveway. My stomach turns a little. *Class act.*

Gina puts the car in park and clutches bat-dog as she exits the vehicle. I can't help but notice her T-shirt. Even after sundown and half-covered by a faded denim jacket, it's hard to miss the shiny blue eyes of Jesus with his famous crown of thorns. That's because parts of our Lord and Savior are embellished with glitter. Wow. Just... wow. I have seen some strange shit, but I have never seen a bedazzled Jesus. Sue comes out the front door with a giant purse hanging across her body and Pepper in one arm. This might be the first time I've seen her without a cigarette in her hand. Thank goodness Gina is there to take up the slack. Jo is right behind her mom.

Suddenly, Tinker bolts out of Gina's arm and onto the grass. At first, I think he is running toward Sue and Pepper. Or maybe he wants a bite of Jo's ankle. But then I remember that there is another canine in the mix. Tinker thinks he is the alpha, and he clearly does not like Roly Poly Oly, who is still lazing in the mulch next to his owner's front door. Tinker stops a few feet away from the bigger dog and starts the patented Chihuahua yap, jaw-jacking the poor beagle while Gina just stands there cough-laughing with smoke coming out of her nose. Roly hardly seems to notice. Sue does not find Tinker's antics funny at all, and she snaps at Gina.

"Get your GD canine under control, Gina! Alice is going to come out here and rip me a new one if your mutt draws blood."

With impeccable timing, Alice's door opens, and she emerges in a pink robe with a leash in her hands.

"SHOO!" she yells at Tinker, and I'll be damned if he doesn't shut right up. Alice hooks Roly Poly Oly to the leash, unhooks him from the cable, and leads him back through her door without a word. I might be wrong, but it feels like she's had about enough of the Mackenzie shenanigans. Sue calls out a half-hearted "Thank you," at which point Tinker breaks out of his Alice trance and starts barking at Pepper. Fortunately for all of us, Tinker is all talk and no action. He doesn't make contact with anyone, just continues to growl at Sue's feet until Gina yells his name. Finally, he stops.

Once Gina has her mutt secured, I introduce myself.

"Walter Bean," I say, holding out my hand. Gina hurriedly taps the long ash from her cigarette onto the driveway, then transfers it to her left hand where she is holding her furry burden. Her right arm goes out, and I swear it's a mile long. The handshake is awkward; her hand is flaccid, like a wet chew toy. I suspect Gina isn't used to such formalities. She looks a lot like the factory rats I work with in my quality director job at Roanoke Forging Company. They are more high-five and fist pump than proper handshake.

"Charmed, I'm sure," she says, and it sounds kind of snooty to me. Deliberately snooty. She drops her cigarette to the ground and grinds it out with the toe of her pointy black boots. *Witch boots.* To my surprise, she leans over to pick up the butt.

"You ready to go?" she asks Sue.

"I'm ready for hours."

Sue looks at Libbi, who has joined us at the top of the driveway. "You have my number. If you need anything, just call me. We aren't but fifteen minutes away."

"Got it," says Libbi. "I'll let you know if we have any questions. Otherwise, we'll see you *after* midnight."

She emphasizes *after,* meaning *please do not show up even one minute before midnight because I will be triggered by the plan deviation and will be in a foul mood for the rest of the investigation.* I know my wife. And truthfully, we need every minute. Three hours in a clean environment is not a lot. Ideally, we'd have five or six. But it almost doesn't matter. One of the dirty little secrets of paranormal investigation is that we rarely—and I do mean rarely—ever have a truly clean environment. There is almost always ambient interference that we are aware of and must factor into the evidence review. Noises like traffic, nature, and loud neighbors are to be expected. This place has all of that and then some.

Jo hops into the back seat of the Pacifica while Sue sits up front on the passenger side with Pepper. She immediately lights up. If this case ever becomes a movie, it will be called *The Case of the Cigarette and Dope-Smoking Hippies and Their Yippy Dogs.* Gina backs down the driveway like a chick in a parking lot—meaning, too fast and a little reckless. Anyone who thinks my statement is sexist, I challenge them to observe the craziest parking lot drivers at their local Target or Walmart and tell me they aren't mostly women. Just sayin'.

Dana and Stan walk out the front door as the minivan drives off. Perfect timing.

"All right," I say, clapping my hands in the setting sun. "Let's wrap up the prep and go dark!"

Excerpt 5 from the *RIP After Dark* Podcast
Episode 72: Case of the Demon Drums

This podcast was broadcast one year after the actual investigation.
Client names and identifying details have been changed to maintain privacy.

Libbi: *I'm telling you, the amphitheater effect of those overgrown trees cannot be overstated. It was a solid wall of bushes and vines and trees.*

Walter: *Oh, I know how you feel about vines.*

Libbi: *Well, okay, aside from the fact that they will choke out the trees—and yes, anyone out there who has vines on your trees, cut those motherfuckers down!*

Walter: *Remember when our neighbor Ed came over and asked if he could cut ours down?*

Libbi: [laughs] *Uh, yeah, Walter. He does it, like, every month. Ed doesn't mess around.*

Walter: *He does not. He takes an interest.*

Libbi: *Anyway, my point being that all the tangled brush was like a big shrubbery bowl that bounced the sound. How could Nancy and her daughter tell which direction anything came from? I thought the radio guy was half a mile down the road in the other direction!*

Walter: *There should be a word for that. When your brain interprets something outside of reality. Like a sound matrix.*

Libbi: *Okay, Neo.*

Walter: *Just sayin'!*

Libbi: *Well, whatever you call it, it's a real thing. Remember that time we were walking on one of the Explore Park trails? When we thought we heard kids playing behind us?*

Walter: *I don't recall that. Remind me.*

Libbi: *We were walking along the river, and we heard kids screaming (like play-screaming) behind us. All three of us—you, me, and Fenny—turned around. Nothing there.*

Walter: *I vaguely remember.*

Libbi: *Absolutely no one in that direction. Then we heard it again, also coming from behind us—but we could see the family ahead making the noise. Maybe a hundred yards up the trail, having a picnic. Yet all three of us heard it from behind.*

Walter: *Yes, I remember now. That was weird. It was like the sound bounced off the trees or something.*

Libbi: *Exactly. I think the Hobarts had the same thing going on. Sound was bouncing off the shrubs and trees.*

Walter: *Ergo, where did the drum sounds come from? Inside? Outside? Back? Front?*

Libbi: *You crystallized my thoughts perfectly.*

Walter: *Okay, so your big aha in the prep was the sound-bouncing thing.*

Libbi: *Yes. Mind blowing.*

Walter: *My biggest takeaway was this: How do you become aware of not one, but two rational explanations for the smell of urine and still deny—adamantly—that it's not the same urine as you smelled? Because you smelled "human" urine (I'm using air quotes for those on audio).*

Libbi: [sighs] *Dude... I do not get that one at all. To recap, we caught the client's dog peeing and pooping in the basement—*

Walter: *—which I witnessed, and it was clearly not the first time either—*

Libbi: *—and the neighbor's intact beagle marked twice right in front of the client's window as I stood there pondering the parallel universe of sound.*

Walter: *And the rug in the basement that lit up like a glow-in-the-dark Picasso painting when I shined the UV light on it.*

Libbi: *Mmmm. Tasty. Yeah, you have to use an enzyme cleaner on urine to break it down.*

Walter: *As you have taught me over the years.*

Libbi: *I have trained you well, Grasshopper.*

Walter: [chuckles] *Riddle me this, Batwoman: With all due respect to our client, how do you know if it's human urine or dog piss?*

Libbi: *You got me. Pee is pee.*

Walter: *That should be part of our podcast tagline. "Ghosts are real, but so is black mold. And sometimes pee is just pee."*

Libbi: [laughs hard] *Oh my god, I might just add that. You are a literary genius, Walter.*

Walter: *I do my best.*

Libbi: [still laughing] *I'm dying! You're going to have to run the show for a minute.* [snorts]

Walter: *I guess that means it's time to go to the Question Coffin!*

Unexpected in the Underground

Saturday, October 4, 9:00-10:30 pm
Investigation, Session One (basement)
Mackenzie Residence, Starry Knob Lane, Roanoke, Virginia
Team 1: Dana, Walter, Maya

The Mackenzie House Basement, Session One

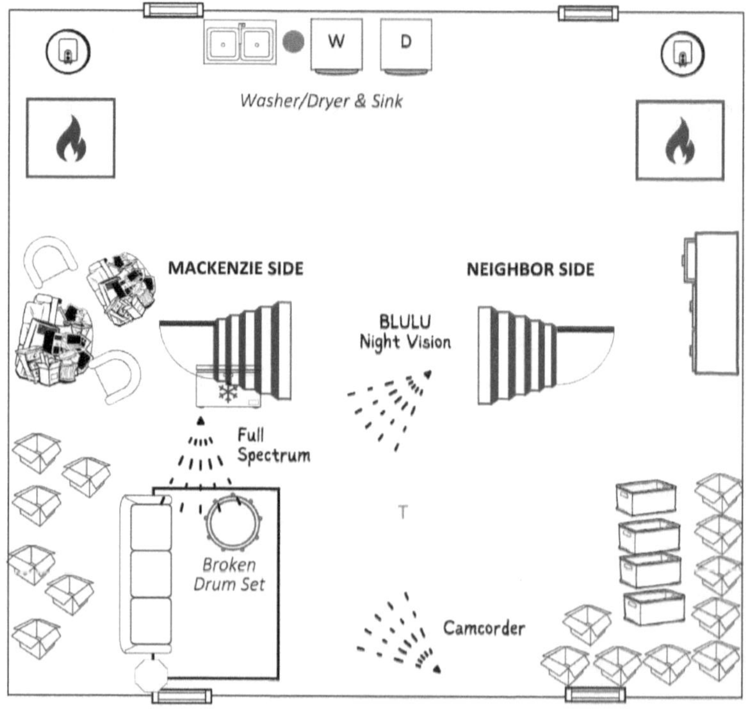

Maya Hill-Goldberg

Walter, Dana, and I are in the basement starting Session One. Walter is standing behind and between the Blu-Lu1 camera and the camcorder, both pointing toward the lounge area. Dana starts off standing behind the icky couch. I opt for the bottom step on the stairwell because that's the only place where I can sit that feels even remotely clean. I have a good view of about two-thirds of the basement. All the lights are out, including upstairs. At first, I see absolutely nothing. After a few minutes my eyes adjust, and I can see a very faint line under the door at the top of the stairs. Libbi is up at the monitoring station (which we call Lighthouse) watching the video stream from the Blu-Lu1; Stan is sitting in the recliner in the living room trying not to make any sound while we conduct the first EVP session downstairs. It is now fully dark outside. We have shut off the exterior lights on both sides of the duplex, but there may still be ambient light from the neighbors' homes and a few streetlamps down the road. The windows are small and high, typical of unfinished basements, and most of them have curtains covering them, although they are a little on the sheer side.

I hear a slight tinkling, like a small wind chime.

"Did you guys hear a bell?"

"Aw, shit," says Dana. "That's me. I forgot to take my earrings off."

I hear her rustling around for a few seconds. Paranormal Investigation 101: Remove any clothing or accessories that might interfere with the evidence gathering. No shiny stuff that might reflect. Skip the tinkling earrings and other jingle-bell jewelry. Turn off light-up watches (mine only turns on manually and is well-hidden under my thick sleeve). Ditch the corduroys (ditch those regardless). Dress for silence and darkness. Sometimes environmental conditions, weather, or safety concerns require us to violate the rule, but on most occasions, we try to blend.

"What the hell, Rookie?" says Walter jokingly.

"I know," says Dana. "I came right from work and just forgot about it. Put me in ghost hunter timeout."

Walter has a nickname for everyone on the team. Dana has been Rookie since she joined the team almost five years ago, and probably always will be. I am Bader because I'm petite and feisty like Ruth Bader Ginsburg and because I'm Jewish with two last names. Stan is Gooch, short for Katagucci. Fun fact, *gooch* is also a slang term for that little piece of skin between a man's testicles and his anus, aka *the taint*. I don't think Stan knows about this, but the rest of the team does (we let that be our little secret). Libbi is some variation of Dear Wife, Gorgeous, or Lib, depending on the occasion. Sometimes I call her Boss or Captain because it pings Walter a little. But it's true. She runs the show. The rest of us sometimes refer to Walter as Professor, because he uses big words that none of us understand, like ubiquitous and chicanery.

"I'm going to start my EVP session if you guys are ready," I say, pulling out my recorder.

Dana and Walter reply in the affirmative. I am the holder of the primary walkie-talkie and need to call up to Libbi to let her know. She and Stan will note any sights, smells, or sounds they encounter above so we can correlate with anything experienced below. I press the walkie button and cringe as the deafening alert beep shatters the silence of the basement.

"Lighthouse, we are starting EVP, over," I say into the unit. I turn the volume down a couple of notches.

"Roger that," comes the tempered response from above.

"SHINY," I call out to Walter and Dana before turning my flashlight on. We always call out a warning when we turn on our lights or use flash photography. A lot of paranormal investigation teams use "FLASH!" The alternate "SHINY" seems a little weird to me, but Walter says it's from a television show *Firefly* that was on back in the olden days, so I just nod and don't ask too many questions that I don't care to hear the answers to.

I point my LED light toward my recorder to make sure it is on and saving to the correct file. It is, so the light goes off.

"Mackenzie Investigation, October 5, 9:08 pm, Session One, basement. I am calling out to any spirits who may be present. We come in peace and mean you no harm. Thank you for allowing us into your home. My name is Maya, and these are my friends Dana and Walter. We are peaceful visitors, here out of curiosity. We would like to ask you some questions."

Just in case there are sentient spirits around, we always start off our investigation by addressing them politely and directly. We wouldn't want a stranger to show up at our home and start barking out questions as soon as we open the front door. We give the same courtesy to any entities who might look at this place as their home.

"We have a device here that will help us hear you." I hold up my recorder in the dark. *"Please get as close to it as you can when you answer and speak as loudly as possible."*

I pause. Dana sneezes and marks it. "That was me—Dana—sneezing. Sorry… dust."

"Bless you," I say, as does Walter at the same time. "Jinx!"

It's not fun unless we make it fun. I talk to any spirits in the room. *"What is your name?"*

I ask our standard list of questions, which we will use for all three sessions, including the seance after Sue and Jo get home. We can (and do) ask questions that are not on the core list, but for consistency, we cover the basic ones first.

I speak slowly and clearly, and I pause for about thirty seconds between questions to give the spirits a chance to respond. It can become tedious, but the silence is necessary.

"How old are you?"

"Did you live here?"

"Where do you come from?"

"Where were you born?"

"Are you aware of the other people living here?"

I continue for nearly thirty minutes. Periodically, someone calls out a marker.

"Car passing outside, lights shining through the front window."

"Walter coughing."

"Dana moving behind the stairwell."

"Maya accidentally dropped her EMF detector."

Other than the random but earthly and normal sounds, the EVP session is uneventful, at least to our ears. A lot of times we catch anomalies and possible responses on the recording, but they are too faint for us to pick up in real-time.

As I am nearing the last few core questions, my heart jumps when my EMF meter makes a sound. I am still sitting on the stairs with the walkie-talkie standing upright next to me, away from anything that would obviously generate the sound.

"My EMF just blipped," I say into the recording. Then, to the spirits: *"Can you do that again?"*

If something supernatural touched the meter, maybe they could do it again. The EMF spikes again, followed by the loud beep of the walkies, both mine and the backup that Walter has in his tool belt. My stomach drops for a few seconds. Even though I choose to do this and I have done it dozens of times, fear can still kick in. As much as I love paranormal investigation, I'm not sure I ever want to encounter a ghost in real life, at least not up close and personal. The walkie-talkies beep again.

"That was not me," I say to my hunting partners. *"Are you trying to communicate?"* We wait a full minute for a response and get nothing.

Walter retrieves his walkie-talkie and calls home base. *"Walter to Lighthouse. Did you register anything up there? Our walkies just went off twice, for reasons unknown. Over."*

A few seconds later, Libbi responds, *"We did not get any walkie-talkie activity up here. I could hear yours through the door, but mine was silent. Over."*

"Very good, we'll note it and move on. Over."

Random walkie-talkie beeps and EMF spikes are not uncommon during investigations, so these will have to be explored amid the bigger picture and recordings.

Walter asks, "Dana, are you picking up anything down here?"

He means, of a psychic nature. I don't know if I fully believe in Dana's abilities, but she has gotten a few good hits on past investigations. I want to believe in a sixth sense, but there are so many fakes out there that it's hard not to be skeptical.

"Nothing is jumping out at me. I felt a sort of energy when I pulled up to the house earlier, and I can feel it here. But what it is, I don't know at this moment. It's a weak, dark energy, but I'm not clear where it's coming from or if it's friendly or not."

My shoulders quiver. I already have the willies, and we're only a half hour into it. Do I want to hear whether or not it's friendly? Not really. But that's part of the thrill. It's the unknown—the possibility that there *might* be something paranormal here, and it might not be nice.

"Maya, go ahead and finish your EVP. When you're done, I want to run a brief experiment."

I comply and pick up where I left off.

"Are you able to show yourself to us?"

"Can you see me?'

"Are there others with you?"

"How did you die?"

"Does time pass for you?"

A short while later, I am done with the required questions. There have been no more unexplained EMF spikes or walkie-talkie beeps so far. Walter takes out his IR flashlight and turns it on. As I watch through the stair rail, he places his KII meter on the floor near the drum pile, positioned so all the cameras have it in view.

I hear the walkie-talkie turn on. *"Team One to Lighthouse. We're about to start an EVP session using the KII and walkie-talkie to try and get them to go off. We are asking for non-emergency radio silence for about five minutes. I'll let you know when we're done. Over."*

"Copy that," comes Libbi's voice.

Walter places his walkie-talkie on the concrete next to the KII and starts talking to any entities that might be present.

"I have placed my walkie-talkie and KII meter on the floor next to the pile of drum pieces. If any spirits are around, please try to make one or both go off. If you move close to the small box on the floor with the light—"

He is referring to the KII, which has a small green light on the side.

"—you may be able to make it blink just by being near it."

He turns off his IR light, and we wait. My eyes have adjusted enough that I can just make out the KII glow from my perch about six feet away. My heart is beating faster in anticipation of a response sound, and I wonder if any of the sensitive microphones will pick up something if my own ears don't. Another car passes, and I log it. Other than the brief rumble of wheels and my mark, you could hear a pin drop.

Something moves behind me, under the stairs. I jump up and away from the open steps because even though it might be nothing, it might also be a demogorgon. I hear more movement, this time farther away, as if my motion caused whatever it is to change direction.

"There is something under the stairs," I say softly but loud enough for the others to hear.

"I heard it too," says Dana. "It went behind the furnace over here. Sounded too big to be a mouse, but maybe a rat?"

She lives on a farm, so I trust her expert opinion on the size of rodents.

"Jesus," says Walter. "I hope it's *just* a rat."

We are all thinking the same thing: Is it a small animal or a small demon? Probably the former, and possibly an explanation for some of the reported noises. But without seeing it, we don't know what's scurrying over there. Regardless of whether it's paranormal (or not), I don't want it coming up behind me in the dark, so I choose to remain standing with my EMF detector and the walkie-talkie still sitting on the stairs. I shudder and wring my hands. I hate mice.

"Let's hope whatever it is, we scared it away," says Dana. She is unfazed. I'm not surprised. Nothing seems to get under her skin.

Walter repeats his request to the spirits to make his KII meter or the walkie-talkie go off. We wait a few more minutes in silence. Just when I think it's about time to change the game, I hear footsteps overhead. Libbi and Stan are supposed to be stationary, and it's mostly carpet up there. This sounds like cowboy boots on a hardwood floor. The steps are slow and deliberate. I can't pinpoint where they are coming from. The ducts on the ceiling and pipes on the front side of the basement vibrate with each step. Finally, after about thirty seconds, the footsteps stop.

Since Walter's walkie-talkie is on the floor, I lean over and grab mine in the darkness.

"Team One to Lighthouse. We just heard footsteps overhead. Was anyone walking around up there just now? Over."

"That's a negative, Team One. We haven't moved."

"Copy that."

"Okay, that was officially weird," says Dana. She says it like it was her kid choosing Froot Loops for breakfast instead of Cap'n Crunch. Meanwhile, the hair on my neck is bristling, and my stomach has dropped into a parallel universe. I am now officially spooked. I try to convince myself that it was Alice, the neighbor, walking around in Dutch wooden shoes with little tulips and windmills painted on top. Because that seems more "old lady" and less "Satan in cowboy boots," I guess.

Walter wraps up our experiment. *"Lighthouse, we are ending our current EVP with the KII and walkie-talkie."*

He picks up his devices as Dana calls out "SHINY" in her deep voice. She has a rich, throaty contralto; very sexy and sultry. I'd describe it as "southern lounge lizard." Her voice gives her authority, and I find it comforting. I sound more like Mickey Mouse. I shrug in my head. People like Mickey Mouse, so it can't be that bad. Dana walks toward where I am standing at the bottom of the stairs.

"I'll be right back. I need to change the batteries on this thermometer."

"Lighthouse, Dana is coming up for a battery change," announces Walter, for both Libbi and the recorder.

Dana heads up the stairs and closes the door behind her when she gets to the main floor. We hear her walking around and then a second set of footsteps, probably Libbi. They sound much different from the footsteps we heard a few moments ago. They also resonate broadly throughout the entire basement, which is curious. Nothing conclusive. Just interesting. I would expect lower resonance with linoleum floors, and especially with carpet. Rugs are sound mufflers. Strange house.

I log: *"I am hearing footsteps above from Libbi and Dana, very loud, and I can easily hear them down in the basement."*

Walter is walking around the back of the couch with his EMF meter engaged as I continue.

"The sound of walking upstairs has more of a boom sound than hard footsteps. It's muffled a bit because of the carpeting but still very audible."

"Maya, do you have your thermometer with you?" asks Walter. "SHINY."

He has turned on his infrared light to see better. My thermometer is in my pocket, so pull it out and walk toward him.

"See what you get in this area."

Walter points to the pile of drums. As I get closer, there is a distinct drop in temperature. I can't feel a breeze, but if I were to guess, I would say it is almost ten degrees colder at the edge of the lounge area five feet away from the stairwell. I point my digital thermometer at the rubble of drums. It reads 52°F. I point to the outer wall. It is 60°F. The couch is at 62°, the concrete floor at 60°. I point back to the drums. Now it's 51°.

I call out the readings and locations into my microphone.

"I'm getting the same," says Walter.

I can feel the hair on my arms standing up underneath my hoodie. The air around me is electrified. My stomach tightens as fear pushes me slightly into fight-or-flight mode. It is noticeably colder near the drums. It's now 49°F, and I back away, shivering. The basement door opens from above, and I see Dana's silhouette as she descends the steps.

"SHINY," she says, pointing her LED downward to light her way. Then: "AAARRGH!"

Dana cries out loudly from the stairwell, followed by a loud BANG! I turn on my flashlight and point it toward her. She is bent over, holding her head in both hands, with the newly re-juiced thermometer lying a few steps below where she stands. That must have been the bang I heard.

"There's something here now," she says. Her voice sounds strained. "Something just hit my brain… and… it is intense." She winces and sucks in air.

I step up so I am just below her. "Are you okay?" I ask, and she nods, but with difficulty.

"Yeah, I think so, but I don't know if I can come down any farther."

She is doubled over as if she has a bad stomachache. Walter comes toward us.

"*GET OUT!*" Dana yells to something we cannot see or perceive.

I breathe in sharply. It's getting wild down here.

Dana Tennant

"GET THE FUCK OUT OF MY HEAD!"

As I started down the basement steps, something hit me. It struck the top of my head with unbelievable force, like one of those anvils Wile E. Coyote throws off a cliff when he is trying to catch the Road Runner. Except the source of my pain is internal. It's not a tangible object. No one dropped a bowling ball on my skull, even though that's what it feels like. It is someone—or something—trying to get inside my thoughts. I can't tell if it's bad energy or good or neither or both. But it is trying very hard to penetrate the protective barrier I have erected around my body, and I don't think it wants to talk. I think it wants us to leave.

I've been able to sense things that others cannot see since I was a child. Usually when I get visual or audio impressions (and I get them almost daily), they don't hurt. I feel a thickness and slight pressure, maybe a light throbbing. It can be uncomfortable but generally tolerable. Sometimes a powerful energy will cause a near-violent reaction. Even harmless souls can wreak havoc on my mind if they are determined enough to make contact. When powerful forces get in, it's like having a major migraine event. Or at least, it's what I imagine a real migraine to be like based on what I have heard from others. The pain is piercing, like sharp needles in my brain. My vision gets blurred, almost as if I'm going blind. Even moderately bright light feels like a hammer pounding behind my eyes. I'm not going to lie. It sucks.

"Easy there," says Maya, coming up another step.

I grab her arm to steady myself and to point her flashlight toward the floor, away from my face. "Yeah, I'll be okay. Something just surged into my brain. Give me a minute; I'll be fine. WHEW! FUCK! This one is for real!"

I sit down on the steps as this... *something*... continues trying to connect with my energy. I can't see enough to walk; my eyes are filmy, like they are coated with petroleum jelly. The more I relax, the better I can handle these waves. They rarely last long before my body adjusts, and then I can attempt some communication. Not all my experiences are paranormal. Meaning, they are not all ghosts or souls of the dead. Living humans can communicate telepathically (knowingly or not, usually not) and they can absolutely create this kind of violent telekinetic energy. Given the circumstances of Sue and Jo's relationship, I would not be surprised if that were the case here.

However, neither of them is present right now. I've never had a living energy come at me so hard when the source is not close by. This is either a living energy from someone else (and I can't imagine who... Alice?) or it's not a living energy. Or I suppose it could be a living energy strong enough to linger after the source is gone. Or maybe *carry* a living energy.

"What are you sensing?" asks Walter flatly. Bless his heart. Even after all these investigations, all the uncanny shit I've pulled out of my ass, he still doesn't fully believe I can pick up ghosts or psychic energy. But he goes through the motions. Maybe someday I'll convince him.

"One sec," I say.

The energy is still clinging hard, but its grip is loosening. I know how to handle these jokers. This isn't my first rodeo with surges of psychic waves. I just need to "let it go" like Elsa says in *Frozen*. Let it go, and it will let go. I focus on my breath while Maya sits beside me. Walter goes about pacing around the stairwell to avoid the awkwardness. Finally, the energy releases and I let out a sigh of relief. It's still there, but now we have an understanding.

I pull my recorder from my side pocket and check that it is still on. It is so I turn off my flashlight.

"Who are you?" I ask. *"What is your business with this family and this house?"*

I sense nothing more in the darkness of the basement; nothing obvious in the darkness of my mind. I faintly see an image of a judge in my head, but it is vague and dull. It could be Judge Judy or an old-timey Revolutionary War era judge with a white curly wig, or even something out of one of those law dramas my husband likes to watch. *Law and Order. Matlock*, the old one or the reboot. *The Practice.* He has watched them all. The visual could also be symbolic of some sort of justice, but for that I would expect scales or the Statue of Liberty. This is an actual judge, which makes me think it's judgement more than justice. Something or someone is being judged, and this energy is not happy about it.

"Who in this house is being judged?"

I don't know whether this energy is being condemned or is doing the condemning, so I choose my question carefully to be open to either. After a few seconds, a toilet flushes from Alice's side of the duplex. The water pipes knock against the wood beams in the ceiling. I try to hold back, but I let slip a laugh that sounds more like a snort. I mark it. The timing is too perfect, and I need some comic relief. I don't think this energy is willing or able to give me any definite answers unless it is trying to tell me it is judging Alice's flushing technique. Or maybe the quality of her bowel movements.

I wait a few more minutes in silence.

"Whatever was here is now gone," I say. "Flushed away like Alice's evening contribution."

Maya laughs with her high-pitched giggle. I like that girl.

Walter says, "Take your time just to be sure. Once you're good, let's run some tests on these pipes."

He radios home base. *"Team One to Lighthouse. Did you hear any knocking just now? Over."*

"Affirmative. I logged it but assumed it was pipes as we could clearly hear the shitter flushing over on Alice's side."

"Copy that."

I am feeling more like my normal self, so I turn the flashlight back on and make my way down the stairs. I don't bother calling out "SHINY" because Maya's light is still on. My petite partner stays with me as we go down, holding my arm just in case. I doubt she could catch my substantial ass if I fell. I've got at least eight inches and fifty pounds (seventy-five?) on her, but I appreciate the effort. I take several deep breaths to clear my mind and put some protective energy around my consciousness. The pipe tests we are about to run are in the here and now, but I want to be prepared in case that rogue energy comes back.

Walter says, "Maya, if you don't mind staying here by the stairs, that way we've got three points of reference for capturing the audio."

He wants to knock on some of the machinery to see if we can recreate any of the reported sounds that Sue and Jo experienced— mainly banging, footsteps, and drums. Maybe some (or all) of that could be caused by the ductwork or pipes. We've already heard some evidence of the banging with Alice's bedtime BM. I hope she is a deep sleeper because this might get loud. If we can hear her pipes this well, it's a good bet she will hear our tests. Sue said she gave Alice fair warning, so I'm crossing my fingers that she doesn't get spooked when I knuckle "Shave and a Haircut—Two Bits" on the furnace duct.

Walter and I make our way to the front of the house where the furnaces, water heaters, and community washer/dryer are located. I briefly contemplate setting my recorder on top of the washer but decide instead to keep it in my hand. Any manipulation of ducts or pipes will vibrate down to the larger equipment and unnaturally affect the sound on the recording. I ask Walter to shine his IR light around so I can pinpoint where I am conducting the test from.

Walter calls up to Libbi. *"Team One to Lighthouse. We are about to start a series of tests on the pipes and ducts down here. Are you in a position where you can log what you hear from above—the time and what it sounds like from your position? We want to capture multiple perspectives. Over."*

"Copy that," says Libbi. *"One sec."*

There is a pause, and we can hear vague mumbling through the ceiling.

"Team One, do you want Stan to do the same? He is in the living room on the recliner. Over."

"Copy that, great idea, thank you. Give us another minute, and then we'll kick off. You might hear us talking down here as well since Dana will be trying to communicate. Over."

"Copy that."

After a couple of minutes, we are ready to start. Walter alerts the team, and I address any spirits who may be listening.

"Hello, my name is Dana, and I am calling out to anyone who might be around and would like to communicate. I am going to ask some questions. If the answer is yes, please knock once, like this."

I knock once on the pipe coming out of the water heater, checking it first to make sure it isn't hot.

"If the answer is no, then knock twice."

I repeat my own directions accordingly. The knocks coming from the water pipe—such as when Alice flushed the toilet—are loud but do not sound at all like a drum of any kind, at least not from down here. They are metallic and dull, with an almost ringing sound.

"Let me check and see if Libbi and Stan can hear this," says Walter softly.

"Team One to Lighthouse. We've begun our knocking test. Were you able to pick up anything? Over."

Libbi replies in the affirmative and confirms Stan heard the two sets of knocks as well, though they were not loud from the upstairs vantage point. We continue in the darkness. The traffic is nil outside, and inside it is eerily quiet. It's rare that we find ourselves in perfect silence. Even here in the basement, in the darkness with a demon possibly hiding in the shadows, there is still ambient noise. A click here and there from the house settling. Rustling of our clothing. Breath. But even with all of that, the stillness is powerful.

"Do you live in this house?" I ask. I pause to allow a response.

"Are you or were you human?"

"Can you see us?"

"Are you a man? Are you a woman? Are you a child?"

I hold my breath after each question and wait for the telltale prickling on the back of my neck, signaling the return of the piercing energy. I am prepared for it now; I've set up some stronger protection around me, but that doesn't mean it won't be intense if it hits again. I must consciously remind myself to relax. It's almost as hard preparing for a soul surge as it is facing one.

"Are there others with you right now?"

A rustling sound comes from Alice's side of the unit, near the toys.

"I think your friend is back, Bader," says Walter.

"She better stay over there," Maya responds. I smile in the darkness. I grew up on the streets of Baltimore, but I married a country boy. Rats and mice are regular visitors to our six-acre spread out in nowhere land known as Catawba, Virginia. The Mackenzies just need a cat.

"Do you exist somewhere outside of our world, like in another dimension or parallel universe?"

Tap, tap, tap. I hear three soft knocks that sound like they are coming from the smaller water heater pipes on Sue's side. Three isn't in the game. That doesn't help.

"Can you repeat that? Do you exist outside of our world?"

There is only silence. I ask a few more questions with no audible response on the water pipes.

"I'm going to try the air ducts now," I say. "They might be a little easier for a spirit to manipulate."

I repeat my directions to whatever might be out there, noting the time verbally so we can correlate with Libbi's and Stan's logs. I suspect the ducts will sound a lot louder and more booming than the pipes, and I am right. When I do my "yes" demo knock, I can feel it resonate through the darkness.

"Damn!" says Walter. "That sounds just like a bass drum."

"Exactly like it," I agree. "It's halftime at the homecoming game and the band is coming onto the field."

We may be onto something as an explanation for at least some of the drum sounds that Sue and Jo reported. I do my "no" knocks and close my eyes. The wave of sound is palpable. I have a theory, so I speak it into the recorder.

"Something to research: It's getting cold at night but still fairly warm during the day. It's likely the furnace is kicking in. Could there be some correlation between the warm air during the day and the furnace kicking on that might have caused the booming bass recently?"

"Ooh, great point," says Maya. "Also—SHINY—look at this duct over here."

She walks a few steps toward us and points her light up at the furnace duct where it crosses the ceiling and branches out to other rooms. There is a slotted vent on the side, about halfway between the stairs and the outside wall. No doubt this is intended for sending warm air into the basement. It's not the most efficient setup, especially if you don't spend much time down here, but if the vent is in good shape and closed, it isn't the worst I've ever seen. And I've seen plenty because my husband did HVAC repair and service for a decade before he started writing fetish novels for a living. Long story.

"Note the vent in the ceiling ductwork in the basement," says Walter into his handheld recorder. *"And it appears to be open."*

I follow his flashlight across the vent, stretching up to get a better look. I'm a hair taller than Walter (and I have two-inch heels on); the basement is roughly seven feet from floor-to-ceiling, if that. I have a pretty good view of the vent, and sure enough, it is wide open. They must have a hideous utility bill in the winter. But hey, at least it's toasty down here in the dungeon for the ten minutes a day they do laundry.

"Maya, your little friend could probably get inside there too," I say. "If there were a rat or mouse running around in there, it would definitely sound like a bass drum, or even multiple drums."

It was a solid theory. Unfortunately, short of removing the vent from the duct and shining a light inside, there wasn't any obvious way to confirm or deny this. Still, it *is* a theory and another potential explanation for events. We heard the scurrying of a critter. We see a vent on the side of the duct, conveniently open and creating the perfect entrance for a small animal. Two and two make four. Sometimes four is a demon, sometimes it's just a rodent's nest.

I continue with more questions and ask the spirits to manipulate the air ducts. In the twenty minutes it takes to get through all the questions with pauses between, we hear a rumbling sound twice. Both correspond with flashes of light through the old curtains on the front windows, and we positively identify them as vehicles passing by. We log both and move on.

Toward the end of the questionnaire, there is a loud boom and rumble, but we see no lights flashing. It does not sound like it comes from inside the basement, but more from upstairs or maybe outside.

BEEEEP!

I nearly soil my Lululemon knockoff leggings when both walkie-talkies go off full blast. Lucky for me, my intestines cooperate. Which they usually do, because I do not crap in strange people's houses or other public places unless it's an absolute emergency. Yes, I am one of those people.

"LIGHTHOUSE TO TEAM ONE," comes Libbi's voice like a tornado siren in the silence. *"Please note we have an Amazon truck delivering a package across the street. The moron does not have his lights on. He was pretty loud, just wanted you to be aware. Over."*

"Copy that," says Maya.

I slowly let out the breath I had been holding. I am more shaken by the walkie-talkie than anything else. Those things are loud as fuck, and I'm frankly a little surprised that my panties are still clean. Apparently, Walter felt the same.

"Turtle almost came out of the shell that time," he says.

I laugh. "Okay, what next?"

There are two additional events worth noting that happen as we get close to wrapping up Session One in the basement. At 10:17, the three of us are standing near the front of the house on the Mackenzie side when we hear a noise that sounds mechanical. It is coming from the other side of the room, but at first, we can't figure out from where. It is rhythmic and somewhat metallic, as if a gear is hitting against another gear. It sounds vaguely familiar, but I can't pinpoint the memory.

"What is that?" asks Maya.

Then it hits me.

"Is it one of the cameras?" I ask.

"Shit," says Walter. "I think it's the Blue-Lu."

"SHINY," I call out, and we both head toward the lounge area with flashlights blazing.

The closer we get to the nasty rug and bashed drum set, the louder the sound becomes. The other cameras are quiet, but the Blu-Lu1 is puking. I think it is trying to send an alert, but the camera is apparently older than dirt, so the tone is faded and sounds quasi-alien. Sure enough, when Walter checks the tiny screen on the camera, it is flashing the low battery signal. The other cameras are plugged into a power strip that Stan attached to one of the stairwell posts, but the Blu-Lu1 runs on batteries.

"Confirmed," Walter says. "It's the Blu-Lu1; needs new batteries."

"Good timing anyway," I say, looking down at my watch. "It's about time to take a break and prep for the next session, yes?"

"Right on target," says Walter.

The second thing that happens as we are wrapping up is that we hear a cat. Or, more accurately, we hear a cat *sound*. Walter is removing the Blu-Lu1 from the tripod for the battery refresh while Maya and I gather up the loose equipment and make final log notes. We all hear what sounds like a cat crying out. If I were to guess, I would say it comes from the top of Alice's stairs (behind the door), or just outside the front basement window on her side of the house. The meow is a little muffled, so I don't think it comes from the basement itself unless it is inside a box. We look around, up Alice's stairs, out the window, and behind some of the clutter, but we never find a cat, nor do we hear any more meowing for the rest of the night. Alice does not have any other pets besides the beagle (at least, as far as we have been told). For now, we chalk it up to a stray kitty or a catbird perched on the oak tree outside. Or something totally not cat-anything that just sounded like one.

We gather our devices and start heading up the stairs.

"Awesome session," I say to the others. "Now let's go get some chow!"

Excerpt 6 from the *RIP After Dark* Podcast
Episode 72: Case of the Demon Drums

This podcast was broadcast one year after the actual investigation.
Client names and identifying details have been changed to maintain privacy.

Libbi: *We have a question in the comments from listener @paranormalkween4815 asking about why we use the word "SHINY" instead of "FLASH" like a lot of other ghost hunting groups do.*

Walter: *A lot of the TV show investigators use "FLASH" as well.*

Libbi: *Yes, they do. Walter, you are the one who came up with this fancy alternative.*

Walter: *I guess I did, didn't I? Well, there was this show back in the early 2000s called* Firefly—

Libbi: *—which sadly only ran for one season—*

Walter: *A shame and a crime. Anyway, it was a sort of Western space series with a ragtag motley crew of the spaceship* Serenity *who took on various jobs in the galaxy.*

Libbi: *I think it was after some big war in the solar system or something like that.*

Walter: *Yep, and there were these creepy, flesh-eating people. Or things. The Reavers.*

Libbi: *The Reavers scared me.*

Walter: *They were horrifying. Anyway, they had some slang words in the series, one of which was "shiny"—used to describe something awesome, if memory serves.*

Libbi: *Like the RIP After Dark podcast: Shiny!*

Walter: *Facts. Well, one day on a practice investigation at a local cemetery, we were explaining to Junior—*

Libbi: *—that would be our team member Dana's son Ralph—*

Walter: *—I was explaining to Junior what Firefly was, and he was the one who started saying "SHINY!" whenever he turned on his flashlight. It just kind of stuck.*

Libbi: *Personally, I like it more than "FLASH." I always expect some guy to jump in front of the camera with his junk hanging out. You know, like a flasher.*

Walter: [sarcastically] *Oh. OH! "FLASH" like a flash-ER! I get it now! Thanks for explaining that.*

Libbi: *Ha ha. Maybe some of our listeners aren't familiar with the classic flasher. It kind of went out of style.*

Walter: *Just in case we haven't explained it, we call out something— whether "FLASH" or "SHINY" or "TURNING ON MY FLASHLIGHT" or whatever—to alert the other investigators and to note on our recordings that a bright light is forthcoming.*

Libbi: *Which could be a flashlight or a flash from a camera.*

Walter: *Either or. When we review the evidence, we'll know it's not a full-bodied apparition manifesting, but rather, just a normal illumination. We mark the event to rule it out, so to speak. And to alert the evidence reviewer that there might be a blinding light about to pop up.*

Libbi: *Thank you @paranormalkween4815 for that question. You know, I think what might surprise a lot of people is how many times during an* *investigation that we see, hear, smell, or feel things that we make note of.*

Walter: *Right... and how many of them are not evidence for the case.*

Libbi: *Yeah, they're mostly noted to rule out something paranormal. Sometimes to debunk.*

Walter: *Just in the hour and a half or so that we were in the basement, we heard delivery trucks, a cat—*

Libbi: *—which was probably a bird—*

Walter: *—rustling in the boxes, dripping, footsteps, knocking on the pipes, the water heater kicking on, and tons more.*

Libbi: *It is insane how much we keep track of.*

Walter: *Not to mention our own movements and sounds. I'm pretty sure I stumbled a few times trying to avoid that nasty rug.*

Libbi: [laughs] *We are not normally "shoes off in the house" people, but after that investigation, I think we both left ours in the garage when we got home.*

Walter: *I sprayed mine with enzyme cleaner the next day.*

Libbi: *Did you really? The stuff for dog urine?*

Walter: *Swear to Odin. I am one hundred percent certain I walked out of that place with Yorkie piss on my Skechers.*

Libbi: [gags audibly] *Ew. I didn't even go down there. I could smell pee a little when I was upstairs monitoring.*

Walter: *You do possess an uncanny sense of smell.*

Libbi: *It's a blessing and a curse. So, without giving away the whole thing yet, what would you say was the most memorable experience of Session One?*

Walter: *Hmmm. I guess I would have to say it was when Dana had her episode on the stairs.*

Libbi: [chuckling] *Her "episode?" Is that what we're calling it?*

Walter: *Well, what would you call it?*

Libbi: *I mean, maybe her psychic event? "Episode" sounds like she got a case of the vapors or had a seizure.*

Walter: *It was kind of like that, if I'm being honest.*

Libbi: *Okay, fair enough. So, Dana was coming down the stairs after changing the batteries on one of her devices when she had an "episode" (I'm using air quotes) where she said it felt like a psychic migraine.*

Walter: *Yeah, it was pretty fierce, from what I witnessed. She was doubled over. Maya had to go up and assist.*

Libbi: *And this "episode" is even more intriguing considering later events and the evidence we found. But I don't want to get ahead of myself.*

Walter: *All in good time.*

Libbi: *Precisely. And we will get to that, good listeners. I promise. We appreciate your patience.*

Bedroom Secrets

Saturday, October 5, 10:45-11:50 pm
Investigation, Session Two (Josephine's bedroom)
Mackenzie Residence, Starry Knob Lane, Roanoke, Virginia
Team Two: Dana, Libbi, Stan

Josephine's Bedroom, Session Two

Front of House

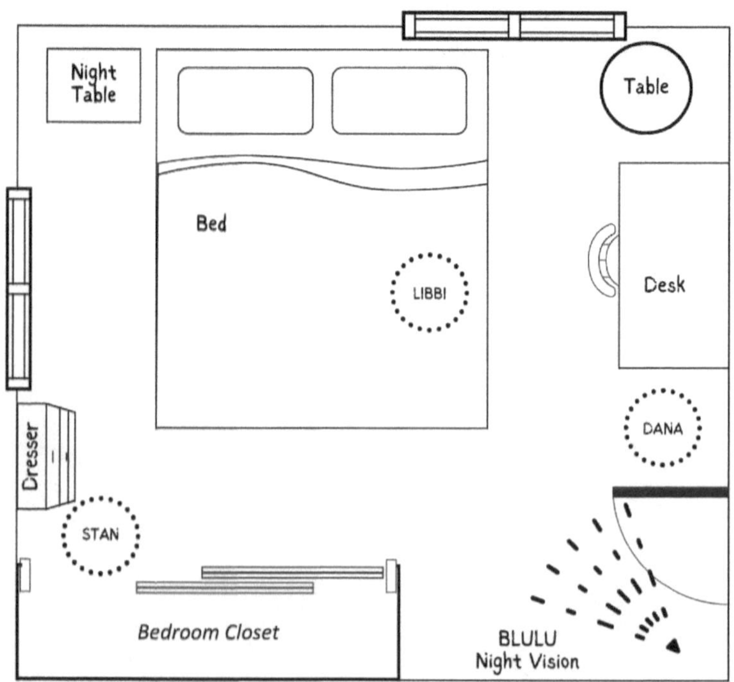

Stan Katagucci

Break time!

I've been sitting in that smelly recliner for the last hour and a half. When Dana, Walter, and Maya come upstairs, I make a quick trip to the bathroom, which is the only room in the house that smells relatively fresh. Ironic, don't you think? When I get back, I pull out a plastic bag from my equipment case—summer sausage from a deer hunt last fall, and smoked cheddar from The Cheese Shop in Stuart's Draft. The Amish sure know how to do cheese right. I cut off slices of sausage and cheese with my pocketknife and stack onto Triscuits, washing down my redneck hors d'oeuvres with some good old American Lipton tea (should have put it in the fridge, but it's still good even at room temperature). No one else is interested in a hearty snack, so I leave them to their chips and candy and Diet Coke. We eat between sessions because all food will be wrapped up and stashed before we start the next phase of the investigation. We don't want the microphones to catch the crackle of Walter dipping into his extra-dark pretzel bag.

At 10:45, everyone takes their last bites and toilet breaks. Maya cleans up the crumbs as Walter takes his place at the Lighthouse command center. Dana, Libbi, and I head into the second bedroom (where the daughter sleeps) to start a new EVP session. Libbi sits on the edge of the bed while Dana and I stand. Dana is near the door, which is closed. I am standing by the exterior side wall, wedged into a corner between the closet and a dresser. There are shades on both windows, and sheer curtains, but some of the outside street lighting from down the road seeps in, so it is not pure dark. I'm not sure why investigations always take place at night anyway, other than there are fewer distracting activities in the environment. But a lot of reported events take place in daylight, so it's just as likely we'll catch something at noon as at midnight.

The plan for this session has two parts: the EVP session and Dana's spirit communication. I will lead the EVP questionnaire. I plan on following the standard list, but I will also ask a few questions of my own. Lib and Walter aren't fans of provoking, but in this case, I think it's worth a shot. Based on my history with the paranormal, I have concluded that angry spirits respond more to an authoritative tone than to touchy-feely statements. When a dog is reactive, sometimes you have to jerk the leash to break them out of it. The same is true for ghosts and other supernatural entities. Docile spirits do well with neutral questions. The aggressive ones just find it silly, so provoking works better.

For the second part of the session, Dana will attempt to communicate with the afterlife or other paranormal energies. She felt something on the stairway earlier. I hope she has the same luck in this room (and later, when we have our seance with the client). I'm still confident that the seance will happen. Sue seemed pretty geeked about the idea.

Dana wants a few minutes to get herself centered before we start, just in case she senses anything during the EVP session. Libbi and I wait in silence after we check our devices and prepare to record. About thirty seconds into our quiet time, there comes a wretched sound from behind the door. It sounds like a violent, demonic puke.

"Apologies from Lighthouse," comes Walter's voice on the walkie-talkie. The bedroom isn't far from the kitchen, so we hear his muffled real voice simultaneously through the door. *"That was the Diet Coke talking."*

I can't see her very well in the darkness, but I am sure Libbi is shaking her head in mock disgust. I say "mock" because for years her favorite prank has been to let out a silent garlic burp after eating Chinese food and then blow it secretly at the person nearest to her. I know this to be fact, as I have occasionally been nearest. It's disgusting.

"Are you kidding me right now?" she says flatly into the walkie-talkie. *"Be professional, Walter. You fucking swine."*

I hear Walter and Maya giggling from the other room. I'm slightly annoyed because these investigations are serious matters. But they can also be heavy sometimes. If you don't have some fun and break the tension of constantly being on alert, tempers will fly. Admittedly, it was an impressive burp. I hope Libbi remembers to cut this from the evidence files, or at least the part where she said the F-word. I'm not sure Sue will appreciate it.

We get back to our silence. I feel a bit of a cold draft and note it aloud while I look around.

"SHINY—*side window has a slight gap at the top of the window, and there is a noticeable cold spot in this area. Temperature near the interior door is—"* I point and click my thermometer. *"—65 degrees Fahrenheit, while at the window gap it is 57 degrees."*

It is getting colder at night as the daylight hours shrink. The weather report says the temperature will get down to 49°F/9°C. That's a little below average for Roanoke, but we typically get some crazy fluctuations this time of year. Fall and spring are especially unpredictable, and I often run both my furnace and central air in the same twenty-four-hour period. Days can still be comfortably warm, but once the sun goes down, it doesn't take long for the chill to settle in. This window gap might explain cold spots. I'm not a huge believer in cold spots as representations of spirits manifesting into the physical world. I guess it can happen, but there are so many logical explanations for temperature variations. People might be surprised at how obvious the source of their mysterious draft is, and yet the obvious gets overlooked all the time.

Something else that often gets overlooked and not reported are smells. People brush off a strange odor, thinking they are imagining it or assuming it comes from something nearby. Smells are actually very common in hauntings. Some of our clients have reported recognizing the perfume of a long-dead loved one, or the cigar of a former resident of a house who was known to indulge in the occasional stogie. Smells of rot are also very common in demonic possessions.

And right now, something rotten is hitting my nose. It is faint, but still detectable. It smells vaguely like roadkill or a decaying deer that died out in the woods. I've come across a few of those in my day.

"Does anyone smell that?" I say, without revealing what scent has come into my nostrils.

Libbi notices nothing from her perch on the bed. I hear Dana sniff a few times.

"I got nothing over here. Hold on, I'll come over." I see her shadow come toward me, and she leans forward. "Wait. Yes. It's very faint. Smells like maybe someone didn't flush. Or Walter's been in here."

"This isn't someone sharting," I say. "It's more like rotting flesh."

See? Everyone dismisses odors.

"SHINY."

I point my flashlight toward the closet, which has two sliding doors, one of which—the one nearest to me toward the exterior wall—is half open. I take a step toward the side that is closed. The smell almost disappears. I walk back to the open side. It is noticeably stronger. What *is* that? I open the sliding door fully to look a little deeper. I probably shouldn't. It doesn't feel right to be snooping in a teenage girl's personal space, but sometimes we need to get into the discomfort zone. The back wall of the closet abuts the only bathroom in the house, and I wonder if it might be a toilet issue, as Dana suggested. Leaky sewage, perhaps. But the toilet is on the opposite side of the bathroom. The tub/shower is on this side, and there wouldn't be any sewage or unflushed turd stink this far over. I assume the tub would provide some sort of buffer.

Libbi, still on the bed, points her light in my direction. "Stan, what the hell are you doing?"

Of course she doesn't approve, and in this case, I get it. Rustling through a teenage girl's closet comes close to crossing a line. But in the interest of uncovering evidence, I feel it is warranted.

"I'm not going to steal her diary, sheesh. Hold on, this will just take a second."

The closet is quite... um... *busy,* so I try not to disturb anything. But the smell is most definitely coming from somewhere inside. I squat down, sensing that the source is toward the ground. There is a massive pile of dirty clothes on the closet floor, and an old plastic dresser on the side wall that appears to be filled with papers and books. I gently push some of the dirty clothes aside so I can see what is behind them next to the dresser. Nestled in the back corner, I find a medium-sized metallic trash bin, about two feet high. The smell is stronger now. I don't want to open this bin, but the curiosity is overpowering me. I point the flashlight and lift the lid.

"OH SHIT," I yell, pushing the dirty clothing back in front of the bin and jumping out of the closet. I almost fall backward as I stand up but catch myself on the bed. I sit on the edge of the mattress and drop my still-lit flashlight onto the blanket.

Libbi stands up. "What is it?"

I dry heave a few times. It wasn't a severed head or anything like that. I almost wish it were.

"Ugh," I say. I stand up and walk toward the front window so I can get as far away from the closet as I can. "There's a bin back there, behind that little plastic dresser. It's full of... *women's products. Used* women's products. You know—pads and tampons, I think. Bloody, very bloody. It's not lined with a trash bag or anything, just thrown in there. There might have been shit in there too; I couldn't tell. It was just a mass of used period stuff."

I dry heave again. I can put up with a lot. If it *had* been a severed head, I think I would have been okay. But personal monthly aftermath? Nope. I don't know how women deal with it; that is why they are truly the strong ones. I don't even want to imagine why a teenage girl would hide all that stuff back there. Because it seemed like it was hidden. My ex-girlfriend put her stuff in the *lined* trash can in my bathroom, wrapped about a hundred times in toilet paper. And it got thrown out every few days. The items in Jo's bedroom seemed like many months' worth of menstruation.

"What are you talking about, Gooch?" says Dana. She says it like she's irritated with me; like I'm some sort of idiot. She goes over to the closet and turns on her flashlight. "SHINY."

She rustles around for a minute, saying absolutely nothing. As a nurse, she's used to seeing such carnage. A minute later she emerges.

"Okay, that is weird. He's right. There is a trash can full of used tampons and pads in there. Dozens, and borderline hemorrhage by the looks of them. That is for sure where the smell is coming from."

She shuts the closet door as I pull a bottle of hand sanitizer from my pocket and squeeze a large drop onto my knuckles. It's ironic that I can shoot and fully dress a deer with my bare hands but need to sterilize myself after being in the vicinity of period aftermath. I fully admit that it makes no sense. Yet here I am.

Dana continues, "I don't know if this makes a difference, but all these clothes piled up in here (which are also a little rank, if I'm being honest) are very feminine. Skirts, dresses, blouses…"

Libbi says, "Okay, we will note that, but let's not include it in the final report or mention it in front of everyone. I'll say something to Sue privately. I don't want to embarrass Jo or get her in trouble. We know of at least one source of the rotten smell they reported; let's leave it at that for now."

This is all very weird, and I am a little thrown. But it's time to get it together and do my EVP.

I grab my flashlight and position myself on the other side of the dresser as I pull a small moleskin notebook from my shirt pocket. Maya, Dana, and Libbi don't use a cheat sheet, but Walter and I do. Must be a guy thing, although I think my memory is pretty good. I have the full set of core questions, plus a few extras that I want to test out tonight.

I switch my light to IR and begin talking directly to the afterlife. *"Addressing any spirits that may be around tonight, any ghosts or disembodied souls, demons, poltergeists, vengeful spirits—"*

"Stanley." This is Libbi's soft warning, which I can't say I didn't expect.

"—and any other beings out there who can hear me. We have been invited into this home by the owner, and we mean you no harm."

But I will get a priest in here posthaste to banish you if you harm this family, I silently promise. I have never done an actual exorcism, but I've witnessed a few dozen performed by an investigation team I was with about ten years ago. Libbi and Walter are staunchly anti-exorcism. And I can sort of see why. A few of the ones I attended seemed more like cases of mental illness than demonic possession. Even the head of that team said as much at a ghost hunting presentation he held at the local library one year. *"Demonic possession can mimic mental illness."* Those were his exact words. Goes both ways, right? Mental illness can mimic demonic possession. Several of the cases we worked *were* legit. My only problem was that one of the team founders—this guy Vince, who was admittedly a little creepy—performed the exorcisms himself. He got his "ordainment" online, but I think it was just a certificate that allowed him to perform wedding ceremonies. There's no way he went through a formal study program at an accredited religious university or organization. He was terrible at exorcisms, and nowadays, I firmly believe that only Catholic priests or other qualified persons should perform these rituals. Not wannabes.

I am about a dozen questions in when Libbi's walkie-talkie goes off after I ask, *"Are you aware of other people living here?"*

We all pause. *"Is that you?"* I ask, and the walkie blips again.

I wait a few seconds. *"Are you angry because you have to share your home?"*

The walkie-talkie beeps loudly again. I wait almost a full minute, but it stays silent.

"One sec, Stan," Libbi says, then calls to Lighthouse. *"Team Two to Lighthouse. Did your walkie-talkie blip about a minute ago? Over."*

"Negative, no blips. I heard it a little through the door, but my unit did not go off. You still on channel 13? Over."

Libbi checks. *"Yep, still on channel 13. Okay, thank you. Over."*

It is not unusual to get occasional rogue sounds on the walkie-talkies. More than once, we've had someone completely unrelated to us talking on our designated channel (which required us to switch). If all our units are set to the same frequency, then a blip should register on all of them. Sometimes when we have more than one device in a large room, we'll get an echo effect. The fact that Walter's walkie-talkie did not make a sound is curious. We decide to continue.

"Can you see me?" Then, a moment later, I ask: *"Are there others with you?"*

Both times there is nothing. We chalk up the earlier blips to something atmospheric or unexplainable (for now). Perhaps something will come out in the evidence review. We continue through most of the basic questions without experiencing any more anomalies or sounds.

Then I ask, *"Do you mean us any harm?"*

The walkie-talkie beeps loudly and turns on as if someone is talking. The static in the background is loud, but it almost sounds like a voice on the other end. I can almost make out—

"What the hell?" asks Dana in the darkness.

"SHHHH!" Dana should know better than to interrupt what could be an important EVP. She might be pissed at me later for shushing her, but I don't care. We need to maintain the integrity of the evidence!

The static continues for a few seconds, then stops. I slowly let out my breath.

"If that was you, make the walkie—"

The device beeps again as if someone is talking, but this time it goes right back to silence like before.

"Try again," I say with increased intensity. If this thing wants to communicate, then we are going to figure out how to listen. But my demand is met only with silence. I'm getting angry.

"SHOW YOURSELF!" I say forcefully. *"You COWARD!"*

"STAN!"

Oh shit, I've done it now.

Libbi Bean

"Jesus! We have talked about provoking!"

I feel like I'm scolding a toddler sometimes with Stan. If Walter were in here instead of me, he would be calmer, quieter, and he would escort Stan out of the room, stat. I will give my stepbrother one more chance, but my fuse is short right now. We have a zero tolerance for provoking, and he knows it. If this happens again, he's going home, and his seance is cancelled.

Stan does not answer, but that's his strategy. When he gets put in timeout, he clams up. More like man-baby pouting if you ask me. But I don't have time for this now. I need to focus on the investigation.

"Team Two to Lighthouse," I say into the same walkie-talkie that just a few minutes ago went berserk.

"What's up?" Ah, the soothing voice of my one and only. *"Sounded like an elephant trumpet in there. Over."*

I smile in the dark. Walter and I have a secret code for Stan. He is "the elephant in the room" (or if we've exhausted elephant references, we use some other obvious zoo animal). Walter's comment really means *What the fuck did Stan do this time?*

"That's exactly what it was," I say, knowing he will get the reference. *"Did you get any calls or beeps on the walkie?"*

"Negative again. Not a sound."

"Anything else you noticed in the past five minutes? Lights, sounds, drums?"

"Not a thing. It has been very quiet out here. Other than Maya's snoring."

I imagine Maya is rolling her eyes.

"Ha, copy that," I say. *"Okay, thanks. We are good. Dana is going to do her thing now. Over."*

"Sounds good, over," he says, and we are back to regrouping in the bedroom.

Stan is in pouty silence as Dana inhales a few times to get herself into receiving mode. I am sitting on the bed and can hear her breathing deeply from above. I'm on the tall side at nearly five feet seven inches, and she's got at least a few inches (maybe four) on me. She's built like a mythical Amazon—muscular and lean—with dark skin and thick, curly hair. In contrast, I'm chubby, pasty (got that Eastern European skin), and my hair only curls with chemicals or heat. She and Maya got the skinny genes, but I got the biggest boobs. Not that it's a competition. I love them both, tits aside.

Dana is still standing near the bedroom door.

"I am here to help communicate," she says, addressing the darkness. *"My name is Dana, and I come in peace. I can sense things that others can't. I may be able to hear what you say. Use me as your vessel and tell us your story."*

I could be imagining it, but it feels like the room is getting thick, like the pressure is increasing. My ears are plugging up.

"There is something here, in this room," Dana says quietly to us. She takes a deep breath and lets it out audibly.

"I feel you," Dana says. *"I feel your pain and your sadness."*

She sniffles a few times. It is not uncommon for Dana to cry while she is communicating with whatever it is she communicates with. She is a true sensitive, which means she picks up emotions, energy, and symbolic communications. I want to ask her if she's okay, but I don't want to interrupt the flow. I say nothing and respect the fact that Dana will speak out if she needs any intervention.

"There is an energy here," she says. "I don't know if it's the same thing that hit me in the basement. It feels different. The first one seemed like something associated with the house, tied to everyone living here or maybe the area. This one is singular. And it is a sad energy, like it's in despair."

I take the opportunity. "Are you good to keep going?"

"Yes," she responds. "I'm fine. Just feeling this deep sadness. I'm going to blow my nose now."

We hear a shuffle as she pulls a tissue from her pocket and then a deep snort as she clears her nasal passages. Stan is still standing by the window, no doubt listening carefully in case Dana's energy even remotely resembles an evil spirit. And I have my third eye on him, ready to haul his provoking ass out if he so much as sputters.

"I know your pain is deep," Dana continues. *"I am here to help you. What can I do to help you ease this sadness?"*

A wind suddenly kicks up outside, and we hear it whistle through the gap at the top of the side window. The room gets a little colder. As Dana sniffles, I point my thermometer around the room. There are no fluctuations that blow my mind, but I do register a slight drop in temperature. The timing is uncanny. I shudder, partly from the cold and partly from the energy that seems to have entered the room.

"Something is hurting itself," Dana says. "Physically hurting itself. To numb the pain."

I have never heard of a spirit hurting itself, and since it has no physical body, it would have to be a remnant of something it did when it was living. Or (and this is fast becoming my prevailing theory) this isn't a ghost energy. It's a living energy. A chill runs through my entire body. Maybe Stan was right. Maybe this energy comes from the person who inhabits this very room—the teenage girl who seems to be having an identity crisis of some sort. She might not be getting the support she needs, at least not from those closest to her. The more I think about it, the more I am convinced we are onto something. Dana is a psychic who picks up energy, and sometimes that energy comes from a living person. If my theory is right, then we might be dealing with someone who is genuinely in pain, who might need help outside a paranormal investigation team.

"Dana, can you tell if this is a spirit energy, or something else… like, human?"

"I don't know. It feels more like an energy of something alive, but…"

She trails off. I give her a minute to absorb it all. I think she is going to come to the same conclusion, but I want it to be hers. No influence. I want her to feel what she feels and figure it out.

Dana is sobbing now. "Whoever this is, they are in deep depression although hiding it well. They are physically hurting themselves— cutting, I think. I keep getting upper leg, like the thigh or hip. And they have thought about taking their own life."

Holy fuck. A suicidal energy. I hope this *is* spirit energy and not Jo.

"We are here for you," says Dana through her plugged nose. *"Whatever you are going through, there is hope. We can help you; we can find someone to help you. You are not alone!"*

The wind is gusting now, like there's a storm coming, except that it was totally clear when we got here and no bad weather is predicted. Sometimes investigations are boring. Sometimes they are freaky. I thought this one was going to be dry and dull, but now I'm feeling anticipation and fear. Not fear of a demon (I'll leave that to Sue). But fear for this force that feels so alone.

"It's not your fault," says Dana quietly. *"It's not your fault, and there is nothing wrong with you. You don't need those. Don't give up."*

I wonder what "those" means. Dana sounds weary, which usually means it's almost over. She blows her nose again and marks it for the microphone. The wind is dying down, and the air is back to normal. The thickness I felt earlier is dissipating, like someone opened the release valve on a pressure cooker.

"It's gone." Dana takes a deep breath. "I don't think it's a spirit. I think it's something generated from the mom or the daughter, or maybe from the conflict between them. Possibly influenced or carried by a leftover force in this house."

She is mirroring my thoughts perfectly, although it had not occurred to me that this could be Sue. Sue, who adorns herself with crosses and has multiple Jesus pictures around the house; who smokes dope to dull some sort of pain and puts out her butts in a cross-shaped ashtray; who is super-religious, conservative, and with a daughter who maybe doesn't want to be a daughter. Or at least doesn't fall into the traditional Christian notion of gender or sexual roles.

"Is she—he, they—in danger?" I ask, not sure which one I'm talking about.

Dana sighs.

"Not imminent," she says. "I kept seeing a bottle of sleeping pills. Someone had an emotional breakdown and wanted those sleeping pills just in case. They knew exactly where the bottle was; they had seen it a hundred times! But when they went looking, they were gone. Whoever this is, they might not have swallowed them. Yet. They wanted to have them just in case. But they couldn't find them."

My logical mind says it's more likely the daughter goes looking for suicide meds rather than the mother. I don't know if over-the-counter sleep aids can kill you, but prescription meds certainly can. And if anyone is going to have a prescription to help them sleep, it's Sue. It just makes sense. Add to that the hidden feminine products in the closet and all the girly clothes piled up in there, and a picture emerges. It could represent shame. Sue doesn't strike me as the type to kill herself, although I'm sure there are many people who have said that about loved ones who have committed suicide. Sue just seems angry and determined to fight whatever comes her way. But if I'm being honest, what little I have seen of Jo doesn't scream suicidal either. She appears passive (other than her outburst over the drums). But if she is realizing a gender or sexual identity, she may be receiving unwanted reactions from her mother and even bullying from others. Things could be escalating.

If (and right now it's a big if) we are talking about Jo thinking about suicide, then where would the pills be, and why couldn't she find them? Did her mom suspect? Did the pills belong to someone else, like maybe the brother or Jo's dad? Is there another energy here influencing any of this? There are many unanswered questions, and at this point it is all speculation.

"Okay," I say. "We have a lot to think about. Before we wrap up, I want to note a few things. You guys tell me if you experienced any of this."

I pull up my recorder.

"At approximately 11:35, as Dana was starting her session to communicate with spiritual energies in the house, I noticed two things. First, the pressure in the bedroom increased noticeably. I could feel it in my sinuses."

I address the room. "Did either of you notice that?"

Stan says maybe. Dana confirms she felt it too. "I thought it was just me, the normal 'ghosts in my head' thing."

"Nope. I felt it too." I lift my recorder. *"Okay, so we confirmed that all three of us noticed a pressure change in the bedroom around 11:35 PM. Dana and Libbi for sure; Stan is a maybe. Second, the wind picked up just as Dana was communicating with this energy. I heard it whistle through the gap in the side window, at the top.* Anyone else?"

"I heard it," said Stan, which would make sense as he was closest.

"I didn't notice anything, but I was a little preoccupied," says Dana with a chuckle.

"Note, Stan and Libbi both heard the wind pick up and whistle. This would be approximately 11:37 or 11:38 pm."

I'm suddenly in need of a break from the activity, so I gather up my devices.

"I think we're done here," I say.

I follow Stan and Dana out and close the door behind me, leaving the lights off and the Blu-Lu2 camera running. We head out to the kitchen to reconvene and wait for Sue and Jo to return. It is now approaching midnight, and I need a drink. A shot of Jägermeister would be nice, but I'll have to settle for some caffeine. I have a feeling I'm going to need it.

Excerpt 7 from the *RIP After Dark* Podcast
Episode 72: Case of the Demon Drums

This podcast was broadcast one year after the actual investigation.
Client names and identifying details have been changed to maintain privacy.

Walter: *Here's an interesting question from @metssuckk68 (and as a Mets fan myself, I can't disagree): "Why are you against provoking spirits? They do it on the TV shows all the time."*

Libbi: *Well, @metssuckk68, they also do fake shit on TV shows all the time.*

Walter: *Good point. We don't provoke (there are exceptions, of course) because we don't want to piss off the ghosts. Our goal is to communicate and to understand and maybe get rid of any spirits that might be present. Not to anger them.*

Libbi: *I mean, imagine a case where there was a sentient spirit haunting a house, probably with frightened homeowners (and maybe even children) living there. Asshole people can die and become ghosts too. Theoretically.*

Walter: *So, in case we are dealing with a ghost who is an asshole, we don't want to increase the possibility that they'll become more of an asshole and magnify the intensity or frequency of their activity.*

Libbi: *Yeah, we're trying to get them to go away or at least live in peace with the living, not throw a temper tantrum.*

Walter: *And we* have *provoked before, but only in extreme cases and with the homeowner's permission.*

Libbi: *Hope that answers your question @metssuckk68. Another comment from @bxren1975field: "What sense are most reported events attributed to (smell, touch, sight, taste, hearing)?" Ooh, good question! Walter, what do you think, based on your experience?*

Walter: *I would say, smell. Almost every case has a smell element. Our clients have reported smelling flowers (where there are no flowers), perfume, pipe smoke, all kinds of things. Urine, feces (as in this case).*

Libbi: *I would agree with that. I think most people assume it's sight, but that just isn't the case. I would put smell and sound both above visual evidence.*

Walter: *Again, both very much at the forefront of Case of the Demon Drums. Like in the daughter's bedroom closet.*

Libbi: *Nope, we're not going there.*

Walter: *You're right, and I really don't want to go there anyway. Sorry, audience, but occasionally we must withhold details that are too personal.*

Libbi: *I can reveal one thing about the closet that was interesting.*

Walter: *I'm afraid to ask.*

Libbi: *There were piles—big ones—of dirty clothes, which had been there a while, from the looks of it. Dana and I both noticed (and we talked about this later) that they were all girly clothes. Skirts, feminine blouses, at least one dress. Not at all like the sporty stuff the daughter wore all the time.*

Walter: *Why is that significant? Help me understand the context. I honestly don't remember.*

Libbi: *Well, it all seemed like fancy clothes that someone would wear to church. Maybe the daughter shoved all that girly stuff in the closet so she could say, "I don't have a thing to wear!" on Sunday. Or maybe just because it was feminine.*

Walter: *I think I see where you're going with this. You think she was hiding her good clothes to avoid church?*

Libbi: *It's all speculation. But if I'm being honest, I think she was hiding her feminine clothes to avoid her femininity.*

Walter: *Ah.*

Libbi: *Just a theory. And how the daughter dressed was a source of conflict between her and Nancy. How that played into the demons and events, well, we'll get to that. But the conflict was there.*

Walter: *Out of my range of emotional intelligence, but I'll trust your instincts.*

Libbi: *Speaking of instincts, we had a second psychic event—*

Walter: *—episode—*

Libbi: *—psychic event during the bedroom session. Dana again felt something, and I'm telling you, I could feel the room getting thicker right before it happened.*

Walter: *Look, no argument from me. I was skeptical of her abilities at first, but Dana is the real deal. She has freaked the shit out of me on more than one occasion.*

Libbi: *Truth. And I'll just tease our listeners with this: Inside Dana's head wasn't the only place where this psychic energy was captured.*

Walter: *To be revealed shortly.*

Libbi: *It's so good! I can hardly wait. In the meantime, we have a couple more comments. From @alanabanana83: "Love your podcast and banter! Don't stop!" Aw, thank you @alanabanana83!*

Walter: *Can you imagine doing Alanabanana with "The Name Game" song?*

Libbi: [chuckles] *Let's try: "Alanabanana bobalanabanana bananafana fofalanabanana—"*

Walter: *Sorry I asked.*

Libbi: *That's it. I'm out. Can't do it.*

Walter: *We appreciate the feedback, @alanabanana83. And from @JoleneJolene—*

Libbi: [singing] *"Jolene, Jolene, Jolene, Jo-leeeene!"*

Walter: *Okay. From @JoleneJolene please don't take my demon Jolene: "Is it possible that the walkie-talkie blips in Session Two were really just more of Walter's burps being picked up?"*

Libbi: [laughs] *YES, @JoleneJolene! Spot on! In fact, it might have been an aftershock from the original earth-shaking belch that caused the beeps.*

Walter: *I guess I deserved that. Let's move on. We saved the best session for last.*

Say What? Seance!

Sunday, October 5, midnight-1:30 am
Investigation, Session Three (seance, living room)
Mackenzie Residence, Starry Knob Lane, Roanoke, Virginia
RIP Team, Sue Mackenzie, Jo Mackenzie, Gina Baymont, Pepper, and Tinker

The Mackenzie House Main Living Area, Session Three (Seance)

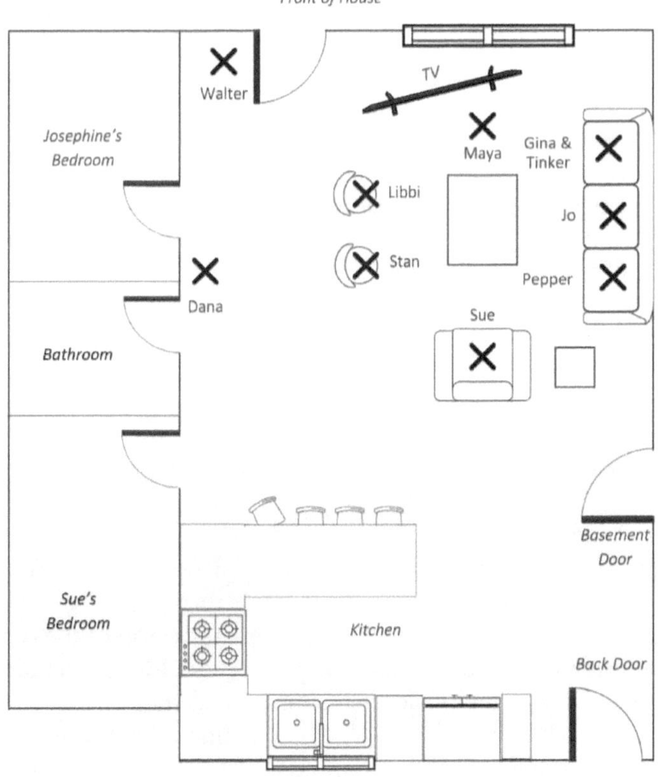

Walter Bean

Libbi fills us in on the events in the bedroom. Neither Maya nor I noticed any pressure change out in the living room or kitchen. Nor did we notice any wind kick up, but this house is up on a hill, so it's likely they have frequent gusts. Libbi doesn't elaborate on any theories about what Dana experienced, but Maya asks if we think the energy is generated (or lingering) from Jo. No one will rule it out. Even though Jo isn't here, it could be a remnant or recording of her energy. We know that all kinds of materials—natural and human-made—can record things in the physical world. Hell, I even heard about a guy who recorded his voice on a potato chip bag once. I guess anything is possible.

As we talk, Dana heads downstairs to look at something in the basement. The rest of us do battery checks, memory checks on our recorders, and get our equipment organized. We are also cleaning up to prepare for the arrival of Sue and the gang. We don't want them walking into the aftermath of a fraternity party, so we grab a quick snack and pack everything else up, including any excess equipment that we won't need for Session Three. Cameras are rolling downstairs and in the bedroom in case we catch anything while we do the client EVP session up here in the living room. Or I guess we're officially calling it *The Seance* now. I am still not happy about that. We have done them a few times, despite my protests. I think they are a waste of time and done more for show than anything else. We are not showy investigators, but just like with the Mackenzie case, our other clients latched onto the idea because they saw something in a movie once. It's ridiculous. If a spirit is going to channel through a human for whatever reason, do we need people to sit around holding hands in a candlelit room for them to do so? Unfortunately for me, the seed was planted (thanks, Stan) and now it looks like we'll have to go through the motions.

It is about ten minutes after midnight when Gina's van pulls into the driveway. The lights make all kinds of shadows around the room as the vehicle turns the corner. Something to note, maybe. There is muffled chatter and barking as the van stops at the top of the driveway and the headlights go out. Chatter is putting it mildly. It sounds more like arguing, with Gina's Cujo-lite chiming in on the chorus. They take forever to finally get to the door, which is fine by me. Every minute they spend out there is another minute my blood pressure stays within a normal range.

Finally, the front door opens and Sue walks in first, holding an exhausted Pepper. But when isn't Pepper exhausted? Only when he's shitting in the basement, apparently. Sue appears impatient and angry and is babbling about something. Jo follows, and she looks terrible, like she just got pulled unwillingly from a hardcore rave. Her face screams, *"I am miserable!"* and I wonder what she consumed (and how much) to make her eyes so red and bloodshot. She looks like a fifty-year-old.

Libbi mumbles under her breath, "Oh, shit, she looks like she's been crying."

Ah, that makes more sense. I am the logical half of our wonderful marriage. Libbi is the emotional intelligence queen, and in this case—given Sue's demeanor storming into the house—I think my wife is right. There was probably a big fight going on before they arrived. Jo's hair looks disheveled, as if she just got out of bed. Or at least, I assume that's what bedhead looks like. Having almost nothing on top and the sides nearly shaved, I cannot relate.

Gina follows the Mackenzies through the front door, tossing her cigarette into outdoor oblivion before stepping inside with Tinker in her arms. Tinker seems more pissed off than Sue and starts barking again as soon as he sees us all standing around the kitchen counter. I bite my tongue to keep from rolling my eyes and letting my annoyance show. Was it necessary to bring the yippy dog? Really, Gina? When it's critical to have as little external noise as possible? Sue puts Pepper on the couch, and he immediately curls up in the same corner where he had been napping during the initial interview. I think Pepper is too old to care about the energy in the house, living or otherwise. Sue tosses her big leather shoulder bag on the floor next to the TV and assumes her position on the recliner. No surprise there.

"Did you find anything?" she asks.

Stan takes his opportunity and jumps in with, "There is something in the bed—"

"We had some interesting experiences," I interject. "We are all eager to see what we caught on the recordings."

I cut Stan off before he broadcasts any premature assumptions. We often experience something during an investigation only to find a logical explanation when we review the audio and video recordings. And vice versa. Stan knows this. He just can't keep his mouth shut; it's like working with a toddler.

Gina sits on the couch at the end opposite from Pepper, nearest the front window, and crosses her right leg over her left. Tinker is still in her arms, now settling into her lap. He has stopped barking (for now;

no doubt we will hear his obnoxious opera again before the night is over) but still growls every few seconds. I don't think he likes Pepper, and he fancies himself king of the Mackenzie castle. At least his snarl is low enough in volume and frequency to be tolerable, certainly better than his ear-piercing bark. But it is still noise. I'm basically chalking this living room seance session up as a debacle. There are too many people (and canines) for a clean investigation. Gina is bouncing her right leg, Tinker is getting all protective with the growling, and Pepper will be snoring shortly. That's all going to get picked up on the microphones.

Jo heads toward her bedroom.

"Be careful in there," I say. "We still have a camera set up."

Jo says nothing and goes into the bathroom instead.

"So, are we gonna have a seance or what?" says Gina. She acts like she's going to Disneyland, but somehow still radiates cast-iron bitch. It's a strange dichotomy.

"I think we should," says Stan. *Of course you would.*

"Let's do it," says Sue. "I'm ready to get in touch with this son of a bitch and see what the hell he wants."

I look at my wife sideways. She shrugs. *Do we have a choice?*

"Lighthouse to Dana," I call on the walkie-talkie. *"We have the client up here and are getting ready to start EVP and the… seance."* I say it with a sigh— like it's a dirty word—with an undertone of dry heaves.

"Copy that. I'll be up in a few, just one more thing I'm going to check."

During our last break, Dana, Libbi, Maya, and I discussed a quick test to run in the basement. Just a theory I have.

Because the seance seed has been planted and is now taking root (much to my dismay), the rest of us gather our equipment together and wait for Dana to get back upstairs. Jo comes out of the bathroom. She takes a seat between Gina and the comatose Pepper.

"I love seances, don't you?" Gina says to Jo, who ignores her.

I wonder how many seances Gina has been involved in where she can say she loves them. Also, would Jesus approve? His glitter-blue eyes look back at me from her shirt, and I wonder if he is giving me a cry for help. Stan asks Sue if she has a candle; she points up to a shelf on the wall between the couch and the basement door where there are at least six half-burned ones on display. Why does that not surprise me? Stan grabs two of the larger ones. We have our own stash of tealights in the tackle box, but if we can use the client's supplies, all the better. I give Stan credit for even asking. He puts the candles on the square wooden coffee table sitting in the middle of the living room. Sue pulls out a set of long matches from the end table drawer and lights them before Stan even asks. On cue, Libbi cuts the kitchen light. The overheads are still on, but the room looks eerie in the glow of the flames.

BANG BANG BANG! THUMP THUMP! Ting ting ta-ting!

I nearly leap out of my pasty Scottish skin at the sudden sound of banging from below. Tinker yelps. Sue stiffens up in her recliner and cries out.

"Did you hear that? The drums! That's the drums!"

Jo and Gina both acknowledge they heard it too. Jo looks panic-stricken in the candlelight. Gina's eyes are wide, and she tries to calm Tinker. Pepper does not budge from his eternal slumber.

BANG BANG BANG! THUMP THUMP! Ting ting ta-ting!

"That's it! That's what we have been hearing!" Sue is rigid as a board, listening. If she had a tail, it would point straight out. She seems genuinely frightened, and I suspect she'll bolt if she hears "Wipe Out."

BANG THUMP TA-TING!

"Are you sure that's what you heard before?" I ask calmly, looking at Sue.

"YES! Yes, that's it! Right before it went into the "Wipe Out" thing, that is exactly what it sounded like! Josie, isn't that what we heard?"

Jo nods. "Yeah, it was like that, but more of it. It was constant."

BANG!

"But you're sure this is the sound that you heard—the drums?"

"Yes, that is the drums!" Sue is adamant. "You hear it too, right? It's not just us?"

I pause for just a few seconds. She wants validation. And I hate doing this. But I must.

"I hear it loud and clear," I say. "That's our team member Dana banging on the pipes and air ducts down in the basement."

Sue looks at me and freezes. Something shifts in her brain, and her eyes glaze over as if she has gone dead inside. I imagine this is what serial killers look like when they get caught. I can't tell if it's relief or if she wants to murder me. Leaning toward the latter. I don't enjoy tricking a client, and in fairness, Maya expressed concern about my little experiment. Libbi didn't think it was the most respectful thing to do, but she knows I'll just do it, regardless. She has lived with me for too long.

"Well, I know what I heard," says Sue, falling back into the chair, surrendering.

We hear Dana coming up the stairs.

"Mom, he's doing it again!" Jo is petting Pepper and becoming distraught. "He won't wake up! Look!"

Jo is pushing the Yorkie with her fingers, nudging him and trying to get him to wake up. For fuck's sake. I'm regretting my pipe-tapping test, because now I fear I've set them all off into a panic.

"Pepper!" Sue calls, leaning over to do her own nudging. "Pepper, wake up!"

She's shouting now. Tinker barks a few times. Not helping, Tink.

"See?" Sue looks at me with desperation, then at Libbi. "This is what I'm talking about! It's like something is possessing him. He won't wake up!"

Her voice is escalating, and I admit, it is strange that Pepper is not stirring despite her repeated yelling and poking.

"This isn't normal!" cries Sue, continuing to shove her dog to get him to wake up.

Libbi walks over to Pepper and pulls something from the pocket of her zip-up hoodie. She puts it under Pepper's nose, and immediately he perks up. Suddenly he's ready to run sprints. He takes the object from her fingers and devours it.

"Zukes dog treat," says Libbi, pulling out another one and giving it to the now wide-eyed and feisty mutt. "I keep a snack bag in my pocket for our dog when we're out walking. Totally forgot it was in there. Pepper's old. He just sleeps well. That's what they do when they get to be that age."

She gives Pepper some ear scratches and then gives Tinker a treat. That calms him down, and he snuggles into his mom's lap for a midnight snack. I hope we can consider the comatose dog events debunked. There appears to be nothing wrong with Pepper other than he's got a lot of years on him. I smile on the inside. I'm proud of my wife for her quick thinking, and we've also got some evidence that might explain some of the drum sounds. It has been a great five minutes of investigation.

Now if we can just get through this damn seance.

Maya Hill-Goldberg

Brava and bravo to Libbi and Walter! Two debunks in less time than it takes to brew a cup of coffee. Which is what I need about now, even though I'm more of an herbal tea kind of gal. But a potent dose of caffeine might do me good. Sitting around waiting to be scared out of my wits takes a lot of energy. I have a Mountain Dew, which helps a little with the fatigue. I am about as petite as they come, so it doesn't take much to pick me up. I guzzle my soda, trying not to burp. We have caught burps on recording before, and they can sound very demonic. Talking to you, Walter.

Stan is leading the seance because, well, I guess he's the resident "expert." Before we settle in and go full lights out, I pull Libbi aside over by the counter and ask, "Is it a good idea to have Jo out here?"

Jo is just fifteen. I don't want this experience to cause any trauma. Even if we encounter nothing unearthly—which I seriously doubt we will—seances can be scary. Plus, there might be a tie-in with Jo herself.

"I asked Sue about it when Stan mentioned it," says Libbi softly. "She said she wanted Jo here."

She shrugs and I let it go. It's ultimately up to the mom. I have said my piece.

"Let's go have one more smoke before we start," says Sue, getting up. "Otherwise, I'll be a wreck."

I don't say *I think you are already a wreck*, but I think she is already a wreck. Also, we are literally about to begin. Maybe you could have done the smoke break five minutes ago? Gina follows Sue out and takes Tinker, who appears to be suffering from a case of "it's way past my bedtime." He has finally fallen silent in his mother's arms. Jo stays on the couch while Dana follows the other women out to the front steps. Dana doesn't smoke a ton on an investigation—not like Sue—but she does smoke. I imagine after the events of the night, she needs a few minutes of deep breathing, even if it is full of tar and nicotine. Stan heads down to the basement, muttering something about checking the cameras. Libbi and Walter are discussing their dog Fenrir by the counter, keeping it light lest Jo overhear.

Jo is alone on the couch, so I walk over and sit on the edge of the recliner, hoping Sue won't consider it an affront. I am wearing long pants, and my Hollins hoodie covers most of my thighs, so I should be safe from any germs or critters running around in the old fibers. And I'm sure there are some down there. If these seat cushions have been vacuumed or wiped down in the past year, I'll buy Sue a carton of cigarettes and smoke one myself.

"So, are you in high school?" I ask Jo. I am only seven or eight years older than her, but I feel motherly toward this teenager. Even if the energy that Dana experienced is not from her, it seems like she is in some emotional pain.

Jo shifts on the couch. "Yeah, I go to Cave Spring. Sophomore."

"Oh cool. I went to Patrick Henry." Patrick Henry High School is north of here, more toward the center of Roanoke proper. Cave Spring is on the south side. "Did you guys have homecoming already?"

I have already passed through the city gate and into Akwardville. Homecoming? It was all I could think of. It's usually around this time of year, right? I was not into sports, what can I say? I helped with the senior float one year, but that was about it.

"It was a couple weeks ago, I think," Jo says, nodding slightly. Does she "think" because she (like me) isn't into the football activities (or dances), or because she can't remember the date? I ponder the thought for a few seconds too long before I decide it is time to change the subject.

"So, do you enjoy living in Roanoke?"

Jo looks down and starts massaging her hands, grabbing one inside the other and pulling out, then repeating as if she has just put on lotion. Except there is no lotion. She pauses, perhaps reluctant to respond to my simple question, or maybe not knowing how. Or more likely, not being in the mood for small talk. Pepper, who is still lounging next to her, raises his head as if he hears something.

"It's okay," is all Jo says.

Roanoke is surrounded by the Blue Ridge Mountains, has a thriving downtown, and the hiking can't be beat. There are lots of great trails within a half-hour drive. Politically, I would call it moderately liberal. Roanoke residents tend to be open-minded, at least within the city limits. However, travel a few miles outside of the city and you see a lot of Confederate flags. I imagine that for someone like Jo, being different from the majority in any way would be difficult. Regardless of the reason she dresses and behaves the way she does, she likely gets her share of bullying.

The front door opens, bringing with it a cool freshness into the Mackenzie's living room. The outside temperature has continued to drop, and I am grateful for my layers. Gina comes in first with Tinker still in her arms. He is miraculously still quiet. Then comes the shorter, stockier Sue, looking a little worse for wear. Finally, the dark tower known as Dana. I see Dana catch Libbi's eye as she enters. She is behind Gina and Sue so they can't see her when she rolls her eyes and shakes her head slightly. I wonder what they talked about out there and make a mental note to catch up with her and Libbi when we have more privacy.

I realize I am in Sue's special spot, so I jump up from the recliner and walk over to the counter. Gina heads to the bathroom—with Tinker still in tow, much to my disbelief—while Sue takes her royal seat on the recliner, as predicted. Dana joins us at the counter. Stan comes up the stairs from the basement, no doubt having heard all the footsteps and not wanting to miss even a second of the seance action. He is carrying the camcorder still connected to its tripod. While we are waiting for Gina, Stan unscrews the Sony from its stand and places the tripod into its case.

When Gina emerges, Libbi gets everyone organized. I can tell she is ready to be done.

"Okay, let's get started. First off, everyone please turn off your cell phones. And I mean off. We don't want to be duped by any vibrations."

There is some rustling as Sue, Gina, and Jo all pull out their phones and shut them off. The RIP team has already silenced our cells, as it is a standard part of our prep.

"Now let's all gather around over here," she says. "Sue, is it okay if we pull a couple of these stools into the living room?" She motions toward the kitchen island.

"Knock yourself out."

Libbi and Stan each grab a stool and place them in the center of the open room next to Sue. Their backs will be toward the bedroom wall as they face the coffee table and couch. Before she sits down, Libbi flips the switch by the front door to turn out the overhead lights. Stan offers me his seat, but I decline and sit on the floor with the TV behind me, just to the right of Gina. Walter stands over near the front door while Dana hangs back by Jo's bedroom doorway. Walter will not be taking part in the seance directly. Dana has opted not to link physically. She feels that if any spirits are present, she doesn't need to be holding hands around a candle to sense them, and the proximity might even be overwhelming. She will stand back and observe only. We all have our recorders in hand except for Stan. His device is standing upright on the coffee table where the candles still burn.

Stan is ready to get the show started. He will use our core questions, and Libbi has reminded him (again) that provoking is off the table. We are all getting tired and a little cranky, and it won't take much for her to shut this show down.

Stan begins, "Everyone, grab each other's hands so we form a full circle."

I clasp fingers with Gina. Her palms are cold and clammy. I try not to think about it. Tinker snuggles next to her as she and Jo join hands. Sue sits up and leans in so she can reach Jo on her right. Then it's Stan, Libbi, and back to me. I laugh a little inside, wondering if Walter offered to monitor the doorway so he could avoid touching Stan's hand. Or anyone's, for that matter.

"Now let's take some deep breaths to relax. In through your nose if you can, out through your mouth. Try to clear your head."

Stan is surprisingly and uncharacteristically mild-mannered when he is in his element, and this is certainly his element. His voice is low, smooth, and calming.

"Keep breathing, relaxing, clearing." He lets out a soft exhale to guide the group. *"I am speaking now to anyone out there in the spirit world who may be listening. We welcome you into our circle of light, to communicate with us. We come in peace and with respect. We mean you no harm and are only here to communicate and gather information. Thank you for letting us be here with you."*

My eyes are shut, but I can feel the tension in the room, especially from Sue and Jo. Whether or not there is anything supernatural in this house, they believe there is.

"We are going to ask you some questions," says Stan softly. *"If you can answer with words, please come as close as possible and be as loud as you can so we can hear you. There is a small box on the table in front of me, near the lights. It will help us hear you better. Get as close to the light as you can."*

Sue coughs and whispers an apology. I can hear Pepper's deep breathing.

"If you cannot speak in words, then please give us another sign that you are here. You could tap something or make the lights flicker. Whatever you do, please do it with great intensity. We have difficulty seeing you and hearing you, so the harder you try to show us you are here, the better."

He waits to see if anything will respond. I hear only a few clicks and creaks from the house settling and people breathing.

"My friend Sue, who lives in this house, is going to ask some questions. Please answer as best you can. Again, talk loudly into the box near the light, or make a tapping sound."

I'm about to doze off when—

ratta-tat-tat

My eyes fly open wide. What the hell was that? It sounded like a drum. Not a pipe or an air duct, but a snare drum. Heading to 34th Street in the Macy's Thanksgiving Day Parade, Big Ten university band snare drums. Okay, that was weird. I am pretty sure Gina heard it too because I could feel her tense up in my hand.

"If that is you, please do it again," says Stan.

We are met with silence. Stan refrains from speaking for nearly a minute just to make sure. Nothing.

"Sue, you can go ahead and start asking questions."

I crack my left eye to peek out. Sue still has her eyes closed, as do all the seance participants. I comply as well.

"Who… are you? Why are you here?"

Stan whispers, "Remember to wait a few seconds after each question to allow time for the spirits to answer. Count to fifteen or twenty slowly in your head if that helps."

I keep my eyes shut but would bet money that Sue's mouth is moving in the candlelight as she counts.

"Why are you here?"

"What do you want with us?"

"Do we know you?"

"Did you live in this house?"

Sue is not following the core EVP script precisely, but I would not expect her to at this point. We have crossed the line from a normal investigation into the atypical. Also, it's difficult to read questions when there is only candlelight to illuminate the words.

*"Are there others with—*what is that?"

I open my eyes and see that Sue has done the same. She is looking around.

"Does anyone hear that?"

At first, I only hear breathing. But then… voices. Muffled voices, like someone is having a conversation inside a closet behind some clothes. And something banging, but more like a thud than a bang. Not the same as the *ratta-tat-tat* or the pipes. Every few seconds I hear a distinct thud that sounds far away.

"I can hear it," I say. "Voices and some sort of thumping."

Gina and Jo confirm they are picking up something too.

"That's what we heard before!" says Sue. "We heard those voices a few times. It sounds like a foreign language. Doesn't it sound foreign to you?"

I'm not sure who she is asking. I can't make out the voices clearly enough to determine actual words.

Jo says, "I heard those voices from the basement under my room. I think it's some ancient language."

Okay, now I'm ready to be done. How would she know if it was an ancient language? Like what? Aramaic? Latin? At best, she's taken a year of Spanish; I would bet my life on it.

"One sec," says Walter. "I think I know what's going on."

Libbi Bean

I hear the mumbling too, but from my perch on the wooden stool it sounds like it's coming from somewhere outside. Walter opens the front door to check. Immediately the voices become louder, echoing in the night.

Thump.

"You suck! You're such a jerk!"

"Whatever."

Thump.

The air is frigid. Walter shuts the door.

"Looks like some older teenagers, a couple of them. They are up the street, maybe six or seven houses, and they are bouncing a basketball."

Crisis averted. But I would not have said the source was down the street into the center of the subdivision. Must be that amphitheater effect again. Also, shouldn't teenagers be home in bed now? Who bounces a ball down the street after midnight? Some manners, please. I'm so glad I never had kids. Have I said that already?

"Let's keep going," says Stan.

"Hold up," I say. "Let's give them a minute to pass. Dana, are you getting anything?"

"Nothing yet," she responds from the bedroom doorway.

"Okay, thanks."

The thumping stops after about thirty seconds, and we conclude that the dribblers have reached their destination somewhere in the subdivision.

Stan gets us back underway. "Sorry, Sue… back to you."

She continues the litany of questions. *What is your name? How many of you are there? Did you live in this house?*

About ten minutes after she resumes, Jo says she sees a light flash across the window. We are all still holding hands, although most of us now have our eyes open. No one else saw anything. Walter looks out the window, but there are no vehicles coming or going. He logs it in his recorder, and we continue.

Another five or ten minutes of slow questions go by. Then Jo again pipes up.

"Do you hear that? The bass drum?"

No one says anything.

"Can you describe it?" I ask.

"It was like *BOOM... BOOM-BOOM*," she says. One beat with a pause, followed by two closer together.

Jo sounds weary and a little afraid. This must be hard for her. Whether the events she experienced are real or imagined, it's a lot of stress for a fifteen-year-old. Not to mention the likely pressure she gets from her mom about dressing and acting like a boy and probably everything else.

"I don't hear anything," says Sue. "You just imagined it." Her tone is curt and unnecessarily bitchy. Whatever tiff they had on the ride back from Gina's is still in the air.

"I did not imagine it!" Jo pulls her hands from Gina's and her mother's and crosses her arms in front of her chest. Oh boy. The defiant teenager has come out. With a smidge of petulant toddler mixed in for good measure. I wonder if we could exorcise *that*.

"Calm down!" snaps Sue at her daughter. Her irritation is obvious. Maybe she still feels embarrassed because we rained on her drum parade earlier. And we debunked the voices. She doesn't want to make the same mistake a third time.

Jo is apparently overstimulated with all the people and her moody mom, because she starts to mildly hyperventilate. Sue just rolls her eyes and shakes her head.

"Oh, for fuck's sake, Josephine. Get it together!"

Suddenly, Jo puts her hands over her ears, leans over, and lets out a primal half-scream/half-yell into her forearms and elbows.

"AAAAAAARRRRRRGGGGGGGHHHH!!!"

This isn't a frightened outburst. This is an explosion of extreme frustration. Teen angst personified. A pure release from the depths of her soul. It is loud, and it is full of rage.

"Holy Mother of God, SHUT UP!" Sue yells with disgust. Jo trails off and stops wailing as Sue sits back in the recliner and shakes her head. I'm sure she loves Jo. But she seems to have zero compassion for whatever her daughter is going through.

Jo is now sitting in silence, still bent over with her hands on her ears.

"If you can't handle it, go to your room!" Sue is livid. I can't help but wonder if she resents Jo stealing her thunder with the outburst.

"Let me check outside," says Walter in his normal, calm voice. That's code for *"Get me out of whack job central."*

He opens the door, and I brace for the chilly blast. He goes all the way out this time and shuts the door behind him. I see his silhouette go past the front window toward Alice's side of the duplex. I hope no one mistakes him for a burglar.

"It could be someone's bass thumping in the distance," says Stan in a rare display of skepticism. "Sue, why don't I ask some questions now?"

"Absolutely," she responds. Her energy seems renewed, although there is still irritation in her voice.

"Why are you here tormenting these people?"

As usual, he ignores my earlier warning about provoking. Starting off with a bang, great job, Stan! I'll step in if he gets offensive, but right now, I think Sue is kind of into it. She is fully in the game, leaning forward as Stan continues.

"What gives you the right to come into this home and harass this Christian woman and her child?"

Sue is rocking now, with her eyes closed. "Yes! Praise God, Amen! Thank you, Jesus!" She repeats her hallelujahs multiple times in the pauses between questions. I'm almost irritated by it. Jesus didn't prevent your alleged haunting, did he? What are you thanking him for? Not to mention, her prayers will overlay any paranormal responses we might get on the recorders.

"Are you a minion of Satan? Do you come from the depths of HELL?"

"Oh yes, thank you, Jesus, for protecting us!"

"What is your purpose? Why have you come here?"

"Mmm… yes, hallelujah, praise the Lord!"

This continues for a while, with Stan asking multiple variations of "Who are you and why are you here?" Jo is sitting back up with her arms crossed. Gina is reaching across Jo to grab Sue's hand. The circle is partially complete, at least. Tinker appears to be done with the show and has curled up between Gina and Jo. Pepper is in his patented coma. Maya and I seem to be the only stable ones in the circle. I keep looking in her direction to see if I can catch her gaze and pass on an eye roll or two, but she has them closed. I think she might have fallen asleep.

"Show yourself and your purpose if you have any courage!" cries Stan. I turn my head to give him a look in the flickering candlelight, but he too has his eyes closed. He is into this.

"Bring yourself OUT!"

He is almost shouting now. We are channeling some good Southern Baptist ministers tonight, aren't we? Stan reminds me of those old-time preachers on TV back in the day—the charlatans who would claim to make the blind see and the deaf hear on their Sunday morning programs. *"I command the deaf spirits to come OUT! HE-AL! HE-AL!"* I don't think they ever actually healed anyone, but they did miraculously turn one-syllable words into two.

"*Show your face if you DA-RE!*" And just like that.

"Thank you, Jesus!"

"*Stop being a coward, and SHOW YOUR DEMON FACE NOW, YOU BASTARD!*"

"Okay, we're done!"

I stand up, walk over to the front door, and flip the living room light switch to illuminate the room. Just then the door swings open, and my stomach drops to my crotch as I cry out with my own "Jesus Christ!" Walter has just walked in after his outdoor check, frightening the bejeezus out of me. Timing is everything.

"You scared the shit out of me," I say, putting my hand on my chest.

"Are you okay?" asks my husband, but not of me. He is looking at Sue. She is doubled over on the recliner, coughing. The rasp in her lungs is wet and deep. I have the urge to go over and pound her back a few times, but Gina and Jo don't seem to be concerned. Sue gives us a thumbs-up signal, so I resist.

"That's normal," says Jo. "She just needs a smoke."

Jo has gotten some of her mojo back despite the late hour and intense activities. How she can go from angst and despair to smartass teenager in mere minutes is astounding. I suspect the light being on is helping her mood. Maybe I should have insisted that we not include her in the seance. Too late now. But this is the last time I'll allow a minor to be involved in an investigation in this way. It can be scary enough for us seasoned professionals, so I can only imagine what goes through the head of someone that young and naïve.

"I do need a smoke," agrees Sue, finally working through all the built-up phlegm and tar in her lungs. She gets up with some effort, grabbing her pack from the end table. Gina rises too, and they both stretch in harmony.

"All right," I say. "I think that's a wrap."

Dana Tennant

I turn on the light to Jo's bedroom knowing that Stan will be in shortly to do his equipment breakdown. Before I help with the packing, I will need a break. A lot of noise has been running through my head in the past few hours, and I need some fresh air to process it all (helped by a Virginia Slim, of course).

"I'm stepping out for a smoke," I say, and follow Sue and Gina out the front door.

It's chilly out here—colder than it should be even for early October—but I don't mind. The house is getting stuffy, and I need a brisk wind on my face. I ignite my cigarette with a pink Bic lighter and inhale my first toke deeply.

"So, you're the psychic," says Gina, lighting her own stick.

I chuckle. "I guess, kind of. I'm more what you call a sensitive. I sense emotions or energy more than anything."

I'm surprised Gina is talking to me. When we were outside before the seance, neither she nor Sue said boo, other than a nod of acknowledgement. Which I find odd. Although it's true we don't know each other well, most smokers I'm acquainted with are on the chatty side. Sue and Gina were chatty, just not with me. I wonder if it's because I'm—how do I put this delicately? I'm not of the *pale* variety. Sue might be the type of person who doesn't hang much with the black and brown folks in the same way that she doesn't care for her daughter to hang with her "fag" friends. I could be wrong; we all know what happens when we assume. I had hoped for Gina to be a little more inviting, but she's even more extreme than Sue, if that is even possible. Glitter Jesus? Come on.

Whatever the reason, they were off by themselves when we were out here before the seance, talking about Jo mostly. I gather they had an argument after they picked her up from the friend's house. The friend sounds like a young gay man who Sue (with Gina's prodding) claims is influencing her daughter to turn into a "dyke." Gina's word, not mine. Sue seems to have no love for this poor teenager, who is probably just living his life and trying to survive in a world full of people like Sue and Gina. They both seem put off by Jo's friends, Jo's attire, and her increasingly negative attitude and behavior. Gina more than Sue, if I am being honest. She quoted scripture at least three times during a five-minute smoke break. I feel like she is a big part of the problem, although Sue is no saint. I feel bad for Jo. Who wouldn't be bitter, having a mother who thinks that what they do, wear, and who they hang out with will ultimately send them to the fires of hell? And if I had to be around that every day, I would be a basket case too.

I heard Gina use the word "fag" twice in their earlier discussion, and she wasn't talking about a British cigarette. She's not smart enough to even know the alternative use of the word; I'm sure of that. She is absolutely an instigator. For what gain, I have no idea. Maybe she feeds off the conflict, and it makes her feel better to console her friend with the tormented daughter. She did most of the talking and most of the Bible-thumping in the conversation. Sue just got angry, and I think Gina likes that. I couldn't make out everything they were saying, but at one point I distinctly heard Gina say, "I told you, the church has a camp for that." I hope she was talking about a band camp. Doubtful.

Despite all the "Amen!" and "Praise Jesus!" comments, I am not sensing that Sue has the worst energy. She is more conflicted. If Gina were not in the picture, I think Sue would be more accepting of her daughter's evolution—or at least ignore it versus act like it's a national crisis.

Sue and Gina are including me in their club during this post-seance smoke break, and I hope the topic of Jo's gender or sexual identity does not come up. All things considered, I'd rather we stick to the demons. I'm much more in control of my emotions and my mouth with the paranormal.

"Did you pick up any energy in the house tonight?" asks Sue as we shiver in the cold. It's still in the low fifties, but there is a crisp wind reminding us that winter isn't too far out.

I pause and exhale. How much am I going to reveal at this point? We rarely give out details until we have reviewed all the evidence. There are too many unknowns and too many opportunities to make incorrect assumptions. But I felt what I felt. I am okay with revealing a few secrets without giving away the keys to the kingdom.

"I did sense a few things that were… interesting," I say. "Some kind of energy hit me on the basement stairs during our first session. Gave me a helluva migraine, but it passed quickly. I couldn't get a handle on where it came from. Could have been something in the basement itself, something physical. There is some mold down there."

I always like to give options when I'm not 100% certain (which I rarely am; there is always room for interpretation, perception, and the unknown).

Sue replies, "Truth be told, I get headaches sometimes when I'm down there too. I will ask the landlord to look at it. Did you get anything else?"

I am not sure how to respond to that question. The stuff in Jo's bedroom might be personal. However, I *did* pick up suicidal thoughts. If that comes from Jo, then maybe her mother needs to know about it. My hesitation and the look on my face must be betraying me.

"What is it?" Sue asks. "I want to know. If there's something in this house—"

"It's not that," I say. Fuck it. Do I want to be a rules follower, or do I want to do what is right? I just wish Gina weren't here. "I did sense something when we were upstairs, in your daughter's room."

"I knew it!" says Gina, smirking. "I told you, Sue. Bad energy."

She doesn't even know what I'm talking about. I'm tired, and I want to head-butt her into the grass.

"No," I say, pointing my fingers, cigarette, and eyes directly toward her. "I did not sense any 'bad energy.'"

I use air quotes to let Gina know what I think of her comment. I am getting a stronger tickle about her. Like maybe she was the one who planted the "demon" seed in Sue's head. I don't just sense paranormal spirit energy or intense telekinetic energy from unhappy teenagers. I can also pick up things from living adults, like the two standing before me. What I am picking up is that Sue is very confused and conflicted, and Gina is a manipulative troublemaker who thrives on other people being in conflict. It makes her feel better about her own shitty life. It is for that reason that I need to tread lightly with anything I say to Sue about her daughter.

"I did sense something," I say quietly, flicking my ash into the air. "I don't think it was a ghost or spirit or anything like that. More like an essence—or an energy—from someone living. Someone going through a very tough time and feeling very conflicted about who they are. Because being who they are might be dangerous around narrow-minded people. If you catch my drift."

I look right at Gina when I say this. I know she catches my drift because she looks away as she exhales a puff of smoke. *Tell me you know I'm onto your game without telling me you know I'm onto your game.* I hope Sue understands the context. But I'm not sure. She just reeks of fatigue. I can't say much more at this point. I would love to cut to the chase: *Your daughter is crying out for help, and you are part of the problem.* But this is neither the place nor the time.

"Someone is hurting and needs help," is all I can say to wrap it up.

"Ugh," says Gina. She rolls her eyes, and I suppress the urge to body slam her into Alice's bushes. "You mean Josie."

I'm not taking her bait. "I didn't say that. Right now, I don't know what or who the source of the energy is. I'm just making *Sue* aware."

I lean down and put out my cigarette on the mulch in front of Sue's window, then put the butt in my pocket. My mama taught me not to leave my shit lying around. I hope that my vague response clicks in Sue's head, and she thinks for herself rather than surrendering to her bestie with the bad intentions. Spending just a few more moments outside with these two has convinced me that Sue is impressionable and easily overwhelmed but not an inherently evil person. She is probably a product of a strict religious upbringing, and true to the famous words of Karl Marx (which I am paraphrasing), her faith in Jesus is the opiate to her trials and tribulations of being a mother to a teenager in an unfamiliar situation.

Gina, however, is a snake. She is a maestro of manipulation, and I wonder what she hopes to gain from encouraging her friend to think that her daughter is evil. Regardless of whether there is anything demonic or paranormal going on, the fact remains that there is a young woman undergoing a significant struggle, and I am convinced that if Gina were not around, things would be infinitely better. Maybe not perfect or even great, but most certainly better.

Since I am done with my cigarette and done with my attempt to get Sue to recognize the pain in her daughter, I go back inside to help wrap up, leaving the dynamic duo to ponder my words. I doubt Gina will have anything nice to say, but as the young'uns say, *IDGAF—I don't give a fuck.* Not my problem.

The crew is making good time with the breakdown, so I make sure I have secured my own devices and then wander around to clean up and double-check each room for any items we might have left behind. With so much equipment, it's not uncommon to forget something, so two or even three sets of eyes come in handy. Jo has disappeared. I assume she has escaped to her bedroom to get some much-needed brain rest. Everyone looks tired. Me, I'm flying. Maybe it's the adrenaline, or maybe it's just that I'm used to crazy hours from being a nurse. Whatever the reason, I will drive back to Catawba with full focus.

Gina and Sue come in from the outdoor smoking lounge. Libbi and Walter are heading out to put the first load of equipment in their car. When they get back, they pull Sue over to the counter to give her a rundown of the next steps and timing.

"Sue, thank you so much again for calling us," says Walter, extending his hand to the client. "As you can imagine, we have a lot of recordings to go over, and it might take us a couple of weeks to do that. We'll call you to set up a time to meet so we can go over what we find."

"That would be great. And thank you so much for coming, especially on short notice. I really appreciate it."

"It's our pleasure," says Libbi. "And please let us know if you have any other incidents between now and when we meet. We may have some resources that might help."

We say our goodbyes, extending to Jo, who has not made an appearance and is probably channeling her inner Pepper right about now. The night is clear, the air brisk, and I am looking forward to exploring the recordings to see what we uncovered. But first, home and a good rest.

"Bye, all," I say with hugs and waves. "Safe travels. Good hunting!"

And with that, we are off.

Excerpt 8 from the *RIP After Dark* Podcast
Episode 72: Case of the Demon Drums

This podcast was broadcast one year after the actual investigation.
Client names and identifying details have been changed to maintain privacy.

Walter: *Quick reminder, you are listening to RIP After Dark, the live podcast where we share the good, bad, and ugly of what it is like to be a paranormal investigator. I am Walter Bean, co-founder of Roanoke Investigations of the Paranormal (aka RIP).*

Libbi: *And I am Libbi Bean, co-host and co-founder extraordinaire.*

Walter: *We were just recapping the final stage of our investigation known as Case of the Demon Drums. Session Three was the now infamous seance with participation from the client, Nancy, her friend (whom we are calling Cher), and the client's daughter Stephanie.*

Libbi: *This was my absolute favorite part of the investigation. Mostly because we debunked so much! I mean, Dana tapping on the pipes in the basement and the client being absolutely one hundred percent sure that it was the same drums they heard—that was EPIC!*

Walter: *That one felt good, no doubt about it. I don't delight in fooling clients like that, but sometimes we need to break them out of the fear cycle.*

Libbi: *Fear is powerful. I almost expected her to double down like she did with the urine smell, but she backed off. I think it was a bit of a wake-up call.*

Walter: *I would agree. Her demeanor from that point on seemed a little diminished.*

Libbi: *Except when she freaked out over the dog in a "coma." Using air quotes for those on audio only.*

Walter: *That was my favorite moment! She's prodding and poking the dog; it's not moving. I honestly thought maybe she was onto something there for a minute. Until my brilliant wife very matter-of-factly walks over and breaks the spell with an ordinary dog treat.*

Libbi: *Well, it WAS a Zukes! Those are like crack to Fenny; I have to give them all the credit. But thank yuh… thank yuh veruh much.*

Walter: *Well-played. Turns out ole—what are we calling it?*

Libbi: *The dog? Paprika.*

Walter: *Right, turns out Paprika was just an old dog who slept deeply and was probably deaf to boot.*

Libbi: *No doubt. That was one of my best debunks ever.*

Walter: *But of course, the climax of the evening was when Stephanie lost her shit and screamed like a banshee. I almost had a coronary.*

Libbi: *Uh, yeah, my anus puckered a bit on that one. That kid had some serious energy to release.*

Walter: *Maybe she needed an old sock or stuffed animal like Fenny does.*

Libbi: *You mean like when you come home for lunch, and she goes apeshit and puts something in her mouth as an offering?*

Walter: *'Zactly. Didn't you say some dogs do that because they have "big energy" and they don't know where to direct it?*

Libbi: *I read that somewhere, yes.*

Walter: *Maybe Stephanie had big energy and needed a sock in her mouth.*

Libbi: [giggles] *Can you imagine? Stan pulls a wad out of his pocket and hands it to her. It's one of his stinky, dirty socks.*

Walter: *Ugh. Now I have a little throw up in my mouth.*

Libbi: *All kidding aside, it was clear that Stephanie had some pent-up frustration.*

Walter: *There was a lot of conflict with the mom. And the friend, for that matter.*

Libbi: *Yeah, from what we observed and heard, I suspect the friend may have played a bigger part in all of this than we originally thought. But, neither here nor there. She isn't here to defend herself, so let's just leave it at that.*

Walter: *Fair enough. That outburst turned out to be gold, though.*

Libbi: [excited] *Yes, it did! And we're going to talk about the evidence we uncovered in just a minute. First, let's take a question from the comments. This one is from @madwayneconklin75, who asks, "What can people do to get rid of hauntings?"*

Walter: *Great question, @madwayneconklin75. And the answer is, it depends. For classic ghost hauntings, we have a laundry list of recommendations that we provide to all our clients.*

Libbi: *For example?*

Walter: *House blessing is one. Our client in Case of the Demon Drums had this done. Twice, if memory serves.*

Libbi: *Yes, I think once by a priest brought in by Cher, and once by the client's pastor.*

Walter: *You can also try talking to the spirits directly to get them to move on.*

Libbi: *Or you can just live with them if they aren't causing any harm or stress.*

Walter: [with a hint of sarcasm] *You talk to spirits in our house, don't you, Libbi?*

Libbi: *Uh, yes, Walter, I do. If I am doing any renovation, moving furniture, painting, that sort of thing. I don't know if there are any hypothetical spirits there, but maybe they keep to themselves because I show them some respect.*

Walter: *The irony.*

Libbi: *I know, I know. Because I don't really believe in an afterlife. But, on the minuscule chance that there are sentient spirits lurking around (like maybe shadow people from an alternate universe), why not say hello?*

Walter: *With that logic, why not just believe in a God? Just in case.*

Libbi: [ignores him] *Okay, let's move on. @madwayneconklin75, there are other things you can do, like installing mirrors. There is a theory that ghosts don't like to see their reflections.*

Walter: *That works for me when I gain a few pounds.*

Libbi: *Facts. You can try sage smudging; that allegedly helps. For hauntings, that is. Probably won't help your weight gain.*

Walter: *And of course, keep in mind that these are all things that we would recommend for a standard haunting. Different paranormal events might require different interventions.*

Libbi: [sarcastically] *Like exorcisms, right?*

Walter: [sighs] *No, not like exorcisms. I'm not saying those aren't necessary (on rare occasions), but not for every situation like some of our fellow ghost hunting groups might like you to believe.*

Libbi: *Don't get me started. I should have just shut my mouth.*

Walter: *My point being, we are here to advise as much as we can and will put you in touch with other experts if we cannot. And remember, if you are experiencing unexplained events in your home, get in touch with us at RIPAfterDark.org.*

Blobs, Blips, & Growls (Oh My!)

October 6-19
Evidence Review
Various locations in and around Roanoke, Virginia

Walter Bean

Libbi and I arrive home from the investigation around 2:30 Sunday morning. Much to my dismay, Stan stays overnight with us in our basement suite but thankfully heads back to his home in Lexington as soon as he gets up. He is gone before my alarm goes off. Libbi didn't sleep in; she never does. Number one, she's a morning person, and number two, we have a silverback ape of a dog who doesn't give a shit that we've been out ghost hunting all night. She's a Labrador, and Labradors will let you know when their next meal is due an hour before it is due. By the time I roll out of bed just after ten, Libbi has been up for several hours, fed and walked Fenny, had two cups of coffee, and started looking at the recordings from last night.

It will take a significant amount of time to get through all the evidence, so it is never too early to start reviewing files. That's why we don't promise delivery of our findings in less than two weeks. We had five cameras set up, with five hours of recording each. Every member of RIP had a handheld recorder. And it's not just listening to and viewing dozens of hours of activity. It's stopping, rewinding, watching or listening multiple times; corroborating on multiple devices; strategically reviewing the reported events and analyzing against the evidence; and logging it all so Libbi can compile it into a cohesive report. Even with five people working on various recordings, it is a substantial effort. Time to buckle up and get going.

Over the next two weeks I'll be reviewing the files from my personal audio recorder and the basement camcorder, plus any files that need a second pair of eyes or ears. It's important to capture every anomaly because we give the client a copy of anything we find.

205

Anything. Some of them will go through the media meticulously, and if we miss something big, it can be embarrassing. On the flip side, some clients claim they hear or see things that just aren't there.

By late Sunday afternoon, Libbi has transferred all the device files to an external hard drive (where we archive our cases) and uploaded copies to the online drive we share with the team. Having everything together and easily accessible is much easier than switching out memory cards and trying to find the right digital file on a device. With so many video and audio apps available, we can find the right one for each medium and easily rewind, fast forward, enlarge, enhance, or clip out our best evidence for our clients. Working online also helps us share files more easily with the rest of the team. Libbi has the most experience with audio and video mixing from her many podcasts, so she gets everything in order on our end. The audio files from the team's personal recorders aren't uploaded yet, and we won't see them for a few more days, maybe a week.

Once Libbi gives me the okay to access the files, I spend much of my free time over the next two weeks reviewing the ones I am assigned to. I log any activity that was marked as well as any audio or video that we did not notice in real time during the investigation.

Pre-investigation Prep Period
Olympus digital recorder, handheld by Walter Bean

It never ceases to amaze me how well the digital recorders pick up sound. This is why they are such great tools and also why we must be so careful. Throughout the pre-investigation prep period (and later, in Session One), the sound of my footsteps on the concrete basement floor is clear on the recorder, but I didn't even notice it during the investigation. As I am listening, I lose count of how many times I hear my lead foot shuffle in the file. I'm not sure if I'm more annoyed that the mic is so sensitive, or that I cannot lift my feet like a fucking adult.

I find nothing new or highly abnormal during the investigation prep, and frankly, I would be surprised if I had. There is usually a lot of noise in the environment as we set up. Logging the prep work is a formality, but you never know what you might find, and it's good to let the client know if we notice anything that might contribute to their experiences. I move on to the actual investigation, Session One.

Session One Basement
Olympus digital recorder, handheld by Walter Bean

9:08 pm: Grrrrrrrrrrrrrr

Whoa! What in the Animal Planet channel is THAT? I wear noise-cancelling earphones when I'm reviewing evidence, so I'm sure the sound came from the recording. Just to be sure, I stop and rewind.

9:08 pm: Grrrrrrrrrrrrr

Just after Maya starts her EVP session, there is a low, guttural growl. It is distinct and eerie, the kind of growl I would not want to hear out on an African savannah. I imagine a lioness giving a warning to another animal that gets too close to her cubs. I don't know what the source is, but I am sure of two things: one, none of us heard anything when we were actively investigating. And two, that is a growl from an animal. If not, it's a spot-on simulation. I make a note in the log and highlight the clip so we can compare with other files from other cameras or audio recorders.

Not long after the growl, I hear Dana clear her throat. She even says "Excuse me" though I didn't hear her mark it explicitly. We try to mark everything verbally, but sometimes we miss. Or the mic picks up a sound that we don't think it will or that no one heard or noticed, like my footsteps. We often sniff or clear our throats—especially in environments like dusty, musty basements. Just another reason why having multiple recordings during the same session is so important to the integrity of the evidence. I remember Dana clearing her throat because it reminded me of what Libbi sometimes does in her sleep when she eats dairy before bedtime, forcing me to sleep in the "room of exile" (aka, the spare bedroom). But sometimes we aren't aware of the noises that we hear frequently in our day-to-day lives, so we forget to call them out.

At around 9:15, I hear unintelligible vocal sounds in a low, whispery tone as Maya goes through her EVP questions. It doesn't happen after every question, but I pick it up after five of them. I rewind and listen again carefully. I can't make out any words or sentences, but I hear some quasi-vocal noises. The timing is precise, meaning the sounds don't overlap with Maya's questions at all—which I would expect if it were something random, like a neighbor talking outside or a distant television conversation. It always happens right after a question. And it's a little different each time, not a consistent rhythm like I would expect with something mechanical, for example. Just like the growl, it is creepy, but I'll reserve my final judgement for after I've compared this file with Maya's and Dana's recordings at those times.

Then… fuck me, there's that sound again. The growl, right after Dana said she got "hit" with something. Sounds like the same big cat, almost purring but evil purring if that makes any sense. Crap, now I sound just like Sue: *"It's not a lion purring, it's a DEMON lion purring!"* Sue said she heard a wolf. I've never heard a wolf's growl in real life, but I watched enough Mutual of Omaha's *Wild Kingdom* back in the day to have some inkling. I have heard dog growls, and I guess this could have been that too, if a dog growl were very low in frequency.

And just like the first one, none of us heard anything in real time.

On the recording, I hear Dana say, "One sec" as she is recovering from whatever attacked her brain. A couple of seconds pass, then the growl. I replay it a few times. It is very similar to the earlier growl but a little strained. Like it was in pain. Like the sound was a release from fighting something. I listen further. The next sound is of Dana asking more questions. At that point, whatever energy had struck her was gone. She had pushed it out.

A crazy thought crosses my mind: What if that strained growl was from whatever hit Dana, and it was resisting her pushing it away? If I just look at it at face value, factoring out the craziness of it all for a minute, that is exactly what it sounds like.

I note it and continue.

It takes nearly four hours to complete the analysis of my audio recorder file for Session One. It is painstaking going through every little sound repeatedly. The camcorder recording went faster; I got that done one evening after work in just over two hours. I don't know why video goes much faster than audio, other than maybe as humans we are more sight-oriented than hearing (when we have both senses). I find little on the camcorder. It's basically a backup in case something happens to the other cameras. The full-spectrum and Blu-Lu IR cameras have much better night clarity, and if there is anything on those, Libbi will catch it during her review. The camcorder file shows a lot of orbs, but there was ample dust in that basement. I don't even mention it. All it does is get the client (who usually doesn't know better) all excited. About dust.

The only thing of note on the camcorder video file comes just as Dana is returning to the basement after changing her thermometer batteries. Just before she cries out—at around 9:47 pm—the video shows something unusual in the lounge area, between the drum pile and the couch. The camcorder was positioned to get a wide angle that included the stairs, so on the video I can vaguely see the abnormality forming just as Dana comes down the stairs and gets hit with her psychic migraine. The anomaly doesn't have any recognizable shape or form; it is just a faint, dark blob. It appears on film like a shadow and shows some movement in the couch/drum area. It sends a chill up my spine, but it could be any number of things—light or focus issues, an actual shadow, even a mechanical glitch. While it is bizarre and the timing peculiar, I am not convinced that it is something paranormal.

Yet.

Libbi Bean

I intentionally take on more evidence review than most of the team. Besides my assigned files, I also check all log reports and flagged items that come in from various team members. I do this because I am the only member of the team who doesn't have a traditional full-time job. Well, other than Maya, but she has a part-time job, *and* she goes to school. I had the amazing good fortune of being let go from my horrible consulting job two years ago. Now I'm a full-time author most days. I've written and published several books already, which do well enough to keep me out of the corporate cesspool. Most days I am afforded the flexibility to put my next bestseller on hold for a few days if we have a lot of evidence to review. I wouldn't give it up for anything. Bonus: I get to hang out with my girl Fenny all day.

I start my evidence review with the audio files from the digital recorder I held during prep time and Session Two in Jo's bedroom. My recordings revealed nothing new during the setup period. Sound bouncing and pee are the star players. My mind is still boggled by Sue's refusal to even entertain the possibility that the "human urine" she smelled could have been her own dog pissing in the house or the neighbor's beagle marking right in front of her window. Unfortunately, this is what we run into more and more these days. Sue is not the first (and won't be the last) to deny clear and overwhelming evidence of a non-paranormal explanation.

I make clips of our setup findings, log the times and details, and move on to Session Two.

Session Two (Bedroom)
Olympus digital recorder, handheld by Libbi Bean

The first anomaly I find is weak at best, but I still note it. During the EVP session, just after Stan asks, *"Do you mean us any harm?"* the walkie-talkie blips audibly. We all heard it in real time. What we didn't hear is a voice saying *"Yes."* At least, it might be *"Yes."* Unfortunately, there is a lot of static. It could be anything—exhale from one of the team members, wind, house settling—and it's probably nothing, but I log it just the same. I pull up a copy of Stan's audio file from our online hub and check the time when I heard the voice. I hear nothing from his recorder, so I add that to the detail.

It didn't feel like it then, but we had a lot going on in Session Two: the trash can in the closet; thickening air; wind whistling; temperature fluctuations; and of course, the intense impressions that Dana was picking up. I'm left knackered after this review. There was nothing blatantly demonic that came out of it (though Stan may interpret it otherwise), but I'm more convinced that there was something paranormal happening that night. Not from a ghost or other supernatural being. Certainly not a demon. It is more likely emanating from Jo. Even without the energy Dana sensed, one could easily conclude that Jo is struggling with something. Her dress; her behavior; the piles of "girly" clothing in the closet along with the hidden sanitary items; and the comments from Sue (and apparently, from Gina as well). If I were to guess (and believe me, it's not my place to guess, but I'll do it anyway), I'd guess that Jo is gay, transgender, both, or somewhere in between, and she's expending an enormous amount of physical and mental energy dealing with the fact that she's different from what her mother expects (or wants) her to be. It is so intense that she may have already tried to hurt herself to bury the pain and at least thought about committing suicide (if she hasn't already tried). Again, this is pure speculation, but I won't sit on this one. Discomfort is the gateway to growth, and this will be uncomfortable. But maybe, just maybe, it will help this family grow a little.

However, right now my focus is on getting through the evidence. I finish the review of my recorder files from Session Two but decide to hold off on listening all the way through the seance portion of the investigation. I want to finish Session One and Session Two as a package. Plus, I think the seance files will be more chaotic, and I want to have everything else behind me before I tackle those.

Sessions One and Two
Blu-Lu2 IR Camera (stationed in bedroom)

As the days pass, I make headway in reviewing the Bu-Lu cameras, starting with Blu-Lu2 which was positioned in the bedroom just inside the doorway pointing inward. It captured most of the room during all three sessions.

The Blu-Lu2 doesn't pick up much during Session One. It's a dull hour and a half of video reviewed on a rainy morning, made tolerable only by cuddles from Fenny and a bag of peanut butter M&M's (shareable size, and no, I did not share). During that time, no one was in Jo's bedroom, and I easily explain any anomalies as normal investigation activity.

During Session Two, when Stan, Dana, and I were actively investigating, things picked up a bit. As always, the Blu-Lu2 comes through and captures multiple incidents that we did not fully notice or mark that night.

- While the team congregates near the closet, there is a light or shadow anomaly near the window on the front wall of the house. It travels over the curtain from the bottom left to the top center of the window. Two team members have flashlights on, and the light is consistent with their movement. There are no vehicles outside.

- Then, just after Stan asks, *"Do you mean us any harm?"* there is a faint sparkle or glimmer coming from the walkie-talkie sitting on the bed next to me. It coincides with the audible beep we all hear. This could be a coincidental reflection from ambient light, although there is no significant motion. It almost looks like a sparkler for a split second. I note the timing with the details of the previously discovered *"Yes"* vocalization, which occurs around the same time. I still think it's something normal, but the timing is uncanny.

- As Dana is starting her communication session and the pressure is changing (which we did notice), there is a weird pixelation near her on the right side of the screen (which would be her left side). It goes in and out a few times, turning a little darker, then lighter, almost like a cloud or shadow. This could be a camera anomaly, or maybe the room pressure affected the lens. Unknown cause or origin, but I am intrigued because of the timing. If this had occurred during a quiet period with no other events, I might have chalked it up to a camera focus problem. Because it coincides with Dana's work, I'll be following up on other devices.

- Just as Dana picks up the energy, the curtain on the side window moves. This aligns with the wind whistling. There is a gap around the air conditioning unit, so it makes sense that the increased wind moves the curtains.

- Okay, stop your grinnin' and drop your linen! There is more pixelation near Dana as she acknowledges the sad energy. It is like the other one—a cloud or shadow. This is worth a follow-up, so I set it aside for further review.

There are no other anomalies caught on the BluLu2 IR camera in the bedroom except for a few faint orbs, which I ignore. I note that there was a motion sensor plugged in during the earlier Session One when no one was in the room, and it did not go off at all during that entire time. I am increasingly fascinated with this case, not only from a psychological perspective but also from a paranormal one. What *is* that pixelation we caught on camera? Is Jo in danger of hurting herself? Or has she already tried?

Sessions One, Two, and Three
Blu-Lu1 IR Camera (stationed in basement)

The last files I go through as part of my core review are from the Blu-Lu1 IR camera which was stationed in the basement starting with our prep and running through the rest of the investigation until we packed up (which included the time during the seance when we were in the living room above). It's a lot of recording time, so it takes a few days to get through it. I can't spend hour after hour looking at the computer screen with extreme focus because my eyes and ears start to spin. I take frequent breaks and do other things to keep my sanity. Thank goodness I have my trusty Labrador to intervene every couple of hours for a quick walk or a trip to the backyard.

While watching the Blu-Lu1 basement files, I see that during the initial prep and walkthrough there are several EMF spikes on Walter's device. The Blu-Lu1 catches nothing on video during those anomalies. There is no video evidence coinciding with the growling at 9:08 (early in Session One), nor when Walter reported the whispery voice around 9:15. The camera did, however, get a clear visual of a small rodent running from the lounge area across the floor behind Sue's staircase. Our little friend is a large mouse or small rat, by my calculation. Dana was correct. I copy out the clip and type it in the log to show Sue. She may want to set a trap down there. If she doesn't outright deny it.

For the entire first half of the ninety-minute Blu-Lu1 video for Session One, there is nothing exciting until—HOLY SHIT! There is that pixelation again! At 9:47 pm, there is an anomaly that lasts about thirty seconds. It is clearer and more distinct than the ones I noted from the bedroom during Session Two. And this is a different device, so that makes it unlikely that the bedroom pixelation was an issue particular to that camera. I love data! We haven't experienced any similar issues with either camera, not in several years of using them. The pendulum is swinging away from this being a technical issue.

The anomaly in the basement appears just as Dana comes down the stairs after changing her thermometer batteries. The Blu-Lu1 video angle only catches the bottom third of the stairs, but I can see the light change as Dana opens the basement door and then shuts it. A few seconds later—around the time she gets "hit" with something—there is a dark, distinct blob of pixelation that appears between the pile of broken drums and the couch. It is low to the floor—two and a half feet high max—and it appears to *roll* from the drum set toward the back wall, across the length of the couch, and then back toward the drums.

A chill runs up my shoulder blade. I pull up the Session One file from Walter's handheld audio recorder and pop it on top of the Blu-Lu1 video in my editing software. I can just make out the sound of the door closing on the Blu-Lu1's shitty audio, so I match it with the handheld recorder (which is much better quality), and run them together. The basement door shuts. Dana calls out "SHINY" as she walks down a few steps. Then she cries out, followed by the bang of the thermometer falling onto the steps. Just after she cries out, I hear the growl that Walter noted, and then the blob slowly forms. As it moves away from the drum pile and then back again, it blocks out the bottom of the couch. Just as Dana yells, "GET THE FUCK OUT OF MY HEAD!" the blob pivots and disappears at triple speed behind the drums. The pixelation is gone. Damn. It sure looks like the blob appears just as Dana senses something, and then it disappears right as she pushes "it" out of her head. The entire event—from door shutting to blob disappearing—was about thirty seconds. It's not one hundred percent conclusive (and if it is, I don't even know what I would conclude it to be), but it has my full attention.

Once I gather myself (and watch the video/audio mashup about a dozen times), I copy out the clip with a few seconds on either side and save to a new file. The others are going to need to see this. I consider myself a level-headed human being, and I am rarely spooked by what we find in our investigations. This blob (or whatever it is) is seriously creeping me out.

Walter reported a minor shadow event on his review of the camcorder, so check that file to see if the timing coincides. Sure enough, I find an almost imperceptible anomaly around the time Dana got hit. From a different angle and distance, it is much, much fainter. If I didn't know where to look, I might have missed it. Great find by Walter. That's two cameras with similar anomalies at the same time. If the full-spectrum camera shows the same—we've got a bleeder!

The full-spectrum camera was closest to the lounge area and positioned to show the side view of the couch and drums, with the lens directed toward the back wall. Stan is going to tackle the full review for that device, but I can at least look at the few minutes around the time of Dana's hit. I pull out a copy of the file and fast-forward to 9:45 pm. Sure enough, there it is at 9:47! The movement of the anomaly isn't as noticeable on the full-spectrum cam because of the more dead-on angle (it travels front to back from the camera perspective), but the video plainly shows some sort of blob or shadow forming between the couch and drum pile. The pixelation is a little different, but that could be due to the nature of the camera. The timing with Dana getting blasted is uncanny. I take another clip and put into the evidence folder.

For the rest of Session One, I see nothing unexplainable on the Blu-Lu1. There are shadows when cars go by, and at 10:17 pm the video goes wonky from the low battery. The team members come into view a few times and then head upstairs for a break. From that point on, the camera sits in the basement in the darkness while we carry on above. Over the next twenty-four hours, I continue to watch the video in pieces, and what I see on the Blu-Lu1 during the next ninety minutes of film absolutely blows my mind. Twice, I see the pixelation blob again. The first time is during our break right after Session One. Walter has just changed the batteries on the Blu-Lu1 and gone back upstairs where the rest of the team is snacking. The blob reappears between the couch and drums, this time moving inward toward the stairwell and then up the stairs until it disappears from the lens view. I am racking my brain trying to think of a logical explanation for what could cause this. Is the furnace kicking in? Water heater? Something from Alice's side of the building? I come up with absolutely nothing, no explanation for the shadow. And if the trajectory caught on video is accurate, it is heading right up to where we are all sitting around eating Little Debbies and Cheetos.

I check the full-spectrum camera and camcorder. The camcorder shows nothing. The full-spectrum lens catches the break-time blob, and damn! It is bizarre! From the camera angle looking out from the side of Sue's stairs toward the back wall of the house, the clip shows this pixelation coming directly at the camera and getting bigger, as if it is going right through the lens. It is much more obvious than in the first instance when Dana sensed something on the stairs. This time, it keeps coming at the camera lens until there is a static wave in the video. The video goes dark for a second, then back to normal. I rerun the full-spectrum file repeatedly—in slow motion, sped up, trying to get a handle on what the fuck this thing is. It just looks like a pixelated shadow every time. And I'll be damned, it seems to go *through* the camera, causing it to burp for a second.

A second anomaly occurs (also when the basement is unoccupied), this time around 11:41 pm during Session Two. This is immediately after the pixelation I noted on the upstairs Blu-Lu2, when Dana picked up the depressed/suicidal energy. On the basement Blu-Lu1 file from that exact time, I see an opaque black shadow—or *something*—fly down the stairs like a swarm of starlings. It is much faster than the slow creep along the couch or up the stairs from the earlier incidents. This time it comes without warning and zips under the couch. Or maybe *into* it, I can't tell. It goes so fast that I have to run the video at quarter speed just to see it. The swarm appears to pass right in front of the camera and then disappears.

The blob has no defined shape in this video. It is fluid with an almost rolling motion. To say it "flies" down the stairs isn't entirely accurate; it's more like it whirls, but with heaviness. There is rotation in the movement. Two of the three blob appearances coincide with other events happening in the investigation, and this is important. When I check the timing of this second swarm on the full-spectrum camera, I confirm that it too has caught this flurry of shadow— although the video did not go blank as it did with the break time event. Maybe the blob didn't go directly through the camera, but over it?

So now we have three instances of this pixelation, each time caught on multiple cameras. One, when the energy hit Dana as she was coming down the stairs after her thermometer battery change. Two, during our break time between Session One and Session Two. And three, during Session Two, when Dana is again sensing the suicidal spirit in the bedroom.

The hair on my arms is standing up as straight as a West Point cadet. We don't get a ton of exciting evidence during our investigations. Sure, we get lots of anomalies. But most of them are your average variety of flickering lights and blowing curtains, things that we can easily explain if we dig a little. Almost as soon as I hear the faint sound of a crying baby in a recording, I'm like, "Catbird!" I see a dog peeing in front of a window, and I immediately know this is a strong likelihood for explaining the smell of urine.

But this pixelation thing? I can't explain it. I've now seen it at different times, on three cameras, and it mostly coincides with Dana picking up something psychically. It *feels* like an energy; it *feels* sentient, or at least purposeful. The good thing is, it doesn't feel malicious, and that's what I'm holding onto right now. My skin is crawling a bit as I watch the last clip several times before taking a copy and putting it in the client evidence file.

The Blu-Lu1 ran alone by itself in the basement throughout the seance session as well, so I watch until the end. I'm almost falling asleep with boredom for most of the remaining footage until I see something that shocks me even more than the last pixelation anomaly.

What. The actual. Fuck.

Excerpt 9 from the *RIP After Dark* Podcast
Episode 72: Case of the Demon Drums

This podcast was broadcast one year after the actual investigation.
Client names and identifying details have been changed to maintain privacy.

Libbi: *When I saw that blob going up the steps during our break, I freaked out a little.*

Walter: *This is why you do the heavy lifting on evidence review. I would have soiled my drawers.*

Libbi: *That's not really a stretch, Walter. At least once a year, you mistake a fart for a shart at work. Don't you remember last month—*

Walter: [interrupts] *—OKAY THEN! So, what you're saying is, they weren't orbs.*

Libbi: *Just sayin'. And no, definitely not orbs. I hardly even know how to describe them.*

Walter: *Just a blob.*

Libbi: *Yes, a black blob but weirdly fading in and out like when people pixelate things in a video to hide them.*

Walter: *Like paintings on HGTV shows. Or trademarked logos.*

Libbi: *Right, exactly. Or dick pics. Butt shots on network television.*

Walter: [surprised chuckle] *Okay, I guess we're going there, folks.*

Libbi: *Well, it was like that. Dark, almost black like smoke or a shadow, except more pixelated.*

Walter: *Coinciding with the times when Dana sensed something.*

Libbi: *More or less. Other than when we were on break. She wasn't sensing anything then, so if there is a correlation, that would be the outlier.*

Walter: *Unless it was just jonesing for some spicy nacho Doritos.*

Libbi: *Who wouldn't be, right? Or maybe it smelled Stan's venison sausage (that no one ate except Stan).*

Walter: *Why have venison when you have Ho Ho's and Yum Yums? It's too gamey.*

Libbi: *It's gross, that's what it is. My mom tried to fake us out once when we were kids. She put ground venison in our spaghetti sauce.*

Walter: *Could you tell it was venison? Even hidden in the spaghetti sauce?*

Libbi: *Oh yeah. No doubt. I was maybe eight or nine, and I think I used a curse word. Not really, but I said something. We could tell, Walter. We could tell. It was icky.*

Walter: *Maybe the pixelation blob thing needed some protein.*

Libbi: *Doubtful.*

Walter: *@potterygirl2022 wants to know if we log everything (like, EVERYTHING) we find, and do we give all that to the client? Libbi, I'll let you take that one since you are the keeper of the records.*

Libbi: *We log just about everything unless it's sensitive in nature (which was the case for this investigation). I will clip out any basic chatter from the files—like when we are on break—unless we catch something during that chatter.*

Walter: *No one needs to hear us burping or see us pigging out like we haven't eaten in a week.*

Libbi: *It's not pretty.*

Walter: *What about swear words? I'm sure that's on someone's mind.*

Libbi: *I will generally leave them in unless it's not appropriate, like if we were arguing about something or it got heated.*

Walter: *There you go, potterygirl2022.*

Libbi: *Getting back to the pixelation stuff. All the anomalies we found during Session One in the basement and Session Two in the bedroom were fascinating, to say the least. But... BUT... what we saw during the last session? UN-FUCKING-BELIEVABLE!*

Walter: *I agree. So, let's talk about what we found in Session Three: The Seance.*

The Seance Stuns

Tuesday, October 15, 6:00 pm
Zoom call originating from Bean Residence, Saddleridge Rd, Roanoke, Virginia
Libbi, Maya, Dana

Maya Hill-Goldberg

Libbi sets up a Zoom call with me and Dana on the second Tuesday evening after the investigation. I have just started reviewing my audio files from the seance session, but I am only about ten percent done (what can I say, I am a busy college student, and I had three princess parties over the weekend). I have fully completed the review of my recorder files from Session One in the basement, and from Session Two when I was sitting in the Mackenzie living room. There was nothing notable other than what Libbi has already reported in the shared log.

Dana is late to the call, so Libbi and I chat while we wait. Libbi jumps right into the details.

"So… we haven't talked in person since the investigation. I'm curious—what is your take on the stuff we found in Jo's closet? From a psychological perspective."

It is not unusual for the team to disconnect somewhat during the evidence review period. We are all busy people. Stan and I both live almost an hour away, so it's not like we just call the team up and ask if anyone wants to go to happy hour at the local brewpub. Dana has a kid; we all have jobs. Plus, we are very different people, both in personality and age. I am in my early twenties, while the rest of the team are in their early to late forties. And we always have a formal team review before the reveal (the one for this case is scheduled for tomorrow night on Zoom). This off-schedule gathering with me and Dana is a little unorthodox, but not unheard of. Sometimes we need to talk face to face about something specific (and without Stan).

"Well," I say, thinking about the closet secret for a few seconds. "I think you nailed it when you said at our briefing at Cracker Barrel that you thought Jo might be working through her sexual or gender identity. Given the hiding of her "stuff," I would say it's more gender. It's like she's hiding the female part of herself. The clothes too. Everything shoved in that closet seemed to be—"

I think for a second, then used air quotes to the camera.

"'Pretty girl clothes.' Skirts, dresses, a pair of patent leather flats if I am remembering correctly. As much as I could tell in the light of a flashlight, anyway. It was consistent with what I saw peeking out when I was doing my baseline with the lights on."

Libbi nods and takes a gulp from a giant white mug that says *This is what a published author looks like*. It is just after six in the evening, so it's probably hot cocoa or decaf. I remember the herbal brew sitting next to me and take a sip from the small, flowered teacup. Libbi puts down her mug and holds up the peace sign with her middle and index fingers. She points them at her eyes, then toward the camera a few times. *We see eye to eye on the Josephine thing.*

"Ah, there's Dana," says Libbi. A moment later, Dana comes online from her dining room table, looking down toward her laptop camera. How can she help it? She's ten feet tall. Her curls are pulled up into a violet scarf, and she is wearing short-sleeved lavender scrubs. She must have had a long shift at Carillion Hospital because the scrubs are a little dirty and look like they've seen better days.

"Sorry I'm late," she apologizes. "The child."

She moves aside and nods her head over her right shoulder, where I can see thirteen-year-old Ralph. He is sitting at their kitchen counter eating what appears to be a bowl of cereal. Cinnamon Toast Crunch, if the box next to him is any indication. I can't help but admire a kid who eats cereal for dinner, and a parent who lets him.

"Hi Junior," calls Libbi. Ralph smiles and waves back.

"So whatcha got?" asks Dana.

Libbi shares her screen and pulls up a handful of files. We watch as she plays the clips from the Blu-Lu1 and the full-spectrum cameras showing the pixelation in the basement during Dana's stairwell episode, the one during our break time, and again when Dana sensed something in the bedroom during Session Two.

"Okay," I say. "You definitely have my attention."

"Yeah," says Dana. "I mean, just looking only at the blobs, it's maybe just dust or something. But the timing compared with my experience is amazing. And twice."

"Those aren't even the best ones," says Libbi. "Not by a long shot. Buckle up."

She gives no setup, just plays the seance audio from her handheld recorder of Jo wailing, stopping, and then her mom yelling at her. Libbi reruns it several times, jacking up the volume as far as she can. Right after Jo stops, I can hear the same rage sound in the background behind Sue and Jo arguing. It is almost a mirror repeat of Jo's howl, about the same length of ten seconds.

"Whoa, that is weird!" says Dana. "It's like an echo of her screaming!"

"Exactly!" says Libbi, pointing at the camera. "And there's more."

She plays a video clip from the Blu-Lu1 of this blob thing materializing in the basement just after the outcry from Jo. It drops from the rafters next to the stairs, and it looks almost like a human form!

Dana and I are speechless for a moment. All we can do is eke out a sound of amazement now and then. Finally, Libbi continues.

"This is exciting for sure. I have a theory. But I need some corroboration. We had a camcorder pointed into the living room during the seance. It didn't catch anything strange—although it confirms that Jo was not screaming when we hear that echo. In fact, she talks over it at one point. It corresponds to the pixelation time. I'd like you two to check your digital recorder files around 1:03 or 1:04 am to see if either of you captured the echo on audio. I think that's a good word for it. The echo."

Dana and I immediately look for the correct files and spend a few minutes reviewing that time frame. Dana had been standing back near the bedroom door during the seance. Libbi was on the stool to my right, across from the couch and on the other side of the coffee table. I was the closest to Jo, sitting on the floor near the front window, next to Gina, who was next to Jo. That's three recorders at varying distances. I would expect the sound to be a little different on each one, maybe loudest on mine, then next loudest on Libbi's, and faintest on Dana's since she was the farthest away.

Dana and I first listen to our recorder audio files around 1:00 am to see if we even picked up the echo.

"I got it!" I say, coming off mute.

I play it for the others. There it is, clear as day, and the echo sounds almost as loud on my recording as the howl that came from Jo herself. It is noticeably louder than the echo on Libbi's version.

"Can you send me a clip of that audio?" asks Libbi. "Start it a few seconds before Jo screams and end a few seconds after the echo."

"Still checking," says Dana. She isn't the most tech-savvy person, so it takes a minute for her to get to the right file at the right time. After she struggles and curses for about thirty seconds, Junior appears on camera to help her. Meanwhile, I take a clip of the echo from my recording and throw it into Google Drive. I copy the link and paste into the Zoom chat for Libbi.

A few minutes later, Dana confirms that she (or rather Ralph) has also found the echo.

"But it's weird," she says. "It's like a wave."

"A wave..." says Libbi, confused. "What does that mean?"

"Hold on, I'll send it to you."

I don't hold my breath. It takes a couple minutes and more help from her son, but Dana eventually sends the entire file link to Libbi, who downloads it, finds the correct time, and takes a clip similar to the one I sent.

I go get another cup of tea, and when I return, Libbi has taken all three audio clips and combined them in her video editing app, overlaid on top of the camcorder video from the living room and the pixelation video from the basement. I think I see what her theory is.

"Okay," Libbi says. "Let's say there is a correlation between Jo's howling, the echo, and this blob-pixelation thing that appeared in the basement around that same time. Could they be the same thing? Meaning, whatever energy created the blob also manifested the sound?"

I nod my head in the affirmative. "Like if Jo manifested this energy—or maybe a combo of Jo and her mom, jury's out on that one—the echo might be emanating from the blob. Or really, from Jo or Sue."

Dana nods in agreement. "From my perspective—based on what I experienced in the basement and the bedroom—it's a strong likelihood that the energy is from Jo. And I agree with you, Maya; the audio and video may very well be connected. The Echo-Blob."

"Good," continues Libbi. "Let's run through these individually first."

She plays the clip called *Maya Echo Audio*. We hear Jo wailing. She stops, but the echo of her cry continues while Sue snaps at her. The echo is loud and distinct behind the argument between Jo and Sue. Then Libbi replays her own audio file. Finally, Dana's, which is the faintest overall. But oddly, on Dana's recorder it sounds very different.

"Wait," I say. "Play them all again, same order."

I hear it again, but it's in all three of them. The wave Dana mentioned. It is much more noticeable on Dana's file, but as I look at the visual representation of the sound waves that Libbi is sharing on her screen, all the recordings have volume variations. Mine starts out very loud (I was the closest to Jo), but then the volume drops—as if the sound is moving away. Libbi's is similar, although it starts fainter, increases slightly, then fades out. Dana's is faint at the start, then has an unmistakable volume increase, then a similar decrease until it fades out.

"Do you hear it?" asks Libbi? Dana and I nod in unison.

"It's like it's… it's moving," I say hesitantly. "From Jo, through the room, and then… away."

"Away, like to the basement," says Dana.

"That's the theory," says Libbi, exhaling as if she had been holding it in. "That is precisely the theory. Although I didn't even think about the *audio* capturing the movement. Good catch, women! Okay, now let's look at the timing of the audio and video together."

Libbi mutes Dana's echo clip and mine, leaving only hers with the volume on. On the editing app, we see a split screen with one side showing the camcorder video of Jo on the couch, the other side showing the video of the stairwell captured by the basement Blu-Lu1. Libbi jacks up the volume and pushes play.

First, we see and hear Jo thinking she heard a drum. Then Sue snaps back, telling Jo she just imagined it. She tells her daughter to calm down, Jo hyperventilates a few times, Sue yells, and then Jo puts her hands over her ears, leans forward, and screams. Sue tells her to shut up. Jo stops—still bent over, but we can clearly see her face on the camcorder. Her lips are pursed, as if she is specifically trying not to make a sound. There isn't anything coming from her mouth at that point, I am sure of it.

And the echo continues.

We hear Sue yell at Jo over the echo. Then Walter says he's going to check outside. The echo is still audible. Almost off camera we see the door open and shut as Walter goes outside to investigate. Around the time that Walter first opens the door to go out, the blob materializes from the ceiling in the basement and disappears into the couch.

With the recording times matched up, it all flows like an assembly line. Or a well-orchestrated scene in a movie. It doesn't prove that the pixelation blob and audio echo are the same, but it certainly doesn't disprove it. And with the other pixelations that Libbi found during Session One and Session Two—which seem to correspond to psychic hits on Dana, save for the one during break—it makes for a gripping possibility. One that is making me shiver.

"Hold up," says Dana as we are watching the sequence for the fourth time. "Can you zoom in on the blob video from the Blu-Lu? Right as it's moving behind the drums after it drops from the ceiling."

Libbi resizes the Blu-Lu1 recording and replays that clip.

"See that? Right there at the bottom of the drum pile. Look at the cymbal (or what used to be the cymbal) hanging off the side of that broken pole. There's a brief flash."

Libbi zooms in a little further and slows the speed to half. The resolution is getting a little blurry, but I see it too.

"Well, fuck me running," she says. "Holy Shit! How did I miss that?"

She leans forward and stares at her monitor, then sits back in her chair and sighs. There is no mistaking what we see, and we are all speechless. Finally, after a long silence, Libbi speaks.

"Dammit. I guess I'm going to have to pull Stan into this one."

Thursday, October 17, 6:00 pm
Evidence Review at Bean Residence, Saddleridge Rd, Roanoke, Virginia
Libbi, Walter, Stan

Stan Kattagucci

The cymbal swings when the blob shadow thing comes down from the ceiling. There is no doubt about it. I don't know why the motion detectors don't go off. I plugged in two of them during the seance, but neither was triggered. It's possible that the location of the blob shadow in relation to the motion sensors put it out of range. Also, it's paranormal, so there is some expectation that it defies what is logical. It wouldn't be the first time I've seen physical evidence of a manifestation, yet the motion detectors stay silent.

Lib and the others might claim it was just a tuft of wind or a coincidence, but the cymbal moves. One hundred percent. While we were conducting the seance, the basement was vacant with the door closed. Any significant air current would have been unlikely. The heat did not kick on, and even if it had, the vent in the basement was only partially open, and too far away to affect the heavy brass. And the timing is too perfect. The blob comes from the ceiling, takes human form, and disappears behind the broken drums. At the precise moment it passes behind the pile and disappears into the couch, the cymbal swings. In the raw video, it is difficult to see but for the slight glare from a corner of the shiny metal that taunts the lens for a split second. With a few filters applied to the clip and a speed adjustment, it is undeniable.

I am over at Walter and Libbi's house looking at evidence clips with the two of them. Libbi offered to do a Zoom call, but my meter repair route covers Botetourt County—which borders Roanoke—so it's easy enough to take the extra twenty minutes to do it face to face. Plus, I get to see Miss Fenny. We are gathered in Libbi's mid-century office, which looks like something out of a *Mad Men* episode. Besides a giant L-shaped desk, she has two leather chairs, a coffee table, and a small table that seats four. For what purpose, I can't imagine. Libbi writes books all day. To each their own, I guess. Libbi is sitting in front of two large monitors, maneuvering the files while Walter and I stand behind her and watch. In just a few days, the Beans will reveal the case evidence to the Mackenzies. We have found a lot—and I mean, a LOT—of unusual exhibits so far: the black blob with the overlaid EVP scream (which Libbi calls "the echo-blob); the other pixelation anomalies; and some things on my recorder from the bedroom session and the seance. There is something at the Mackenzie house. Maybe it's not a demon, but it is most definitely supernatural. The cymbal movement all but confirms it.

In the week and a half since the investigation, I have reviewed the files from my handheld recorder, both the Blu-Lu cameras, and the full-spectrum file from the basement. I also discovered (on my own) the pixelations that correlate with the echo and with Dana's spiritual communication. I had put my findings into a folder on our shared drive (and labeled it "MIND BLOWING" no less), then alerted Libbi. If she had checked her personal email or her texts before she had her Zoom call with Maya and Dana, she would have known that I knew about this powerful evidence several days before she did. I reached out three times. Sometimes I think she ignores me on purpose.

So, nanny nanny boo boo; I figured it out before she did.

But I also got one more thing on my audio that no one else has brought up so far. It happens during the echo. The echo is behind the chatter. What I found is behind the echo—a long, groaning sound like a great metal machine grinding against itself; a massive gear coming to life after sitting in a junkyard rusting away in a frigid death. The sound is deep and cavernous and almost undetectable behind the echo sound and the amid tension of the seance conversation. But it is there.

"It sounds like someone's stomach growling," says Libbi. "Or gas."

Sometimes Libbi outshines even her husband in the "dick" category.

"You know what it might be?" says Walter. "That nasty old chair Sue sits in. It's a recliner; there's probably something straining inside that ancient leather."

Sometimes the two of them are just a little *too* skeptical.

"It's not the chair," I say. "I ran the audio parallel to the camcorder; Sue barely moves during the echo. Play it again if you don't believe me."

Libbi sighs and looks up at me. "It's not that we don't believe you, Stanley. We just need to make sure we have ruled out everything else before saying it's an unearthly growl. I mean, I can hardly hear it let alone decipher it."

She plays the video/audio mashup again. The camcorder file shows Jo doing her wailing thing, then she and Sue have words while the echo plays underneath. The groan is in the shadows, barely there—but it *is* there. Sue does sit back briefly, but it happens before the grinding sound. After that, she does nothing but tilt her head.

"You might be right, dear wife," says Walter. "I think that's when she pushed it out."

"Pushed what out?" I ask, and then immediately regret it.

"Her fart," says Walter, taking a sip of coffee from a large mug with some sort of Nordic symbol on it. He's going to be up all night. "She dropped a zipper fart right then. That's what it sounds like. Once again, my wife is right."

Libbi turns over her shoulder and gives her husband a fist pump. I roll my eyes.

"I don't think it's a fart," I say, defeated.

"Maybe not," says my stepsister. "Let's just make sure we get the clip into the evidence folder and maybe Sue or Jo will recognize the sound. It's so low and soft that it could be anything. Even something outside or down the road. A car on the freeway in the distance, or maybe an engine brake."

I can hardly contain my frustration, so I bite my tongue—literally, almost drawing blood—to keep from going ballistic. ENGINE BRAKE? This is not an engine brake. I know the difference between a semi-truck and this sound, which is most definitely not related to shifting gears on a large vehicle. My only consolation is that we agree on the echo-blob. That is indisputable. When Libbi told me that both Maya and Dana had reviewed the files and could not debunk the echo, I was grateful beyond belief. Finally, we get something that can't be explained by dogs pissing in the mulch or a rat skulking in the shadows.

I leave the Bean residence shortly thereafter. In retrospect, it was hardly worth the drive considering I already knew the big secret. At least I got a few minutes to wrestle with my four-legged niece and toss her a ball about a hundred times.

I have completed the review of my assigned files and corroborated most of what Libbi and Walter found. There are a few things from the log I want to check again, and then I'll be finished.

The first verification is from Session Two in the bedroom, when Libbi thinks she hears a response of *"Yes"* after I ask, *"Do you mean us any harm?"* I check my recorder, which has the best likelihood of catching the sound. I didn't notice anything on my first blind review, but maybe I missed it. I loop a clip from the two walkie-talkie events around that time (11:09 and 11:13 pm). There is nothing vocal on the first one. On the second one, there is something coming through faintly under the static, right after the device beeps. It could be a female voice saying something like "Ooh-ya." But I'm pretty sure it's just the wind. I note it in my log.

See? I know how to be skeptical as well as the rest of them. I don't think *everything* is an evil spirit.

I find nothing else questionable in the reported anomalies on Libbi's list, but I am obsessed with the pixelations, particularly the one coinciding with the echo. Now that I have the timestamp, I can run my own tests. After compiling a mashup of the basement Blu-Lu1 camera, the full-spectrum cam, and the audio recordings from the seance, there is no doubt in my mind that the black blob thing is directly related to the echo. And it likely came from Jo.

I no longer think this is a demon. Might there be an evil spirit here? Sure. But I don't think Sue or Jo (or their house) is possessed. I'm not a hundred percent on that on account of a few things, like Jo being touched on her leg. But there is a growing amount of evidence supporting the idea that people—particularly adolescent-aged kids—can generate incredible amounts of telekinetic energy, especially when they are in distress. Like in that Stephen King book *Carrie,* or that other one they made into a movie with Drew Barrymore. *Firestarter,* that's it. That stuff happens, and more often than we think. It's rarely as drastic as in books and film. Usually, it's subtle enough that the adults don't even notice—or at least, it never occurs to them that there is anything supernatural going on. The dining room chair gets moved or the drawer is found opened, and they just assume it's the teenager being careless.

Is this energy from Jo dangerous? That I don't know. I think it could be, but it's hard to say. So far, the person most in danger of being harmed is Jo herself. Self-harmed. Sometimes the telekinetic energy is directed inward. If Jo is suffering because of an internal conflict about her identity—even if the lack of acceptance originates somewhere outside (like her mom or classmates or society in general)—the nature of the conflict could direct the energy toward self-mutilation. Or invoke an urge to take it even further.

I truly hope it doesn't come to that. And I think our findings might influence the outcome.

Excerpt 10 from the *RIP After Dark* Podcast Episode 72: Case of the Demon Drums

This podcast was broadcast one year after the actual investigation.
Client names and identifying details have been changed to maintain privacy.

Walter: *I gotta say, you did a great job finding that echo-blob thing. And synchronizing it with the audio.*

Libbi: *Thanks! I give credit to Stan, too. Technically, he found it first, although I didn't realize it.*

Walter: *Because you didn't read his emails or respond to his texts.*

Libbi: *What's your point?*

Walter: *Well, you mocked me for having a full voicemail box not one hour ago.*

Libbi: *[pauses] I did do that. I apologize. I am supposed to be the one keeping it all organized, and I failed the team. Can you ever forgive me?*

Walter: *Just sayin'.*

Libbi: *So, thank you, Stan, for corroborating our evidence! That was a good analysis, if I do say so myself.*

Walter: *Absolutely. And when you synced up the audio from Maya and Dana too? That was pro-level.*

Libbi: *Maya and Dana figured out that the echo came in waves and was likely moving. And Dana noticed the cymbal moving. The power of estrogen.*

Walter: *All brought together by my brilliant wife. You should have a TV show. PSI—Paranormal Scene Investigator.*

Libbi: *Maybe GSI—Ghost Scene Investigator. We already used PSI for Poop Scene Investigator, like when I inspect Fenny's shit piles for earplugs and rocks.*

Walter: *That's right. I blocked it out because it involves fecal matter. You know I can't deal.*

Libbi: *I am aware. Remember the time Fenny came home from daycare and shit out an everlasting gobstopper?*

Walter: [fake gags] *Stop! I'm gonna start dry heaving!*

Libbi: *I had to inspect it. With rubber gloves, in case anyone out there is concerned about my attention to germs and bacteria.*

Walter: *When your Labrador doesn't want to be touched, you know there's something wrong.*

Libbi: *Facts. A story for another day, perhaps.*

Walter: *Or today, since you just told it.*

Libbi: *Churlish. Moving on!*

Walter: *So, do you think it was a demon?*

Libbi: *Uh, no. Not a demon.*

Walter: *Fair enough. What about the metal grinding sound that Stan heard on his recorder? Maybe that was a demon?*

Libbi: *Mmm... doubtful. I'm going to call engine brake in the distance or your stomach gurgling.*

Walter: *I did have a lot of junk food that night.*

Libbi: *Including extra-dark pretzels. Guaran-TEED to cause bowel inflammation.*

Walter: *I do like my extra-dark pretzels. In spite of the side effects, which I cannot deny.*

Libbi: *Intestinal flatulence, yes. Demon or devil, no.*

Walter: *Anyway, we somehow got through all the evidence in two weeks. That was a lot of work.*

Libbi: *And then it was time to do the reveal.*

Walter: *Believe it or not, folks... that's when things REALLY got crazy.*

Demons and Delinquents

Friday, October 18, 2:45 pm
Roanoke County Juvenile and Domestic Relations District Court

Josephine Suzanne Mackenzie stands before the Honorable Helen Halloran at the Roanoke County Juvenile and Domestic Relations District Court in Roanoke, Virginia. Her mother, Sue Mackenzie, is beside her. They have waived representation by an attorney (as is their right), and the judge has agreed that this waiver is consistent with the interests of the child. The charges are relatively minor: habitual unexcused absences from school; a person less than twenty-one years of age in possession of an alcoholic beverage; and a juvenile driving a car without a valid driver's license. These are all misdemeanors and will likely result in fines, warnings, promises made, and promises broken.

Josephine stands before the judge, scratching the back of her neck near the tag on the button-down blouse she borrowed from her mother. Her khaki pants make a papery sound as she shuffles her feet nervously. Her mother insisted that she dress up for the occasion, and they compromised with the shirt and slacks after arguing for ten minutes over the alternative (that being a dress). The judge is silently reading Josephine's file, which the teenager finds nerve-racking. The absolute quiet of the small courtroom is only adding to Josephine's agitation. She isn't certain whether she is more afraid of the legal consequences or the parental ones. She scratches her neck again. Sue gives her a not-so-subtle elbow nudge as they wait for the judge to finish.

The judge is not aware that Josephine does not feel like a Josephine, but more like a Jo or maybe even a Joe with an e. The judge does not know that Jo finds it unbearable to wear the overly feminine clothing her mother keeps buying for her, so she finds ways to "accidentally" ruin the skirts and dresses—or she simply stuffs them into the back of her closet. Out of sight, out of mind. The judge has no idea that Jo hides the evidence of her monthly cycle, not because she is ashamed of it, but because it is a frequent reminder of her biology, which doesn't play nice with her psychology. It is as if her body is giving her a big *Fuck you!* every four weeks. Judge Halloran is oblivious to these facts and how they factor into the defendant's behavior.

The judge is unaware that Jo feels wholly unloved and unaccepted by the person closest to her, that being her mother. Jo believes Sue hates her short hair, hates her basketball shorts, hates her. She senses that her mom's best friend is disgusted by her too—even more so than Sue (for now)—and she has heard the two women talking in hushed voices about church camps and private schools. Jo believes that her mother would rather she were dead than "different" in the way she feels different. Sometimes Jo doesn't want to be alive in this world anymore. Because what is worse than the rejection of who we truly are inside by those who are supposed to love us the most? The judge has no clue that Jo has already taken steps to rid the world of herself, unsuccessfully. The judge doesn't know that Jo believes with all her heart that her mother would be better off—even happier—without her around.

The judge has no knowledge of these things. She sees only what is in front of her. But Helen Halloran wasn't born yesterday, and she makes some assumptions. Before her is a tall teenage girl with short hair who dresses like a boy, standing next to a bona fide literal Bible-toting mother wearing a glaring Swarovski crystal cross around her neck. The cross is unavoidable in all its angelic sparkle, and Her Honor wonders if the mom feels it will somehow channel Jesus in her favor for these proceedings. *Not in my court.* But it is a valiant effort.

The file on Josephine Mackenzie is short. She is not a chronically troubled child. Judge Halloran has seen thousands of juvenile cases over the years, and many of these kids begin their habits of rebellion in elementary school. Jo is not one of them. Until this year, she was an honor student with no priors. Not even a minor charge of shoplifting, which is a rite of passage these days for just about every teenager—even the ones who don't graduate to more serious activities. Her Honor thinks she knows what is going on here, and she feels for Josephine Mackenzie. She reminds herself to give her wife an extra-big hug tonight when she gets home, and to thank whatever gods or energy may be out there that she had parents supportive of her being different from them.

The Honorable Judge Helen Halloran addresses the Mackenzies.

"Ms. Mackenzie—the younger, Josephine—this is the first time I've seen you in my courtroom. Have you been in trouble before?"

She must always ask. Records from outside the state or county are painfully slow to get updated. Judge Halloran feels relieved when Jo responds, "No, Ma'am."

Her Honor is not a biological mom, but her maternal instincts have kicked in with many of the children who have come before her prior to this one. She has seen this scenario dozens of times. The boy who likes boys; the girl who wants to be a boy; the child who isn't sure about anything. It is heartening that it is becoming more acceptable for them to feel comfortable expressing their true selves—but disheartening that being authentic is still met with conflict both internally and externally.

She addresses Sue now.

"Mrs. Mackenzie, it appears that Josephine has no priors…"

(She is careful not to say "your daughter" just in case she is right.)

"… and has been until recently an exemplary student with an equally stellar record."

"Yes, Ma'am, that is correct."

Judge Halloran takes off her reading glasses and sets them next to the paperwork. "Is there something going on that may have triggered the behavior? Because honestly, I'm perplexed."

She is not perplexed, but her job is to go by what is written on the paper in front of her.

She looks at Josephine. "I would ask the same of you, Josephine. If you feel comfortable talking about it."

They rarely do—talk about it—and Judge Halloran is not a psychologist, but she always asks. Out of respect.

Sue speaks first, which doesn't surprise Her Honor. "There *is* something going on at home," she says without hesitation.

The judge instinctively scans back through her decades of experience for what might come next. A recent divorce? She knows from the paperwork that Josephine's father is not living with them, but the split was over two years ago. Statistically, if any divorce-related behavior is going to manifest, it will start with a vengeance as the parents are splitting, not this long after. What then? Sexual abuse? That is always a possibility, and all too common. The Judge prays that this is not the case. There is no one else living in the home, and her gut says that the mother isn't the type. Maybe someone at their church? The Judge would bet good money that Mom is singing hymns every Sunday, ten o'clock butt-in-pew, on the dot. God only knows what predators are lurking there. And there *is* an older brother.

But Judge Halloran's instinct is still very much leading her toward a different conclusion, one that involves gender or sexual preference.

But if that's where the mother goes when she responds, Her Honor will eat her neatly pressed judicial robe and swallow it down with a glass of sweet tea.

"What is going on at home?" the Judge asks, keeping her tone neutral, gentle, curious.

Sue Mackenzie crosses her arms and fidgets. Josephine Mackenzie lowers her head and avoids looking at anything except the gray industrial carpet on the floor.

"Well…" Sue sighs, appearing to find some conviction. "It's because of the demons."

Miraculously, Judge Helen Halloran's expression does not waver—although she does have a brief *Twilight Zone* moment when time freezes as she processes what she just heard. There is silence in the nearly empty courtroom. It goes on almost too long before the Judge speaks.

"I'm sorry. Did you say *demons?*"

"Yes, Ma'am," says Sue, nodding her head and standing tall, as if to underscore her conviction.

Her Honor presses her lips together and then purses them as her expression turns quizzical. "When you say 'demons,' what do you mean? Is this metaphorical, like 'inner demons?' As in a mental health concern?"

She hopes the mother knows what metaphorical means.

"Not metaphorical," says Sue, shaking her head. "Literal. We've had demons haunting our house."

Judge Helen Halloran bites her tongue to keep from making a sound. She isn't sure if she would laugh or audibly sigh with unabashed sarcasm (and maybe utter, "Oh, for fuck's sake!"), but those responses would be neither helpful nor appropriate. *Well, this is a first.*

Another moment passes in silence before she speaks.

"All right, Mrs. Mackenzie. Tell me about your demons."

Revelation

Saturday, October 19, 4:30 pm
The Investigation Findings and Reveal
Mackenzie Residence, Starry Knob Lane, Roanoke, Virginia

Libbi Bean

We asked Sue to meet with us alone first because of the sensitivity around what we found in Josephine's closet. When we arrive, I am happy that Jo is not sitting in the dark living room that reeks of week-old (month-old?) cigarette smoke and sweat. I don't know what happened in the last fourteen days, but I don't remember it being this bad when we had the investigation. It is stuffy inside despite the cool late-October weather. Even the pedestal fan running next to the kitchen island isn't dissipating the thick stink of stale nicotine as it blows quietly toward the front of the house.

Sue and her friend Gina are puffing away in unison almost as soon as we get inside. I'm a little annoyed that Gina is here, sitting on the couch near the front window with her anorexic mongrel and her righteousness. A giant gold keychain in the shape of a cross is hanging off the strap of her cross-body purse. I have this irrational (or is it?) urge to sucker-punch her in the gut. She is part of the problem in this family; I would bet money on it. From what Dana overheard during the smoke breaks on the night of the investigation, Gina is an instigator. I stalked her Facebook profile last week, and to call her a religious nutjob would be a severe understatement. Gina is either not smart enough to lock down her social media (I could read and comment on anything, even though we are not connected as friends or even friends of friends), or she just doesn't care. Every other post is about her going to church or a Bible verse (or meme or video). She doesn't say anything blatantly biased (plausible deniability), but the undertone is unmistakable: She hates liberals, non-Christians, Christians who don't pray or go to church, LGBTQ+ (they are just

238

"throwing it in her face," which is ironic), "the illegals," feminists, and just about everyone else. There is a tone of superiority running throughout her social media: *I'm better than you because I'm a devout Christian.* As if she's got a direct line to Jesus. In one of her posts, she actually said she was praying for her keto cookies to come out right, and she knew God would help her. If there *is* an all-powerful, supernatural being, I very much doubt it invests its time and energy in the successful execution of someone's low-carb recipes. Honestly, someone who must constantly remind everyone (and themselves) of how deep their faith is probably isn't very sure of their faith at all. In Gina's case, her rhetoric is toxic.

As we get settled in for the reveal, I sit on the opposite end of the couch to allow a little space between my agnostic heathen soul and God's apparent right-hand woman. I feel bad taking Pepper's favorite spot, but I spy him nestled under the kitchen island between two of the bar stools. Sleeping, per usual. Gina puffs on her cigarette with long, slow draws. After each time, she flicks her ashes exactly three times into a square, pewter ashtray balanced on the arm of the couch. It's almost obsessive-compulsive. She seems very comfortable blowing smoke into Sue's already-funky living room, but I'd bet money her own house is immaculate. It catches my attention that she does not look in Sue's direction at all. I am sensing tension between the two, and now my interest is piqued.

I open my laptop on the coffee table next to the two candles we burned during the seance. Walter shoots me a look, no doubt wondering where he should sit. I say nothing. Sometimes I have to let him figure it out for himself. Finally, he grabs one of the bar stools rather than sit in the middle of the couch next to the thirteenth apostle and her holy rodent. I'm disappointed that I won't have a buffer between me and Hellhound, but I get it. Walter is an introvert, and this is a lot of people for him.

Sue is sitting in her old leather recliner. She and Gina are each wearing jeans and a long-sleeved shirt. Gina's white knit top has a carved cross printed on the front, in black with the words **"The Way, The Truth, The Life"** stamped on one side. Her jeans look like they were dry-cleaned and pressed. Sue's jeans look like they were last washed a year ago, and her pullover graphic is so faded that I can't tell what it's supposed to be. It might be a version of the classic Rolling Stones' lips logo, or it might be Shrek; only she knows. But I *can* say with reasonable certainty that she slept in it.

Before I open the files, I ask Sue if anything has happened since the investigation two weeks ago. She tells me that things have been quiet. They smelled urine a few times (human, obviously) and there have been some vague voices and a cold spot or two, but that's about it. No drums, nothing significant other than they had to go in front of a judge on account of Josephine's recent truancy and a few other behavior issues. I ask how that went.

"Well, I told 'em it was the demons' fault," she says.

She says it so matter-of-factly, like she might say, "Pardon me" to a stranger passing on the street or let someone know the bathroom is out of toilet paper. It was that indifferent. I glance up and catch Walter's eye as I open the evidence directory. He doesn't even try to hide his disbelief. He shuts his eyes and shakes his head back and forth—almost imperceptibly, but I see it. I'm sure Gina can see him too, but I don't think he cares. I know what he is thinking. *See, I told you! Whack job! She told the judge—THE JUDGE—that her daughter's behavior is because Satan's spawn is invading her house.* I give him credit for holding his tongue. If someone like me finds it difficult, it must be nearly unbearable for him. I defended Sue many times these past few weeks, but now I am questioning my own critical thinking. She must really believe, from the innermost part of her soul, that she has demons in her house. To reveal this in a truancy case is madness.

"Okay," I say, hiding my disbelief, but narrowly. "So how did it go?"

Sue shrugs and takes a long drag. "I don't think she believed me, but she was sympathetic to our... situation."

She taps her cigarette into the cross-shaped ashtray. Her eyes are half-closed. I'd bet money she downed a couple of adult gummies before we arrived. How would Jesus feel about that, I wonder? Meh, what am I saying? He wouldn't give a shit.

"Josie doesn't have to go to juvie, but she has to take a drug and alcohol class and do community service. Plus a fine and probation. It's now on her official record, but in a few years, it can be..." Sue squints her eyes and waves her half-smoked cigarette in a circle, like she's trying to remember something. "... exssspunged! That's it."

She is nodding her head and smiling slightly, probably proud of herself that she came up with an uncommon, two-syllable word in her current state. Well, almost came up with it.

"Great news! That is wonderful!" says Walter with fake enthusiasm, like he's attending a Tony Robbins rally. He is looking directly at Sue, nodding his head and smiling. I feel like I should give him an Academy Award right now.

Sue nods back at my husband with satisfaction. "Yeah, it is good news. Just what we need for a fresh start."

I'm not sure what that means, but when Sue blatantly looks in Gina's direction, I sense Gina shifting uncomfortably. She is being exceptionally quiet, not so much as a peep other than the sound of her sucking on her cigarette. I'm not a psychic or medium, but I get the feeling that Sue and Gina have had words since our last visit. I don't believe for a second that suddenly Sue turned into Mother of the Year, but maybe she told her friend to calm the fuck down and back off. Whatever the case, I am enjoying the silence.

And then Sue surprises us even further. "We're moving to Wilmington next month. North Carolina, that is. Gonna stay with my mom for a while until we figure things out. I got a job managing a Marriot for the holiday season. I'll figure something out after that."

I am surprised at the announcement but also sort of not surprised. I can't explain it, but this is exactly what I imagine someone like Sue doing in a situation like this. And I don't mean the alleged demon situation. This is running away from something. I hope Sue doesn't think that she can escape the reality of her daughter's circumstance (whatever that may be) by moving to another state.

"Wow! Congratulations," I say, glancing at Walter with the speed of light, then back at Sue. "Sounds like a great opportunity." I shift my body toward Gina, still looking at Sue. "For a fresh start."

I don't like her. Gina. It's a vibe. I mean, I hardly know her. But now it's all making sense. I don't think Gina is the reason Sue is picking up and leaving the state, but I damn sure think it's a good idea to have Her Bible Thumpness out of the Mackenzie's lives.

"Okay," I say, leaning forward and double-clicking a file in my Mac Finder window. "Let's show you what we found."

Walter Bean

Here's a rundown of the reveal, in a nutshell: Sue disputed just about everything for which we had a boatload of evidence to debunk; she obsessed over little things that we couldn't explain with 100% certainty (like the crying baby sound, which was probably someone's actual crying baby or a cat or a catbird); she damn near bit Libbi's head off when my wife shared a clip Sue was positive was a bass drum but turned out to be the water heater turning on; and Gina is a religious fanatic who has hyped this entire thing up to a new level of crazy. Her exaggerated sense of religious superiority has most certainly escalated this whole situation.

I feel like I'm sitting here next to the Whack Job Twins and the worst part of it is, the innocent daughter who doesn't fit into her mom's norm—or more accurately, her mom's nutjob Jesus-freak friend's norm—is the one who is suffering. Despite Sue's upcoming "fresh start" (which I suspect is just her trying to escape the perceived embarrassment of her daughter's delinquency from her church cohorts), I don't get the sense that her new outlook included any evolution of her critical thinking skills.

When we first arrive, Sue is stoned, Gina acts like she just got friend detention, and they are both chain-smoking as if their lives depend on an intravenous drip of nicotine. The inside of the duplex smells like lutefisk. As we drive up, the neighbor's greasy beagle is again chilling in front of the Mackenzie's window almost as if it were expecting us. One of the neighbors is blasting Eminem from their backyard; or maybe it's from the opposite direction. Hard to tell with the giant bush wall behind the Mackenzie duplex. Either way, the entire scene is a cliché of working-class hell. I can't wait for this case to be over.

I didn't think it could get much worse than Stoner Mom and Tammy Faye Baker puffing away in the middle of Shag Carpet Central, but when Sue tells us about her experience with the judge, I almost spit-take my own spit. Even with my teeth clenched, I can't help but let out a small, sarcastic sigh. I'm pretty sure even the dogs are thinking, *Is she for real?"*

Libbi walks Sue through the investigation from start to finish, pausing occasionally to show her the evidence examples. Our findings are more than enough to debunk most of the experiences Sue and Jo reported. Some of the evidence (such as the urine events) points overwhelmingly to a logical explanation. The neighbor's dog marked twice in front of their window. Their own dog peed (and pooped) right in front of me in the basement. And they live across from acres of farmland. Any of these facts would give the average client pause (and, frankly speaking, relief—because who WANTS a demon in their house?) before assuming something is paranormal.

But not Sue Mackenzie. She just keeps saying, "That's not what I smelled. It was human urine."

"Fair enough," I say. "But hear me out."

I tell her the story of a recent investigation we did with the team for practice at a cemetery in Buchanan the previous summer. Dana and her son were there. Libbi and I both did a double take when we smelled human piss. We were sure of it. It smelled like every alley in every major metropolitan that has a significant unhoused population.

"We were all perplexed until Junior pointed out that we were surrounded by active farmland—and it was peak fertilization time. We're the professionals, and we sometimes get duped. Temporarily, anyway."

"I can appreciate that, but I'm telling you, that's not what I smelled. I know the difference. Full stop."

She turns away from me, and I think she is annoyed. I'm speechless. I thought sharing our experience would help Sue see the light on what might reasonably have caused the urine smell. But no. She is as stubborn as a Labrador with a dead mole in its mouth (I speak from experience). We provide evidence of multiple dogs pissing in the vicinity or fertilizer. She smells urine put there by a demon. I damn near throw my arms up right in front of her.

What boggles my mind the most is that of the few events that we *do* find intriguing, she almost totally brushes them off. I'm not sure she fully understands what we are saying. When Lib goes through the pixelation evidence, I expect Sue to respond like we just proved that Bigfoot exists. *"Yes! See? I told you so! That's a demon! Look at it! I'm not crazy!"*

But she doesn't do that at all. She barely acknowledges the stark coincidence of the visual blob and the audio echo, and how they both travel across the room and into the basement. Caught on multiple devices. This is one of the most startling pieces of evidence we've captured since we started ghost hunting, and all our client can do is shrug her shoulders like we just showed her a picture of a cow.

And she still insists that she heard drums when Dana was testing the pipes. The level of denial in this case is over the top.

This type of negation is the most frustrating thing about ghost hunting. While I would love to capture a full-spectrum apparition on multiple cameras with corresponding audio in every case, the fact is, irrefutable evidence is rare. Maybe even nonexistent, because there is always the possibility that even the most compelling examples could be reasonably explained. Even the pixelation leaves room for doubt. It could still just be a coincidental anomaly—like something in Jo's voice pitch that caused the cameras to malfunction or metallic particles floating in the air. If we really brainstormed it, we could come up with a hundred possibilities.

With most of our investigations, we end up debunking the majority of reported events. And our findings are usually very well received. Why? Because no one wants to live in a haunted house. We've known people ready to move out of their homes because of their crushing fear of paranormal activity—activity that we found absolutely zero evidence for. Most people are grateful to hear that when they woke up and saw a shadow figure, it was just sleep paralysis (a perfectly normal phenomenon). They are thrilled when we find raccoons in their attic instead of tiny, mischievous goblins. We bring great relief to genuinely frightened people who appreciate the myriad plausible possibilities that we provide.

Sue is not those people. She still insists that she smelled human urine. The random walkie-talkie beeps are communications from beyond. Cold spots couldn't possibly be from gaps in windows or horrible insulation. The tapping sounds they heard were most definitely not a rat running across the drum set in the basement, or a neighbor blasting "Wipe Out" from their garage, or knocks from their old, rusty pipes. Must be demon tribal drums then! That makes the most sense.

It is all very awkward. The worst part for me is when we talk about what we found in the closet. Lib saves that one for the end. I don't want to be here during that discussion. This is one for the women and, frankly speaking, I would rather let them work it out. I do think my wife is right; something is going on with Jo. Something that she is suppressing, maybe, and certainly causing a lot of stress. The pixelation we saw could be some sort of psychic manifestation of that inner conflict (intensified by the outer conflict with her mother). Poltergeist? No, not quite. But something we can't easily explain. The coincidence in timing with her wailing is too stark to ignore. If it isn't emanating *from* her, then at least it is connected *to* her somehow.

And I am happy to be involved in any discussion about paranormal energy expressed by an angry teenager. But I am not comfortable talking about… *women's stuff.* I feel like I'm intruding on the secret life of the female. As soon as Libbi brings it up, I feel myself tense up, and if I could think of an excuse to get the fuck out of here, I would use it. But in the end, I'm glad I stayed. Because I would have missed the end-all, beat-all reveal.

Let's just say it doesn't go well

Sue Mackenzie

Thank you, Jesus, for the strength to hold back from putting Gina in a chokehold and dragging her and the miniature kraken out the front door. The more I think about it, the more I believe she brought these demons into our home. She is a wolf in sheep's clothing and a heartless bitch. Forgive my cursing.

I am happy that the RIP team found nothing blatantly demonic in their evidence. No devil manifestations, no audio of anything speaking in tongues. I am disappointed that they still think the human urine and shit smells were caused by Pepper. I call bullshit on that, no pun intended. But no matter. I feel that we have fended off the evil forces for now, at least long enough for us to get out of Dodge. The day after the investigation, I had the house blessed and cleansed again—this time by the minister from my church, Pastor William Gerber (or Pastor Bill as we call him). Father of Cliff, my weed supplier. I don't know what kind of voodoo Gina put on her priest, but our activity didn't stop after he did the first blessing early on. But since Pastor Bill has been out, we haven't had so much as a bulb flicker. Makes me wonder.

The Beans went over a lot of stuff. A lot. My brain is throbbing from all their "evidence." I'm numb. If I hadn't quit drinking back when Jared went off the rails with his drugs, I'd pour myself a Jack & Coke right now and repeat that until I was three sheets to the wind. For now, I'll stick with a little *Last Dance With Mary Jane* and my Marlboros. The weed doesn't call to me like the drink does, so I allow myself that solace every so often. Today is one of those occasions. I needed something. Even before they started with the rundown, I was fit to be tied. And it's all Gina's fault.

She started in on me right after the RIP team left in the wee hours after the investigation. Harping on me about Josie again, trying to convince me to put her in Catholic school (like I can afford that) or one of those conversion therapy programs for the gays. I had to get a little curt with her. It was 2:30 in the morning, for Christ's sake! I could hardly keep my eyes open, and she wanted to plan the next four years of my daughter's life. MY daughter. I told myself she was just trying to help, and maybe I would feel more open to it in the morning after a good night's sleep. But I couldn't stop thinking about what that RIP psychic said: *"Someone is hurting and needs help."* I think she meant Josie. Even Gina understood that. Josie is hurting and needs help. Well, fuck me, aren't I the one supposed to be doing the helping and not the hurting?

I didn't see Gina much in the week after the investigation. She was working long hours to train a new employee, and I was grateful to have the time to myself. To think. We talked on the phone a few times, but I shut her down when she started asking about Josie or the investigation results. This past Wednesday, I took her to IHOP for lunch. I owed her for all the times she gave me a ride while Randy's van was in the shop, and Gina wanted some pancakes, so the girls got together. It was nice for a while. She can be a great friend when she wants to be. But then she started asking if the RIP team had found anything yet. She flat out asked me when I was meeting with them to go over the evidence. She wanted to be there. For me, she said.

But it isn't about me.

I told her I'd rather handle it myself. Then she started in on Josie. With the camp thing. She even had a brochure in her purse! Pulls it right out of her Mary Poppins magic carpet bag. Pack of smokes, lighter, travel pack of tissues, and a shiny trifold with big letters on the front: *PRAY AWAY THE GAY!* I don't even know that she is gay! Gina sets the pamphlet right on the table, in all its glory. What did that bitch think she was doing, pushing that shit on me in a public place?

My daughter is a tomboy. She's fifteen, only just got her boobs last year (and with a fury; she's hardly caught up to the fact). She's got PCOS, which likely has her body all confused. Josie will be fine. She doesn't know what's what right now because of the hormones. Even if she is gay—and even if I thought those programs were worth half a shit—who the hell is GINA FUCKING BAYMONT to tell me how to raise my kid? I've been called a Bible thumper before, and I wear the badge proudly. But I'm not stupid. The Bible was written by men, and men are flawed. Don't I know it? I married two of them, and they both turned out to be Jackasses with a capital J. Men have egos the size of Canada and are as fragile as a robin's egg. And they lie. I know all those words written about God and Jesus (*praise Him!*) didn't come directly from God's own mouth. The Bible has more than a few falsehoods, misinterpretations, and poor translations—and if I believed otherwise, then I'd have to be quite an idiot.

Gina doesn't see it that way. She's a pusher. She has an agenda, and I wish I had seen it sooner. We might have been spared all this madness. She's never liked Josie because she assumes Josie is something that Gina was told was evil and unholy. But the truth is, Gina is the evil one. I don't want her to be here for this. We haven't spoken since IHOP. But I made the mistake of telling her when the Beans were coming. Sure enough, she shows up out of nowhere, and in a moment of fear and weakness, I tell her she can stay. I've been nervous about this; I can't lie. *The reveal*, they call it. I wasn't sure what the ghost hunters would find, and I've been worried that it's not over. The Beans didn't want Josie to be here when they go over the evidence—and I don't disagree—but that also gave me even more anxiety. Was it so bad that they couldn't even talk about it in front of her? So, I leaned on Gina for support, against my better judgement.

That will never happen again.

Libbi goes through what they found from start to finish. I say Libbi because even though her husband is present, he doesn't say much. I get the feeling he isn't interested in being here. Maybe this is his golf day or something. He looks like a golfer. Or a police officer, with his shaved head and plain, dark clothes. A few times I think he is rolling his eyes at me—every time I disagree with their findings, in fact. I don't claim to be a ghost-hunting guru. But I am not cosmically aligned with all their assumptions, let's put it that way.

With nearly all the evidence Libbi and Walter show us, I can at least *process* it in my brain. I accept some of it, don't accept some of it, but it all makes sense in my head. I get why they might think pee is just pee, even though I know better. When you have a drunk husband and an addict son (both with horrible aim) you experience a few pissing events over the years. But I understand their perspective. We agree to disagree on a few things.

The drums? I'm not sure. I know what we heard. RIP says it may have been a neighbor down the street, echoing up to our duplex because of the way the trees and bushes are all congested around the back of the houses. I don't buy it. On the night of the investigation, Walter said it was pipes. Again, I disagree. We've lived in this house for almost two years; you'd think we would have heard pipe knocking before now. And this wasn't just tapping. It was a full-on drum solo; there's no way that was pipes. We heard drum tapping *after* Josie went postal on that old set in the basement, which rules out anything coming from the only actual drums that have been in the house. It wasn't Alice's grandson, and it wasn't the dog hitting the cymbals while it chased a mouse or some other bullshit.

But the drums have stopped. That's how I know the demons are gone. At least for now. They have stopped. I still hear them in my sleep sometimes. I wake up with that wicked "Wipe Out" riff running full volume in my head, and it takes me a few minutes to realize it's just a dream. When the pipes or ducts knock, it startles me (and I KNOW it's the pipes; I am not a fool). But the *ratta-tat-tat* has been silent since

Pastor Bill came out the day after the investigation. Still, I won't feel fully safe until we've moved on and all this mayhem (including Gina) is out of our lives forever.

The thing they called the echo-blob? That seemed like a stretch to me. Libbi thinks this is some sort of psychic energy coming from Josie. I don't buy it. For one, they saw a blob before we even got home. Where was Josie then? Nowhere near the house. I think that black mass was the last of the demons being driven out. That was me taking my power back. They knew I was coming for 'em, and I most certainly did the very next day. *Yippee kay-yay, motherfuckers!*

All that said, nothing they showed me was concerning. It's there for interpretation, just like the Bible. You've got to try and make sense of it all.

Libbi goes through all the evidence, and when we get to the end of the list, she pauses. Her demeanor changes, like she's about to tell me something bad, like they got a video clip of Lucifer himself taking a piss on our basement wall or something like that.

"There is one more thing we want to talk to you about," she says, all serious and concerned. "And this is going to sound like a strange question but bear with me. Has Josie ever physically hurt herself—like maybe with cutting? Or has she ever talked about hurting herself? Or even…killing herself?"

I lose my breath for a moment. Good thing I wasn't taking a toke off my ciggy. The answer is yes. I believe Josie might have tried to hurt herself last summer.

The last time we went to the doctor for her cysts—mid-July, I think—Dr. Wiley, the gynecologist, noticed some marks on Josie's upper thigh. Looked like three or four long scars running vertical along her skin just below the groin area. They were not fully healed from what I could see—which wasn't much because Josie got embarrassed and kept trying to hide behind that pathetic excuse for a modesty garment they give us for our female exams. But I saw it. The lines were the same length and equal distance apart, as if someone had taken a fork and dragged it from upper mid-thigh toward her hip bone. The thing is… a fork wouldn't do that. It had to be something sharp, like a knife or razor.

And then I remembered the Swiss Army knife I got Josie for Christmas last year. The doc asked me later, when we were alone, if Josie was going through anything because it looked like she had been cutting herself. It was all I could do not to break down. I am familiar with cutters. Jared was a cutter; hell, he might still be. But he's a boy, I didn't put too much worry into it because that's what boys do. Testosterone makes them lose fear and sensibility, so why would I be concerned that my young son was giving himself a knife tattoo when he got a little stressed?

It was different with Josie. The thought of her maiming herself with a knife that I gave her was heart-wrenching. Josie adamantly denied it when I confronted her later; said she fell off her bike and landed on one of the pedals. That was most certainly a lie because her bike has been sitting in the back shed gathering cobwebs along with my treadmill and all those bins of clothes I might someday fit into again. But I didn't press her. We'd already had too many fights, and I knew she was in pain from her cysts.

When Libbi asks about suicide, my stomach drops. Dr. Wiley asked the same thing. She said it was probably nothing, not to be worried. But I should keep an eye out because self-injury can lead to "more serious things." Is Josie hurting herself to mask the physical pain? Or is it something more emotional… or in her mind? And am I part of the reason?

I choke as I answer. "You aren't wrong. Dana wasn't wrong. Josie *has* cut herself. I don't think she still is, but she did last summer."

I don't tell them any of the details. Neither the place nor the time. Gina scoffs softly and shakes her head. I didn't tell her any of this. I don't think she's happy about being kept in the dark.

Libbi continues. "Thing is, Sue… we also found something in Josie's room that may or may not be related. It's sensitive, and that's another reason we didn't want her here for the reveal."

I see her glance over at Gina, who is leaning forward like she's waiting for the jury verdict for a serial killer. She looks like she's out for blood and almost happy about it. I want to make her leave before Libbi says anything more, but I'm frozen. I want the other Gina—the one I trusted to have my back and who gave me a shoulder to cry on. But all I have is a strange woman who seems to *want* me to get bad news. I'm confused, but my need to hear what is coming next is greater than my confidence in hearing it alone.

"Understood," I say. "You can say it. I'm ready."

I'm not sure I am ready. But I need to hear it all.

"During the session in Josie's bedroom, our investigator Stan smelled something coming from her closet. It was faintly rotten."

Holy Father! Please do not tell me there is a dead body in there!

"Don't worry, it wasn't a dead body or anything," Libbi says, reading my mind. I relax slightly. "We found a trash bin with… how do I say this? With a bunch of used sanitary products stuffed inside. That's what we smelled."

Wait, that's it? I pause for a moment. Libbi doesn't speak. Gina looks like she wants to, but I give her a glare.

"So… you found a trash bin with her dirty pads and tampons in her closet? Is that it?"

Libbi nods, but in a way that tells me that's not it.

"Yes, but they were hidden way in back, behind some piles of clothes. There were a lot of used… *products*… in the bin, and it seemed like they were being hidden."

I nod. I understand what she is getting at. I'm not shocked by what she tells me; it is sinking in. I have asked Josie about her period many times, because of the cysts. Just making sure she's regular. She told me they were barely there and irregular, which I assumed was normal in her condition. I realize now that "barely there and irregular" isn't the exact truth.

Libbi goes on. "There were piles of clothes in the back of the closet that also seemed hidden. Those clothes seemed to be dresses and skirts that are more feminine."

I feel Gina's eyes on me, and I'm getting hot.

"I don't mean to get into your business; that's not our place. And I'm not certain if there is a correlation between this energy that Dana sensed and your daughter. But what Dana *did* sense is that this energy or presence feels sad; despair would be more accurate. It believes something is wrong with itself. Something bad, like it hates itself. Dana picked up that this energy was hurting itself—maybe on the leg—to numb pain. Not physical pain, per se, but more mental pain."

I let out a small gasp and put my hand over my mouth. Libbi reaches out and puts her hand on my arm for comfort. Much as I don't want to break down in front of Gina (or anyone, for that matter), I am having a hard time keeping it together.

"That's where she cut herself," I eke out. "On her leg."

Libbi lifts her hand and sighs with sympathy.

"What else?" I ask.

"Dana said that this energy had thoughts of… killing… itself. She saw that it went looking for some prescription sleeping pills somewhere, but when it got to where the pills were, they were gone. I don't know if this is a past thing or a future thing or even a real thing. But we wanted you to be aware just in case."

My stomach drops even further. I know exactly what she's talking about. My eyes close and the tears come hard. I let them flow for a few seconds and then wipe my eyes with my shirt. The room is silent but for the sound of the dogs breathing. I take a deep, stuttered inhale and pick up my smokes from the end table. I light one and inhale, knowing it will help regulate my breathing.

"I had some Ambien in the nightstand by my bed," I say, blowing out the smoke in a long exhale. See? Feeling better already. "The pills were expired. I hadn't taken any since right after we moved into this house. I like my gummies too much, and it's too risky to do both. Forgot to toss them…the Ambien. Right after I found out Josie had been cutting her leg, I remembered they were in the drawer and I flushed them down the toilet. They'd been sitting there for two years. I just had a feeling, I guess. I know she went through my nightstand after that because I kept the pills under a folded bandana. One day I saw the bandana was unfolded and messed up, like someone had been looking inside it and didn't bother to put it back right. I knew it was her; who else would it be? But I told myself she was just looking for a phone cord or something like that."

Libbi nods. "Given what Dana picked up, we just thought you should know about what we saw in the closet in case they were related."

I can't think about it anymore right now. Gina scoffs again. Her toxic energy is palpable from across the room. I mentally scream at her, and my head hurts from it. I am cursing myself for even telling her when the reveal was taking place. Even more so now, because as soon as the words come out of Libbi's mouth—that my daughter is hiding her monthlies, and her secret girl clothes might be related to our paranormal activity—Gina just can't help herself. She has to give me a big ole "I told you so!" It's like she's been saving it up so she can have one last colossal word.

"I knew it!" Gina finally lets her venom loose and hisses like the rattler she is. "I KNEW it! She is denying her true self, her womanhood. Following the devil's path, Sue. Right to hell. That's why you have demons!" She points at me with her bony hand and her lipstick-stained cigarette. "You have got to get this under control."

I am more embarrassed than angry at first. Walter lowers his head into his hand and shakes his head back and forth. Very slightly, but I see it. I can almost hear him thinking, *crazy bitch* in his head. Or maybe *bitches* plural. I'm sure I am being lumped in with the truly deranged.

Libbi just mutters, "Okay, then." She sits back from her laptop like she's about to grab a bucket of popcorn and watch the shitshow.

And I'm about to give her one. My anger is rising like a tsunami wave, and when Gina points her nicotine fingers at me, I inhale deep—

like, Grand Canyon deep—and let it out slowly lest I break the Sixth Commandment and commit murder right here in my own living room.

"I told you, you should've put her in that camp," says Gina, looking right at me. Tinker is now alert and getting agitated. It's like he knows when Gina is angry, and he's ready to back her up. Stupid little fucker. He makes one move, and I'll strangle that little neck of his with two fingers. He growls as if he can hear me. There's the demon right there.

"You know I'm right," says Gina with her teeth clenched. I half expect drops of spit to spray out of her mouth, she's so full of rage. I don't get it. She's still looking at me like she expects me to validate her craziness. Oh, no. We are done with that, Medusa. I take another long, deliberate drag from my cigarette, all the while looking at her calmly. There's a lot of silence as I draw in. Silence can be powerful. Something I learned from being a mom. Sometimes the brats don't listen when you yell. But they pay lots of attention when you go quiet.

I let out my smoke in a long, leisurely stream and then I answer low and slow, just like my toke.

"I've had about enough of your horseshit, Gina. Keep your damn tongue in your piehole or get the hell out."

"I do not believe this!" Gina all but slams Tinker onto the couch and stands up. The little mutt growls again, his little pointy teeth bared like a rabid raccoon. "You are blind, Sue! That… *abomination*… is gonna bring the demons right back into your house!"

Oh, no, she did not.

"You did not just call my daughter an abomination," I say, controlling my voice and body with every ounce of mental strength I have left. I've punched people for lesser offenses. If I were twenty years younger, I'd already be on my feet.

"You know what I'm talking about," she hisses. "Mark my words. This won't end well, Sue. You need to take care of it. NOW!"

She's pointing at me again. Well now, I got her all fired up, didn't I? Tinker too, he looks fit to be tied. Standing on the center cushion like he's a wolf with his little shark mouth. I crush out my cigarette prematurely, glancing over at Walter, who looks uncomfortably out the window the other way. I'd lay money he's stacking the odds in his head that the chubby, chain-smoking mom is going to score a TKO against the bony chick. He would be right about that. I never lost a fight from kindergarten through high school graduation, and I had plenty of opportunities. Today is not the day to crack my record.

Libbi looks almost excited, like she's watching a big fireworks show on the Fourth of July. I'll give her a show if Gina doesn't back off. I'm a patient woman, but it's wearing as thin as Gina's flat ass. I look at her directly, my last offering for her to get herself under control.

"I'm only gonna tell you once more, Gina. Either sit the fuck down and shut the fuck up—or get out. Or I'll pick one for you."

She looks at me with utter disgust. I'm seriously wondering what I ever saw in her. I'm more convinced than ever that she sucked this evil energy into our lives. She is the demon. She is the drums.

"You are a coward," she says with gritted teeth, like I've committed the ultimate transgression against her. I'm sure I did in her mind. I'm not sure why she cares so much, other than her inherent need to be right. Maybe she gets a referral fee for the "PRAY AWAY THE GAY!" camp.

"God sees you! And He will send you both to HELL! I hope you know that."

She grabs Tinker from the couch and steps around the coffee table toward the door. She might have gotten away clean if she had just cut her losses when she had the chance. But no. She cursed me, and for that she is going to get a little of Sue Mackenzie's sweet revenge. I am out of that comfy old chair before she has Tinker fully secured under her arm. I step in front of Walter, who leans back to give me space. I stretch my arm out, grab a clump of Gina's greasy black hair, and yank it back harder than I believe my middle-age self is still capable of. Gina stumbles backward, taking an awkward step before letting go of Tinker so she can catch herself on the TV stand. The little four-legged piranha goes airborne the other way, straight toward Walter.

But Walter is on it. He slides off the stool and moves aside with unreal reflexes just before Tinker lands half on the seat and slides to the floor after a valiant attempt to claw his way up the stool leg. That will leave a scratch mark, but I give it no attention. I move forward like The Flash as Gina gets herself fully upright. For a few seconds, she looks like one of those giant flapping people you see at the car dealership when they're having a sale, waving her arms around to get her balance. And I am right there. She's got a few inches on me, but I am still up in her face—so close I can almost smell her cheap makeup.

"Don't you ever—" I point at her with my right index finger, almost touching her cheek. "—EVER—slander me or my daughter like that again."

I step up a little higher. She is scared now; I can feel it. *Good.*

"And how dare you come into my home, where I have welcomed you like a sister… and curse me in God's name. You filthy, worthless piece of trash."

Gina is quivering now. I'm a big mama bear with nothing to lose, and she knows it. She prays under her breath.

"In Jesus' name—"

"YOU FUCKING HYPOCRATE!" I scream it, probably terrifying the Beans, but I don't care. If I don't let it out, I will seriously hurt this sorry excuse for a woman and get myself taken to jail. My face is hot, my heart racing, and my body more tense than it has ever been. Tinker is barking at my feet, ever the protector. I feel like I'm about to have a heart attack. There is a loud *BANG* and for a split second, I fear the drums are back.

"MOM!"

Josie is standing just inside the front door, horrified. My energy collapses. Gina takes the opportunity. She grabs Tinker and nudges Josie out of the way so she can reopen the door and make her escape. The door slams again, even louder, and the thickness in the room dissipates.

"What's happening?" Josie asks, her voice trembling. I'm immediately exhausted and taken back to when she was just a little girl, afraid of nothing except the wrath of her mother. She would try anything with a level of confidence I didn't think possible—but her voice would waver and crack when she got in trouble. How much of this have I caused? I wonder. Is she the energy Dana sensed? Is it my fault that she doesn't want to be alive anymore?

I am overcome with shame and guilt. Not at this innocent girl who Gina called an abomination. But at myself for letting it get this far. Is there anything my kids could do that would tear my love away? I almost let that happen. But no more. It stops here.

"I'm sorry, Josie," I say with a weary sigh. "I'm so, so sorry."

She takes a step, and I take a step, and she puts her arms around me. She's taller than I am now. And I think she's got another inch or two still to go. That's good. I like that she'll be the bigger person than her old mom both physically and mentally. I hug her tight. No matter what, she's a part of me. Part of my heart and soul.

"It's okay, Mom," she says with her neck nestled into my collarbone. "It's okay."

I feel a tear roll down my cheek. "I'm so sorry, Josephine Suzanne Mackenzie. Please forgive me."

"Always, Mom," she says. "Always."

Final Excerpt, the *RIP After Dark Podcast* Episode 72: Case of the Demon Drums

*This podcast was broadcast one year after the actual investigation.
Client names and identifying details have been changed to maintain privacy.*

Walter: *I think that was the closest we've ever come to a client almost getting in a fistfight with someone over a ghost.*

Libbi: [laughs] *Right? I don't even know which one I would bet on. Nancy had more the weightlifter body, and she was breathing fire, so my money's probably on her.*

Walter: *Yeah, but Cher could have been one of those scrawny people you don't expect to be that strong until they get that icy look in their eye, and suddenly five people are dead. Like Jynx in* Arcane: League of Legends. *She might have been like that.*

Libbi: *Yeah, Cher may have lost the fight, but she would have left some scars.*

Walter: *I have no doubt. Thank God the daughter came home when she did, or we might have had to call the cops. And you know how I feel about cops.*

Libbi: *Story for another time. For those just joining us, this is The RIP After Dark Podcast coming to you LIVE on Instagram and YouTube. We are recapping a case we did last October in Roanoke, Virginia. Which was nice, having a local case; we didn't have to travel far.*

Walter: *I would have been pissed if I had to follow that train wreck of a seance with a three-hour drive home.*

Libbi: *Oh, come on. It wasn't that bad. You just hate the woo-woo stuff.*

Walter: *True. Although I guess it's all woo-woo, if you really look at it.*

Libbi: *You said it, not me.*

Walter: *And we got something on video, so I guess I can't make fun of it.*

Libbi: *So, the daughter, Stephanie, comes in right before Nancy and her—I guess now ex-best friend, Cher—are about to come to blows. And the whole fight was because... well, let's be honest. Because Cher was a religious—*

Walter: *—whack job.*

Libbi: *Right. A religious whack job. And I think Nancy was starting to realize how much Cher had influenced her regarding Stephanie. Can you imagine if they had started throwing punches?*

Walter: *I told you my money was on Cher. Her dog would have jumped in to help its pack leader. Two against one.*

Libbi: [snorts laughter] *Unless Paprika wanted to get in on the action.*

Walter: *Nope, he would've slept right through the kerfuffle. In fact, I think he did. Just like at the investigation.*

Libbi: [laughs] *Truth! Until I stuck a chicken chew under his nose.*

Walter: *That was such a bizarre reveal. Nancy hardly blinked an eye at the pixelation videos or the echo sound, but she doubled down on the urine and other relatively minor things.*

Libbi: *And yet, that is somewhat typical of our clients!*

Walter: *Well, I wouldn't go that far.*

Libbi: *I meant, because we have had so many situations where our clients are so afraid and so distracted that they are in denial about the obvious.*

Walter: *Ah, yes. I guess it underscores how powerful fear is.*

Libbi: *You know, sometimes I think fear itself creates paranormal energy.*

Walter: *Whoa, now you're getting deep! I think you just created a paradox in the universe.*

Libbie: *Well, I mean... think about it. If we believe a stressed-out and confused teenager can generate enough paranormal energy to show up on camera and audio recorders, why wouldn't we think the same is possible with fear?*

Walter: *Good point. Energy is energy. My brilliant wife strikes a blog-worthy observation yet again.*

Libbi: [laughs] *Okay, now you're just mocking me. Smart ass.*

Walter: *Well, at least we got through the reveal unscathed. Mostly.*

Libbi: *Yeah, it was iffy there for a minute, but the daughter saved the day. I do feel for her, you know? I really think she was just trying to figure herself out.*

Walter: *I'm sure she'll be fine now that the chain-smoking, demon-mongering friend is out of the picture. They moved away, right?*

Libbi: *I believe so, yes. At least, that was the plan when we did the reveal.*

Walter: *And now they can put the demon drums behind them and get back to plain old mother-daughter fighting.*

Libbi: *That's a thing, Walter. The mother-daughter dynamic.*

Walter: *Oh, I know it. I had a mom, and I have a sister.*

Libbi: *Sometimes I couldn't stand to be in the same room as my mom. I loved her very much, and I would give anything to have her back. But her mere presence sometimes drove me to madness.*

Walter: *My sister might say the same.*

Libbi: *Anyway, I wish our clients well. Anything else from your end?*

Walter: *Nope, that's about it. Good recap. It was an outstanding case. One of the most bizarre pieces of evidence we have found to date.*

Libbi: *For sure. Alrighty then, time to wrap up the RIP After Dark Podcast. Thank you so much for watching (or listening to the replay). If you're catching this on YouTube or Instagram, please LIKE and SUBSCRIBE or FOLLOW, and drop us a comment—we appreciate it more than a full-bodied apparition on video! If you are listening to audio only, please also consider giving us a review on Apple Podcasts or your favorite streaming platform.*

Walter: *If you are in the greater Roanoke, Virginia, area and have unexplainable events happening in your home or business, get in touch with us at RIPAfterDark.org and maybe we can help. Our services are always free.*

Libbi: *Thank you again, and remember: Ghosts are real, but so is black mold.*

Walter: *Stay skeptical, but don't run toward the noise. Take it easy, ghost lovers.*

Final Report and Recommendations

Case Number: 0076-RIP-MACKENZIE
Client Name: Sue Mackenzie
Address: 1031 Starry Knob Lane, Roanoke, Virginia
Phone: 540.882.XXXX
Email Address: MackSueFaithGirl24018@yahoo.com
Investigation Date: Saturday, October 5, 7:00 pm-Sunday,
October 6, 2:30 am

Summary and Conclusion of Findings:
RIP found no conclusive evidence of paranormal activity caused by an
external source, such as a ghost, spirit, or demons. There were many
minor incidents that could not be explained, but for which there were
strong logical explanations.

RIP investigators do agree that there is evidence of paranormal
(telekinetic) energy present in the house caused by an *internal* source.
This internal source would be someone living in or near the house
(either Sue or Josephine, or both). RIP believes that the source is likely
the latter (Josephine) but that the energy is intensified by the conflict
between the two.

Evidence was captured that confirms physical and audio manifestations
of the telekinetic energy. There is a strong correlation between the
stress energy from Josephine (exacerbated by conflict with Sue) and
audio and video events caught on multiple cameras and recorders.
These could be telekinetic in origin; RIP believes this to be the case.

Telekinesis is, by definition, the ability to manipulate something
physically (move it or change its shape, for example) without physically
touching it, using the power of the mind. Telekinesis is often associated
with teenagers and/or stressful situations.

RIP believes that telekinesis is the strongest explanation for some of the unexplained events experienced by Sue and Josephine Mackenzie.

Evidence and Explanations:

<u>Snare and bass drum sound:</u> Possible explanations include car or neighborhood music; car bass thumping; rat or other animal in ductwork or hitting drums (when they were intact); pipes knocking; distant traffic noise from highway; noises from duplex neighbor; and/or the washer or dryer running. Telekinetic activity could also be at play.

<u>"Wipe Out" drum solo:</u> Possible explanations include a neighbor's TV or radio/speaker (misconstrued directionally due to the thick foliage throughout the subdivision); someone physically playing the drums in the basement (e.g., the neighbor's grandson) prior to the drum set's destruction. Telekinetic activity could also be at play.

<u>Bible thrown or propelled across the room from an unknown source:</u> Visual and audio evidence suggests the presence of telekinetic energy (likely emanating from one or more occupants of the home). While the RIP team did not experience (or capture on film) any similar events during the investigation, we know from research and other reports that telekinetic energy *can* be powerful enough to move objects. Other explanations include Josephine throwing the Bible and blacking out; or someone else being in the house.

<u>Sound of footsteps running up and down stairs:</u> During Session One (basement), the investigation team heard footsteps multiple times. All but one instance could be attributed to other team members walking overhead. Regarding the one instance that could not be explained, nothing conclusive was captured one way or the other. Explanations include pipe/duct sounds; the duplex neighbor's grandson/friend; other noise from the neighborhood; car bass; and/or the washer or dryer running. Telekinetic activity could also be at play.

<u>Growling:</u> The RIP team captured several growling sounds on audio recordings that seemed to coincide with possible telekinetic events (when psychic/sensitive Dana Tennant was communicating with an energy in the house). Other explanations include dogs growling (if not

Pepper, then the neighbor's beagle); engine braking; or the neighbor's TV or radio.

<u>Random strong urine smell and/or fecal smell</u>: The RIP team experienced several events which provide sound explanations for the reports of urine and feces smells.

- The duplex neighbor's unneutered beagle marked (peed) in front of the living room window twice during the investigation setup (witnessed by three RIP members).
- Pepper urinated and defecated in the basement during the investigation setup (witnessed by two RIP team members).
- Adjacent to the subdivision are several large swaths of farmland. Farms often use urine-based and manure-based products. RIP acknowledges that at the time of the events (early to late September) the farmland was likely dormant (although some farmers apply fertilizer in the off season).

<u>Nightmares</u>: Josephine reported dreams that included being possessed by a demon and wanting to kill her mother. Sue believes they are prophetic dreams and stated that her daughter had experienced dreams that came true in the past. RIP suggests these dreams are psychological, not prophetic or indicative of paranormal events. The conflict between Sue and Josephine is apparent and could be the cause (as could other stressors in the household or with family members). RIP recommends seeking professional therapy or similar help if dreams continue or become disruptive to daily life.

<u>Hearing voices, conversation; foreign language (indecipherable)</u>: During Session Three (seance) a similar sound was witnessed by the RIP team, Gina Baymont, Sue, and Josephine. Both Josephine and Sue felt the sound was what they had heard on earlier occasions. RIP determined the source to be the voices of two young men walking down the street. Other explanations include the duplex neighbor talking; neighbors' TVs; other people talking outside (amplified by the dense foliage in the subdivision); someone leaving their phone on unknowingly; or another sound that could be mistaken for conversation.

<u>Woman screaming "GET OUT!"</u>: RIP team members heard (and captured on audio recording) the sound of a cat or baby or possibly mockingbird or catbird. These could explain the sound. Other evidence

suggests telekinetic energy, which could also have generated the voice. See also above for "Hearing voices…"

<u>Sue Mackenzie being pushed from behind on multiple occasions:</u> Physical events have not occurred since RIP was initially called. RIP believes there was telekinetic energy present, which could be the source of any perceived physical touch. We found black mold in the basement, but the location and small quantity would not suggest a strong possibility of hallucinogenic effects. Additional possibilities include hallucinations or dizziness caused by stress, medications, or drugs.

<u>Josephine being grabbed on her leg, leaving fingertip bruises:</u> No further events have occurred since RIP was called. RIP believes there was likely telekinetic energy present, which could be the source of any perceived physical touch. Additional possibilities include Sue touching her daughter's leg (not realizing it during events); Josephine touching her own leg (perhaps in fear); or earlier bruising that was not noticed.

<u>Cold spots, particularly in Josephine's bedroom:</u> The RIP team observed a gap in the side bedroom window during Session Two of the investigation. The temperature near the window was significantly colder than at the center of the room. At least some of the cold spots are likely due to inadequate window sealing around the air conditioner. Because extreme cold was reported around the time of major paranormal events, it is possible that the temperature fluctuations were caused by telekinetic energy (as described above).

<u>Pepper (dog) acting differently; being fearful; sleeping too deeply and not waking easily:</u> The RIP team witnessed this event just prior to Session Three (seance). RIP Team member Libbi Bean easily roused the dog with a dog treat. Likely these "coma" events are because of Pepper's age, hearing loss, and possibly secondhand exposure to THC.

<u>Light in the basement going off/on by itself:</u> The RIP team found no damage or bad wiring and did not witness any anomalies with lighting or electrical work during the investigation. Nothing conclusive one way or the other. Explanations include old light bulbs; dirty or corroded sockets; faulty wiring behind the socket.

<u>Electrical anomalies, phones or other</u>: The RIP team did not experience any electrical anomalies with phones or other equipment. While it is possible that the presumed telekinetic energy mentioned above could have negatively affected Sue's phone, we also suggest that phones are notorious for having issues before and after upgrades, when not properly charged, when space is limited, and for a variety of other reasons. No evidence was found to conclusively explain this phenomenon one way or the other.

Mediation Options:

Roanoke Investigations of the Paranormal does not make any claims about the validity of these methods, nor do we make any formal recommendations. The options below are general and may or may not apply to the Mackenzies' specific situation. RIP provides them as a courtesy only.

For traditional haunting, spirit presence, ghosts, or other external paranormal activity:

- <u>Smudging/space cleansing</u>: This is usually done with dried sage, but lavender or sweetgrass can also be used. There are complex rituals involving cleaning, sage, and bells that can be found online (RIP will provide links upon request).
- <u>House blessing with holy water</u>: It is preferred that this be performed by a trained clergy member. However, it can be done by anyone, provided the water is blessed appropriately.
- <u>Prayer/religion</u>: Ask for help from your ancestors, deities, saints, etc. This is a common mitigation and works well for the devout.
- <u>Protection methods:</u> Remove the fear, become empowered; meditate (surround yourself and your property with white light); some believe garlic can help.
- <u>Ghost rescue:</u> Get the spirit to move on. This works best with a medium or sensitive who can communicate with the spirit(s). Ask the presence firmly to leave. The physical domain is YOUR world. Take ownership.
- <u>Mirrors:</u> There is a theory that some ghosts dislike seeing their reflections. Strategically placed mirrors may help rid the house of the entity.
- <u>Sea salt:</u> Best if blessed by a priest or clergy. The theory is that ghosts cannot cross a line of blessed salt.

For telekinesis or other energy originating from a living person:

- <u>Remove the cause of the stress in the telekinetic individual.</u> Telekinetic activity can be triggered and/or increased in correlation with a high-stress emotional state (usually negative and involving conflict or trauma). Removing or mitigating the cause of the stress often helps to eliminate the telekinetic activity.
- <u>Psychological intervention and counseling.</u> If the cause of the stress cannot be easily removed or resolved, seek the help of a trained psychiatrist, psychologist, or therapist to address any internal conflict or trauma. Because the originator of this type of psychic energy is often unaware and/or incapable of controlling it, getting to the root cause of the stress is imperative. NOTE: It is also worth considering counseling for other individuals (non-telekinetic) who may play a role in the conflict or trauma.
- <u>Emotional regulation.</u> There are proven techniques to help control outbursts and train the telekinetic individual to respond thoughtfully to situations (rather than react with intense emotion). These can be helpful in lessening the activity.

Time To Move On

Friday, November 15, 8:30 am
Former Mackenzie Residence, Starry Knob Lane, Roanoke, Virginia

As the movers pull the last few boxes out of the house and load them into a large U-Haul truck, Sue emerges from the front door of the duplex dragging a large black contractor bag. The broken snare, bass, and cymbals of the old drum set make a dull clanking sound as they bang against the concrete steps and down the asphalt driveway. Sue seems unconcerned about the noise at this early hour and hoists the bag slightly off the ground before tossing it to the curb. Anyone observing might think she was pissed at it. Josephine steps out of the house wearing a Detroit Pistons jersey under a faded red hoodie. Her navy Converse high-tops look new. As Sue looks at her daughter with newfound ambivalence, Jo wheels her oversized suitcase down the driveway and heaves it with some effort into a ten-year-old Jeep Rubicon that is already stuffed to the hilt with bins, boxes, and bags. Just enough to keep them going until they reach North Carolina and settle in.

Sue yells over to Josie from the other side of the driveway. "You ready?"

Josephine gives her a thumbs up and climbs into the passenger seat. *I call shotgun!* The days of fighting over the front seat are over. There are just the two of them now. Well, two and a half if you count Pepper, who is comfortably sleeping in his car carrier on top of a Snoopy and Woodstock blanket in the back seat. Sue spits on the contractor's bag, which has spilled open a bit. Her phlegm hits a dented cymbal dead on. *I should compete in a spitting contest.* Then she spits again and only hits the edge of the black vinyl-like bag. *Maybe not.* She sighs for the umpteenth time that day and heads up to the house for one last walk-through. She doesn't nag Josephine to help. That girl has been through enough. Everything accounted for, Sue pays the movers and confirms the address to the truck driver. She locks up and puts the key in a planter under a cluster of dried-up chrysanthemums. She gave up her security deposit in exchange for not cleaning the rental, a fair deal as far as she is concerned. Time is money, and it is time to go.

Sue walks back down to the curb with her hands in the pockets of her plaid barn jacket. It is chilly now, and the flannel lining will come in handy as winter grows near. Underneath the coat is a new t-shirt that says, *"I'm mostly peace, love, and light... and a little go fuck yourself."* It was a gift from Tina for their new life. Sue wants to focus more on the peace, love, and light these days. The "go fuck yourself" will always have her back, no need to worry. She's not crazy about leaving her son and grandson. It's less than six hours from Wilmington to Blacksburg even with the Raleigh-Durham traffic, but that's a lifetime when you're used to family popping in and out on a moment's notice. Change is hard, but change is good. Someone once told Sue that discomfort is the herald of opportunity. If that's the case, there ought to be archangels singing from the heavens by the time they hit the Atlantic Ocean.

She climbs into the pumpkin-colored Jeep, reminding Josie to fasten her seatbelt. It's going to be a long ride and a new start. Might be a good idea to arrive alive.

"All righty, Jo-Jo," she says. "It's time."

Jo smiles a little. She hasn't been called Jo-Jo for a few years. It feels nice.

Sue slowly pulls away from 1031 Starry Knob Lane and glances in her rear-view mirror as the Jeep comes to a stop at the end of the cul-de-sac. The demon drums are finally behind her, literally and figuratively. *I hope they get buried in sewage,* she thinks, picturing the crumbled snare drowning in a sinkhole. The sun is still low in the sky, and it hits the shiny black bag behind her on the curb, reflecting its warm light against the protruding brass. Just for a second, it looks like the drums are on fire. Sue's heart skips a beat, but when she blinks, it's gone. And she feels just a little stronger as she turns her gaze forward. *Never look back,* she reminds herself, veering the steering wheel to the right. Her foot presses down on the gas pedal.

"Here we go," she says to Josie, who turns and gives her a rare teenager smile.

Time to move on.

About the Author

Beth Anne Campbell is an award-winning author, corporate humorist, podcaster, and unapologetic truth-seeker who's spent as much time chasing spirits as she has chasing deadlines. Her debut book, *Where the Hell Is My Bacon?*, won an International Impact Award in 2024 and cemented her reputation for blending humor, heart, and honesty in everything she writes.

After publishing two nonfiction books about leadership and corporate life, Beth Anne decided it was time to channel her inner novelist. *Case of the Demon Drums* is the first book in *The RIP Files* trilogy and draws inspiration from her decade as a paranormal investigator. During those years, she discovered how much fear and psychology can affect hauntings. This inspired her to write about ghost hunting with realism, empathy, and a touch of dark humor.

Beth Anne Campbell lives in Virginia with her husband, Sean, and their dog Moxie. She's a proud ally and firm believer that everyone deserves to live—and love—as their authentic self.